KT-228-469

Between Enemies

ANDREA MOLESINI

Translated by
ANTONY SHUGAAR & PATRICK CREAGH

Atlantic Books
LONDON

First published in Italy in 2010 by Editore Sellerio, Palermo.

First published in Great Britain in 2015 by Atlantic Books,
an imprint of Atlantic Books Ltd.

Copyright © Andrea Molesini, 2010
Translation copyright © Antony Shugaar and Patrick Creagh, 2015

The moral right of Andrea Molesini to be identified as the author of this work
has been asserted by him in accordance with the Copyright, Designs and
Patents Act of 1988.

The moral right of Antony Shugaar and Patrick Creagh to be identified as
the translators of this work has been asserted by them in accordance with the
Copyright, Designs and Patents Act of 1988.

All rights reserved. No part of this publication may be reproduced, stored
in a retrieval system, or transmitted in any form or by any means, electronic,
mechanical, photocopying, recording, or otherwise, without the prior
permission of both the copyright owner and the above publisher of this book.

This novel is entirely a work of fiction. The names, characters and incidents
portrayed in it are the work of the author's imagination and not to be
construed as real. Any resemblance to actual persons, living or dead,
events or localities, is entirely coincidental.

10 9 8 7 6 5 4 3 2 1

A CIP catalogue record for this book is available
from the British Library.

Trade Paperback ISBN: 978 0 85789 795 4
E-book ISBN: 978 0 85789 796 1

Printed in Great Britain

Atlantic Books
An Imprint of Atlantic Books Ltd
Ormond House
26–27 Boswell Street
London
WC1N 3JZ
www.atlantic-books.co.uk

Prelude
Friday 9 November 1917

He loomed up out of the night. And for an instant there was nothing to distinguish him from it. Then a glint, a reflection from the lantern the woman was holding up close to the horse's nose, attested to a monocle. The man addressed the woman in impeccable Italian, flawed only by certain gutturals that revealed his German mother tongue. There was something fierce and splendid in that face bathed in the swaying lamplight, as if the stars and the dust were met together there.

'I'll call the mistress,' said Teresa, concealing the fear she habitually felt at the doings of the gentry. She lowered the lantern, and darkness once more swallowed up the captain and his horse.

A torch, then a second and a third, cast shadows beneath the vaults of the portico. Teresa hugged her shawl to her breast to repress a shudder. In the road outside the gate came other torches, the squeaking of cartwheels, soldiers' voices, the headlights of a lorry, the heavy silence of mules in the icy drizzle. As she closed the oaken shutters behind her Teresa noticed I was watching her, crouched beside the window in the hall. She put a finger to her lips and grunted her annoyance in my face.

Aunt Maria was still up, in a black dress, the collar fastened with an ivory pin. She was at the window watching the army as it filled the piazza, where the light of fires now outshone that of the headlights. As we came in she turned towards the door.

'Madam, madam, ma—'

'Don't panic, Teresa, leave it to me. Go and tell the horseman that I'll be down in a moment.'

The cook left the room with lowered eyes, dragging her feet, the lantern dangling beside her knees. With a slight movement of her eyes my aunt told me to go out with her. Stock still in the saddle, the captain watched the coming and going of the troops without so much as the flicker of an eyelid, attentive only on keeping his horse under the stone arches of the portico. His distant immobility issued orders that everyone – officers, men and mules – seemed to grasp without hesitation.

'The mistress…' Teresa gave a cough. 'The mistress says she's coming.'

She took a step backwards to distance the smell of horse. The men were unloading the mules and machine guns under the shelter of the arcade, kicking aside the rakes and shovels leant against the wall. The cook gave a groan that expressed all the scorn she felt: those tools were humble and dear to her, faithful dogs driven away by wolves. Their army-issue spades broke down one door after another and in the soldiers went with their heavy packs, emptying cupboards and smashing things; and their voices were an uncouth hubbub of harsh syllables. One of them, his helmet covered with sopping wet leaves, drove his chugging motorbike right into the dining room and pulled up a metre from the oak table.

Aunt Maria went outside.

'Herr Captain.'

The captain gave a soldierly salute, without a smile.

'Captain Korpium,' he said. 'There are eighteen of us, counting officers and batmen. We shall be lodging here.' He took his monocle from his pocket. 'If you think you are unable to fit us in,' he added, inserting the lens between eyebrow and cheekbone, 'you will be obliged to leave the house.' His voice was calm and cold. Each syllable sounded detached from all the others, as if his thought required all those tiny pauses to get itself organized.

Half a dozen motorcycles roared in through the gate. The captain's horse shook its head.

'You may be a great warrior,' said my aunt, 'but you are certainly no gentleman.'

'My non-commissioned officers will sleep at the inn in the piazza, the officers in the Villa, and the men in the nearby houses. We will erect tents in your grounds, as well as a camp kitchen.' He readjusted his monocle between eyebrow and reddened cheekbone. 'Maybe tomorrow we shall cross the Piave and nothing here will be as it was before.'

'Maybe,' said my aunt, adding to herself under her breath, 'Or perhaps the war will have the flesh off your bones.'

The captain dug in his spurs and turned towards the mules still streaming in and the soldiers lit by the lanterns of the non-commissioned officers yelling out orders.

I heard the distant barking of a dog. Then another, with a cavernous voice. Then came a rifle shot, then a second, and far away a third. The stench of the mules had crept into the dining room. The soldiers were smashing up tables and chairs to light the fires with. They made way, however, for the two women who walked bolt upright in front of me; and one of the men, flaxen-haired, his eyes bulging like a toad's, actually stood to attention.

'In the midst of this tragedy', murmured my aunt, 'there is a touch of the ridiculous.'

'A mouse's bum is better mannered than them,' said Teresa. 'These boys didn't even have mothers.'

'The war will see them off tomorrow. Tell Renato to keep his eyes peeled. You and Loretta will sleep upstairs with me. Put two palliasses on the floor: we'll barricade ourselves in my bedroom. Paolo, you will sleep with your grandfather.' She turned to give Teresa a straight look. 'Have you hidden the copper?'

'Just as you ordered, madam.'

'Very good.' There was no trace of emotion in my aunt's voice. Her nerves were steady, her mind cool: the cook had to understand who to take orders from. 'Guns are mere trifles, but this rabble doesn't know it.' She paused for a moment to give Teresa time to work that out and get the message. 'We'll get the better of them.'

The cook lifted the lantern high above the time-worn steps.

Part One

Part One

One

GRANDMA'S THIRD PARAMOUR HAD SUCH BIG FEET THAT he could not be considered intelligent. He was not altogether stupid, for he knew how to hang about with elegance and steadfastness, but owing to the size of his feet there had not been a great deal of care left over for his head. Grandpa Gugliemo, who boasted a number of mistresses, said that *that fellow* – he never called his rival by name – only ever opened his mouth to emit hot air: 'Fools like to parade their folly, and there's no better medium for it than words.'

Grandpa liked to pigeonhole everything. He used to pigeonhole away while chewing a cigar and wearing the air of a sailor who had sailed the seven seas, though in fact he had an aversion to water, the stuff in the washbasin being no exception. An ironclad liberal, he poked fun at Grandma's mildly Socialist sympathies: 'Put three of your lot in a room together and half an hour later you'll get four different opinions.' He spent hours each day writing a novel which he never finished, but according to Grandma he hadn't even written a line of: 'It's a sham, to keep away boors and children.' No one, however, dared set foot in the Thinking Den, the little room where Grandpa spent almost all day, except when it rained; because then he would go out walking alone, without an umbrella, in the felt hat with the tattered brim. He was a Buddhist, though he didn't know much about Buddha. But his knew his cards and his history, and used to write letters to the *Gazzettino*, which were never published because they were full of abuse about the city councillors of Venice: all 'stinking sons of brainless priests', in his opinion.

Grandma, on the contrary, fizzled about everything. If it was a case of spending half a lira she would say 'Better not', and that 'Better not' came a couple of dozen times a day. Despite her seventy years she held herself erect and tall, she was strong and handsome, a white-haired panther of a woman. Her bathroom was a poem: bedecked with beige, ochre, black and flesh-coloured enema bags. There were two or three of them on every arm of the enamelled clothes hanger, whereas pyjamas and knickers were relegated to a green chest of drawers, on which sat a Murano glass bowl containing a dozen strings of artificial pearls and glass beads. The enema bags, in their days of glory, were as many as sixteen, with their different-sized rubber nozzles for ¼, ½, ¾ and a whole litre. The bags were rounded, pear- or pumpkin- or melon-shaped, and made of oilcloth. Reflected in the white tiles, the opaque rubber tubes looked like the tentacles of sea creatures with hooked beaks.

The three servants – Teresa, her daughter Loretta, and Renato – did the work of six. Loretta, twenty years old, was a buxom lass with cross-eyes which she kept lowered, though when she did turn them on you, you knew they hated you, that they couldn't do otherwise. Renato had one leg slightly shorter than the other, so he limped. He was my favourite, and knew how to do everything, how to fish in the river with harpoon and knife, and also how to pluck a chicken ready for Teresa's stewpot. And she herself, Teresa, was a prodigy. Ugly beyond belief, she bore her fifty years well, was as strong as a mule and no less obstinate. On the contrary Aunt Maria – Donna Maria to outsiders – was fine-looking, the victim of a haughty manner which both fascinated men and kept them at a distance. She was courted with circumspection by even the boldest and most passionate spirits: not a light cross to bear.

And then there was Giulia. Giulia was a lovely, crazy redhead and a mass of freckles. She had fled from Venice on account of a scandal no one dared talk about, but quite a few in town would spit on the ground as she passed, and there was no shortage of bigots who would cross themselves to ward off *Pape Satán*. She was six years older than me and when I caught sight of her, even at a distance, I blushed. She wasn't in a madhouse because she was a Candiani, and gentlefolk – at least in those days – did not end up inside. Indeed they were not even mad: simply eccentric. A gentleman was a kleptomaniac, not a thief, and a lady was a nymphomaniac, never a whore.

That night of November the ninth, when the Germans took over my room, I went to sleep up in the loft, a long room nine metres by five, with four dormer windows and such low larch-wood beams that I had to mind my head. There Grandpa and I shared a palliasse dumped straight on the attic floorboards, splintery as they were, whereas Grandma was allowed to stay in her own bedroom.

The defeat of the Italian army was an ignominy that each and every enemy soldier cast in our teeth. I was then seventeen, going on eighteen, and to see the enemy lording it in my own home was excruciating. Those born in 1899 were already in the trenches, and in a few months' time it would be my turn.

'In a little while they'll be in Rome to free the pope, so they say. Well, there's honour among thieves, say I.' Grandpa considered the priests only a step – and a rather small one at that – above tax collectors. 'Those ugly customers in skirts have as much imagination as a turkey, but the cunning of a fox and a snake combined. They are the great pestilence of creation, worse than Job's boils…See here, Buddha doesn't have priests,' and he looked me straight in the eye, something he rarely did since I lost my parents. 'Or if he does they are not Austriophiles.' He spat into the palm of his hand, which he wiped on his enormous handkerchief.

I was fond of Grandpa. He abandoned his nightcap only at about ten in the morning, and even then unwillingly. That night, however, he had to manage without it. A private and a corporal had tied him to a chair, and while one jabbed his rifle butt into his breastbone and the other tickled his throat with the point of his bayonet, they had tried to force him to say where the family jewellery was hidden. It was lucky that Grandma, unbeknownst to him, had managed to hide the most precious things – along with a handful of gold sovereigns – in the bag of one of her enemas: objects too humble, and too closely associated with faeces, to tickle the appetite of the predators.

'I am concerned for Maria…Of course, if there's anyone who can put a scare into a German it's her,' said Grandpa, flopping down on the palliasse. The dry maize leaves of the stuffing crunched beneath his weight. He gazed up at the beams with moist eyes, but he didn't want me to sense his fear: our lives, our property, everything was at the mercy of the enemy. 'War and loot are the only faithful married couple,' he said.

I lay down beside him. Grandpa was really fond of my aunt: 'She's a woman of grace and initiative,' he would say. She was the daughter of his brother who had gone down in the wreck of the *Empress of Ireland* in May 1914, along with his wife and my own parents, during the voyage which everyone in the family called the Great Disaster. Since then she had been entrusted with the running of the Villa, perhaps because my education was seen to, albeit with fitful zeal, by my grandmother. 'Have you ever looked closely into your aunt's eyes? So green, and as firm as two stones. D'you know what sailors say? They say that when the water turns green the storm engulfs you.' Grandpa had never been to sea, but his talk was full of nautical slang and sea-captains' oaths: 'steady as you go', 'splice the mainbrace', 'if I catch you at it I'll hang you from the yardarm'; though this last one had been banished from his discourse ever since, immediately following the Great Disaster, he had asked me to address him with the familiar *tu*.

Everyone had become very kind to me after the sinking of the *Empress*, and I had made the most of it. The best part was that I had not suffered, at least not as much as might be expected. My parents were practically strangers to me. They had sent me to boarding school to relieve themselves of a burden, or – to be more charitable – because they thought that a father and mother are unsuited to the task of educating their children. My school was run by the Dominicans, and the good Fathers considered physical fitness at least as important as that of the soul, regarding which they were, amazingly enough, inclined to admit a certain degree of ignorance.

On that fatal day the headmaster – an authority on St Dominic de Guzmán, who to us boys seemed a hundred years old because of his snow-white beard and his stoop – sent to fetch me. His study, lined with large leather-bound books, measured about three paces by four, in which the smell of mould, paper, ink, armpits and grappa struggled for dominance. He looked up from the manuscript he was consulting, gave me a square look with great blue eyes further enlarged by his lenses, and said, 'Sit down, young man.' He made no preambles and did not soften the blow with any rigmarole about eternal life. He spoke firmly, without a pause.

I made no pretence at feeling sad. 'I won't miss them,' I said.

He blinked, then gave me a stern look. 'There are things one comes to understand only with time,' he said before burying his nose in his manuscript again. Perhaps he didn't even hear me leave the room, but those words of his stayed with me. He was right, the blow came later; the wound opened little by little, and little by little it healed.

Grandpa didn't take his eyes off me.

'So what happens now, Grandpa?'

'Now, laddie,' (as he liked to call me) 'we keep our mouths shut and let them loot us. This lot wouldn't think twice about skinning us alive. Have you heard what they do with the farmhands? Make them stand up against the wall and then throw buckets of water all round the house in search of their copper cauldrons and other treasures. Where the soil is freshly dug the water sinks in at once.' He smiled, because he smiled when he was afraid. 'Two kilos of copper can buy a pig…but I put my trust in your grandmother. She told me where she'd hidden the artificial jewellery, making out that it was the good stuff. They won't find the real stuff even if they dig up the whole garden.' He heaved a sigh. 'Luckily they'll be leaving tomorrow.'

'But then . . . our front line! Do you think it won't even hold along the Piave?'

'The war is lost, laddie.'

Donna Maria didn't get a wink of sleep. She told me so the next morning. It wasn't fear, for in her mind there was simply no room for fear. She was afraid neither for herself nor for us. 'These jackals have other things to keep them busy, but if they reach Venice there'll be no end to the looting. And now they are here, in my garden, in my rooms, in my kitchen, and they're digging the latrine in the soil which is the resting place of my mother and of yours.' It wasn't true. Teutonic efficiency had not yet envisaged drain fields, but my aunt had a meticulous imagination, thirsty for details, and especially the most disagreeable.

In the dead of night she had heard a horse neighing. The sound came from the portico. The neighing of horses always gave her gooseflesh because she loved horses. She had seen them dragging the last of the rearguard's carts; she had seen them refusing the bit, tossing their heads, digging in their hoofs when they passed by the corpses of mules with their thighs slashed open by the bayonets of hungry infantrymen. 'They have a sense of foreboding at the death of one of their own kind, just as we do ourselves.' It was so unjust that they were made to suffer. 'It is men who make war; animals have nothing to do with it. And then…maybe they are closer to God…they are so simple…so *direct*.'

At about three in the morning Donna Maria had got up, taking care not to wake Teresa who was sleeping at the foot of her bed. She went to the window. There were bonfires everywhere. The troops were unloading huge crates marked with the arms of the House of Savoy: the municipal warehouse had only partly burnt down. She saw the captain on horseback among the tents. The ground-floor windows were aglow with the yellow light of paraffin lamps. All of a sudden she felt she was being watched. She turned. Loretta was standing only a metre away, stock still, her long, long hair dangling and her eyes fixed on her. 'What's the matter?'

The servant lowered her eyes.

'They won't harm us,' said Donna Maria softly. 'They'll take it out on the Villa, and with the farmhands' houses, but nothing will happen to us. Go back to bed.' And back Loretta went to her palliasse, which emitted a crunch of dried leaves.

Grandpa's was a laughing face even when he was sad. Not even he slept a wink, but he pulled his sheet right up to his moustache and made a gentle pretence at snoring. I watched him in the darkness. Grandpa's moustache was a bristly rake, the tips of which attempted a risky handlebar effect. It was a sign of his contrariness, his wish to poke fun at the conventions which his plump chin, carefully shaved, paid homage to. I was amused by his childish eccentricities, partly because they constantly irritated Grandma, who would retaliate by inviting the Third Paramour to dinner.

The doors were no longer banging, the German voices sounded more sleepy, as did the noise of the boots, of the hoofs and even of the motorbikes.

I listened to my thoughts buzzing around in the muddle of somnolence. Big thoughts, about faraway things, sufficiently intangible as to not make me feel responsible. I thought of the rout of our Second Army more than of the occupation of the Villa; I thought of the ceaseless stream of peasants and infantrymen, the carts of the poor and the motor cars of the generals, of the wounded men abandoned in the ditches. I had never seen so many eyes ravaged by terror. The eyes of women with bundles slung round their necks: lifeless bundles and whimpering bundles. I would never have believed that the pain of a whole people in flight, a people to whom until then I had not been aware of belonging, could have affected me so deeply as to become mine, a pain of my own. There was no believing in what the generals Cadorna, Capello or the Official Gazettes said, but in pain, yes there was. It was like a massive boulder on my breast. The voices of the barbarians rang in my ears, those abrupt orders, the squeal of brakes, the thud of packs dumped down on stone. Images of stamping men and mules, and doors smashed in. My lips were parched, my tongue a piece of bark. I was a fly in an upside-down tumbler, twisting and turning on the mattress, dashing myself against the glass.

Two

RENATO LIT HIS PIPE WITH A PIECE OF BURNING STRAW and his face vanished into the smoke, from which there first emerged his long, sharp nose, then his pale eyes. He had arrived to act as steward at the Villa in mid-October, with references from a Tuscan marquis, an old friend of Grandma's. Although maintaining a proper distance, the very heart of authority, my aunt didn't manage to conceal her liking for this lame giant with his one metre ninety and over a hundred kilos.

'What are they doing with those big tubs?'

'Looking for copper. They think we're simpletons like the farmhands, who bury the stuff near their houses. Your grandfather told them about some valuables and now they're hunting for the bits and bobs. They're methodical, but not very astute.' His voice was of a sombre baritone, yet each syllable came out clear and clean. He was very observant, and uncommonly intelligent, so it was not easy to think of him as a servant. And then his vocabulary was too precise and extensive. Grandpa and Aunt Maria said he was a true Tuscan, but there was something else about him I couldn't put my finger on, and that perplexed me: he was too clear-minded, too sure of himself.

'Did they threaten you?'

'I gave them a couple of things of small importance, the mandolin and the big copper cauldron from the cowshed, which I'd hidden under the straw to make them think they were more valuable than they are. They stuck a barrel right between my eyes. I put on a show of reluctance at first, but didn't overdo it. You don't get yourself killed to save your employer's possessions.'

'They don't look so ferocious today.'

Renato disappeared behind the smoke again. I liked the shape of his pipe, with a four-inch-long almost vertical mouthpiece and a blackened brier bowl. 'The ones who left here this morning had a nasty look to them,' he said. 'And tomorrow we'll know whether, as rivers go, the Piave turns out a better barrier than the Tagliamento was.'

'Grandpa says the war is already lost.'

He looked me straight in the eye. I looked at the ground. 'Italy is feminine,' he said, raising his voice a little, 'whereas Germany is masculine. Where women are concerned,' he added, almost in a whisper, 'you can never tell. We have lost one army, but if the rest of our forces rally…The front is far shorter now, and we could prove a tough nut to crack.'

I turned towards the gate, where there was a sudden hubbub. I made out the silhouette of Giulia, who was hugging some dangling object to herself, something the two sentries were trying to wrest from her hands. 'I'll go and see…'

'You will do nothing of the sort. Donna Giulia is quite able to fend for herself.'

His tone conveyed an order, not a piece of advice.

'Better to leave the women to it. And that one doesn't speak much, but when she does, it's fireworks.' He chewed on his pipe-stem. 'Poor sentries,' he added, fanning the smoke away with his big, horny right hand. His eyes were smiling. I realized that he guessed what I felt for Giulia, and I blushed again. 'You see? She's already got out of it.'

18

I went to meet Giulia. She had the sun behind her and it took me a while to make out what it was she was holding. A gasmask, one of those with a snout. 'Hello,' I said, suppressing my excitement.

Giulia held up the gasmask to hide a rather crafty grin. The snout hung down onto her swelling breasts, which even her padded jacket barely restrained. The two glass eyepieces made her look like a giant insect, and the pot at the end of the snout added a Martian touch. 'I picked it up for half a bucketful of carobs. This German wanted a kiss and I slipped him the carobs. Even horses don't like them much.' She laughed, and taking the mask from her face released a swarm of freckles.

'A bit macabre, your headdress.'

'I think it suits me. You told me yesterday that my eyes are too blue. With this I've got eyes like a hornet.'

'Come on, let's go indoors. Too many soldiers here.'

Out of the corner of my eye I caught a glimpse of Renato following a sergeant towards the wood with a shovel over his shoulder.

'Let's hope they're not making him dig his own grave,' said Giulia.

'They're going to dig a trench further off, in case the wind blows this way. These toff officers have delicate noses,' said Teresa as she stood aside to let us in. It took a little while for my eyes to adjust to the darkness of the kitchen. There were five men round the fireplace, one of them Italian, a prisoner. They looked at me unseeingly. They were blotto. One of them, his tunic unbuttoned, was stirring polenta over a sparkling blaze. Without weapons on their belts they had a cheery look, as if the war had gone away along with the officers who had left at dawn.

With the staring eyes of famished men the soldiers gazed at

Giulia as she made her way between the blackened pillars. To take the edge off my agitation I took a deep breath of the odour of mould and polenta. The Italian gave us a sketchy greeting, while the others looked away, pretending a sudden interest in the cauldron. In them I no longer felt the arrogance of the marauders of last evening, but more the embarrassment of uninvited guests, prisoners of a foreign language, almost regretful at being unable to exchange courtesies. Bavarians or Prussians as they might be, their firesides at home couldn't be all that different from ours, and their employers must have had kitchens no less spacious than this one. Giulia went through into the drawing room, and I followed her.

'Is it German, that pendant of yours?'

'No. It was on the corpse of a *bersagliere* officer. Would you rather have a rag doll?'

I wasn't interested in what she said, but only in her voice. Giulia was chaos personified, an irresistible force. Grandpa had described her as the crupper of a horse, the shudder it gives, the lash of its tail on a horsefly. But she was far, far more than that: she was beautiful, she was ablaze. She regarded me with the hauteur of one who, knowing herself desired, strives not to reproach the unrequited lover.

'I must see your grandmother. At once!'

'She's been shut up in her room ever since…this lot arrived.'

'They've kidnapped some girls. Over at the church. And knocked out the priest.'

'How do you know?'

'What I know I know.'

'Go upstairs then. Try knocking.'

I was left alone in the dark room. They had carried off the carpets and nearly all the chairs were smashed. The pianola had vanished. The great oak table was still there, and on it two filthy mattresses which made me think of the kidnapped girls and what it said in the *Corriere* about the iniquities committed by the Huns in Belgium. I had never really wanted to believe it, even if at the inn they spoke of certain details…

I left by the back door, wound my scarf around my neck and buttoned up my overcoat. I took the path that goes up to the little temple. It wasn't far, but it took me almost ten minutes. I saw Renato digging the latrine along with a German soldier and an Italian prisoner with his neck swathed in grey, blood-stained bandages. I exchanged a glance with the steward and almost unwittingly turned to look at the church, one whole side of which adjoined the rear of our porticoed *barchessa*. Six or seven soldiers were sitting round the apse, chewing on pipe-stems. From their helmets I realized they were prisoners too. If they were outside the church, it meant that the story about the girls was true. I looked up at the bell tower, and made out the bell in its belfry. Whenever anything extraordinary happened, it was that bell that first spoke of it. I wondered how soon the value of its metal would rob us of it, leaving Refrontolo without its ancient voice.

I noticed they were digging a second latrine right up against the wall of our cemetery. 'Aunt won't like that,' I said to myself as I walked on. Muffled by distance, the din of the artillery sounded like the rhythmic hooting of ships' foghorns. Every cloud, be it large or small, left its dark shadow on the empty plain. Nearly everyone had fled the village. But not the peasants. All they had was that patch of land, three farm animals and four chairs: how could they possibly leave them? Of people of any standing in the village only the priest was left, apart from a few with their heads not screwed on properly, such as the Third

Paramour, who was not the type to become a refugee. His feet were big enough, but his pockets were not deep.

Only one cow was left in our cowshed, because the Germans had taken the other two off to a nearby farmhouse; but the milk of that one cow, which Loretta milked at dawn, was enough for us.

More noise from the big guns. It came from over Montello way. I sat down on the empty altar in the middle of the little round temple, so tiny that when I stretched my arms my fingertips brushed the pillars. The sun was paling in a sky growing greyer by the moment. The air was heavy with the odour of stabling and sweaty clothes. And also that smell like iron filings that even today – more then ten years later – makes me think of the war. The roads were choked with refugees then and I learnt to recognize the stench of iron and piss that got right into your throat, tasting of sweat, and terror, and rags clogged with excrement.

I lit a cigarette and tried to think about nothing.

The darkness was as dense as the breath of cattle. There was no one in the streets. The windows were all shuttered up. Only from the church windows filtered some wan and ominous light. The drizzle had intensified the smell of mule dung. The Villa was almost empty, and my grandparents didn't even have supper. Aunt Maria and I ate in a corner of her room, where the frescoed ceiling depicted a jungle with huge red ibises and water buffalo. Among the tangle of boughs there was also a little temple that was perhaps Hindu, in the shadow of which were two Barbary apes and a blue parrot. Loretta served us a dish of rice, with a few drops of olive oil from a jug which Teresa at once went and hid behind the dresser, where a brick had been removed to make a secret hiding place.

A sudden din of engines and crunching gravel brought us to our feet. Motorbikes. Then two, three, four lorries. The rain was rebounding on the window sill. I watched an orderly file of lorries drive into the grounds. 'They're a different sort from yesterday's. No mules, no bicycles,' I said.

'Germany here on our doorstep, whoever would have thought it?' My aunt's voice betrayed more anger than sorrow. Then the noise of the rain came crashing against the windowpanes, drowning even the roar of the engines.

Three

THE MEDALLION CLINKED AGAINST THE DOG'S COLLAR. IT
was a messenger dog belonging to the Imperial Army, a sheep-
dog with the tips of its ears folded down, part Alsatian and
part retriever. Giulia, sitting under the magnolia tree with her
gasmask in her lap, stretched out a hand. 'It's a medallion with
a picture of the Madonna,' she said.

I leant down and took hold of the medallion as the dog raised
its nose. I read the inscription: 'To Luisa, for her First Communion, 9 May 1908'. I looked over at the sentries standing guard
at the gate. 'What bastards! How dare they hang it round the
neck of a dog.'

'They've got guns.'

'How many are there in the church?'

'What does it matter? There's nothing we can do.' At that
moment the dog, alarmed by a rifle shot, darted away. Giulia
dropped the mask.

One of the two sentries at the gate fell to the ground. The
other unslung his rifle, dropped to one knee and fired twice at
a window on the other side of the road.

The fire was returned from the window.

'Let's get out of here,' said Giulia. We ran back into the Villa
and up the stairs, two at a time. We entered the loft without
knocking, and crowded in close to Grandpa, already at one of

the dormer windows.

'That must be Rocca. The fellow who works at Pancrazio's. They've got one of his nieces in the church.'

'What can we do?' said Giulia and Grandpa in unison.

A platoon of infantrymen was surrounding the house across the way; a few of them broke down the door.

Another shot, then one more. Then silence.

Five minutes passed, or perhaps ten. Then we watched as the soldiers, led by a dark-haired lieutenant, emerged with their rifle butts thrust into the ribs of two old men with their hands up, and an old woman not just bent but crippled.

The officer barked two orders. The prisoners were pushed under the portico of our barchetta. One soldier forced them to sit against the wall while another started kicking the younger man, who looked about sixty. The old woman hobbled out and stopped right in front of the officer.

'This has nothing to do with the kidnapped girls,' said Grandpa, turning away from the window. 'I bet that if one were to prick her belly with a pin a barrel of grappa would spurt out.' He chuckled. 'If that German has them shot there'll be three corpses ready for bottling, but if he decides to hang them the old girl will get away with it. Just wait and see.'

Grandpa was right. The lieutenant was partial to the noose, and the woman was spared. 'You'll find they leave them hanging there in full view,' said Grandpa. 'Shootings are soon forgotten, but the bodies of hanged men…There's no more explicit threat.'

The trial lasted a bare minute or two. Just enough time for the young officer to bark out three orders and draw up his small troop at the edge of the street that a little further on widened into a little piazza. The old dame was escorted into the inn where the non-commissioned officers were lodged, even though some said she too had fired with a revolver towards the great magnolia tree in our grounds. The soldier was not seriously wounded, and that evening I saw him on a camp bed by the drawing-room fire, surrounded by his mates, who were laughing and handing him one glass of wine after another.

It was a hanging without ceremony. Almost no one spoke up in their defence. Only the innkeeper said that they were drunk on his grappa, that they certainly didn't know what they were doing, that the guns were only shotguns that wouldn't really hurt anyone, and that they didn't deserve to die.

The officer listened, silent and motionless, and when mine host had finished he saluted him, clicking his heels as though the man before him was a general. The innkeeper went back inside with dragging feet and a hung head, and the troops burst out laughing, every man jack of them. Then the officer shouted one single brief word and all fell silent. Men, women, donkeys, everything.

It may be that, drunk as they were, they died without realizing it. The soldier who tied the knot did not show them the noose. No one murmured pious fibs into their ears. They remained there hanging, their breeches sodden with urine, until evening. And until darkness fell no one crossed the piazza, where the lime-tree branches creaked without ceasing in the Sirocco wind.

That night we held a family conference. Grandma called us into the only room where she was sure of not being disturbed, her own bedroom. She was wearing a blue dress and high heels. At her neck she wore a black lace frill and in her ears two artificial sapphires that competed with her eyes for blueness. Grandpa, with ill-groomed moustache, was seated beside her on the bed, clasping an old issue of the Touring Club magazine with a picture of a column of Alpine troops and mules heavily laden with Talmone chocolate. I stood next to my aunt, who was sitting by the chest of drawers containing Grandma's underwear, priceless possessions that only Teresa was authorized to iron and replace. Although not 'family', the steward was standing at the door – his enormous hands clasped behind his back, his felt jacket buttoned up to the neck, and his feet apart – as if to say, with his embarrassingly huge bulk, that no one was setting foot in here, not even if they mobilized the whole Alpenkorps. I think it was the first time I had seen him without his pipe.

'I have called you here to explain to you how we must behave from now on,' said Grandma almost in an undertone. 'Between these people and us I want there to be a barrier of tight lips and sour looks. After what has happened we cannot behave otherwise. We will put at their disposal whatever they would take in any case, which means to say everything – except our dignity. And this we will defend by maintaining a scornful silence. The village is virtually deserted, and the remaining old people cannot and must not attempt foolish actions like today's. To get oneself hanged is downright stupid.' She gave each of us in turn a straight look, and time for it to sink in. 'Do nothing rash.' And Grandma looked at me, just me. 'We will have as little contact as possible with the enemy. Signor Manca,' and she nodded towards the steward at the door, as she smoothed out the folds of her skirt with her bony fingers, 'has offered to act as our ears and my voice, talking to the farmhands and referring to me alone, every day, as to what is going on. We have to be careful and circumspect.'

All eyes turned towards Renato. All except those of Aunt Maria, who stared fixedly at some spot on the wall. The fact that the steward was there at all was already strange, but this

28

investiture by Grandma bordered on the astonishing. 'Our ears and my voice,' is what she had said. I couldn't believe it. I noticed that Grandpa looked saddened; not surprised, just saddened. He kept his eyes low, fixed on that old copy of the Touring Club magazine until it slipped from his fingers and ended up on the carpet.

Grandpa didn't take to Renato. 'That fellow doesn't say much and looks around him too much,' he told me a few days after the steward's arrival. 'I bet my moustache that he could have the shoes off me while I was walking in the rain, and I wouldn't know it until my feet were sopping.' The truth is that it was Grandma and Aunt Maria who had a liking for that giant; it was they who had decided to employ him, despite the fact that the references from that Tuscan marquis were, according to Grandpa, rather nebulous.

A heavy blow shook the door, once, twice, three times. A curt order in German. Renato undid the bolt and Aunt Maria went to stand at his side. The door creaked open. The soldier said something to my aunt which I didn't understand. The steward stood aside and she followed the soldier down the stairs.

'We mustn't show any curiosity,' said Grandma. 'Paolo, catch up with your aunt and pretend you've got something to tell her. She'll like to have you close by.'

Grandpa looked at me with great sad-dog eyes, and leant down to retrieve the crumpled magazine with the mules and their loads of Talmone. 'Run along, then,' he said.

There was a great coming and going in the garden. Swarms of troops with mud-spattered boots and uniforms, their faces drawn with exhaustion. I went to the gate. No one took the least notice of me. Aunt Maria was standing between the two sentries guarding the entrance, who were rigidly at attention.

The captain, upright in the saddle, screwed in his monocle and brought his right hand up to his temple, as stiff as an iron wing.

'Captain Korpium,' said my aunt.

The captain, with a twitch of irritation, ejected the monocle.

'Madame, your river Piave was not favourable to us, but I am still in one piece. I dare say you are not pleased.' He pronounced the Italian vowels with a studied precision that endowed them with a roundness hard to credit in the mouth of a foreigner. The hard edge of his voice struggled with a warmth diminished, perhaps banished, by the brutality of war.

'Captain, have you had me summoned just to let me know you are still alive?'

'I want you to enter the church immediately after me…Fetch the girls out: they will need to hear a woman's voice. Call your maids, give me five minutes and not a second longer, then enter.'

He turned his horse with gentle pressure of the heels, and went off at a walk.

Aunt Maria turned swiftly to me. 'Call Teresa and Loretta. Quick!'

But they were both there already, as well as Renato.

'Renato, we won't need you at the moment.'

The steward nodded. I noticed that Loretta was trying to catch his eye. Teresa gave her a *diambarne de l'ostia* accompanied by a snort.

Teresa never took the name of the devil in vain, but preferred to use that nickname lest she should inadvertently conjure him up.

I too started off towards the church, and Aunt Maria made no attempt to stop me. Teresa's looks were black as a thundercloud.

And the hoofs of the bay horse climbing the church steps

30

were like the crackle of thunder that follows the lightning. Like drums out of rhythm, as if the trident of hell itself, fallen from the hand of Lucifer, were tumbling step by step down a rocky stairway.

The captain shouted an order. Two privates and a sergeant forced the church door, which opened with a grinding of metal. The church within was almost as bright as daylight. I sidled in behind a pillar. There were candles everywhere, on the pews and on the altars. The bay reared up, and the captain drew his sabre. I saw the girls clinging tightly to each other, five of them, sitting on the steps of the high altar. They were naked. Four soldiers got to their feet in various places. I heard the sound of a wine fiasco rolling about. The captain's horse approached the tallest and burliest of the men, whose jacket was open and chest bared as he held out his hands to ward off the blow. The flat of the blade struck him on the head. There was a sharp cry. It didn't come from the soldier, who crumpled to the ground, but from the girls. The fallen man tried to struggle to his feet, but his legs folded beneath him and he fell again, face down as if he had a broken back. I saw another two men get up in different parts of the church. They quickly formed a group, reached the high altar and stood shakily in line at attention.

The captain walked his horse round among the overturned pews, extinguished a cluster of candles at one swipe, and drew up with his horse's nose almost in the soldiers' faces. The girls were all gazing silently towards the door. The captain uttered a few words which I didn't understand. The men might have been made of wax, like candles gradually melting. I watched them leave in Indian file, completely mute, heads hanging; a squad resigned to an ancient tradition of discipline and death. The struck man lay still. The captain rode over him, the horse taking a long step to avoid the body. In came my aunt with the two servants. Spotting me, she said, 'See to Don Lorenzo. Look in the tower.'

I found the priest bound to the circular staircase of the bell tower. I pulled out the piece of rag he was gagged with. He said not a word, but panted like a thirsty dog. He avoided my eyes. It took me a good three minutes, maybe more, to untie all the knots. When I had finished he gripped my shoulders with both hands and croaked something, of which I only understood the word 'water'. I realized that the poor man had not had a drop to drink for two days. With me supporting him we tottered round the forecourt, he with his cassock encrusted with urine. The sacristy door was ajar, the lock smashed. In we went and I led him to the locker where the pump was. I have never seen anyone drink as he did. Then he put his bald head under the icy water and kept it there, motionless, while I pumped the handle.

Yellowish trickles ran down into his collar and down his cassock. He raised his head and heaved a heavy sigh.

'Don Lorenzo... Will you be all right?'

He turned his small eyes on me. 'Those girls... The godless bastard Huns!' he whispered in the distracted tones of pious old dames telling their beads. 'And in the Lord's house!' he added with effort. 'Under the very eyes of the Blessed Virgin! But He' – pointing up towards the mould-blotched ceiling – 'He sees all and He provides.'

'If it's any consolation to you, Father, I think their captain also sees and provides. One of the Huns is laid out in the middle of the church with his head split open.'

Don Lorenzo wrinkled his 'alopecic pate', as Grandpa liked to call it, and hurled in my face a mephitic blast of syllables: 'Don't be insolent!'

I followed him into the church. The candles were guttering out. With the help of Teresa and Loretta, my aunt had taken the girls away. I felt something warm on my fingers. It was a dog's tongue.

'All these candles, these tiny flames…Do you hear their voices too?' The priest clutched my arm so hard it hurt. 'What happened here…' He fell silent for a moment. Then: 'A legion of angels will destroy them utterly,' he added, his eyes fixed on the ground. And he sat down heavily on the altar steps.

The dog, an army Alsatian, started licking his folded hands. It was then that I noticed Don Lorenzo's eyes were welling with tears. I left the church on tiptoe, as if I were disturbing a dying man. A weary sadness took possession of me, as when one thinks of a friend who has died, of how unjust his absence is, of the voice we shall never hear again, of how he left us without any reason in the world.

Four

THE DAYS PASSED UNEVENTFULLY. IF IT HADN'T BEEN FOR the helmets, rifles and uniforms, one would scarcely have thought there was a war on. The artillery barrages became rarer, and always in the distance. Hordes of prisoners, commanded by Austrian non-commissioned officers with the rough manners of gang overseers, were clearing the roads, ditches and footpaths of the wreckage left during our retreat. Most of the carts, bicycles, motorbikes and lorries abandoned by our routed forces had been removed during the earliest days of the occupation. Everything was engulfed by the repair shops which the victors were busy getting into operation again. The enemy troops had plentiful rations, Italian foodstuffs which had survived the destruction of the army depots, while trains loaded with flour, cows, fabrics and furnishings were making their way to Vienna, Budapest and Berlin.

The homes of the country people, but even the big houses of the gentry, were ransacked again and again. Resistance was out of the question; the least one could expect was a jaw smashed with a rifle butt. The young women in the outlying farms were smearing their faces with pig-dung and stuffing bundled-up rags into their clothes to make them look disgusting, pregnant, altogether unappetizing.

'Opening their legs has never done women much harm,' said

Grandpa in dialect, which he used to fall back on for his lewder utterances. He had always liked to scatter his good-humoured sarcasm over the world, especially when the world seemed even more scared than he was.

Captain Korpium had given Don Lorenzo a safe-conduct for the raped girls. After a brief visit to the medical officer's tent, his problem cleared up with a drop of cordial, the priest had taken them off in Grandpa's gig just as dawn was rising over the hills. He got them out before their parents and siblings could see them. 'Better not to rub salt into the wounds,' he said to Donna Maria as he climbed onto the driving seat. My aunt saw the girls off with the ghost of a wave. They did not reply, or say a word, or do anything at all except keep their staring, bewildered eyes fixed on the back of the priest's hat. When the gig passed through the gate the sentries sprang to attention. I followed the whole scene from up above, glued to the window along with Grandpa, who was stroking his moustache to give it some semblance of shape. Neither of us had slept a wink. A silence more stolid than that of the mules had fallen upon the garden, the streets, the Villa, the entire village.

It took three days to recover all the medallions of the Madonna, because two of the dogs had ended up at Pieve di Soligo, and were only found by a company of Bosnian pontoon-bridge builders returning, decimated, from Segusino.

All that had taken place in the church had to be erased from the memory of the village. The medallions were collected up by the priest's housekeeper, a woman of sixty or so about the height of a tub of cheese and with a face carved out of boxwood, who hung them all round the neck of the Virgin, a blue and white wooden statue standing beside the altar in the left-hand nave. In this way the little housemaid-like face of the Queen of Heaven was suffused with the light of reflected gold. But it didn't last long, because Aunt Maria was furious: 'A hen has more sense than you,' said she, towering over the housekeeper. 'Take away those foul baubles. Give them to the blacksmith and have him melt them down, at once! Don Lorenzo will find a good use for the metal.' My aunt then spent half an hour in church telling her beads. She thought it a point of honour, a personal matter, to mollify the affront suffered by the Virgin Mother. Poor Aunt, she really did believe in the Church. She thought of it as a relic of the Roman Empire, and the only political institution worthy of respect out of all that have set up house in this martyred peninsula of ours. Besides, after the Battle of Caporetto it was not easy for anyone to put their trust in a dwarf king and his pack of imbeciles.

'It's odd,' I had heard Grandpa say more than once, 'that such a tough customer as your aunt is such a God-botherer.' Grandma, on the other hand, had her own ideas about it: 'Ever since she was little Maria has relied only on herself, on what one can see and touch, not on the twaddle of the black beetles.' She had studied with intention to become a schoolteacher, but then – the war in Libya had begun just two days after her thirtieth birthday – she joined up in the Red Cross. I was very fond of her, because she was different, as if there were something masculine in her, and then because our parents, hers and mine, had all died together in that shipwreck. I don't think I ever met anyone more conscious than she of her rank in society. She knew in her innermost being that privileges are paid for by responsibilities, and these were two things to be borne with grace. But, 'Grace,' she would make a point of saying, 'is a gift from God, not something to be come by on request.' In the melancholy of her features I could discern a barely concealed trace of despondency which ill fitted the generosity of her nature.

Donna Maria had left the house in Venice a month after the Great Disaster and had taken me with her to Refrontolo. Grandma had immediately entrusted her with the running of Villa Spada. Partly to distract her thoughts, of course, but also because this came in very handy, as she herself was rather devoid of practical sense. Since then Aunt Maria had administered the Villa and the farm with a firm hand, thrift, and a touch of daring, managing even to make a success of the miserable patch of vineyard that stretched from the little temple as far as the ditch that marked the border of our grounds. Of her passion for horses, which she bought, broke in and sold, the malicious tongues in the village used to say, 'She mounts them because no one mounts her.' Unlike intelligence, to quote one of Grandpa's maxims, stupidity knows no bounds.

Those were days when the *tramontana* was blowing, and time and again the sleet beat and beat against the windowpanes. 'Paolo,' said Grandma, 'just think of a swarm of birds that veers round in the twinkling of an eye and in perfect formation; and fish do the same in a stream. It takes the mathematics you hate so much to describe such a wonderful thing. Only a formula can capture that miracle of nature which your Fokkers and your SPADs try in vain to imitate.' She spoke from her bed, her back against the headboard, the blankets pulled up to her waist. She was wearing a white dressing gown bordered in pink and topped off with a lace collar. In her eyes as she spoke I saw that same sleet that whirled against the windowpanes. I was on my feet near the chest of drawers, staring at the coat-stand hung with enemas, in full view through the open bathroom door.

'You sneaked it away under their very noses, didn't you, Grandma?'

'You are very good at changing the subject,' she smiled. 'Yes, they searched everywhere. They even unscrewed the legs of the bed, but they're better at fighting than they are at thinking, because thinking takes more effort. You don't want to make the effort to get to like maths, but it's worth it. You have to work hard to understand the simple things, which are the most difficult, and then suddenly, when you least expect it – just you see – everything falls into place.'

There was no way of dinning it into her head that I just wasn't cut out for maths, and if I had gone on protesting how hopeless I was it would have upset her too much. 'Human beings don't give up their illusions, even on the point of death,' Grandpa used to quote from the dictionary of proverbs stored in his head. The family legend was quite clear on one matter: Grandma Nancy had shown an outstanding gift for numbers even as a little girl. The daughter of a Venetian astronomer, at sixteen she had gone with her father on a journey through the deserts of Mauretania, along with some English friends of her mother, who was a Scot of the Clan Bruce.

Great-Grandma Elizabeth had died rather young, at forty-two, of a disease the doctors had not managed to diagnose in time, perhaps leukaemia. So when she was twenty-one Grandma Nancy found herself motherless, with a father in great distress. She took care of him and, in no less a place than Burano, managed a small corn-meal biscuit business which had belonged to her mother. They went to Edinburgh to take possession of their Bruce inheritance, sold what was left of it and returned to Italy. Nancy realized almost at once that it was not easy for a young woman to work with a bunch of men accustomed to regarding the gentle sex as divided into three categories: mothers and sisters; wives and daughters; maidservants. Her father died barely two years after her mother, at which point – managing not to get too badly swindled – she sold her business to the owner of the bakery. On the advice of a Venetian notary friend of her father's she used the money to buy property, including the Villa at Refrontolo.

The years that followed were the happiest of her life. She resumed her studies and spent every spring and summer in London, where she was one of a group of mathematicians, who recognized and appreciated her talent, thus helping her to allay the suspicion which – even in England – a lady with great intellectual endowments was likely to arouse. She used to spend the winters in Venice and Paris, along with the gilded youth of half of Europe, until finally she married Grandpa Gugliemo, who was two years her junior.

With the outbreak of war the exchange of letters between Grandma and her mathematician London friends had become more intense. At the end of the summer of 1917, after the eleventh Battle of the Isonzo, she had a visit from one of them, by the name of Sir James, who spoke good Italian because he had lived for a while in Tripoli. He was a tall, thin man with snow-white hair and an impressive nose. He smoked great rolls of foul-smelling tobacco and wore grey pullovers, never a jacket or a tie. I don't know what they talked about, but they spent the evenings together, and several times I came across them strolling along the stream. They often went all the way to the old mill, and Sir James always came back with a bag of flour for Teresa's store-cupboard. One thing was abundantly clear to me: the two of them shared more than their common passion for mathematics, which they managed to talk about even at dinner, raising more than one protest from Grandpa.

During those days Grandma seemed to have shed twenty years. On one occasion I came across the 'two old sticks' – a definition coined, not without malicious intent, by Grandpa – nattering under the chestnut tree in the garden. They were speaking in hushed tones. I had hidden behind a box-bush which Teresa trimmed and cared for like a son, but I was in for a complete let-down. The subject of their animated, whispered conversation was the shutters of the three-mullioned sixteenth-century window in the façade of the Villa overlooking the village piazza, and the underclothing we all wear, associated for some reason with the washing lines stretched across the courtyard at the back of the building.

Five

TERESA BROUGHT ME A BOWL OF HOT MILK BARELY TINTED
with black barley. 'Drink up, before these Krauts pinch the lot!'
Then, seeing her daughter tidying her hair reflected in the water
in the sink, she burst out: 'Stop admiring yourself, Loretta, don't
you know it's Old Nick who combs hair!' She knew her daughter was vacuous, and that it's hard to do much with a vacuum.

I drank my milk and barley at a draught, got to my feet and
stepped round Teresa. She was a mule of a woman, with greyish
complexion and a long chin, shoulders custom built for burdens,
and a grimace of rage mingled with soot. She was a noble, obstinate animal, tamed only if you knew how to get on her right side,
a gift which only Grandma and Aunt Maria seemed to possess.

A loud outcry rang through the kitchen. Then another, then
a third. I was already at the door when Renato's arm barred my
way.

'Don't go out. Aunt's orders.'

'What's going on?'

'The men from the church have served their sentence and
the sub-lieutenant has told the troops the captain is packing the
lot of them off to Monte Grappa. There's a hint of rebellion
in the air. But nothing will come of it – this lot were born in
uniform.' Renato lowered his pipe. 'They think this is unfair
punishment, but he is their C.O. so nothing will come of it. If

he knows his stuff he'll allow them to let off steam, and in half
an hour it'll all be over.'

The soldiers' voices grew more numerous, some coming
even from the inner courtyard.

'They're getting off lightly, these Krauts,' said Teresa as she
dried the last dish.

'Lightly? Monte Grappa?' The steward rammed his pipe
back in his mouth. 'It's hell on earth up on that mountain.'

I really liked that man. I was used to seeing people from above;
at seventeen I was already a metre seventy, but he towered over
me. Everything about him seemed to speak to me. His appearance, the look in his eyes, the quick, strong movements of his
arms, even his limp. If he was the steward at the Villa...But who
was he really? Why did Grandma think so highly of him? Even
Aunt Maria hung on his lips, a privilege I had never seen her
grant to anyone.

'Like a bowl of milk, Renato?' asked Loretta.

'Be quiet, girl,' snapped Teresa, flaring her nostrils.

'But...Mum...'

'Quiet, I tell you!'

The soldiers' voices grew louder and louder, interrupted at
intervals by sharp orders.

'Signor Manca, won't you let me in?'

It was Giulia with her hair bundled up under a fur hat. She
was wearing a jacket with a fur collar, and her trousers were
rolled up over a pair of riding boots. I had never seen her in such
a get-up, but Giulia was Giulia and no one showed any surprise
at her odd breeches.

Renato stepped aside, and she came in saying, 'I'll light the
fire.'

'The fire is my job,' said Teresa, stooping over the firewood.

To help her mother, Loretta moved the swinging arm on which hung the cauldron. It squeaked and Teresa gave a snort. All of a sudden the voices of the soldiers fell silent.

'Just you see, they'll get off scot free, this rabble!'

Loretta couldn't take her eyes off Renato's face, his hands, his manly chest.

'What is it these youngsters put into your noddle?' grunted Teresa. 'Beelzebub's business, that's what.'

Giulia smiled, looking hard at the steward.

'Would you like some milk?' I asked her.

She lifted the gasmask to her face, then lowered it again and bared her teeth.

'We could do with a walk,' I added in a shaky voice.

'I'll have a bowl of milk first.'

Giulia took the bowl from Loretta's hands and I went upstairs to fetch my overcoat. I said hello to Grandpa who told me to take care, and when I came down again I saw only Teresa and her daughter at the fireplace. This surprised me. I went outside, and as I closed the door I glimpsed a pout on Loretta's face. Giulia and Renato were at the gate talking to a sentry who had ordered arms. Renato was waving his pipe in front of his face. The soldier was laughing. I started towards them.

'Come along quick,' said Giulia, coming to meet me. 'That fellow's asking too many questions.'

We set off. To my surprise and disappointment I found that Renato, despite his limp, was as agile as an ibex.

We climbed up towards the cemetery, passed the front of the church, and then took to the main road. There was still the sweetish whiff of corpses, whether of man or of mule, and still wrecks of carts and lorries, though many had been cleared away over the last few days. Every so often we spotted a line of prisoners, easy to distinguish by the unmistakable Adrian steel helmets weighing down their heads. They were raking the fields and filling huge sacks with fragments of the flesh and bones of men and beasts all jumbled together. But when in the grass they came across a human head those makeshift undertakers stopped for a moment, crossed themselves to a man, and a metal chest was set down beside those pathetic remains.

Giulia was on ahead. Renato and I, instead, were walking side by side. It began to snow. Just a little at first, but then heavily.

'Let's get back,' said Renato.

Giulia, four steps ahead of us, had begun to fool around with her pet gasmask. Renato reached into his pocket and took out a flask of grappa. He held it out to me. I shook my head. But I was cold, and when he had taken a long swig and was shoving it back in his pocket I asked for a drop.

'A little more and you'll become a regular Alpino.'

'Just a year to go for that…but right now we're in Germany.'

'This bloody war isn't going to last a year.'

'Do you mean we've lost it?'

'I didn't say that. The armies might hold out but not the empires, they've run out of steam.' He put the flask back and rammed his pipe into his mouth. 'The Central Powers, the Western Powers, all of them are broken winded.' He stabbed the mouthpiece in the direction of Giulia as he gave me a clout on the back. 'You fancy the young lady, eh?'

Six

Teresa's stubby fingers smoothed the wrinkles out of the lace on the little table. 'Is it all right here, madam?'

'Yes, it's just right there. A small table for a grand occasion.'

'Those poor girls. Who ever will take those poor girls now?' Teresa waved her open palms towards the ceiling.

'Don Lorenzo has taken them to a convent near Feltre,' said Donna Maria. 'But we have many more troubles ahead of us... and when those poor girls come back there will be a lot else to think about, and a lot to be done.'

'But those medallions round the neck of a dog...'

Donna Maria had moved to the window. 'Put on a bit more wood, Teresa. It's getting chilly.' She stroked the thick, rough woollen shawl that fell over her still firm, fine bosom. 'Put out the German's soup tureen as well as his silver...he'll have stolen them from some other Italian house. Those bastards,' and she lowered her voice, 'call looting a requisite of war. They have a nerve.'

'They ought to be shot,' grumbled Teresa, and vanished through the doorway.

Aunt made a tour of the room lighting one candle after another. She told me she was going to ask the captain to provide more paraffin for the lamps. She used the bellows to liven up the fire burning on the terracotta firedogs, embossed with the faces of two centurions wearing helmets not unlike those of the Prussians. And she began to talk about the eagle of the Roman legions, of the two-headed eagle of the Hapsburgs, and the German eagle. 'No one uses the horse as a crest,' she said with a smile. 'And the horse is the noblest of animals, the one all armies exploit, even unto death.'

'Even the Americans have an eagle, Aunt.'

Grandma Nancy burst in without knocking. 'It's all the fault of Rome,' she said. 'All these countries have the Scipio complex.' Grandma liked history and politics almost as much as mathematics. 'If we of the gentle sex were in command, wars would be made for self-interest, or perhaps for reasons of jealousy.' And her eyes fixed on me. 'You men, though, make war to show off your strength, you like killing, you act like brainless children almost all your lives, especially when you stop playing, which is in fact the only serious thing you do well. Don't be in any hurry to grow up, my boy.'

The two women exchanged glances. Grandma's face had the strong features of an ardent race, fierce Border raiders accustomed to command; while my aunt's warm eyes, set between prominent eyebrows and cheekbones, held a grave look of loneliness, gracefully borne though it was.

'If I didn't know you so well I'd think you were out to seduce someone.'

Donna Maria responded with a wan smile. 'I've invited Captain Korpium to dinner.'

Grandma stiffened. 'I thought I had enjoined silence.'

'I want those men shot.'

'It's none of our business. Why are you poking your nose in?'

Donna Maria put her fingertips to her cheeks. 'You must understand…I have to do it…or at least try.'

Grandma was aware of Aunt's deep-seated melancholy. 'I would prefer to be informed next time.' She turned and reached the door without deigning to glance at me. Her dress with its shot blue reflections rustled on the parquet. The candlelight flickered ever so slightly.

The moon was already high when Loretta announced the German.

'Come in, Captain,' said Donna Maria, upright with one hand on the mantelpiece and the other touching the ivory brooch conspicuous against the dark blue of her long dress, with its lace collar caressing her chin.

Korpium clicked his heels and stood for a long moment at attention, his cap under his arm. 'Thank you for the invitation, Madame,' he said, accompanying the words with a nervous little bow.

'Please be seated, Captain.'

They sat down face to face, Loretta standing beside her mistress and Teresa beside the captain. And the dance began.

I followed the scene from a hiding place – we called it 'Grandpa's cubby-hole' because he kept his cache of cognac there – where I had concealed myself with the complicity of Teresa. Not even Loretta was in the know. Teresa was very fond of me, spoiling me by making me biscuits and doing me almost countless favours, which I repaid with smiles and – every now and again – a few ten-minute sessions devoted to listening to her woes. There in Grandpa's cubby-hole Grandma and Aunt Maria had stacked old rugs and rolls of cloth, a dozen table-lamps, a tiny showcase containing three broken teeth – the brass plate read 'Relic of the Thirteenth Century' – and a burst armchair in which I accommodated myself. I had a good view of the little table through a hole in the wooden door where a knot had fallen out. This hole was a thumb's width, so I didn't even have to put my eye to it, while it was concealed by the yellowed gauze hung from the ceiling to hide the cracks.

'I see that you are wearing regulation uniform.' Aunt's voice bore a trace of vexation.

The captain coughed into his gloved hand. 'A soldier takes pride in his war uniform, though this is a profession at which your people do not shine.'

Donna Maria responded with an artful smile. 'Perhaps we should stop fencing, don't you think, Captain?'

The captain screwed in his monocle: 'Touché, Madame.'

'On the Piave, though, you have met with some resistance.'

The captain dropped his monocle into his left palm. 'Shall we savour the Marzemino, Madame?'

'With pleasure. Indeed, I must thank you for not having commandeered our demijohns.'

The captain poured two fingers of wine into Donna Maria's glass.

'Are you so very attached to your headgear, Captain?'

Korpium realized he still had his cap under his arm. He handed it to Teresa. 'I am jittery. Punishing these men…'

'Punishing? And in what manner, for goodness' sake?'

The captain removed his gloves and handed them also to Teresa. Then, clearing his throat, he said quietly: 'I am posting them to Monte Grappa. The men say that whoever goes up there doesn't come back down.'

'You ought to shoot them,' said Aunt in a firm, clear voice. 'An example needs to be set.'

The captain pretended not to have heard, and helped himself to a ladleful of the steaming risotto which Loretta was offering him. Then, following my aunt's lead, he swallowed a mouthful and his features relaxed. 'I have demoted them and transferred them to the most dangerous section of the front line. They have been with me for a year.'

'Those medallions round the dogs' necks. How cheap!'

'It was…unworthy…on the part of those men. I knew them all personally. They knew their job. I have led them in attacks on enemy trenches. They had iron truncheons and daggers and… How do you say it…guts! Yes, they had guts! It was a great grief to me to punish them, but discipline is discipline. Do not let it distress you, Madame. The priest removed the girls at once, and you will see, the village will soon forget it.'

'You ought to have shot them. Refrontolo would have been grateful.'

'You do not shoot a soldier for…and I do not require the gratitude of this village.'

'Do not forget, Captain, that I am a woman. There are some things a woman does not forgive.'

'But they have *been* punished!'

I thought I heard a snort from Teresa.

I felt like having a go at our Buddhist's cache of cognac – I only had to reach out a hand. But I didn't, for fear that even the rustle of a sleeve might be heard; the wooden partition was so very thin. I even tried to breathe quietly.

The captain raised his fork to his mouth, seeing that even my aunt couldn't resist the risotto.

I saw her make a sign. Teresa and her daughter left the room, Loretta dragging her feet.

'Monte Grappa has a curse on it. There's a little while left before the snow puts a halt to the manoeuvres. In action an officer gives life-and-death orders every day, and every day he demands immediate, absolute obedience. When there is no action, when the men are…resting…I have to be lenient with them, because the next day I might have to order those same lads to swim across a river, even if it's in flood, even under a full moon. And what I tell them to do, they do, even if it means death.'

I didn't manage to see my aunt's expression, but her tone of voice softened as she said, 'Men like you, who are on close terms with death, have an appeal all your own…doctors, soldiers… murderers…every woman feels it.' I heard her sigh. 'It has something to do with waiting. A soldier waiting for the battle or a woman waiting for her man's return. The terror is in the waiting, while action leaves no room for fear. I have seen terror. It was there in the eyes of the wounded men our troops abandoned by the roadside. I have seen it in the eyes of horses, when they are dying. And I have felt it within myself, Captain.'

The captain laid down his fork and adjusted his monocle. I suspected that he used that gadget as a shield. Perhaps he was afraid of his eyes betraying him, of being caught with his guard down.

'Do you think, Captain, that a woman does not know what it feels like to crouch in a hole while grenades are out to get you? Do you think I cannot imagine what it is to hear those blasts, those explosions, get nearer and nearer? Or to find yourself with the head or the arm of a friend in your lap, a bodiless head or arm? I am a woman, it is true, but I have seen what happens to soldiers. It is not their words that speak to you, but their eyes. Eyes which ask you, "Why now, why here, why me?" But one dies simply because one dies. A grenade carried off your hands, your legs…So it is up to us to speak out, to us mothers, and sisters, and fiancées and…even prostitutes. It is us, we women, all women, who give the answers. We do not give them with

52

words, Captain, but with womb and with voice, with our lips and the very hair of our heads, we are your yearning and your consolation.' Aunt was speaking quietly, but passionately. The candlelight flashed in the German's monocle as he sat still and silent. 'What is the fuel of war?' Aunt went on. 'Cynics say it is alcohol. Because you go drunk into the attack, don't you? But I think it is something else.'

The officer removed his monocle. 'When you are there in the mud,' he said, 'and preparing to go over the top, what you think of is staying alive, and you fight with and for the man on your left, with and for the man on your right. Because they and they only can help you to stay alive. Then and there you have no fatherland, no emperor, but only a rifle on your left and another on your right, and your own rifle, and bayonet, and hand grenades.'

'But that is not all there is to it. You fight also to discover how far you can hold out, to understand who you are. But maybe I am talking nonsense, maybe you fight only because you cannot help it…'

'We shoot cowards.'

'Yes, that's another thing. You cannot bear being thought cowards…However, no soldier has ever got himself killed just for his pay, has he, Captain?'

There followed a long moment of silence. I watched the glasses coming and going to their lips. I imagined that they were avoiding each other's eyes.

'I lived for a while in Tuscany, and I got to know the Italians: staunch people, much attached to their homes, their fields, their children, as well as to money, but you are different… You are eager and curious… You have in you an impulse towards abstraction which is rare in a woman, very rare.'

'It is that I…I know horses. There are times when I seem to feel their sadness, their fear.'

A thunderous blast shook the windowpanes.

'Excuse me, Madame.'

The captain stood up and went to the window. 'Artillery!' He turned, and added, 'It has begun to snow heavily again. If it snows in the mountains…'

Aunt Maria rang the brass bell standing near her glass. 'Can the snow stop the big guns?'

'Oh, yes, indeed the snow can. Only the snow. But it will not happen. What has been begun must be brought to a conclusion.' The captain resumed his seat.

Teresa entered, followed by her daughter. She was carrying a tray, and on the tray was a chicken, or perhaps a turkey. At that moment I remembered that during the afternoon I had seen the steward leaving the Villa with an empty sack over his shoulder.

Another rumble, further away. 'If winter brings the war to a halt in the mountains…'

'But have you not already won it?'

A shadow fell across the captain's face. It was that of Teresa, in the act of serving him.

'Do you like guinea-fowl?'

'I have not eaten so well for months, Madame. For years, I should say. Ever since…'

'Since…?'

'Forgive me, I was about to…to bore you with personal matters.' The captain's voice broke slightly.

'You are not boring me. You have said you have stayed in Tuscany. Is that where you learnt our language? You express yourself with extraordinary correctness, and I do not say it to flatter you, believe me.'

'You are too kind.' I saw him screw in his monocle. 'Yes, as a boy I spent many of my summer holidays at Piombino, where a friend of mine called…Anselm, Anselm von Feuerbach, had a villa. His mother came from Grozeto.'

'Grosseto.'

'Ah, Groseto indeed! You had just paid me a compliment, so I made a mistake.'

'I assure you, Captain, that I would be very happy to speak your language as well as you speak mine.'

Loretta refilled the wine glasses. I felt a sneeze coming, and stuffed a hanky into my mouth. All I heard was the clatter of knives and forks, and then once more the captain's voice, slower now, with a note of sadness.

'Von Feuerbach, a great friend. It is to him that I owe my Italian. We were always together, every summer, on the Tyrrhenian. There was sweetness in my life in those days. In those days I used to read Horace.'

'Horace?'

'Yes, I used to read the Latin poets. There was still room in my head for books. I remember the rocks, the undertow. We would dive in at night, Anselm and I…swimming naked, just the two of us…I remember how huge the moon was.'

'Hearing you talk like this…the war is far from your thoughts…just now.'

Something made me turn my head; I seemed to have heard a sound of scuttling. It was a sparrow! Inside Grandpa's cubbyhole! If I don't let it out it'll die of hunger, I thought. It was hopping about on an old dust-laden newspaper folded over the top of a lamp, and with hefty pecks with its beak was digging a tiny crater in that relic of the freedom of the press.

'Do you know what is good about war? That it makes things

simple. It puts the good men on this side, the bad men on that. You know you have to kill that man: your uniform tells you so. You know you have to give orders to this man and you owe obedience to that one. You only have to glance at his insignia. A soldier even has time for reflection. Civilian life is dull because it is too full of – supposed – liberties.'

'In peacetime people don't die, though.'

'People die anyway, always, all of them.'

'You have no children, have you, Captain?'

'I have my men.'

I seemed to see my aunt smile. The captain lifted his glass to his lips. 'A little more, please,' he said, turning his eyes to Teresa. I heard not a sound, but I'm fairly sure that the cook, through clamped lips, uttered a *diambarne de l'ostia*.

Loretta replaced some of the candles. The light became colder, stiller.

'We need some coffee. We have a little coffee today…real coffee. Let us seat ourselves more comfortably.'

The captain slipped his monocle into his pocket as he rose. 'I am fond of coffee.'

My aunt went over and sat in front of the fire. The captain did likewise, and cleared his throat.

'You know, Madame Spada, you remind me of a French lady I knew in Agadir, in Morocco. It was in 1910…'

'Morocco?'

'Yes, there was one of our destroyers in the harbour…On military business…I would have liked to marry her, but she hated the army, she hated people who give orders…She had just such a brow as you have, and the same grave look in the eyes.'

'You wish to flatter me, Captain. But…do you find me so sad?'

A long moment of silence.

'She is dead.'

I could have heard a pin drop.

Then came two thumps on the door. A few words in German. The captain shot to his feet. There was a brief exchange.

'Madame, I have to go. This dinner has been…Well, thank you.'

I heard the click of his heels, and pictured him stiff at attention.

'Teresa, Loretta, get a move on…clear the table.'

Seven

THERE WAS MUCH TALK ABOUT THE VANISHED GIRLS. Whispered talk, which made its way to Teresa's kitchen. But when Loretta mentioned what had happened in the church her mother shut her gob with a swipe of the dishcloth. At the bar they were talking about the monastery in the mountains and the way the rapists had been reprieved: in the streets the hatred was as thick as the stucco on the walls. Sour looks and silence dogged the footsteps of the troops. The church was still closed. Children were running round and round it, happy because no one was hearing their confession. And it is very likely that the fetid blast that issued from the priest's mouth – his bad breath was legendary – was not missed even by the most pious old biddies.

I spent as much time as I could with Renato. I was captivated by his physical strength, his brief, clipped mode of expression, always to the point, and by his Tuscan accent. I noticed that as soon as Loretta came into the kitchen her eyes sought him out, while her fingers never missed a chance to brush up against his jacket. He, however, always moved away.

I also spent some time in my aunt's company. After that evening I felt rather guilty towards her for having eavesdropped. One day, as we were walking together to the old mill, I asked her about the German captain.

'You're curious about that fellow Korpium, aren't you?'

Without realizing it, Aunt Maria quickened her pace. She knew that love is a fool's game. She knew it because beneath the surface she was a burning fire. The formality that restricted her manners was frail armour. One that made her feel a kinship with the dispositions of men bound by a discipline of death. Grandma said Aunt Maria had in her something of a retired colonel. I think she was wrong, and if anything she was like a colonel out to win medals. She had a high forehead, prominent brows and cheekbones, thin lips and a melancholy smile. And in her look, though sharp at times, there was always a trace of sadness. She preferred dried-up plants to those in flower: 'To make them bloom again is my business,' she would say, almost as if it were a mission. She was devoted to simple pleasures, to books, a plate of risotto, risqué conversation and the algebraic strictness of the liturgy. And she was fond of cats: 'A cat is always elegant, even when it licks its backside.'

'Did you really think you'd persuade the captain to shoot them?'

'No. Not for a moment. I wanted to force him to show his hand. At present we have no choice but to live with these men, these Germans. The future may be rather arduous; we must know them well so we might better fight them.'

'But the army…Will it manage to check them?'

'Don't you hear the big guns? They are firing from the Montello, from Monte Tomba. They are fighting around the Quero Pass. As long as we can hear the guns it means they have not broken through.'

A magpie flew off from the fence at the edge of the wood. I followed it with my eyes. It perched on the rooftop of a ruined house masked from view by an array of hornbeams.

'Who lives there?'

She turned to me with a slight smile. 'It belonged to an English family, but it's been empty for quite some time. Abandoned. Can't you see the state it's in?'

'People you knew?'

'Yes. I knew one young man. Some years ago. He said he was descended from a famous poet, and quite gave himself airs about it. He was nice, though. We got on well. He was short and tubby and not good-looking, but he had shrewd eyes and was fond of horses.'

'How is it you love horses so much?'

'They are beautiful, and full of courage.' She cleared her throat. 'They haul great cannons, and ammunition, foodstuffs and grappa and the carts carrying the wounded, and to see them suffer and die like this…It goes to my heart, that's why.'

'You pity them more than you do the soldiers.'

'Yes,' she said. And she didn't smile.

When we got home the garden looked like the main square of a capital city. Much coming and going of carts and soldiers. All the men without their helmets or greatcoats, with shovels in hand. And there were some sweeping the portico, some polishing door handles, others trundling barrows laden with munitions. The sentries saluted Donna Maria with a click of the heels, while the captain came to meet us. Slowly, so as to keep us waiting. My aunt took advantage by pretending not to notice him.

'Madame Spada.' With a single movement the captain saluted and whipped off his cap, holding it by the peak.

I went on into the kitchen where Renato was plucking a chicken, leaning against the door jamb, with his greatcoat buttoned up to the neck and his pipe smoking like a chimney. In the remaining light hung the odours of soldiers, diesel oil, animals and wet wood. Looking back, I saw my aunt standing very close to the captain. Their coats were almost touching, though perhaps that was a trick of perspective, or else my secret hope of finding chinks in Donna Maria's armour.

From a cloud of smoke and feathers, chewing on his pipe, the steward said, 'After supper I must have a few words with you.'

'Very well,' I replied, attempting to hide my surprise.

'Pretend to go to bed, and we'll meet behind the house, outside the silkworm hatchery. What time do you make it?' But he gave me no time to pull out my watch. 'Never mind, I'll just expect you after supper.'

I felt gooseflesh all up my arms. I crossed the kitchen without paying much attention to the German soldiers, who were also busy plucking chickens. What was going on? I hunted for Teresa. No luck. Not even Loretta was around. Had they been turned out of the kitchen? Grandpa was waiting for me at the top of the stairs, sitting on the top step. He had a big, black book in his hands. I recognized it at once: it was his Gibbon, that bible of his which by way of corrupting us he often liked to quote from, even at random, when he wanted to attract attention. 'There's a mass of things in here that don't make any sense,' said he, closing the volume and waving it in front of me, 'but there are a lot of truths as well, and truth is something I have very much at heart, even when I can't grasp it.' He rapped his knuckles on the binding of the book. 'There's no finer English than this,' he said, raising his voice a little. 'The frontiers of that extensive monarchy were guarded by ancient renown and disciplined valour...' He gave me a stern look. 'Just what was needed at Caporetto... and at the Saga Pass.' His crouching bulk continued to block

62

my way. 'It's these Germans who are the heirs of Rome, that's the fact of the matter. It is they who have the renown, and as for the disciplined valour…there's even less doubt about *that*.' He shook his head and got to his feet with difficulty. 'Come along, laddie, your grandmother wants a word with you.'

Grandma had a red shawl over her legs and body as she leant back against the bed's headboard. Its vivid colour combined with the pallor of her face to give her a devilish air. Grandpa sat beside her and held her right hand in his left. She was wearing her sapphire-coloured earrings and just a touch of lipstick. 'Come closer,' she said.

I went and stood beside her. 'Aren't you feeling well, Grandma?'

'A bit of a sore throat. I have to talk little, and quietly. Listen, Paolo, I know you're not short of guts, but having guts doesn't mean underrating danger. It doesn't take much for these people to hang you.'

'Why are you telling me this, Grandma?'

'Don't pretend you don't follow me. Renato can be relied on…but he has a mission to perform. Your mission, on the other hand, is to stay alive. Italy needs its young men to live. At present the heroics can be left to the youngsters on the Piave, and up on Monte Grappa.'

'Are you telling me to trust the steward, but not to chance my arm too much?'

A smile spread across Grandma's face. 'Just that. You're still a boy, Paolo, and we love you.' She took hold of my hand and pressed it between hers, looking up at me and trying to hide her emotion.

Grandpa got up and saw me to the door, patting me on the shoulder. 'See you get something hot to eat. Teresa has put aside a bit of rabbit for you. These Huns are more ravenous than landsknechts.'

The gasmask hung from her belt and the glass eyes, those huge hornet-eyes, brushed the top of the grass. Renato walked fast, three or four steps ahead. Every so often I looked over my shoulder at the lights of the Villa, but very soon even those of the village faded from sight, dim as they were due to the shortage of paraffin. We skirted the woods, following paths through the underbrush. Heading north-northwest. At one moment I thought I recognized the bell tower of Corbanese off to the right. High up, in the belfry, a speck of light glittered then almost went out. Someone was smoking up there. A sentry, maybe. The sight of that sort of firefly, alone at the top of the tower, cheered me up. The tranquillity of that glow coming and going, tiny but distinct in the darkness, went to my heart, so that I thought not of an enemy but of the man who, with a cigarette for company, was fashioning his own peace.

'We're nearly there,' said Giulia at a certain moment. 'I'll take the lead now.'

Renato stepped aside to let her pass. The moon was high and almost full. A rocket burst and a flare lit up the wood. Renato shoved us both face down on the ground. A second rocket opened like an umbrella above the streak of its trajectory.

'What are they looking for?'

'A friend of mine,' said Renato. 'A pilot... These patrols come from Mura, or perhaps from Cisone.'

Another flare. Then the brilliance faded and became one with the bright moonlight. Giulia rose and followed the edge of the wood for two kilometres or so before turning almost back on her tracks and taking us into the thick of it. It consisted mostly of beeches and hornbeam, and the lower branches lashed me in the face. I warded them off with my upraised hands, so my wrists became a mass of scratches. But I didn't bat an eyelid. Then, all of a sudden, a clearing.

There before us, about fifty metres away, loomed the black bulk of a cottage. The air smelt of burning paraffin. Suddenly a rectangle of light appeared, and in it the dark silhouette of a man. His shadow stretched out through the darkness until it almost reached us. His head practically touched the lintel of the door, even though he was short and thickset. Renato went ahead to meet him, while Giulia and I hung back.

'Brian,' said Renato.

'There is special providence in the fall of a sparrow,' quoted the man in English, stepping back from the doorway to let us pass. 'Come in, take a pew.'

After a fusillade of jokes in English that made Renato laugh, the man offered us tea. One single chipped cup, which we passed around. Giulia did not partake.

'Assam,' said the Englishman, patting his cartridge-pouch. 'Never go anywhere without tea.' He spoke a somewhat basic Italian with a strong accent. And he eyed Giulia hungrily.

'Where is the plane?' asked Renato, holding his palms towards the camping stove, from which arose a mighty stink of paraffin.

Brian pointed to the window beside the fireplace.

'But if they go round behind the house they'll see it,' said Giulia.

'Forgotten magic wand on battlefield of Montebelluna.'

'The Fokkers will spot it tomorrow,' said Renato.

'Tomorrow maybe it'll snow,' said the Englishman. 'Got any tobacco?'

Renato pulled out a leather pouch, stuck his pipe in his

mouth and handed the pouch to the airman, who weighed it in his hand as he asked, 'Any news?'

There was an odour of damp cloth and rotten wood in the room, competing with the reek of the paraffin.

We were sitting elbow to elbow, Renato and I, while the Englishman was standing at the fireplace with his left elbow on the mantelpiece, eyeing Giulia. She, for her part, seemed all taken up by the portable stove, only twenty centimetres by ten. 'Italian women good housewives,' he said, puffing smoke up over his head. Then, turning to Renato: 'Well, go on. News from Florida?'

'I haven't set foot there since. Tampa wasn't the place for me. Those disgusting cigars turned my stomach.'

A heavy silence fell on the room. Giulia's eyes met mine. Neither of us knew anything of Renato's past. But now we were almost sure of one thing: that he was working for the Military Intelligence Service.

'It was a lucky landing.' Brian took off his white scarf and threw it onto a chair, on which I saw his leather flying helmet and goggles. 'There is special providence in the fall of a sparrow.'

'Oh, have done with it…You and your spouting poetry…' said Renato.

'Don't forget I am a Herrick, the poet of Cheapside.'

'Yes, yes. I know all about your ancestor. You've bored us all stiff with him, every time you had one too many up he popped… How does the poem go again?'

The Englishman took a stance with his feet apart, lifted his chin and rhythmically intoned:

> *Gather ye rosebuds while ye may,*
> *Old Time is still a-flying;*

And this same flower that smiles today
Tomorrow will be dying.

Renato repeated the last two lines in Italian for our benefit.

But a sudden burst of light whitened the window. 'Flares!' cried Renato. 'Outside! At the double!'

Out we scrambled. Giulia first, then the Englishman and Renato. I was last out. Two shots sounded from the edge of the clearing.

'Hold on a tick,' said the pilot. He darted round behind the house. I saw the spark of a lighter and then the flames that in a trice engulfed the aircraft. He had left the fuel tank open. 'No free gifts for the enemy.'

Renato led us off among the trees. The Englishman was just a step ahead of me. Short and stocky, with small, swift hands; more like a cutpurse than a knight of the skies. Then, behind us, the explosion.

The wood suddenly became bright as day. Not from the fire rising from the burning aircraft, but from the rockets of the Germans searching for us.

'These Huns know how to make war.'

Renato quickened his pace, and we followed suit, and finally we entered a ravine.

The crash of the bursting flares echoed among the branches and off the rock walls. I was wondering why Renato had wanted me to come along with him. I learnt next day that the cottage where Brian had hidden up had belonged to Giulia's mother. So she was there because she was the only one who really knew the last part of the way through the woods, and also because she wanted to come anyway. But I felt nothing but a burden.

We went ahead slowly, following the stream and careful not

to make any noise. The water was flowing beneath the ice, with a gentle, muted gurgle. Every so often Renato called a halt, and stood listening intently. Nothing. Only the faint *plumf* of snow falling from the branches and the voices of night-hunting creatures. All the same, they were searching for us. A pilot is a lion, not a mere hare, and calls for highly skilled hunters. And the zone was occupied by two battalions of Feldjäger.

At a certain moment I realized we were near Refrontolo. I made out the form of the ruined house I had seen with my aunt, the one belonging to a young Englishman with a poet in his ancestry, and I understood. We reached the ruin in very few minutes, sidling along the black hedges that bordered the abandoned farms. Bare rock walls, leafless trees, the tops of the beeches shattered by lightning. We passed empty sheep-pens, empty cowsheds. The hunger of both victors and vanquished, of the soldiers and the peasants, had made a clean sweep.

'*Ergiebt Euch! Kommot mit!*'

Stock still, I held my breath. If a blade of grass had bent beneath the weight of a grasshopper, I would have heard it. Pitchy blackness. A hand touched my right ear. A cold hand. I turned, and Giulia put her lips to mine and murmured something I didn't catch. I felt myself blushing to the roots of my hair, but I was concealed by darkness and was seized by an uprush of joy that came from deep inside me.

Then, muffled, the voice of Renato: 'Crawl after me, slowly, single file as far as the rise. They haven't seen us. They're smoking.' Keeping on all fours, I peeped over the hedge. Ten metres away, two cooking-pot helmets were outlined above the intermittent glow of two cigarettes. Renato told me later that they were imitating our soldiers trying to say in German that they wanted to surrender. They hadn't heard us.

Brian brushed past me, forcing Giulia to move away. I felt a quick surge of hatred for him, until I saw that his forearm ended in an eight-inch blade. He was about to attack, but Renato held him back: 'Don't move, they're leaving.'

The two cigarettes disappeared along the mule-track. I turned to Giulia, and felt her hip pressing mine, her shoulder too. We dipped under the fence and entered the house. The door hinges didn't squeak. Renato went over to a cupboard, took out a paraffin lamp and struck a match, the flare of which lit up the room. The window was blocked up with boards covered with tarred sacking. The steward had prepared everything down to the last detail. That explained why we had seen so little of him at the Villa.

'Look here, Brian, no one will come looking for you here, but don't light the fire. I've given you a couple of blankets.'

Brian gave a nod. His eyes shone merrily. The room was spotless and on either side of the fireplace long black moustaches stained the white paint of the walls. The top of Renato's head brushed the beams. The palliasse was broad and thick, and Giulia threw herself on it to test it out, making the stuffing crackle. Brian and Renato lit their pipes as a man. I would have liked to have had one myself. It wasn't like lighting a cigarette; there was something both sensual and soldierly in the way they handled the smoking bowls. Their gestures were affectionate, at one and the same time both tender and masculine. Renato read my thoughts. 'You ought to smoke a pipe too,' he said, giving me a steady look.

Brian said, 'It's so nice to be home.'

A jute sack also emerged from the cupboard. 'I've left you some rusks and a pot of honey. There's also a slab of cheese and half a *sopressa*. That should last you a day or two…Then I'll take you to Falzè, where there's always a lot of bustle, and you ought to be able to get through. The boat will be there for you.'

Brian answered Renato with a machine-gun burst of English and the pair of them ended with an exchange of jokes too private for us to understand anyway.

I edged closer to Giulia, but she bounced off the palliasse at once. Then she moved to the door and said to the steward, 'I'm sleepy, and there's nothing more to do here.'

Renato checked her with one look. 'We'll come too. Better not to be caught by daylight,' he said almost under his breath. 'I'll be back tomorrow, Brian. At dusk.'

The pilot replied with a broad grin. I left with Giulia. Renato caught up with us almost at once and went swiftly on ahead. Dawn was still a long way off. We reached the Villa in less than twenty minutes. 'We'll go round behind the church,' said Renato. He had no wish to wake the sentries dozing against the gateposts in the flickering glare of torches.

Giulia went off down an alleyway, without so much as a wave. I followed her with my eyes.

'Women scarcely ever match up to one's hopes,' murmured the steward.

Now he's starting to talk like Grandpa, I thought.

We crouched down behind the chapel and then, on all fours, skirted the family graveyard wrinkling our noses – for the drainage of the latrine was far from perfect – and finally got behind the camp kitchen, where two men were already at work. We crept past a sergeant sitting on the ground, his legs apart and his back against a wall, a pipe in his mouth; he was snoring. When Renato drew back the bolt I thought the rasping sound would have woken the whole camp. A clip on the shoulder. 'See you tomorrow, Paolo.' His familiarity surprised me. I felt flattered.

I went up the stairs two at a time, without a lamp. It was already first light in the attic.

Grandpa was sleeping, smelling of beans and sauerkraut. I undressed and slipped under the bedclothes. In no time at all I was asleep.

Eight

DON LORENZO HAD RETURNED. TO THE GIRLS' PARENTS HE had merely said that they shouldn't worry, the girls were in safe hands. He had skipped the ritual needed to reconsecrate the church – the bishop had given his dispensation in view of the war conditions – and he had reopened the school. He was fond of children, and he liked teaching.

He had prepared for the event by visiting from door to door. He, the parish priest, was after all the sole Italian authority left in Refrontolo, and the lessons – he thought chiefly of the catechism – had to start again, as life had to start again. Bertaggia the schoolteacher had taken to his heels even before the advance guard of the army, followed in turn by the pharmacist, the village doctor, and anyone else who had two pennies to rub together. The only remaining people of any education were my grandparents, my aunt, Giulia and – technically enrolled in the class – the Third Paramour, even though Grandpa used to say, 'If that fellow can read and write, then call me Marcus Aurelius.' Our cook and her daughter had also had a smattering of education. Loretta, however, showed no sign of it. Teresa, on the contrary, was mad on Mastriani and De Amicis, and I once took her by surprise with a copy of D'Annunzio's *Il piacere* in her hands. It was the only time I had seen her blush.

The children turned up in dribs and drabs, half an hour

before the evening rosary. Two novice nuns from Sernaglia acted as sheepdogs, rushing round the church forecourt and driving the tousled sheep towards the pen. The church doors were flung wide, with the priest towering in the middle. The notoriety of his bad breath threw panic into the little creatures being pushed and shoved up the steps towards the alms box, which Grandpa dubbed 'God's nest egg'.

His breath was not the only acid thing to issue from the priest's mouth. He once said to an Alpino guilty of having pinched his housekeeper's bottom, 'May your bayonet be thrust up your backside and turn into a hedgehog!' And when confessing a certain woman of his flock, as sure as death he would load her with a barrelful of Ave Marias, not suspecting that fleeing from what came from his mouth was a prize, not a penance.

With slaps and with scoldings the brisk sisters from Sernaglia, as anxious as anyone to make a getaway, wove the net that captured the last of the shivering lambs.

Until at last all were gathered in the dim light of the church. The front rows, those of the young recalcitrants, filled up in no time. I watched the scene from the rearmost pew, along with Giulia. The priest was afraid that the novices might not be able to ensure the conduct that befitted the holy place. They didn't know our village children, and besides, with the war on they needed a box on the ears to keep them in line. But the younglings of the flock well knew what wolves and fanged jaws were about in the streets, in the fields, in the mountains. They all had a couple of brothers in uniform, and almost all had seen one of them buried.

Don Lorenzo's figure loomed large in front of the altar. A stick of chalk served him as a baton. Without so much as a how-do-you-do? he launched into a description of hell that made the press-ganged lads' flesh creep. He spoke of the eyes of the

74

devil, as cold as bayonets, and of his flaming whip that lashed off chunks of flesh. 'It will spell trouble for you if I catch you eyeing the...' – he flavoured the pause with a rotund gesture which they all understood – 'the...of the baker's girl! It is a Sin, a Sin!' He then attempted to define this Sin using words which the lambs had never heard before: 'grave matters', and 'deliberate consent'.

'First the fire and then the smoke,' I whispered in Giulia's ear.

The priest's voice grew clearer, his speech slower, as he went on to speak about worldly temptations: 'Because one day the devil comes disguised as a woman knocking at your door, her dress all torn, and another as a rich man wearing a top hat, and the one will promise you the pleasures of the flesh and the other riches and power. You must be as alert as a sentry on watch, because the Enemy is crafty, seeking out our weak spots and scenting it when we weary. If we lower our guard he knows it. Yes, and he knows how to lie in wait, and how to strike!' Don Lorenzo heaved a deep sigh, and the lectern was shaken by the weight of his hands. 'You, Attilio...yes, you...' – and he aimed his chalk at a child sitting in the third row – 'You, sitting there yawning without putting your hand over your mouth... the demon will come for you too, you who yawn and imagine that he's not thinking of you. Fool! He will come for you too!' He broke off to stab the chalk at him once more. 'I see you've finished yawning. Good boy, that's the way, be attentive, like our soldiers on the Piave, who never let their rifles out of their hands, or it would be the end of our country. Be vigilant, Attilio, and the devil will not come for you.'

Don Lorenzo furrowed his brow. 'Do you understand, lads? The devil is cunning and comes furtively, like a thief in the night, and if you are not watching out, then you can kiss goodbye to the crock of gold, and goodbye to Paradise, the only place where there is no sin.'

'Bloody bore, this Paradise,' muttered Attilio.

Don Lorenzo started walking to and fro in front of the altar. Saying nothing. All of a sudden he halted and raked us all with his eyes, right down to the back pew. Like a cow chewing the cud.

'However, the universal evil…' Here he raised his chalk towards the ceiling before pointing it at all of us. 'The universal evil comes knocking at all doors, even that of the smallest cottage hidden in the woods.' Thereupon, to bring grist to his mill, he launched into an invective against the war: 'The mayor has bolted, the doctor has bolted, they have all followed suit, even before the army bolted, but your priest is still here, the Church is still here, because the Church is a rock in the torrent.' He had scored a point in his favour. But the very next moment he got bogged down in one of his proverbial demonstrations of the existence of God, which Grandpa called 'sacristy garbage'.

'Have you any idea, lads,' began the priest, pointing his chalk at the astonished stucco angels on the ceiling, 'how much money that young man at the back of the church has in his pocket?'

They all swivelled their heads towards me, including Attilio who was yawning again. Don Lorenzo lowered the chalk. 'Do *you* know?' And he stabbed the chalk at a boy in the front row. 'Or do *you* know?' pointing at another. 'Or maybe that sleepyhead Attilio knows…Ah, no!' And the chalk made a full circle, describing a halo above his bald head. 'But He knows.' And pointing once more to the stuccoed ceiling, he confirmed: 'Yes, He knows all right!'

Even if this proof of the existence of a superior being had not been forged in the metal of incontrovertible logic, the children appreciated it, because whenever Don Lorenzo brought up the subject of money it meant that the sermon was near the end, for our vicar did not let a day go by without telling us that 'money all comes from the devil's own coffers'. Except, of course, what came by way of God's nest egg.

The whish of the devil's coat-tails and the clinking of his money were still with us when Atillio raised his hand. 'Father,' said he in scarcely more than a whisper, 'you always say that the devil is more cunning than a witch…So why couldn't he disguise himself as Don Lorenzo?'

In three bounds the priest thrust his face almost nose to nose with the child, who hastily withdrew with a grimace. 'What's that you say, boy?'

'That Don Lorenzo might also be…' A great wave of laughter threatened to sweep through the church. But the priest lifted his head and the look in his eyes raised a bulwark and checked the wave. His face returned nose to nose with the child's, his lips drew back and showed his teeth, yellow and crooked. When the blast of his breath struck the boy with the ready yawn, I realized that Atillio had hit the nail on the head: the priest's breath came from the sulphurous depths of Gehenna.

Back at the Villa all was a-bustle. Beside the gates a majestic motor car glittered in all its chrome-plated splendour. It was a Daimler, guarded by a soldier with rifle slung on one shoulder and uniform crisply pressed. With short, nervous steps he paced back and forth from one bumper to the other. I wanted to take a closer look at that marvel of machinery, but my aunt grasped my arm and held me back: 'Have you lost your mind?'

All the soldiers to a man had their capes buttoned tight, the buckles shining, their cartridge pouches aligned with unaccustomed symmetry and their boots might have come straight from a shop window. The machine guns, set up in line under the portico, were oiled and spotless, and if the evening light had been a little brighter the bayonets would have glittered like the chrome fittings of the Daimler. They all spoke in subdued tones, even the sergeants.

'I'll go and find Renato,' I said in my aunt's ear.

'And I'll find the captain.'

I made a tour of the garden, playing with an Alsatian which was let off its chain every evening by a sergeant who couldn't bear to hear it barking. I ran here and there to get the dog to follow me, whimpering with pleasure, and every so often it would try to knock me over by planting its huge black paws on my chest, then on my back. In this way, under the astonished eyes of non-commissioned officers and sentries, I got right through the camp, now reduced to half a dozen tents. Many of the troops had left during the afternoon to relieve a company of Schützen stationed at Pieve. I spotted the medical officer, a tall, lean fellow of about fifty, with impressive side-whiskers, sitting on a pile of wooden boxes and peeling an apple with a barber's razor. Through the windows of the side chapel came the faint glimmer of lighted candles. I got rid of the dog by throwing a stick over the ditch that marked the northern edge of the garden, and hurried in.

Loretta and Teresa were telling their rosaries and mangling words in Latin. Teresa gave me a cross look. Loretta pretended to be rapt in prayer, pulling her dark headscarf so far forward as to cover her cheekbones. I approached the cook.

'This evening we got generals,' she said.

I gave her a questioning look: 'Generals?'

'Teresa says it and Teresa knows it, those landsknechts have no manners.'

'Are they going to eat in the big dining room?'

78

The cook nodded. 'They've killed the sucking pig. I'd hidden it to celebrate Christmas with.'

'Where had you hidden it?'

'You…don't have to know. It's Teresa who knows and has to know.' She shrugged her shoulders and stood up. Turning to the Christ figure frescoed in the tiny apse, she made the sign of the cross accompanied by the snort with which she always expressed her vexation. She went out without waiting for her daughter, tearing the kerchief from her head.

Loretta got to her feet and followed, crossing herself hastily.

I stayed where I was and sat down. The Christ figure staring at me was of the Byzantine type, doubtless copied by inexpert hand from a photograph of some famous icon or other. There was something out of shape about his face that deprived him of any aura of divinity.

I heard the door creak behind me. 'Renato.'

'Von Below, Krafft von Dellmensingen and von Stein…top brass…' The steward paused to get his breath back. 'They'll be here this evening. They'll be staying in the Villa. There are nine divisions between Sernaglia and the Piave. They're planning a breakthrough in the area of Vidòr, Moriàgo and Falzè, because further north, between Fener and Quero, their offensive has bogged down.'

Renato's eyes were burnt out with worry. We spoke for a minute or two. He explained how by opening the door of the dining room stove one could hear what was going on from the floor above, from my aunt's very room. 'Unluckily none of us is much good at German, not even Madame Nancy. But Brian, now…His mother comes from Hamburg. Donna Maria and your grandmother have concealed him where Signor Guglielmo hides his brandy. Is it a safe place?'

'Only Teresa knows about it. We can trust her implicitly. But how did you manage to smuggle him in?'

'Never you mind. The fewer people who know, the better.' He took out his pipe and lit it.

'We're in a chapel,' I murmured.

Renato took it out again and regarded the creator of all things visible and invisible, tobacco included. He winked his right eye, I don't know whether at me or at the painting, poked me in the chest with the stem, and said firmly, 'I've got far worse things to be forgiven for.' But he didn't put his pipe back in his mouth. 'I need you, right now, to go to the dining room, find some way of leaving the stove door ajar, and tell the maid not to close it even if she's told to.'

I left and headed towards the *tempietto*. I didn't want to go in through the gates. The shadows of the trees and the houses were starting to merge with the dusk.

I went at once to the kitchen and took Teresa to one side, not telling her more than need be. '*Diambarne de l'ostia,*' she commented grimly. She asked no questions.

'Who is there in the big dining room?'

'Soldiers all smartly got up.'

'Is the stove alight?'

'Yes. Now I'll send the girl to bring logs.'

'No, I'll do that.'

'But it'll look odd.'

'I've got to do it myself, and that's that.'

I went out into the courtyard sinking my boots deep in the mud, smeared a handful of it on my cheeks and forehead, then dirtied my knees and jacket, tearing a strip off the sleeve and a couple of buttons. The oak table had already been laid. The tablecloth was of Burano lace, doubtless the spoils of war. And the silverware was indeed silver, and I wondered for a moment whether the Germans hadn't found Grandma's hiding place after all. In any case I was glad to notice that they had not managed to find any carbide for the bright lamps, so that there were candles everywhere, possibly stolen from the house of some bishop, they were so much finer than those of our priest. The four soldiers putting out the plates and glasses took no notice of me, though finally one of them, who had loosened his collar, gave me a contemptuous glance and muttered: '*Wallischen.*'

A few resolute paces took me to the stove. From the neat pile of logs I picked two small and one fairly large one, opened the upper door, puffed once or twice at the embers and closed it again. Then, without delay, I opened the bottom door and ostentatiously used the hearth brush to empty the ashes into the metal bucket, which Loretta had left perfectly clean. There was very little ash to remove, but I had to pretend to be doing something. I was not nervous. I never even glanced towards the soldiers, who went on laying the table. On my way out I saw that two of them had lit cigarettes and were chuckling as they looked at me, maybe because for once in their lives they felt themselves superior to someone.

The guard on the Villa had not been increased. The usual two sentries were at the gate, while at the back a single rifleman strolled back and forth, smoking one cigarette after another and playing with the Alsatian.

Grandpa met me upstairs with a napkin tied round his neck and a chicken wing between his teeth. He looked pleased with himself as he walked round and round the table with his Gibbon open in his left hand while he chewed away. It occurred to me that the Germans were looking more and more civilized while we were beginning to slip back into barbarism; but it was a silly thought. It was just that I needed to calm down. I was seeking for some trace of symmetry in the swiftly changing world.

Without removing his face from the book or his teeth from the chicken, Grandpa favoured me with a glance. 'Now look what a state you are in…Have you been rolling in the muck-heap? I thought I was the only one allergic to water,' he said, sitting himself down. He put down the Gibbon, and what was left of the chicken wing described an arc and finished up in the waste-paper basket. He jerked his chin towards the window. 'Have you noticed? It's starting to snow.'

'Only a sprinkling. Have you heard that three generals are expected? The steward says they're top brass.'

'These creatures preen their feathers day in day out, as if they were expecting the late emperor's ghost for dinner.'

One by one Grandpa wiped his fingers on the napkin.

Grandma entered the room without knocking. She had her hair up, her eyes were shining, and the blue lace collar of her black dress reflected colour on her face. She was of an elegance only slightly marred by a dab of powder on her cheekbones. 'Guglielmo, you've been in my bathroom!'

The wind rattled the windowpanes. From the kitchen rose the odour of roast pork.

'You know very well I never set foot there. That hatstand hung with those things turns my stomach,' replied Grandpa.

Two raps at the door prevented Grandma from giving full vent to her wrath.

The door opened a little and Loretta timidly poked her head in. 'The steward says he wants the young laddie.'

To be called 'laddie' by Loretta! I pretended I hadn't heard.

Only then did Grandma notice me. 'Be off with you! And clean yourself up, you're a disgrace.'

I followed Loretta downstairs. It was not Renato waiting for me, but Teresa. She spoke in an undertone: 'That mad English-man is in your grandfather's cupboard and there's Renato waiting for you…Where, I don't know.'

I put on my overcoat and crossed the courtyard. One of the guards pointed his rifle right at my chest. He didn't recognize me and gestured at me to make myself scarce. I didn't need telling twice. I went straight to the silkworm hatchery without looking back, turning up my collar and thrusting my hands into my pockets.

Renato pulled me inside with a jerk and rammed home the bolt. 'About time, too!'

'What now?'

'We wait. This is Brian's moment.'

'Do you expect any problems?'

'No.'

We sat down on the matting, our backs against the wall streaked with sulphur fumes. It had almost stopped snowing. Every now and then a car's headlight lit up the little window.

'You're in Intelligence, aren't you?'

'Yes…Paolo. Do you mind if I call you by your Christian name?'

I felt both flattered and a little offended. This familiarity was so sudden. 'Yes, call me Paolo.'

'Our intelligence system is about as slovenly as our army… but maybe I'm exaggerating.'

Renato's voice was as composed as could be, even though he must have been on tenterhooks about Brian.

The stench of sulphur seeping from the walls of the hatchery, out of use since the arrival of the Germans, joined forces with that of the petrol and diesel oil coming from outside. Renato took off one boot, the one with the higher heel, and scratched the sole of his foot.

'Does it hurt?'

'It itches. It's the fault of polio. I was five years old, or maybe six. We lived above a stable, and my father was a vet. When I began to recover we moved to Livorno, in the centre of town. We had a terrace, and we could see the sea.'

He lit his pipe. And said nothing more.

'How was it you became a spy?'

He laughed loudly. 'Do you think a spy lets on about those things?'

'Well, at least tell me why you took me with you to fetch Brian. You needed Giulia, of course, but what about me?'

'If they had caught us your presence there would have made your grandparents and your aunt speak up for us, and we would have had a chance, however small, of getting away with it. No one likes to shoot the children of the gentry. If these Germans win the war, as they think they are going to, they will have to govern this territory with the complicity of some.' He produced a great puff of smoke. 'And who do you think they will try but the people who govern it already?'

'Do you mean they don't want to make too many enemies?'

'It's not the number of enemies that worries them, but the quality, the rank in society. The Hapsburgs know how to govern; or at least, they did. There are about fifteen languages spoken within the empire, and it is only loyalty to the emperor that holds the lid on that stew pot. If the ruling house falls – and I tell you that it will – then the various nations grumbling in its belly today will all turn against one another and tear each other to pieces.'

He broke off to look straight at me in the semi-darkness. The smoke engulfed me and made my eyes water. He smelt of tree-bark and grappa. 'You see, Paolo, for some decades now the Kingdom of Hungary has been too important. Vienna is not as firmly in command as it used to be. It's a Dual Monarchy in fact as well as in name. For this reason it's not as strong. And there's more to it than that. However, they have the pope on their side.'

'But the pope is Italian…So you think like Grandpa, you think the pope's a traitor?'

'I don't know your grandfather intimately. He's a…an eccentric. I like him, even if he doesn't take to me at all.'

'It's because of Grandma. Grandpa is jealous.'

'I've no hard feelings.'

'Tell me about the pope. Do you think he's with them, with our enemies?'

'No. I don't think it's that simple. But Italy is Ghibelline, born of a Ghibelline vision of things. It's either us or the Church!'

He went back to his pipe. In silence. I could hear his breathing.

'They've always known, those slyboots of priests, that if the northern part of our peninsula joined up with the south, they could kiss goodbye to the Pope King and his temporal power.'

'I don't follow you.'

'Italy was united by the House of Savoy and the freemasons, and it was united in defiance of the priests. But behind it we always find Britain, anxious to stick a knife into what was left of the Holy Roman Empire. During the century that has just ended France and Prussia have given us a helping hand, I admit, but only for a moment. Whereas Britain always looks ahead, into the future, and sees clearly. Do you think it's a coincidence that Sidney Sonnino, our Foreign Minister, has a Welsh mother and isn't a Catholic? Have you never heard of the Treaty of London?'

'It's the one that led to the Entente...Am I right? Grandpa told me about it just a few days ago. The Russians have just published it in a newspaper, in French. Grandpa says there's a revolution going on in Russia, and they're really laying into their king.'

'Secret treaties, my foot! The fact is that very little in this world is secret. What is put down on paper comes from more than one head. Heads give voice to words and words pass from mouth to mouth. The last...or rather the next to last article in that treaty states...I can't for the moment remember the exact words...but it says that when the war is over Britain and France pledge to help Italy to exclude the pope from the drawing up of the peace terms.' He fell silent.

A roar of motors outside. They passed us by.

'Please go on.' I liked his lively, lucid way of talking. I even liked the aroma of his pipe, which kept at bay the stink of diesel oil and sulphur and sodden earth.

'Do you think the two British warships which were at Marsala the day Garibaldi landed were there by coincidence? Or to protect the wineries, as their captains professed? That old freemason wouldn't even have set foot ashore except for the British. They positioned themselves between the Bourbon guns and Garibaldi's ship.' For almost a minute he was silent and motionless; I couldn't even hear him breathe. 'Ever since the time of the Spanish Armada, the war between Queen Elizabeth and Philip II of Spain, the Protestants and Catholics have never let slip a chance of getting at each other's throat... And don't think it's over and done with! There's a lot more to come.'

The darkness had become more intense. I could no longer even make out Renato's profile. 'Go on,' I said.

Once again the roar of engines, and headlights dazzling in the windows. Then the sound of motorcycles, and of a car drawing up. 'It's them!'

'Let's hope Brian manages to overhear something useful. When the moment comes it'll be up to you to go and fetch him. You won't be noticed on the staircase, as long as you change your clothes and have a wash! Then bring him to me here. The rest is my business.'

'Very well.'

We got to our feet to watch. My legs had gone numb and I felt cold. I flapped my arms around my chest and jumped from foot to foot.

The guard of honour had drawn up, rigid in the freezing night. Korpium was stalking back and forth, his uniform reaching to his gaiters, his sword at his side.

And at last they arrived, heralded by a long, slow screech of brakes. They arrived with calf-length greatcoats and badges of rank that glittered in the light of the headlamps. The *tramontana* had cleansed the air. I simply gazed. I didn't even feel myself breathe. It seemed to me impossible that those men with their chiselled features could be cruel or barbarous, or even just run-of-the-mill men whose destiny it was to be wearing uniform. No, they were warriors marked by the branding iron of legend – the ancient, bearded, childish legend – of military valour and honour. Everything within me, every ligament and every cell, told me that those men were the enemy and that I ought to hate them. But in the tension of the moment the force of their mythical image imposed a truce, so that there in the darkness I abandoned myself to an inward surge of admiration.

Nine

FILTERED THROUGH THE LEAFLESS TREES, THE EARLY MORN-
ing sun cast a piano keyboard on the snowy street. I was sitting
at the window, chewing a slice of *sopressa* nicked from the
Germans' table. And it was all the tastier for being stolen. I
saw Grandma's Third Paramour coming up the road. He was
walking slowly. I could recognize him from the attic by the long
cigarette holder that gave his emaciated figure a somewhat
womanish air. Grandpa was by my side, wearing his comical
cap and holding a cup of coffee. 'See him, laddie? You can tell
he's a nitwit from the way he smokes and walks. But what's he
doing around at this time of day?' Grandpa's voice was still
thick with sleep, not yet ready for the business of the day.

I watched the motorcycles leaving the village and heading
west, towards the front line, and others – many more of them –
that took the road to Conegliano. The tracks they made in the
frozen snow destroyed the sun-shed keyboard pattern. My eyes
were still heavy with sleep.

'The generals are not up yet,' said Grandpa, taking off his
cap and tapping a forefinger against the windowpane. 'They
take things easy.'

'Have you ever been to war, Grandpa?'

'Certainly not!' he replied, piqued. 'But I know what I'm
saying, laddie. Just look at those men. That one is polishing

his boots, that one shaving, another curry combing his horse, another writing a letter, another eating an apple and watching the clouds, and the one sitting on the sixty-pounder is combing his hair as if his girlfriend were waiting round the corner. For every minute under fire there are a thousand minutes of…nothingness. Bullets cost money.'

At that moment in came Grandma and said cheerfully, 'What are you hatching, you two?' She was wearing a close-fitting black dress showing her slender ankles.

'Off to a tryst with Pagnini?'

'That's none of your business.' Grandma always acted like that when she wanted to be affectionate.

But Grandpa was ready for her: 'That fellow has a noddle full of noodles. Perhaps you could use him as a messenger boy, now that you've taken up playing spies.'

Grandma smiled. She was up to something. She went down the stairs with a clatter of heels on every step.

'Stay here, Paolo!' commanded Grandpa, giving me a steady look.

He put an arm round my shoulder and drew me back into the window embrasure.

Grandma went out into the garden. She had put on her grey overcoat, and walked to the gates. The sentries barred her way with crossed arms. A sergeant came up making expansive gestures, a rare thing for Germans in uniform. Grandma pointed to the Third Paramour, just arriving. The sergeant gave a bow and let her pass, while the sentries snapped to attention.

The Third Paramour offered her his arm, and with slow steps they set off towards the church.

'What d'you bet that that woman has got even Bigfeet involved in this business?'

★

'I'm going back to my novel,' said Grandpa, opening the door of the Thinking Den, where he co-habited with a desk, an Under-wood and his little statue of Buddha. On one occasion Grandma had pulled his leg by saying that his typewriter didn't even have a ribbon in it. Grandpa got back at her by ordering from a shop in Milan two dozen red and yellow tins stamped with the blue eagle and the legend: Made in USA. He left them about here, there and everywhere, on all the little tables that occupied stra-tegic points in the Villa, like the cigarette butts that betray the presence of an inveterate smoker.

Grandpa's Underwood was a Creature of Myth. The day it arrived the mayor and the pharmacist had been invited to dinner in order to see it. It had been set up in the middle of the oak table and shrouded with a green headscarf. When the time came to serve the dessert, which had cost a dozen eggs, a whole pat of butter, five bars of chocolate and goodness knows how many *diambarne de l'ostias*, the Creature was jointly unveiled by the hands of Grandma and Aunt Maria, who thus presented it to the master of the household. Grandpa rose, bowed to the assembled company and, unsheathing his crafty smile, said: 'Many thanks to the Spada girls, whom next year I will repay with a novel written on...on...but we must give it a name!' And with both forefingers he pointed at the Creature. 'Come on, help me choose a name.'

The pharmacist said, 'Babel.'

The mayor said, 'Alcyone.'

'Alcyone,' echoed the mayor's wife.

Grandma said, 'Bidet.'

Aunt Maria said, 'Nerina.'

I said, 'Greymouth.'

From her corner, silent and motionless, Teresa followed the whole scene. And while Loretta was starting on her round with the Sachertorte, Grandpa, resuming his seat, said, 'Beelzebub.'

And Beelzebub it was.

Before being put to use, Beelzebub was subjected by all the men present to a close inspection. It was measured with a ruler which they sent me upstairs to fetch. The base measured 30cm by 27cm, and it stood 26cm in height. 'It's almost a cube!' exclaimed the mayor, at which his wife assented gravely.

The pharmacist was very interested in the mechanics, and loved the little wheels, whether they were smooth or toothed, and he ended up getting ink from the ribbon all over his fingers.

Grandpa, on the other hand, was bewitched by the keys. He stroked them one by one. Four rows of them arranged in four tiers. In each little white silver-edged circle a black letter, including even Y and J, K and W! The semicircle of little hammers already made his fingers itch. His eyes sparkled.

I felt an urge to join Grandma and the Third Paramour. For no particular reason I thought they might know something about the Englishman. Grandpa followed me, saying that his novel could wait until the afternoon. 'I'm not in the mood today. I can feel it when Beelzebub isn't going to be helpful.'

All muffled up, coat collars up to our ears, we entered the church. It was dark in there, but not so much that it hid the way things had been neglected. The windows were almost black, the altars dulled with dust, and not even the candles of the tabernacle were burning. Grandma was kneeling at the confessional, her upright shoulders draped with black lace. I knew that her attitude to religion was occasional, and merely for form's sake.

When I saw the priest emerge from the sacristy my suspicion became a certainty: inside the confessional was the Englishman. We sat down in one of the rear pews. When Don Lorenzo spotted Grandpa he made a face like one finding a rat in his soup. 'What brings *you* into the House of the Lord?'

Grandpa cleared his throat, though he would have liked to have cast in the priest's face one of Teresa's *diambarne de l'ostias*. I held my tongue, hoping only that the priest didn't come anywhere near me. Even his cassock stank of wet dog. Grandma stood up. She crossed herself, and slipped a piece of paper into her handbag. Before she could close the bag Renato, appearing suddenly from the other side of the confessional, snatched it from her and crumpled it up in his fist. Grandma pulled an indignant face, but did nothing. She came and sat in the pew in front of us. Renato approached the priest and, stooping a little, said rather loudly, 'Don Lorenzo, I would like to light a candle to Our Lady.'

'Those filthy swine used them all up, but I had just a few put aside.' He rolled one fist around in the palm of his other hand. 'I'll be back in a moment.' And indeed he was. He emerged from the sacristy with three candles, which he set up under the statue with its perpetual dozy smile. He knelt for an instant. Then he rose and said to Renato, 'Here you are then.' The steward lit the middle candle. Then he made the sign of the cross and whispered something into the priest's ear that made him rush off, scowling furiously. Renato opened his fist, read the message, then held it to the flame as the priest went back into the sacristy. At this point the pilot emerged from the confessional.

'Is it all clear?' asked Grandma.

'As crystal,' answered Brian, and followed Renato into the sacristy.

At that very moment, in the doorway two steps from Grandma and me, appeared Captain Korpium.

Had he caught sight of Brian? My fear was banished as soon as the captain, with his exquisite accent, addressed Grandma: 'On Friday the Swedish ambassador is due to arrive at Refrontolo. Would you care to join us for dinner? Your husband, your grandson and Donna Maria would also be most welcome. Your company would cheer up this old soldier.' The captain straightened like a ramrod and clicked his heels. Then he let out the magic words he had saved till last: 'There will be roast pork.'

'I do think you might have waited for us to leave the church before issuing your invitation, Captain,' said Grandma Nancy. 'However, I thank you, also in the name of Donna Maria.'

Grandpa got to his feet with a fearful glower.

'And that of my husband,' added Grandma.

Korpium departed, somewhat ruffled.

Grandpa scratched his belly and threw back his head a bit, saying, 'I sometimes catch myself adoring your sharp tongue, my dear.'

Grandma got up too. While she was marching out through the doorway the Third Paramour – who all this time had been sitting some way back – followed her with an air of challenge.

Ten

THE CODE. THE CODE WAS THE KEY TO EVERYTHING. GRAND-
ma was the brains behind it, Brian the messenger, Renato
the intermediary. Less clear were the roles of Donna Maria,
Grandpa and myself. We were certainly in a sense accomplices,
but I got the impression that we were nothing but the garnish-
ings to their roast.

Our attempt to gain strategic information had gone badly,
very badly indeed. The three generals had talked about wine,
women, the weather, and even exchanged a few titbits of gossip
about wives lying in wait to cuckold their husbands at the front.
They had also spoken of how well-stocked the Italian army's
stores were, and had even mentioned how our resistance along
the Piave was stronger than expected. 'They didn't risk discussing serious matters at dinner; they just enjoyed their food and
talked hot air,' was the steward's comment.

The real motive behind Brian's dare-devil landing was quite
different. I later learnt from Renato that the generals' visit was
not known either by our Intelligence Service or by British Intelligence (though I never learnt how Renato kept in contact). It
had been simply a stroke of luck which they decided to profit by.
Brian had come to memorize the code worked out by Grandma,
and a month later was to start flying over the Villa with his
squadron twice a week, to photograph the three-mullioned

window in the façade and the washing hanging out to dry in the courtyard.

The code was fairly simple. The first inside shutter open and the second closed meant 'troop movements towards the front line', the first closed and the second open meant 'movements from the front to the rear zone'. All shutters closed meant 'no troop movements observed'. Then, however, it became more complicated with the part played by the other shutters. The first window indicated the troop movement and its direction, the second the number of divisions or battalions involved in the movement, the third the type of movement (and I don't know what was meant by 'type'). The code invented for the washing, on the other hand, entailed the colour and nature of the garments hung out. Jackets, shirts, trousers and long-johns, easily distinguishable from the air by their long dangling sleeves and legs, referred to the Imperial Air Force (in her confabs with her London friend Sir James, Grandma had associated legs and arms with aircraft wings), while sheets, dishcloths and hand-kerchiefs gave indications of the enemy supply system. Colours had their importance also. A white shirt and red breeches combined with a yellow handkerchief – the only such combina-tion I can remember – meant 'shortage of aircraft fuel'.

'Why don't we use pigeons?' I asked.

Renato laughed. 'Don't you read the posters on the walls? There's martial law! If they find a single pigeon at a farm they shoot the head of the family on the spot. Then they start on the children, so in the end the mother tells them where they've got the birds hidden. And furthermore, don't you know that all the way from Belluno to the sea everyone is on the hunt for food?'

Giulia threw her head back, burying it in the hay. Her firm

breasts gave a testing time to the mother-of-pearl buttons of her coat. Renato was seated between us, which I didn't exactly like.

There was a movement under the hay, from whence came a protesting voice.

'Not now, Brian,' said Renato quietly, without removing the pipe from his mouth.

'What's going on?'

'Troops…at the gates.'

Giulia sat motionless, looking straight ahead of her, hair full of bits of hay. There was something both reckless and tender about her beauty. I searched Renato's face for any sign betraying an interest in Giulia. Then the motorcycles began to move out, in double file. Next came the Daimlers, followed by a lorryload of soldiers and a single motorcyclist, forming the tail of that gigantic lizard that blackened the street. The sentries clicked their heels beneath the eagles of the Hohenzollern and the Hapsburgs, flapping indolently in the freezing dawn.

'We'll wait another minute or two,' said Renato. The English-man's round face emerged from the hay.

'It's prickly.'

The sentries lit up their cigarettes and the guard of honour, which for all too long had been frozen to attention to salute the generals' cars, broke up in a scramble to get some hot coffee.

'Even Captain Korpium's leaving.' Renato's voice was less brusque now.

'Can we start?'

'Yes, we can go now.'

Giulia and I jumped down from the haystack together and exchanged happy grins.

We climbed to the little temple, skirting the woods. The pilot walked alongside Renato, keeping to the side nearer the trees so that the sentries down below would make out three people, not four. We entered the woods as soon as we could.

'We have to stay in the thickest cover.'

'Are we going to the river?'

'Yes, we're making for the river. In a couple of hours we'll separate, and you and Giulia will turn back,' said Renato.

The idea of being alone in the woods with Giulia was my idea of heaven.

'I', announced Giulia with a despotic air, 'want to see the Piave.'

'No.' Renato's tone brooked no rejoinder. Giulia held her gasmask to her face and overtook us with a burst of speed. Then she turned, lowered the mask, and jeered, 'Slowcoaches!'

The climb began to tell on us, but we didn't slow up. We walked west for three hours, then took a breather beside a road that ran between the woods and some bare fields patched with snow. A hundred metres away, directly ahead of us, was a run-down farmhouse with a smoking chimney.

'This is where we part company,' said Renato. 'You two go back, and if you don't find me tomorrow morning,' he said, looking me in the eye, 'tell your grandmother.'

I would have liked to raise some objection, but I had no time. The steward set off briskly for the farmhouse with Brian in his wake.

Giulia had hung her gasmask from her belt. She walked quickly without looking at me. Suddenly we heard voices, German voices, approaching us through the dense woods. We exchanged glances. 'Let's go this way,' I whispered.

'They're already here,' she said, hugging me to her and pressing her lips to mine. I felt the tip of her tongue, warm and sweet, lick at my front teeth, enter my mouth. But the chill of a rifle barrel forced our necks apart.

'Pretty vuman, zehr pretty,' said the soldier standing beside the one prising us apart with his rifle, who was staring dumbly at Giulia, his lips drawn back in a grimace.

'Me from Pola,' continued the other soldier, his rifle slung on his shoulder and his filthy greatcoat with sleeves torn in several places. 'Pretty redhair vuman, like our vumans,' he said, stroking Giulia's hair. She went on hugging me close to her, looking into my eyes with an air of being pleased with herself and not a trace of fear.

I felt the cold steel of the gun's muzzle against my chin. I didn't know what to do. 'When you're up to your neck in trouble,' Aunt Maria had once told me, perhaps to get back at Grandpa, 'it's no good either praying or panicking, but praying is certainly more practical.' I mentally clutched at that dictum of hers and began to laugh. I laughed without thinking. Giulia, quicker on the uptake than me, promptly seized on the occasion and laughed even louder, again and again, louder and louder, her eyes flashing from me to the soldiers, until in the end they were laughing too. At which point Giulia took a pace back, her face suddenly serious, and with two fingers gently pushed the gun-barrel down from my neck. The Austrian slung his weapon over his shoulder. Giulia leant her head on my shoulder and, in the unexpected silence, grinned.

The one with the Istrian accent said something in German to his companion; then, eyeing the two of us, he shook his head. 'I love you, I love you,' he chuckled, and gave a punch on the shoulder to the other, who was gawping at us with two tiny, expressionless eyes and baring all his teeth, few and yellow as they were.

Giulia was a blazing fire, and they hadn't seen such a woman for goodness knows how long.

I pulled out my cigarettes, and the one from Pola removed his gloves and grabbed the packet, offering it to his friend. But the other jerked his chin towards Giulia: he wasn't thinking about cigarettes. Whereupon the Istrian put one between his lips, lit it, and at once took his mate by surprise by jamming it into his mouth. 'Go, go,' he said, lighting another for himself and putting my packet in his pocket. '*Raus, raus!*'

I took Giulia's hand and we made our way leisurely into the trees. We didn't look back. Behind us, beyond the woodland sounds, the two German voices were interlocked. The toothless fellow was jabbering hoarsely, while the Istrian tried to calm him down with brief interjections. After a few minutes the woods reasserted their sovereignty with the sudden whirring of wings and the murmur of water flowing beneath the ice in frozen streams.

We walked on for ten minutes or so without speaking. Then Giulia gave my hand a hard squeeze.

'You don't know much about women, do you?'

'Not much.'

'Liar,' she said, and laughed that mocking laugh of hers.

It was still dark when Teresa woke me next morning. It took me several attempts to shake the blankets off.

'There's an emergency!'

Grandpa turned over with much crunching, but didn't wake up.

As I got up I realized that I had gone to bed almost fully clothed. I put on boots and overcoat and caught up with the cook.

Waiting for me in the kitchen was a tall man with dark, steady eyes, a badly shaven chin, a dirty cloak, and patched sleeves and breeches. But his smile showed an array of strong, white straight teeth. He was not a peasant, even though he wanted to pass for one.

'You must come with me, some friends are expecting us,' he said in dialect. But he wasn't from the Veneto, though he was pretending to be. On our feet we drank the hot milky coffee prepared by Teresa, who eyed me in silence, without even a little grunt.

'You have to go,' she said, speaking for once in Italian. 'The mistress knows about it, and Donna Maria told me,' she added, returning to dialect.

The man walked swiftly, but I had no trouble in keeping up with him in the woods, which he seemed to know like the back of his hand. He uttered not a word, and after the first few minutes I saw it was better to say nothing and save my breath for walking.

And walk we did, for many hours, with very few breaks. When we stopped it was always in dense forest, away from roads and clearings. The man would produce a knife and a slab of hard cheese, offer me two mouthfuls – always two, and always the same size – and then hand me a dented flask. 'Just a sip,' he would say, for there was a taste of wine in the water. There was a meticulousness about whatever he did that I found reassuring.

We joined Brian and Renato at dusk, in a mountain hut up against a cliff face. I was worn out. I flopped down onto the straw mattress beside the Englishman, who no longer wore the cheerful expression I had come to know. The tall, ill-shaven man saluted Renato and clicked his heels: 'Major...'

'Seen any patrols?' asked Renato, scrambling to his feet and returning the salute.

'No, but we never left the woods.'

'You did well, Lieutenant. Back to your duties and…thank you.'

The lieutenant left without a word, and made no gesture towards me or the Englishman. He closed the door behind him soundlessly, as if afraid of waking someone.

I then realized that one of Brian's legs was in a splint from the knee downwards, his ankle swollen.

'What happened?'

'Lucky if the ankle isn't broken…anyway, he can't walk on it. That's why I sent for you. Have a bite to eat, we're leaving in ten minutes.'

Even though Brian was using a makeshift crutch, in places where the going was tough almost half of his weight was on my shoulders, and that was no feather-weight. Because of his ankle we had to skirt the woods of the Soligo valley without ever taking cover in them. The sky was clear, black, with a half-moon that, though it helped us to see the path, might betray us at any moment.

Within three or four kilometres of the Piave the enemy was everywhere. The cart-tracks, the mule-paths, and the walks along the river banks were bright with a network of fires which patrols of four to six men gathered around. Near them loomed the forms of picketed mules and horses, tents, carts, lorries, and motorbikes and bicycles propped up against the hedges and fences: survivors of the hard-won peace treaty which bound hard-working folks to the world of nature.

Renato had his unlit pipe clamped between his teeth. Brian was sweating as he leant partly on me, partly on Renato. We slid down into a gorge, sure that that route was not guarded. For a quarter of an hour we slipped between sheer cliffs covered with moss and lichen, heartened by the silence of the vegetation and the gurgling of water under the crust of ice. Until we were arrested by a sound. We froze in our tracks. A metallic click, like the cocking of a revolver. I turned to look at Brian, and found he had a barrel aimed at his temple. 'Who are you?' It was a woman's voice.

'Refugees on the run,' said Renato with a sigh of relief. 'We're making for the river.'

It was too dark for me to see the face of whoever was threatening us. 'Hands up! Above your heads! I want to see them,' said the woman, moving with a rustle in the dry underbrush.

In less than a minute we were forced into a fissure in the rock not even a metre wide, though after a few steps it broadened out into what might have been the lair of some large animal. At one side was a fire made of a handful of brushwood. Behind us, in the half-light, something stirred. Covered by an army greatcoat, two young girls were lying hugging each other tight, their faces bloodless. They gazed at us with the blank eyes of the blind, and appeared to have lost their wits. The woman with the revolver ordered us to sit down but not to lower our hands.

'Mariapia, Giovanna, liven the fire up a bit. Don't be afraid… If they move they're dead men.'

There was a note of tenderness in that voice. The woman's face was gaunt, with the same look of desperation as that of the girls. 'Who are you?'

'Brian, Royal Flying Corps.'

'My name is Renato Manca. I'm the steward of Villa Spada at Refrontolo. This lad is the grandson of the owners. You have nothing to fear from us, we are —'

'At this time of night? Creeping about…'

'We're escaping from the Germans,' I put in, without moving a muscle.

And Renato added, 'But what are you doing here in this den, madam, with two young children?'

Renato lowered his hands, very slowly, for even in the dim light he had observed the woman's face: 'How long since you last ate?'

The woman burst into tears, and the girls got up from under the greatcoat and held tight to her.

Renato stood up, but he saw the pistol barrel rising. It was a Montenegrin revolver. Renato drew a piece of hard tack from his pocket and held it out to the woman. The revolver was too heavy for her skinny fingers, and she put it down on a slab of rock. Then she seized Renato's hand and kissed it. The girls grabbed the hard tack and started to nibble at it before even breaking it in half.

'Gently now, Giovanna, Mariapia…gently,' said the woman.

'I think I can imagine what has happened to you, madam,' said Renato, picking up the revolver and lowering the hammer. 'We'll take you with us to the Piave. There'll be a boat to meet us.'

The woman could not stem her tears.

'What happened?' queried Brian, who knew nothing of the brutal way the country had been sacked and pillaged.

'First two deserters, Italian, two bastards from the Second Army, came saying they had lost contact with their company. I asked them in for a bowl of soup while I gave them directions. They dragged me into the bedroom and…at least they didn't touch the girls…Then came Slavs, five of them…no, six. There were six of them, curses on them! They abused the girls, the filthy bastards! Oh, damn them, damn them!'

Renato turned to the girls: about thirteen, the elder perhaps a little more. From what was left of their clothing, and from the lifeless but composed look on their faces, they came from a wealthy family. The woman was not the mother. Perhaps she was a governess. 'Where are their parents?'

The woman looked at the children, who stared back at her in terror. Then, turning to us, she raised her first finger to her lips, while Renato poked the fire.

'It's cold here,' said the woman.

Renato stared into the flames. 'If this war doesn't end soon,' he said, 'we'll all become savage beasts.'

Brian, sitting with his back against the rock so as to raise his aching foot a bit, reached out a hand to shift the revolver, which Renato had left too near the fire. But the woman beat him to it, aiming it at him for a moment. But then she gave it to Renato, holding it on the palms of both hands as if offering a dish of food. Renato put it in his pocket. 'Let's go. Once across the river you'll find a doctor.'

The girls got to their feet again. The elder one gave her little sister the greatcoat, who put it round her shoulders, giving her sister the last mouthful of tack.

Renato led the way out, the revolver in his fist. To be found with a weapon on you spelt death.

'Are you wounded?' asked the woman, noticing his limp.

'No, I'm not, but the Englishman has a badly injured ankle.'

'Where will we be crossing the river?'

'Falzè. They're expecting us there with a boat.'

'I know the way, I'm from these parts. But it's going to be a long haul with your limping friend.'

'Then lead on...madam.' There was a catch in Renato's voice.

Leaning on me, Brian reached his side in two hops: 'Can we make it?'

Major Manca made no answer.

Holding the hands of both girls, the woman went on ahead. 'I know how to avoid the enemy troops,' she said, her voice now clear and strong. 'And I know where to find a cart, too.'

Eleven

IT WAS AN ARMY STOREHOUSE THE ENEMY HAD REACHED before our rearguard had had time to set fire to it. Its southern side was scarcely more than a dozen steps from the wood, and was unguarded.

In a whisper Renato asked the woman where the horses and mules were.

'Behind the store.' That woman knew her onions. 'The men here are always drunk. They go inside and drink themselves silly.'

I followed Renato to the building. There were four sentries. Only one was awake, smoking.

'Wait for me among those carts. I'll lay my hands on a horse.'

I slithered into the ditch. Several minutes passed. No sign of him. The carts were really a heap of wrecks, but two were serviceable. I inspected the wheels, the axles. I crawled in under the one with a bench nailed to the floorboards. I was thinking of Brian's ankle.

Renato joined me half an hour later. He had a horse, and the others were with him. The Englishman let go of the woman, who was hard pushed to support him, and grabbed on to me. He was sopping wet and dead on his feet. Maybe he had a fever. He smelt of hay and decay.

The girls climbed onto the cart while Renato backed the horse between the shafts.

He then had to help me with Brian, who lay back on the boards with his throbbing ankle up on the seat between the two girls.

The woman got up on the box with Renato and me, and took the reins from him.

'I know how. Falzè?'

'Falzè it is.'

The horse was a bay, iron-shod carthorse. It moved off at the merest murmur from the woman, her head now covered with a piece of sacking.

'She knows horses,' whispered Renato in my ear. He was tense, but relieved.

We slid off into the darkness. After nearly an hour the woman drew up beside a haystack. 'We need to get some hay. Over that hump there's a bridge, and it's guarded.'

Renato looked at her for a long moment. He turned towards Brian. He was asleep, or maybe he had fainted. 'All right, let's get a move on.'

I dismounted with him and the elder of the girls. In a few minutes the cart was piled with hay. We all scrambled under it except for Renato, who rubbed a bit of soil over his face and into his hair, and then climbed back on the box beside the woman. 'I'd better take the reins now. I'm your husband, a woman carter would look odd.' She handed him the reins without a murmur.

The first, slow moments of daylight. The horse's hoofs clattered on the cobbles and the hay bulged out over the sides of the cart. In less than ten minutes we reached the bridge. I poked my head out. No one there. A hundred metres away on the left was a sleeping encampment. I saw a fire burning and three men warming their hands at it. One of them, the only one wearing a helmet, raised his head to look in our direction, but he lowered it again almost at once and lit his pipe. I could make out from even that far away that it was a large, curved pipe. Work was beginning again, but the intense cold made the men too lazy to be interested in what was on a cart.

As daylight grew the roadside pickets thinned out. Every so often there would be some mechanical carcass blocking a ditch, and a patrol surrounding it wielding spanners and hammers, and the occasional soldier looking up at the cart. As for Renato, he observed everything. Those infantrymen had a well-fed look to them; the sacking of the Italian army stores and the houses was still boosting their rations. 'But not for long,' he said, pushing my head back under the hay. 'They're getting indigestion now, but food shortage is going to come, and it will be long and hard, for everyone.'

In the warmth of the pungent hay I nodded off. I dreamt of Villa Spada, I dreamt of Giulia who was giving herself to me, until I was woken by a jolt. I heard Renato's voice: 'Only Schüt-zen.' I peeped out again. He was lighting his pipe and speaking to the woman: 'No Germans here.' He turned round. 'And you, Paolo, pull your head back under!'

The pilot's chubby face emerged beside mine.

'How's it going?'

'Better.'

The woman nestled up close to Renato. And seeing the pair of us with our hair full of hay, she laughed. For the first time. I noticed she had good teeth. Comfortable life and healthy food, I thought.

'How are my girls doing?'

'They're asleep.' The pilot's accent made us laugh, all three.

'This is what I like about war,' Brian laughed along with us, 'when you get a laugh. That's the best thing.'

A 'Sshh!' from Renato sent us all ducking back under. I held a hand over the mouth of one of the girls in case she woke up, and Brian did the same with the other. A rumble of engines. Less than a minute later, after a bend, the cart drew into the roadside. Lorries, lots of them. A motorized convoy climbing up the valley. Our own silence became oppressive. The girl whose mouth I was stopping woke up. But she remained motionless, or almost. I pressed my fingers to her lips, trying not to hurt her. Behind the lorries followed the mules, an entire battalion, I later learnt, of infantry with pack-animals.

The minutes seemed never-ending. But at last the cart moved on. I waited a while and then poked my head out. A church steeple pointed upwards from a knoll. 'Barbisano?'

'Yes,' answered Renato. 'It's Barbisano.' Then, in a lower voice: 'Honvéd, Hungarians, coming from Falzè, Moriago or Mercatelli. Sickeningly filthy uniforms.'

I dived back under the hay and released the mouth of the girl, who first stroked my hand and then squeezed it without letting go.

The horse was moving at a trot, and I nodded off again with the girl's breath on my face.

Half an hour later I poked out my head again. 'How much further?'

'Not much,' said the woman.

There were no longer any wrecks by the roadside. We saw no one and made good progress. It was as if the war had simply gone away. No more tents, no more sentries, the sky was clear and the air less chill. We heard no gunfire, not even in the distance, and there was no stink of diesel oil, of wet leather, of urine. Peace had returned.

Suddenly came the loud roar of the Piave. The pilot and the two girls thrust their heads up out of the hay, looking around them and spitting out bits of stalk like threshing machines. 'Have we got to the river'? asked the younger one.

'Very nearly,' replied the woman, gently solicitous.

'Not long now,' said Renato, and cracked the whip over the horse's ears.

Evening had come to our aid. Here and there, the first stars. And at last Renato, who had halted the cart a hundred metres from the river and had gone with the woman in search of food, came back with a sack containing blessings galore: *sopressa* and cheese, and dry black bread which hunger melted in our mouths. There was even a bottle of wine, slightly sour but good. We waited for darkness. The Piave was in full flood, and the noise of it drowned out every other sound. Renato was nervous, Brian was acting impatiently, while the elder girl struggled to hold back her tears and the other slept curled up on the knees of the woman, now crouching in the hay. The cart was drawn up behind a boulder only a few dozen metres from the river bank. The Hungarian trenches stopped three or four hundred metres further south. To the north, less than half a kilometre away, was an Austrian outpost where the soldiers were making merry round two fires burning almost on the river banks.

'The flood waters are a help to us. There's not even a patrol boat,' said Renato, though I could sense the tension in his voice.

'With such a strong current…will the boat make it?'

'It'll make it,' he assured me, giving me a pat on the shoulder.

The two Austrian fires were in plain view. Quite enough to scare one.

Brian staggered to his feet and joined us, giving Renato a light punch on the chest. 'Somebody's coming.'

Indeed, someone was crawling along the bank. Renato crouched low and went to meet him.

'Are you the Englishman?' asked a boy's unbroken voice.

'Yes, that's us,' replied Renato. 'It's four people who have to cross,' he added at once. I stretched out flat on my belly and wormed my way forward to join them. The boy might have been eleven or twelve.

'They're sending us children to do war jobs now,' I murmured, and for the first time I felt myself to be a soldier.

'There's room for two,' said the boy, putting on a man's voice.

'You have to fit in four. Two are little girls.' The major's tone of voice allowed of no dispute.

While I was helping to lower Brian into the boat – it was long and narrow, a kind of flat-bottomed pirogue – Renato went back to lend a hand to the woman.

In the stern was a boy of fifteen or sixteen, holding the tiller, while the younger one helped the woman to scramble down and told her to crouch down on the floorboards. The sides were scarcely more than half a metre high, and the bow was filled by half a dozen sacks. Brian put his arms round the two girls, so relieved that his ankle wasn't hurting so badly. The boards were sopping wet, and I felt a shiver of cold run down my back.

Brian and the major brought up their right hands in salute at the very same moment. The boat left the bank. 'So long.' And the current swept it away.

'Good luck,' I murmured.

Renato turned to me: 'We've got a long trek ahead of us. We must get back before dawn.'

'What about the cart?'

112

'It stays here.'

I tore off a piece of *sopressa* with my teeth and put the rest in my pocket. 'Do you know the way?'

'Lieutenant Muller, the man who brought you to me, is expecting us four kilometres away, but we're late.'

The light caught us just as we reached the garden. The Villa was still sleeping. We made our way round it and approached from the direction of the little temple. We parted without a word. I was so weary that my legs were numb, and all I wanted was to sleep. Grandpa heard me come in. He stroked the back of my neck as I sat on the palliasse taking off my boots. 'Welcome back, laddie.'

I flopped face down on the pillow. I hadn't the strength to undress. The crackly mattress stuffing seemed to me like goose-feathers.

Twelve

WHEN I WOKE UP THE VILLA WAS IN FERMENT. THE ambassador was expected in the afternoon. I breakfasted on hot milk and coffee in the kitchen where Teresa and Loretta had, only recently, regained possession. Their expulsion, lasting two whole days, had enraged the cook: 'That spawn of hell's belly, they'll pay for it I tell you – *diambarne de l'ostia* – them hellkrauts'll pay through their snotty noses, they will!'

Grandpa appeared, capless and with his jacket smartly ironed. He had shaved off his moustache. 'All cleaned up like this the master looks like a stripling,' commented Teresa.

Standing in the doorway he looked us all over from head to foot, and gave a sniff of pleasure: '*Caffellatte,* what a treat.' He took a seat facing me. 'You know, at home, when I was knee-high to a grasshopper, there was a book – I can't recall the title, but it was as thick as this…' – and he formed a C with his thumb and first finger – 'and in the middle of the last page, otherwise totally blank, was the legend, "Revised and corrected edition without any prunting errors." Do you know, laddie, that we've got an ambassador coming to dinner?' He knocked back the entire cup of milky coffee at a single draught. 'In my opinion this invitation is a bad *prunting* error,' he said, with the accent on the prunting. 'The front line is only a few kilometres from the village, and who comes to visit? The ambassador of a *neutral* country.' He rose to his feet and clicked his heels like a German colonel. 'There's not even a whiff of neutrality in this matter. Sweden is friends with those…krauti-chompers, as the cook calls them.' And a placid expression settled on his face. 'Any news of the fighting?' He resumed his seat. 'And is there any more of this coffee?'

While Teresa was pouring it out, Grandpa stroked the moustache he no longer had.

'The krauti-chompers thought our river was just another Isonzo, another Tagliamento, or maybe the Livenza or the Monticano. It's been a surprise…for them too.'

'But do you know anything for certain?'

He sat back heavily, making the chair creak, and once again stroked his non-existent moustache. 'I am a haunter of *bottiglierie*, and much may be learnt among bottles, the whole world goes where there are bottles to be found…Well then, on the twelfth they tried to cross at Zensòn, where the river makes that big loop, the next day at the Papadopoli sink-holes and at Grisolera, and then a few days ago, on the sixteenth or seventeenth, I think, at Fagarè. Pinned down on the river banks, thrown back everywhere. They've got at least twice as many big guns as we have…' He raised his coffee cup aloft, then brought it down on the table with a crash. 'But we stopped them, the dirty mangelwurzels…' This patriotic outburst took me aback, coming from Grandpa, who was usually given to irony.

Grandpa heaved a sigh and continued his discourse, which threatened to turn into a harangue. 'Now all their main force is up on Monte Grappa, and if the Alpini hold out until the Christmas snow the Huns will end up…' He broke off and gave Teresa a challenging grin.

'Frying in hell, *diambarne de l'ostia*,' they said with one voice, and for exclamation mark the cook snorted.

Thumps at the door. A blast of cold air ushered in three soldiers with grim expressions. The shortest of them, with flaxen hair and Franz Joseph side-whiskers, wore a leather apron reaching to below the knee. 'Ich cook,' he said. 'You out. *Raus!*' He pointed to the fire. 'Ich want that.' Grandpa got up and left the kitchen, slamming the door behind him.

Teresa reopened it at once to let me and her daughter through. Out of the corner of my eye I saw her turn to the German cook and say in dialect: 'Cook, you've got a face like a profiterole made of mouse shit.' She turned to me and added, 'The priest's not the only one knows the right words.' Indeed, she had rolled the word 'profiterole' around in her mouth. It was a pastry she made well, having worked as a girl in a pastry shop in Turin.

Korpium and Donna Maria were walking side by side. My aunt was careful never to leave less than a span between their coat-sleeves, but I fancy she was a little disgruntled because the cold forced her to muffle up, detracting from the grace of her natural gait. I was sitting on the barn roof, legs dangling over the edge, and itching to smoke the pipe which I didn't have. I was not thinking about Giulia. I was watching my aunt and the captain as they walked the bounds of the park. I watched some soldiers shovelling snow; two of them, instructed by a corporal, were sawing a branch off a tree that was blocking their way. I watched the mules picketed with their muzzles towards the railings that gave out onto the village street. It occurred to me that I felt the same empathy towards those creatures as Aunt Maria did for horses. Their steadfastness, their patience, their strength, these did not spring from stupidity, but resembled the qualities shown by the men in the trenches. And as for the trenches I had heard many stories – terrible stories – from infantrymen returning from the Kolovrat, the Matajur, the Carso.

And then, I personally had learnt something from the war. My bed was now a lumpy mattress, prickly and noisy, the soles and uppers of my shoes were worn out, the few scraps of meat I got to eat were as tough as leather, I drank unsweetened coffee, and everything, absolutely everything, stank. The streets stank of rotting wood, sweat, men, mules and dung, and there was the stench of clotted blood in bandages, of rotting flesh, of piss, of stagnant water. Even in the garden I smelt cigarettes and tar, diesel oil, burnt rubber and dust. Wartime dust was different from the dust I knew. It got right under your clothes, penetrated curtains and walls, pervaded fields and woods. Even in winter, with the roads half iced over, the columns of lorries and mules managed to raise dust.

To my surprise I saw that the captain and my aunt were making for the barn. They had spotted me. I scrambled down the ladder to get there first and steer them away from Renato's quarters. I didn't know if he was still sleeping.

Korpium had no love of peace and quiet, not even the hectic peace of just behind the lines. He was restless, and even awkward in his movements. He needed the swift, clear-cut, obligatory rigour of action.

'Good morning,' said the captain.

'Good morning to you, Captain…And Aunt…'

'You've got rings under your eyes, Signor Paolo. Did you sleep badly?'

'Not too well.'

'He's thinking about that girl,' said Aunt Maria, scenting the danger.

Korpium smiled. I got the impression that he suspected

something. I tried to smother every trace of concern and looked him straight in the eye.

'Women are difficult,' he said, taking his monocle out of his pocket. 'But you will win through,' pausing to screw it in, 'if you keep at it.'

'Does your horse have a name, Captain?' Aunt Maria had come to my rescue.

Korpium switched his gaze to her, adjusted his cap, and with a bewildered air said no.

'It ought to have one.'

The captain swallowed and removed that ridiculous lens from his eye.

'May I suggest one, Captain?'

'Please do, Madame.'

'Torrente. Call him Torrente.'

'*Torente, torente,*' repeated Korpium, looking sightlessly at me.

'*Torrente*, with two Rs. It's a good name for such a lively bay. It's got three syllables, one O, two Es and two Rs. It has that murmuring sound that horses like so much.'

'You are a poet, Madame.'

'No, no, for heaven's sake, But I like to listen, with care… That's all.'

'Oh yes…yes, of course.'

Aunt Maria shot me a look. 'Now I am afraid that matters at the Villa require my attention, Captain.'

A click of the heels, a little bow.

'Until this evening,' I said, following her in.

The Swedish ambassador was seated in the back of the car of von Below, the victor of Caporetto, commander of the

Austro-German 14th Army. On the bonnet the blue and yellow flag of the Baltic monarchy fluttered side by side with the red, black and white standard of the Kaiser. The fusilier corporal who opened the door for him stiffened to attention.

The great general was the first to emerge. He was bare-headed despite the cold, with receding white hair and deep-set eyes stamped in a face both tranquil and absorbed. He didn't have the look of a Caesar acclaimed under a triumphal arch, but that of a tired man who perhaps already foresaw his final victory was in doubt. The ambassador, on the other hand, was on the portly side, and the chestnut curls emerging from under his hat-brim gave him an air of frivolity. He had blue eyes and wore a long camelhair coat with a fur collar.

I saw not a single helmet, but only caps with the battalion badge. Korpium sprang to attention before his commanding officer, who returned his salute by raising two fingers momentarily to his temple and smiling thinly.

Grandpa was flaunting his dark frock coat and Grandma a mauve silk dress that covered her ankles; round her neck was a string of artificial pearls. Donna Maria and I were also equal to the occasion. Grandpa had lent me a dazzling bow tie, while my aunt was wearing a long blue dress, the lace fastened at the neck with an oval enamel depicting a swallow soaring into a blue sky above green fields, a church tower and the motto *Je reviendrai*. Von Below kissed the ladies' hands with studied gravity, while the ambassador's gesture was hasty and clumsy. He seemed in a hurry to flee from the cold of the garden and get his teeth into a tasty morsel.

In the middle of the oak table stood two silver candelabras. The tall, deep fireplace was giving out a pleasing warmth. The candelabras did not belong to us, but were part of the general's furnishings, and it occurred to us all that they were spoils of war – they were of Lombard or Veronese workmanship – as were the tall candles. To be guests of the enemy in one's own house is perhaps more embittering than the sorrows of exile.

Grandma had imposed on us a polite, though firm, refusal to collaborate. Thirst for information, however, had altered her strategy. This excited me, and I was proud to be taking part in an enterprise far greater than me, the limits of which were beyond my ken.

Our places at table were marked with cards bearing the names of those present elaborately inscribed in sepia ink. Capitain Korpium, Monsieur Spada; the ladies and I were spared the embarrassment of a surname, called merely Monsieur Paolo, Madame Nancy and Madame Maria, while the bigwigs, seated at the top of the table, were Monsieur l'Ambassadeur and Monsieur le Général. For conversation French was *de rigeur*. Grandma was seated on von Below's right, Madame Maria to the right of the ambassador, while Grandpa was placed on the left of the former and Monsieur le Capitain on that of the latter. I was between Grandpa and Aunt Maria, rather glad to be breaking up the symmetry of the dinner party.

The flames from the fire boosted the illumination of the room, their light rising from behind the general and conferring on him a Luciferian aura. On the wall facing me, between the two windows, in the wavering candlelight hung the portrait of Great-Grandma Caterina, which did more honour to her bewildered girlish face than to the skill of the painter. On the general's left, dressed in black with a white apron and frilly white cap, stood Teresa, ramrod stiff, while Loretta, whose cap gave her the air of a frog with aspirations to queenship, held the opposite fort, between the Swede and Aunt Maria.

After the first hesitant openings, the conversation, ably steered by Donna Maria, turned to matters of war. The ambassador was drinking Marzemino like water; Loretta had already uncorked two bottles. Monsieur le Capitain let slip the remark that in the near future the Villa would pass into Austrian hands. 'The Austrians have a conspicuous talent,' said von Below in impeccable French, 'for making a mess of a good job.' He said it with the corners of his mouth turned down and his eyes fixed on some distant, invisible point. He said nothing more for practically the whole dinner, and no more did his captain, who took refuge behind his monocle.

Grandpa chuckled away beneath the moustache he no longer had but never ceased stroking. He was amused by the ambassador, whom wine had bereft of more than a few inhibitions. His curly locks, which he continuously thrust back with his chubby, twitchy left hand, kept flopping forward over his rather low brow and ending up in his eyes. He started talking about Sweden and butterflies. He told us his country was like an overfed horse, asleep on its feet in a spotlessly clean stable. He went on to say that in Italy he loved the butterflies in summer but hated the churches, because they were too beautiful. 'The result is that as soon as you leave one you feel sucked down into the maelstrom of barbarism. There are too many angels in Italian painting, too many angels and no butterflies. You Italians are strange people: practical people who have no love for reality.'

The roast pork was delicious, served with egg sauce and potatoes. There was even a dessert, an apple tart, which Teresa served to the Prussian warrior accompanied by a *diambarne de l'ostia* which, though uttered in an undertone, caused both Grandma and Aunt Maria to look daggers at her. But the general took no notice of the cook. A broad brow crowned his distinguished features and melancholy expression. That bold, meticulous strategist was courteous more by calling than by custom. Though his warrior skills and instincts were legendary, what I saw before me was nothing but a worried man.

At a certain moment the ambassador, dropping the etiquette, addressed the conqueror of Rumania in German. He spoke rapidly for a long minute, amid the stunned silence of the rest of us. The general responded with a few brusque remarks. His face had hardened and his eyes suddenly glittered. The smattering of German possessed by our family was enough to make out that they were discussing an exchange of coal and steel and a large consignment of machine pistols needed by Sweden for purposes of defence. To observe the new German automatic weapon in action was, very likely, the reason for the ambassador's visit to the front line. All the same, we were amazed that they didn't mind being overheard. Even if this was not priceless information for the destiny of Italy, it was certainly a message worth entrusting to the shutters in the bay window, and we were thankful for it.

Then, after a rather long lull, the Swede said something that infuriated the general. Otto von Below shot to his feet, wide-eyed as if seeing a ghost. He crumpled up his table napkin. We all got up, like musicians obeying an imperious gesture from a conductor. Only the ambassador dithered.

Monsieur le Général gave a hasty bow to Grandma at his side, who returned him an astonished look, then walked round the table to raise Donna Maria's hand to his lips, retaining it just a moment longer than necessary. He stalked to the door, turned, and with a barely audible click of the heels said, '*Mesdames, Messieurs, je vous remercie.*' And, turning his back on us, he added a whispered '*Adieu*'.

The captain and the ambassador followed him without deigning to say so much as a word.

'*Diambarne de l'ostia,* may they burn in hell,' muttered Teresa, as Grandma signed to us to sit down.

'Loretta, shut the door,' ordered Aunt Maria.

'New automatic pistols…no great matter, is it?' said Grandpa, stroking his upper lip. 'But after all, in this business we're just raw recruits.'

Aunt Maria got up and blew out some of the nearby candles. 'So we'll soon be taking orders from the Austrians.'

'But if the Germans are moving out' – and there was barely concealed jubilation in Grandpa's voice – 'it means that at the front…everything's going to pot for them.'

'However that may be,' said Grandma irritably, 'we will face matters a day at a time.'

Thirteen

THE GENERAL LEFT BEFORE DAWN, ALONG WITH THE AMBAS-
sador and the escort.

I got up late, at about nine. The machine guns were already
loaded onto the mules. Of the camp hospital and kitchen there
was no trace. When I came down to breakfast Teresa was like
a hen seeing her chicks emerge from their shells. The pots and
pans, ladles and wooden spoons had been restored to the expert
hands of their rightful sovereign, who with a few well-placed
diambarne de l'ostias was swearing to herself that no one would
ever again dethrone her. Her daughter, on the contrary, was on
edge. She no sooner saw me than she asked where Renato was.

'Probably gone out to do some bartering.'

Loretta covered her face with her hands.

My grandparents came down at about midday. It had been
snowing for a little over an hour. The captain had only just finished inspecting his men, drawn up ready for departure. The
motorcycles were the first to leave, followed by two lorries and
the long file of mules, about thirty of them. His second-in-
command had stationed himself near the sentries at the gates,
and the snow, little by little, turned him into a snowman with a
glassy stare and a carrot-coloured nose. I did up the top button
of my overcoat. Korpium circled the garden at a trot. He went
out as far as the graveyard, passed in front of the chapel, then

cantered all round the main building and slowed to a walk beneath Donna Maria's windows. I looked up. She was there, upright and motionless, visible through the falling snow. The captain, standing in his stirrups, brought his right hand smartly to the peak of his cap.

When the officer's bay horse left through the gates, the sentries had already gone. Korpium turned for an instant, raised his eyes towards my aunt's window. It was empty. Then, for a moment, he looked at me. I was strolling towards the railings, and he gave me a salute. I stood to attention, and without thinking I whipped my right hand up to my brow, stiff as a knife-blade. I seemed to glimpse a smile on his lips. Then a light tap of his heels and the bay started off at a trot.

The Villa was ours again. But I was feeling upset, low-spirited. I maundered around the huge empty rooms, passing my fingers over the few pieces of furniture not filched or used as firewood by the invaders, and over the oak table where we had dined the evening before. The general's candlesticks were no longer on it. In the huge fireplace two blackened logs still smouldered. The odour of musty fabric, which had always reigned supreme in the Villa, was gradually regaining possession of the rooms, which one by one surrendered to its dominion, contested for three weeks past by the odours of war. Those soldiers had taken much from the house, but also left something behind them. And soon others would arrive, wearing different uniforms but speaking the same metallic-sounding language. The ownership of things had returned into our hands, but nothing any longer had the feel of being ours, of being mine.

That evening we all ate together. There was a festive air, a feeling of freedom which we had quite forgotten. We ate up the leftovers from the previous evening, reheated pork roast and slices of polenta toasted over charcoal. We laughed about everything. Loretta had to open the last three bottles of Marzemino, survivors of the thirst of the Huns. And so for two long hours, in the room where generals and ambassadors had lately dined, we abandoned ourselves to merriment. And we were lunatics, children, drunkards, poets.

Part Two

Fourteen

GIULIA'S HOUSE WAS HIGH UP ON THE HILL, LESS THAN three hundred metres from the Villa as the crow flies. It was an old farmhouse converted into a small neo-Gothic dwelling in the early years of the century. Despite the wooden embellishments around the doorways and windows, it retained its rustic character, and the balcony all round the upper storey bore witness to its peasant origins. The first time I set foot there was at the end of a long walk. The Germans had departed a few days before. Giulia asked me in. It was early in the morning. We climbed some rickety steps to the balcony and entered the house from there. I noticed that the doors and windows of the ground floor were bolted and barred.

Inside it consisted of a single large room, with larch-wood flooring, a ceiling of terracotta tiles, a table two metres by two surrounded by half a dozen rustic chairs, and a large sofa in front of the broad fireplace in the centre of the north wall, which was the only one without windows. On the other side was a spacious Empire-style bed, the counterpane neatly ironed. Giulia put a flame to the carefully laid log fire and hung her overcoat on an iron hook hanging from a tie-beam.

'So this is where you live.'

'It's enough for me. I let the downstairs. I don't like to be surrounded by things…I find them suffocating and oppressive.'

'Oppressive? Really?'

She stretched out on the sofa. 'Come over here, I'll make coffee later.'

I went and sat by her without taking off my overcoat.

'You've got a fine nose, long and finely chiselled. It's worth having a face to carry around a nose like yours.'

She looked into my eyes. Her blouse was unbuttoned down to the cleavage between her breasts. In the fireplace the wood was already crackling. I shot to my feet and went over to the window. From there I could see the Villa, with the big garden forming an L-shape around the main building, and the *barchessa* backed up alongside the church.

'What's so fascinating about your grandparents' house? You ought to have eyes only for me.'

'It looks different from here. Now the Germans have gone the garden looks smaller, but maybe it's only the perspective,' I replied, still gazing out. 'I like your home. It's so neat and tidy… you know…I thought you were…'

'A savage? It feels like a boat, doesn't it? My grand-father was a rear admiral, and when he came here he used to bring his mistresses, and maybe he felt some nostalgia for his ship.'

'A rear admiral?'

'Yes, at the Battle of Lissa he was a junior officer in the Austro-Hungarian navy, just think of it! He died in July 1914, two months after your mother and father.'

She got up and joined me at the window, pressing the tip of her nose against the pane. 'Your house is so huge…What do you do with all those rooms? And that three-mullioned window on the façade…It's ridiculous, it looks stuck on.'

I put an arm round her shoulders.

'Please don't,' she said, and the look she gave me hurt. I took my arm away.

'Do you live here all alone?'

'But didn't you know? Pagnini lives downstairs.' And she gave a coarse laugh.

'*Whaaat?*'

'Yes, it's him I let the ground floor to. But I come in that way,' pointing to the little door onto the balcony which we had entered by. 'We never meet. He keeps to himself down there, as quiet as the dead. I don't even hear him coming and going. I sometimes think he likes living in the dark, because day after day he never even opens a window.'

She took my hand and we sat together on the sofa in front of the fire. She unbuttoned my overcoat and brought her lips close to mine, but without touching them. So I kissed her, and she let me do it; but she was distant, she was playing with me. I drew back. 'Don't you like me?'

'Silly! Of course I like you, but you're just a boy.'

I kissed her again, and again she let me.

'I don't like the way you laugh. You seem afraid of showing your teeth, but you've got lovely teeth and have the look of a lady-killer.' She almost tittered, and again I pulled back, feeling she was only teasing me.

'Did you do those?' I asked, nodding at two watercolours hanging above the mantelpiece, the only purely decorative objects in the whole house.

'Yes, a few years ago. I don't paint any longer. When I was in Venice I liked to, but not now.'

She ran her fingers through my hair and brought her face close to mine. I smelt her breath and her eau de cologne, and could feel myself blushing. 'Don't you dare kiss me any more, not today at any rate…You've got really beautiful hair. I'd like to paint those black curls of yours. But you've got the thin lips of a cynic, and sometimes you give a crooked smile, as Renato does. But then, he's a grown-up man, and is entitled to.'

Those last words were like daggers. I got up and without thinking up an excuse walked out through the door to the balcony and down the steps without looking back.

I reached the piazza in just a few minutes. I strode along quickly, thinking of those two brief stolen kisses. The morning air sneaked in at my coat collar. I was miserable, deeply miserable. I stopped at the inn and entered the place to get a taste of the loneliness one feels in the company of strangers, and to be forced to show it a bold face.

The intense cold had moved Don Lorenzo's school into the sacristy. Adriano, who ruled as the king of the youngsters from the pinnacle of his fourteen years and 170 centimetres, was put in charge of the stove. The priest had asked me to give him a hand with history and geography. I had said yes because it would put me in well with Grandma, who at the beginning of the summer had intuitively plumbed the depths of my mathematical skills and had immediately drawn back appalled: 'Perhaps you are more cut out for non-Euclidean foolishness…' and ever since then there had been no mention of exponents and logarithms, abscissas, ordinates or sines and cosines.

The priest, his mood as black as his cassock, strode up and down grasping a tailor's measuring stick which he whacked against the blackboard at regular intervals to assure himself of the attention of his pupils.

'You!' And he aimed the measure at Adriano, who was puffing at the embers. 'Come here to the board.'

This boy's face was long and pale. He slammed shut the stove door. He got to his feet. His body too was long and skinny.

'Get a move on! Have your feet turned to lead? Now write!' I was sitting at the back of the class awaiting my turn. I had to do a bit of Roman history and was trying to concentrate. 'Write, boy, write. My dog is good.'

Adriano wrote the sentence on the blackboard. One word under another, each on a separate line. He knew the way. Grammar was Don Lorenzo's torment and delight.

Adriano's letters were all out of shape, the A spindly, the O obese, and he forgot to put an accent on the E. When he had finished writing he pressed the chalk to his forehead in search of inspiration.

'IL is the subject,' he said after a long minute.

The priest didn't move a muscle. The class was frozen in the silence that comes before a battle.

'MY means that it is mine.'

Silence.

'DOG is its name.'

Silence. They all knew that Adriano's dog, a grey Pomeranian, was in fact simply called 'Dog'.

'IS...is a verb.'

Silence.

'GOOD is a complimentary object.'

The boys were as silent as the walls. The priest strode towards the blackboard. Adriano saw the tailor's measure transformed into the lance of St George attacking the dragon. He turned tail and fled, vanishing through the doorway. The saint's lance clattered to the floor. Don Lorenzo rubbed his bald pate with both hands, his shoes astraddle beneath his cassock, his eyes cast down and haggard. 'Give me patience,' he said. 'It takes all the patience the Good Lord can give!' And he shooed the class out with his hands: 'Out, out with you!'

Thus it was that the children of Refrontolo were spared my little learning, and Dog received an unexpectedly large ration of snowballs.

While I was on my way home that same afternoon, a sergeant and a private in the army of Karl I of Hapsburg, the thirty-year-old emperor, arrived at the Villa mounted on a couple of donkeys – one of which was missing an ear – and with unusual cordiality, the result of a hefty dose of grappa, informed Aunt Maria that General Serda Teodorski had decided to make Villa Spada one of the headquarters of the Sernaglia sector of the front. Then the sergeant asked Aunt Maria for an egg for himself and one for the private, and Teresa allowed them to sit in the kitchen, on the most uncomfortable bench, the only one she hadn't yet cleaned. For no one scents – and despises – the hoi polloi sooner than a consummate servant.

The Austrians arrived at about seven o'clock. Three companies, only one of which stayed, the others going on towards Pieve di Soligo. The troops were drawn up in the piazza, only a few dozen metres from the gateway by the old façade, beneath the three-mullioned window which in the near future would begin to transmit Grandma's code. They came from Codroipo, and for a good quarter of an hour were kept there stock still in the cold, lined up before a major who was shouting orders about what I took to be the allotment of quarters and the sentry posts.

For a month already, two thirds of the houses in Refrontolo had been empty, stripped of everything that could be loaded onto a cart, everything a donkey could possibly drag away. The new arrivals spent the whole evening forcing doors and gates to lay hands on what little was left. Four officers and their batmen came to take up quarters in the Villa.

Donna Maria received their commanding officer seated in an armchair beside the burning fire. The room – upstairs, above the dining room with the oak table – was lit by a few candles and the tremulous flame of a lamp just about to run out of paraffin.

I was sitting on a rather uncomfortable little sofa, pretending to read a book Grandpa had thrust upon me, when in came an officer. Crisply ironed uniform, shining buttons. He sported, hanging from a blue-bordered triangular yellow ribbon, a two-headed eagle with a gold F on a shield in the middle. There was something un-military about him, maybe the hesitant way he moved his hands. They almost seemed to embarrass him. He was not much more than thirty, had the insignia of a major, light chestnut hair cut short, and no moustache or sideburns. His pink complexion didn't give the impression of a warrior, but rather that of a young man who had just bid his mother goodnight.

He crossed the room with short, quick steps. I got to my feet. My aunt remained seated, but raised her eyes, put her book down open astraddle the arm of her chair and offered him her hand. The officer, clasping his cap to his left side, bowed and executed an awkward hand-kissing. Aunt Maria bowed her head ever so slightly. 'Major,' she said.

The major brought up his right hand in a smart salute. 'Madame, allow me to introduce myself. I am Rudolf Freiherr von Feilitzsch, Baron von Feilitzsch, aide-de-camp to General Bolzano, and in the name of His Imperial Majesty Karl I of Hapsburg I am taking possession of this Villa.' In his Italian – which Grandpa defined as 'stuff with all the subjunctives in the right place' – there was barely a trace of a German accent. 'I hold myself responsible for the wellbeing of yourself and that of your family.' He swallowed. 'My officers and I,' he added, raising his voice a little, 'are aware that it is our duty not to put you to any inconvenience other than those demanded by the state of war.' He then turned to me, and his face broke into a smile less of circumstance than of amusement. It was as if he were asking, 'Did I do that well?'

All at once I felt him to be my fellow, thought of him as a youngster merely playing at making war.

'My duties as commander call me away, Madame,' said the baron firmly. And with a click of the heels he vanished.

Giulia joined us for supper, along with the Third Paramour. The officers ate in the big dining room on the ground floor, served by their batmen. We were confined to the upstairs, with Teresa serving at table and Loretta running back and forth to the kitchen. The grandparents were in high spirits. The purple lion on the shield borne by the two-headed eagle lacked the tenebrous glower of the Prussian eagle. 'The damsel has chased away the dragon,' was the maxim of the evening. And though Aunt Maria did not share our Buddhist's enthusiasm, she appreciated the gentlemanly manners of the new master of the house: 'The baron is aide-de-camp to a general and has exquisite manners.'

The Third Paramour objected that manners aren't everything. 'A curious statement,' commented Grandpa, 'coming from you, who are a bundle of good manners and nothing else.' Grandpa's well-bred ferocity intended to leave his rival no room for manoeuvre. Grandma didn't interfere; those squabbles amused her, as homage to the last stirrings of her womanhood.

When Giulia, sitting opposite me, stretched out a foot to touch mine, I felt the blood rise to my cheeks. Teresa, who was offering me the soup tureen, noticed it and grunted one of her grunts. Giulia was radiant, and I was longing for her lips, to touch her skin. I couldn't even follow what was being said. At a certain point I stood up. 'Excuse me, I don't feel very well.' I dumped my napkin on the table and left the room.

I was hoping that Giulia would follow me. A woman of her stamp has no need of excuses. Without thinking I set off towards the barn. I was wearing only a sweater. I broke into a run to ward off the cold. About thirty metres ahead I saw a point of light coming and going. It was Renato's pipe.

'Do you want to catch your death? Come inside.' Renato stooped slightly to avoid the oaken lintel. He took off his overcoat and lit a paraffin lamp in a stone niche beside the door. I breathed in the odour of embers, garlic, dried figs. He offered me a flask of grappa. One sip and my throat was on fire. I handed it back at once. It was a large room, seven metres by five. The hearthstone in the corner was about fifty to sixty centimetres higher than the brick floor. I was struck by the cleanliness of it all: the hood over the fireplace was redolent of Marseille soap. I see a woman's hand here, I thought. The window, right opposite the door, was masked by a heavy curtain of sacking brushing the floor. The bedstead was of iron, long and broad like the giant who occupied it. The fawn blanket had the same rust-coloured stripes as mine. It came from the Villa.

'Let's have some heat,' he said, with a nod at the logs in the fireplace. 'Close the door.'

The chimney drew like a dream, and the wood was ablaze in an instant.

He pulled a green-painted bench out away from the wall

and we sat down side by side. 'Would you like a puff at a pipe? I've got a Peterson, a present from Brian. The tobacco smells a bit like manure, but it's not actually mule dung. Considering everything I've put you through, you deserve a present.'

He showed me how to fill it, and how to keep the smoke in my mouth without inhaling. 'Gently...you must smoke gently, feel the calm effect between your teeth. As when you touch a woman's breast,' he smiled, 'you have to go gently with the nipples, circle round them...and then downwards over her curves, until you reach the cleft you're after. The gradual assault pays off. And the pipe is quietude, rhythm, restrained passion... It helps you think.'

The Peterson was curved, with a dark brier bowl which came down to just under my chin. I smoked as slowly as I could, so as not to disappoint my teacher, and every now and again we caught each other's eye and laughed like children with a new toy.

'So you are a major...'

'I am the steward of the Villa. Nothing else.'

We chatted for a while about the officers who had just arrived.

'Austria, like Italy, is a woman...Two women, in fact, because there is also the Kingdom of Hungary...But Hungary is more like a peasant girl, while Austria is a great lady. Two women coming to blows with Italy, a pretty hefty woman herself, despite everything.' With the tip of his pipe-stem he sketched the outline of our boot-shaped peninsula.

'When it's between women...' I began, but two raps at the door shut me up.

'That must be Loretta...This is when she brings me a bowl of soup with polenta.' He undid the bolt.

'Signorina Candiani!' Renato turned to me and registered astonishment.

I stood up.

Giulia shot me a withering glance.

Renato shut the door. 'What are you doing here?' From his voice he seemed genuinely taken aback.

'Looking for Paolo.' She was tense, but I didn't want to think she was lying. 'Your aunt's asking for you,' she added.

'How did you know I was here?'

'I'm a witch. Haven't you realized that yet?'

I nodded.

'What a lovely pipe.'

'A present from Renato. It came from Brian.'

'An Irish pipe...A good dry smoke,' said Renato. 'But don't keep your aunt waiting...Off you go.'

'Thanks for the pipe...and everything.' But the door had already closed behind us.

I was glad that the darkness concealed my blushes. Giulia took my hand and started to run. Then, suddenly, she stopped and planted her lips on mine. So firmly it almost hurt. She was trembling with nerves. I felt her warm, soft tongue on mine. I slid a hand in under her overcoat. A moment, then she broke away, pushing me away with both hands on my chest. 'Quiet! There's someone coming.'

We were in the middle of the garden. The light shed on the snow from a single window was all that broke the darkness. We strained our ears, heard a crunching sound. 'Quick, let's get inside,' she whispered. As soon as we reached a door at the back Giulia let go my hand and gave me a hasty kiss. 'See you tomorrow...Donna Maria is expecting you.'

'But you can't go home now...There's the curfew.'

'What I can do and not do is up to me and only me.' Her voice was cold. It stung me. She turned and ran off in the direction of the hill, since she couldn't go out through the gates.

I glanced back towards the barn. For a moment I thought I could discern the intermittent glow of a cigarette, or a pipe. Then nothing but darkness. I went indoors.

Fifteen

ON DECEMBER THE EIGHTH THERE WAS UPROAR. THE Germans of the Silesian division had been called home and let off their entire reserves of ammunition. After that the month passed uneventfully until Christmas. Action on the Piave was slackening off. The salvos from the Montello, from Vidòr, from Segusino were rare enough to be remarked on. Only in the foothills and valleys around Monte Grappa, as far as Monte Tomba and the narrow valley at Quero, was the battle still raging.

Grandpa was the most optimistic of the lot of us. 'If they haven't broken through yet, they never will. There's two metres of snow up there on top. With snow that deep it's not easy to survive, let alone fight.'

On December the fourth a few British and French contingents had joined our front line; or at least so they said in the *bottiglieria* Grandpa haunted, in the conviction that 'barmen know more than generals'.

At that time no one knew that the Emperor Karl had as early as the second issued a 'secret' order to halt the Austrian offensive. If they were still firing up in the mountains it was only to improve their positions while awaiting the thaw.

Giulia and I met every day, and every day I was granted the taste of her kisses, but she didn't let me touch her very much, and this began to get on my nerves. Meanwhile, Don Lorenzo had caught me in his net: I was recruited for the fourth. I gave history lessons to all the boys left in the village, about thirty of them, although never more than ten or a dozen turned up. The troops were billeted in the abandoned houses round the piazza, and the few officers quartered in the Villa were all but invisible. 'They are very well-mannered,' said Aunt Maria, with a touch of admiration. Grandpa had once said that if she had seen a hangman proffer the noose politely she would have lauded his exquisite manners.

Donna Maria was attempting to break the ice with Major von Feilitzsch. She had been urged to do so by both Grandma and Renato, but she made her own special contribution: the baron too was fond of horses, and in the stables there were now five of them, one for each officer, in addition to the carthorses.

Since the beginning of December the Villa had become a staging post, and two Imperial Army grooms were permanently lodged in the *barchessa*. The mules of contingents passing through were tethered under the portico, or in the courtyard of the inn, the only source of provisions in the whole place.

The invaders were thirsty for grappa and ravenous for polenta. Things that the innkeeper's wife – he himself was stuck behind his bar counter all day long – obtained from the peasants' wives in exchange for bags of salt and white flour, pretending not to know that thereafter, amongst the mules in the courtyard, every good wife got two sips of grappa and a slice of polenta if she offered the customer a little entertainment.

Everyone said the paper money printed by the Austrians was 'bum bumf'. So it was that in that December of 1917 – after twenty centuries of ready cash – exchange and barter was rediscovered, even if there was little left to barter with: a few sacks of vegetables, oats, eggs, chickens and eros. 'A chick with an empty purse is an easy lay,' said Grandpa. 'Even if a full purse is no chastity belt.' And exchanges of eros and polenta – not restricted to the inn yard – had become a matter of 'see no evil, hear no evil'. Don Lorenzo had good reason to shout and yell in church. Hunger had triumphed over honour.

The British fighter plane roared over at rooftop level. All eyes were glued to the skies, including those of the officers smoking by the window. Near the red, white and blue rings on the fuselage I noticed a blue bird set in a red oval. The SPAD flew over again twenty minutes later, but this time it was going in the opposite direction, towards the Pieve. Aunt Maria had barely had time to position the shutters, and there was nothing on the washing line. To hang out laundry just to have it freeze would have aroused suspicion.

Once past us the aircraft waggled its wings once or twice. The SPADs often did this on their way back to behind our lines. We'll chuck the bastards out, was the message.

Grandpa and I, who were stretching our legs back and forth over the hundred metres between the chapel and the stables, both waved madly to return the greeting. The steward was coming towards us, a shovel and a rake over his shoulder. As he passed he gave me a wink and murmured, 'The blue kingfisher...Our friend made it to safety.'

While Renato was on his way towards the latrine, the officer of the day caught up with us and, slowing to our pace though keeping eyes front, said quietly but distinctly: 'N'oubliez pas Karfreit.'

'Don't worry, we remember Caporetto all right,' rebutted Grandpa loudly, 'but it's not over yet. Not by a long chalk.'

The morning of Christmas Eve surprised us with its

unseasonal mildness. Grandpa and I went to the *bottiglieria* in Solighetto, while Aunt Maria went out riding with the major. On the way we came across a group of prisoners busying themselves around the mangled bonnet of a lorry. They begged us for cigarettes. Grandpa, who smoked only Toscano cigars, and used cigarettes in lieu of tips, pulled out a packet which was torn to shreds in a brace of shakes. One fag even went to the lackadaisical Hungarian overseer, who grinned at us happily with his few remaining teeth.

The *bottiglieria* consisted of a huge dark room, ten metres by five, panelled in wood from floor to ceiling. It had only one window, with iron bars as thick as two fingers. On the oaken shelves behind the counter was a row of half-empty bottles with handwritten labels, and were one to believe the writing there was even whisky and cognac. But it was grappa that claimed the lion's share, with at least twenty or thirty bottles. There were also two demijohns which gave off an acrid tang that turned my stomach. The beaten earth floor was saturated with alcohol at five pfennigs a flask, the ferocious stench of which contested the field with that of the few customers.

The hostess was short and robust. A lock of snow-white hair sprang from under the kerchief knotted beneath her chin, while in her oval face dark eyes expressed the melancholy born of much mourning. She asked what we wanted in the educated voice of a person who reads. Her husband approached her, seventy kilos of muscle for a metre and a half in height: 'Give 'em some wine, woman!'

'Cognac,' said Grandpa. 'For two, one of them with water.'

'With what?' barked the host in dialect. 'Water will do for washing in, if you have any.' And off he went with a sneer. 'And to rot the piles, as they say in Venice.'

I hadn't the least desire to drink. I gave Grandpa a glance.

'We're not here for the fun of it.'

So I had no choice.

'Malingerers are the first to spot trouble,' he said. 'And to get wind of troop movements.'

We spent the morning in that stench of sour wine and sweaty humanity. I was nearly sick, my head was spinning. Luckily, at about midday Grandpa thought he had laid his hands on something to communicate to the three-mullioned window. Three Hungarian army battalions were expected at Sernaglia at the beginning of January. It wasn't the kind of news to change the outcome of a battle, but at least it was something to transmit to the kingfisher.

For the festive occasion the baron had arranged a concert last thing before midnight mass. All of us were invited, but only Aunt Maria and I attended. We arrived a little late so there was no time for introductions. The dining room was lit by two carbide lamps. The oak table had been shifted to the side opposite the fire, which sparkled away behind the quartet.

The cellist was a lady of thirty at the outside, with hair as black as her silk dress and a décolleté gleaming with a double string of pearls which reflected the tenuous wavering of the flames. The fire gave the silhouettes of the musicians an almost sinister appearance somewhat at odds with the music of Mozart.

Seated with us in a semicircle were seven Austrian and three Hungarian officers, summoned from the neighbouring commands. I couldn't keep my eyes off the cellist; her face enthralled me. At the end of the concert we discovered that the mystery woman was von Feilitzsch's wife, who had been permitted to join her husband for Christmas. This had not pleased the major, who would rather have had leave to join her in Vienna, so he had said not a word about it to anyone, maybe because he knew she would be off again the next day. Madame von Feilitzsch had assembled her musician friends – amateurs, but esteemed in many drawing rooms in the capital – and obtained a pass thanks to her friendship with a colonel in the emperor's graces.

We drank 'à la fin de la guerre' in sharp-tasting red Tyrolese wine. For the sake of politeness the officers forced themselves to talk French, but it was obvious that they couldn't wait to get rid of us and chat amongst themselves. What's more, Madame von Feilitzsch knew little Italian but was determined to speak it, making things hard for my aunt and me, scarcely able to under-stand what she was gabbling about. In the end, after the ritual formalities we took our leave with a sigh of relief.

'Well, that's something done,' said Aunt Maria. 'Now let's go to church.'

I went with her as far as the church forecourt and said goodbye.

'But it's Christmas!' she cried, her eyes shooting sparks at me. But I had a tryst with Giulia, and the threat of hell in another life little availed against the promise of a heaven, however brief, just round the corner.

On the evening of the thirty-first – a freezing Monday which I had spent reading in front of the fire – we went into a huddle in Aunt Maria's room to review the situation. A frugal repast. Grandpa did his level best to raise our spirits, but whatever story he told, whatever joke he pulled out of his hat, he couldn't make us forget we were guests in our own house, reduced to dependence on the goodwill of enemy officers. Loretta served at table. She was more self-confident now, and seemed pleased with herself, as if happy to see us downhearted. We were eating leftovers, as she had often had to do, and our sheets were a little less white than usual – for even lye was hard to get – and now we too were not our own masters.

Teresa, on the other hand, was unhappy for her own sake and for ours, and one could see it in her face. Our feeling of loss, of humiliation, was hers also.

Sixteen

THE SLANTING EVENING LIGHT STRETCHED THE SHADOW of Beelzebub across the whole width of the desk. I picked up the top sheet of the pile, and as Grandpa followed my every gesture while fingering his long cigar, a smile came to his lips. I was the first person in the world to read one of his pages, the first to be admitted into the Thinking Den. At Grandma's instigation we had thought his book a myth. He didn't take his eyes off me, even if he pretended to busy himself with his cigar, which remained unlit, or with Beelzebub's ribbon, which blackened his fingertips.

'But your book then…actually exists!'

Reaching out his right hand, while his left snapped the cigar in half, he tore the page from my fingers and laid it atop the others, beside the typewriter. For a long moment he glared at the pile, then thrust it into a drawer which he closed with tremulous hands. I attempted to say something, but the words stuck in my throat. I still had to take in the emotional impact of the event.

I would have liked to tell him his style was really original, to tell him I loved him, but instead – in his bizarre and simple way – he said: 'Dinner will be on the table.' His voice showed no disappointment. 'Don't let's keep them waiting, you know our womenfolk…We'll talk another time.'

He raised his trouser seat from the cherry-wood chair which caged him round.

'Tell me, how's the redhead at kissing?'

I felt my cheeks burning. I started down the stairs.

'Forgive me, laddie...I never did learn to mind my own business.'

Teresa had stirred some raisins in with the polenta. 'Said to be good for you.' After that came a stew of suspect flavour.

'Rabbit,' she said firmly. And we asked no questions.

After dinner I went for a smoke with the steward. The priest was with him. They were sitting on a bench before the fire, eating a leftover of stew. They were talking nineteen to the dozen, their plates on their knees.

'Good evening.' I came in, bringing the cold with me. I sat down on the stone hearth, my back to the barely flickering flames. Both men had long faces. 'Bad news?' I asked.

Don Lorenzo raised his fork to take the last mouthful. He put his plate down beside me on the hearthstone, picked up his glass from the floor under the bench and drank a long draught. I smelt the heavy odour of the wine.

'All church bells weighing over fifty kilos are to be taken away,' said Renato. 'Orders from Boreovic.'

'All the bells expropriated,' Don Lorenzo began to read from a printed sheet he had taken from under his cassock and spread on his knees, 'will be examined by a specially appointed art expert.' He read one syllable at a time, and I had never heard such a note of sadness in his voice. He held the paper at a distance so as to focus better: 'Bells certified as being cast earlier than the year 1600 will as a rule be considered objects of value, whereas bells of more recent date will be considered as such only if they are of real historic and artistic value.' With a greyish handkerchief he wiped his brow, which was perfectly dry. 'It is forbidden to proceed with expropriation during divine service, on Sundays and on Feast Days.'

'If you were to say one mass after another without stopping...' I pulled myself up short. It wasn't funny.

'The bell is the voice of the whole village, not just of the church,' said the priest, folding up the printed sheet.

'That's why they're taking them.' Renato spoke with a spurt of anger. 'Take away the voice of the people, the voice that announces their festivals and funerals, the voice that sounds the alarm...it's like tearing the heart out of them.'

Don Lorenzo got to his feet. 'No bells, no voices but those of the guns.'

A knock at the door. Renato said, 'Come in,' and a blast of cold air brought in Loretta. She was carrying a steaming dish, a slice of pancetta on a thick slab of polenta. 'I've brought you some supper. A nice Kraut boy put it aside for me.' Then she spotted us and her eyes widened. 'You here too...' Her eyes flicked back and forth between me and the priest.

Renato cut the pancetta into three pieces, taking a large knife from a hook on the wall. I made the most of the mouthful by taking a sip of wine. Loretta just stood there, sulking. The priest gave her a look of disgust to match her mother's *diambarne de l'ostia.*

'Scrumptious pancetta, this. I wonder who they stole it from,' I said.

'From the mayor.' Loretta's voice betrayed the poison of rancour. 'The mayor's larder was chock-full of every blessed thing, I tell you. All stuff stolen from the labouring folk, poor ducks.'

'Pancetta...Haven't had *this* for a while,' said the priest with his mouth full. His pleasure-loving nature loathed abstractions.

His god was in things themselves, as in that mouthful of pancetta that had put him in a good mood. Renato, though, was troubled. He had something on his mind that wouldn't let up. However, the pancetta acted on him, and on me, like a healer's balm. And all of a sudden we began to sing:

> *They say, they say that she fell sick*
> *Because she didn't eat polenta.*

And then, with the priest joining in at the top of his lungs, we followed it up with:

> *A graveyard lies beyond the bridge*
> *The graveyard of us soldier-boys.*

I wondered what could be the source of the magic of such sad, disconsolate songs. Maybe in the dark we all feel at one with the river, the woods, the beasts of the field. Maybe we too are there in the mule that catches the scent of death and refuses the bit.

Seventeen

IN THE MIDDLE OF THE WHITE SILK FLAG WAS THE COAT OF arms of Franz Joseph, the gloomy Apostolic King of Hungary, known to us as Ceccobeppe, topped by the crown of St Stephen. Giulia and I were walking together so close that our elbows brushed as my fingers furtively sought hers while hers kept making their escape. We circled the flagpole. The Austrian banner mesmerized us. 'With a flag that beautiful,' said Giulia, taking my hand, 'they can't win.' On the other side, the middle of the white space was occupied by the arms of the Kingdom of Hungary, supported by two angels in flight, the outer one in profile, while the one nearer the flagstaff gave us the same embarrassed look as so many Madonnas who haven't quite made up their minds how to hold the Babe. The background colours of the shield peeped through a mass of crowns, towers, heraldic beasts, and symbols of the feuds of Dalmatia, Croatia, Slavonia and the grand-duchy of Transylvania, in which the gold of the crown, embellished with red, blue and green inlays, was at odds with the silhouettes of the angels, who seemed eager to wilt into the cloth, harbingers of fading glories.

'This lavish display of symbols jars with the shoddiness of the present,' I said.

'Now you're starting to talk like your grandfather.'

The blood rushed to my cheeks. I didn't know what comeback

to make, so I ran on ahead and into the *barchessa*, on my own. A few mules were tied up there, along with a stomach-turning stench of piss and a dozen bicycles leant against the wall. I waited for my eyes to adjust to the semi-darkness. A soldier with a pipe in his mouth was stroking a dog, whispering in its ear as if it were a restive horse. I left. I looked around me. Giulia was no longer there. Two non-commissioned officers were leaning against the boundary wall, smoking their long pipes.

It seemed as if the war had simply gone away. But as I approached the kitchen I heard the noise of crockery being smashed. In the corridor two soldiers with rifles and cartridge belts slung crosswise were rummaging in the dresser, among the pans and dishes. They glanced at me without the slightest interest and made no room for me to pass. I squeezed myself against the wall and entered the kitchen. Teresa was yelling, 'To hell with you, misbegotten mangel-wurzel mashers! There'll be no Madonna for you, you'll be supping with Satan!' A pile of casseroles, coppers, wooden spoons and pots and pans of every shape and size blocked the area between the hearth and the table. 'But what're you after, eh, you scrofulous thimble-riggers?'

I went and stood by her. 'Just as well they can't understand you.'

Teresa regarded me with ill-concealed contempt. 'Don't know what these pilfering piddlers want. It's been ten minutes they been messing among my pots, and him with the emperor moustache has said if they don't find what they want they'll go and stick their noses upstairs, may his moustaches moulder!'

The sergeant now came up and thrust his chest to within a centimetre or two of mine. He loomed above me by a hands-breadth. 'You, out!'

I was about to obey when in came Grandpa. 'What's all this hullaballoo, Teresa?'

'They're just hurling everythin' to hell here, and won't even deign to tell me what they're lookin' for, the curs!'

'It here, I know!' growled Whiskers, glaring at Grandpa with his huge blue eyes.

'Franzi-fancy Whiskers,' murmured Grandpa. 'What are you hunting for? Rather than turn everything upside down, wouldn't it be better to ask?'

'You, quiet. We search gun,' he said, cocking up his thumb and pointing a pretend revolver. 'You know where is? You say!' And he smoothed down his moustache, challenging Grandpa's scowl with his bright blue glower. 'We know it be here,' he added, repeating that childish revolver gesture.

'We are hiding nothing. We have no weapons,' protested Grandpa mildly.

The sergeant stopped stroking his moustache and his glower darkened. He seized Grandpa by the lapels, and this time Grandpa paled. I had never seen him like that. He was more surprised than frightened. I took a step towards him but Teresa beat me to it. She shouldered the sergeant off and stabbed a finger straight at his nose. Staggered, he took a step backwards.

'Cowardly scoundrel!'

'Calm down, calm down, nothing's the matter, Teresa. Take it easy and let them search for what they want. We have nothing to hide.' Grandpa straightened his jacket collar. 'There are no weapons here, Sergeant.'

The search resumed, even more wild and violent. The men now hurled the pans onto the floor with greater rage and fury than ever. It was their way of showing us who was top dog. After the kitchen came the turn of the downstairs rooms, one after another. I took Grandpa out of doors, into the garden, and we strolled around for a while.

'Defended by a servant! If this is what this world is coming to, I don't mind going to another,' said Grandpa, then clammed up. After half an hour we went up to the attic. The search, with din and devastation, continued far below. Grandma and Aunt Maria had been to protest to the baron, who had stayed immured in his office and hadn't even received them.

I followed Grandpa to the Thinking Den. We sat and smoked, he an inordinately long Tuscan cigar, I my pipe. On the desk between us towered the black bulk of Beelzebub, reducing the little Buddha to the status of a minor god. Grandpa had an urge to talk, to give an account of himself. Even he, who in one of those aphorisms good for the dinner table had said that men do not do so, and that if they do it is to conceal, not to reveal.

'I have always been a prisoner,' he said quietly but clearly, with a tiny pause after each word. 'Yes, a prisoner, you heard me right.' He was not even seeing me, but fixing his gaze straight ahead, on the smoke from his cigar. 'I have never been able to kick the current Kraut in the teeth.'

'What do you mean, Grandpa?'

'A man who is really a man soon learns to fend for himself, to cast aside all safety and convenience…He has to learn it early!' He blew a smoke-ring. 'I've been scared of the truth…When you tell the truth you lose friends, you lose everything. The truth hurts, because it brings you right back down to earth. And that's what we all try to avoid.' He still wasn't seeing me.

'You mean, back to reality, not dreams.'

For an instant, a bare instant, he saw me there. 'Defended by a cook…a servant…' He sighed, as if to get a load off his chest. 'That woman Teresa is worth more than me, she's got more guts than me, she's of more use to the world than I am.'

'Her rabbit stew wasn't bad…in its wartime way.'

'You know what the trouble is, Paolo? The trouble is that we have the priests sitting on our heads. They're the ones who school us, and they it is who have least faith of all. They believe in God's nest egg all right, because it's useful, but for the rest… Just draperies and incense to dress up all their natter about nothing. What do they know of the fire that burns within us? They don't see their wives and children die. What do they know of the kingdom of the dead? They fear it and they avoid it, as do we all, but what do they know of it? They believe in the Church, yes that, because their Church has walls and money, but when they turn to their god…They've always burnt visionaries alive. If a peasant sees the Madonna they don't pat him on the back, they put him on trial! But then if other people start to see Madonnas where the peasant they burnt saw his, then they say, "Yes, the Madonna appeared here," and build a chapel, then a cathedral, a monastery. That's how it works with them. They think they are lambs among a pack of wolves, but in fact they themselves are the wolves. There is no hellfire, but the truth is a flaming fire, and the truth is our hell. Our cook showed me today that she has more truth to her, more life in her, than I have.' He looked at me then, and he saw me.

'She's a very special woman. I'm fond of her too.'

'She is a great-hearted woman.'

'Heart' was a word Grandpa never ever used.

'We Italians are the progeny of priests, we detest joy. It scares us. Foreigners say we're a happy-go-lucky people, but they're wrong. We clip the wings of happiness as soon as it's heard in an infant's cries, because they're a disturbance. But the world needs disturbing, and how!' He looked at me, but again without seeing me. 'These bars that imprison me I have fashioned little by little over the years, day by day. They are forged out of my fear of disturbing the world.' He stubbed out his cigar in the ashtray he kept beside Beelzebub. He laced his fingers at the back of his neck, leant back in the creaking chair, and raised his eyes to the ceiling. Something resembling an expression of serenity spread across his face, and a smile appeared beneath the moustache he no longer had. He was my old Grandpa again, with the face that laughed even when he was sad.

'Grandpa, do you remember when you were teaching me geography?'

He roared with laughter. 'You refused to learn the word "antipodes".' His hands described a globe above Beelzebub. 'Italy and New Zealand,' he said, pointing his index fingers at each other, but from a distance, to convey the notion of a map of the world. 'New Zealand and Italy, you couldn't grasp the idea. And then suddenly you said, "New Zealand is a boot upside down, Grandpa; it's Italy fallen onto the other side of the ball." It was a wonderful moment…You'd made me see something I'd had in front of my eyes all the time.' He laughed again, and added in the grave tones of one of his grand pronouncements: 'War also is like a child. A child who every so often shows us what we've had before our eyes and never seen, because we're too careless or cowardly.' He sighed. 'Two things which, at bottom, are very much alike.' He fell silent for a while to mark the change of register, then said: 'How's it going with Giulia?'

'Well.' I was expecting to blush, but I didn't. With him I felt safe.

'I'll see for myself when you've been for a good ride on her…You must be ingenious. As I told you, that one is a mare's crupper!'

Eighteen

I HAD WOKEN UP WITH A HEADACHE. 'WHAT I NEED IS A good walk,' I said to Grandpa, who without deigning to glance at me went straight to earth in his Thinking Den. I left the house without breakfasting. I wanted to be alone. It looked like rain. I went as far as the little temple and lit my pipe. I began to feel better, and after a few minutes I set off walking again, doing the round of the park. With the air making my eyes smart and firing up my mind, I thought back over what Grandpa had said. That a man had to learn to fend for himself early in life. I'm too meek, I thought.

I stopped outside the barn. I knocked at the steward's door but got no answer. On the floor above his quarters the hayloft was divided in two by a thin partition of larch-wood planks; on the left was usually piled the fresher hay, on the right the seasoned stuff, which had all been carried off by the Germans. I climbed the wooden ladder and went and sat in the right-hand part, the empty one, as I didn't want to get my breeches full of hay. I spread my legs and leant back against the partition. It began to rain. I loved the smells that the first rain reawakens, of wood and grass and soil and dung and leaves: everything revives. But suddenly I was startled by the voices of Loretta and Renato, talking excitedly. I thrust my pipe into my pocket, still burning but with my hand over the mouth of the bowl, and flattened myself against the partition.

Between the planks there was a gap of a finger's breadth. She was clambering up the ladder. He was following. 'If this is what you're after…But you'll take me up the bum…I'm not taking any chances, see?' He didn't even remove his overcoat, just unbuttoned it. With quick, precise movements worthy of a gunsmith he stripped off her cloak and blouse, revealing her enormous milk-white breasts. He bit them, eliciting a little cry which he stifled by turning her round and pressing her head down in the hay. She spat out bits of hay, while he spat in his hand and took her brutally. Again he stifled a cry from her, pushing her face right into the hay. I saw his heavy boots grazing her ankles, saw the skin reddening. And when she, spluttering out hay and sobs and saliva, managed to moan, it was only to mingle her pleasure with his. Then, for a long moment, I fancied I could hear the woodworms at work in the rafters amid the rain battering at the tiles.

Buttoning himself up, Renato lowered his head slightly so as not to knock it against the beams. Loretta could not find the strength to get to her feet, or to look at the man who had taken her in such a way. She kept spitting, wiping her eyes with her fingers. With trembling hands she felt for the knickers rolled down round her ankles. With a handful of hay she wiped at the blood already drying at the backs of her knees.

Renato went down the ladder first, disappearing into his quarters. From my perch I saw Loretta walking slowly, weeping and hobbling in the rain. I saw her heading for the latrine. She couldn't go back indoors at once, because her mother would have guessed all.

Nineteen

GRANDPA AND I WERE WATCHING GRANDMA COUNT UP THE gold sovereigns. They were her little nest egg, craftily wrested from the fury of the plunderers. Grandma had sent for Renato. When he entered the room Grandpa turned his face to the wall and stared at the whitewash. Grandma handed two gold sovereigns to Renato, who was limping more heavily than usual. 'You know how best to use them...We've run out of flour...and get a few pieces of dried meat too.'

Renato glanced down at the coins. 'It's not enough, madam. The prices are going up along with the risks. This quartermaster in Sernaglia...If they find him out they'll shoot him.'

Grandma avoided his eye. 'Take care not to get yourself killed, Signor Manca,' she said quietly.

Renato looked at me. He didn't know I had seen what had gone on in the hayloft. He gave me a long look, with hard, cold eyes.

'Where I come from, madam, we slaughter the boar, not the pig, and falcons for us are chickens. If there's something to be done we do it, or something to be said we say it.' He tossed the two sovereigns in the palm of his hand until a third one stopped him.

'That's settled, then,' she said.

'I'll be back at midday tomorrow.' Renato took another look at the coins. 'This is Queen Victoria,' he murmured.

'Old savings…but gold doesn't age.' Grandma dismissed the steward with a brusque gesture, which she then softened with a smile. But he had already left the room.

Grandpa protested: 'I could have gone myself.'

'Real life is *my* province.'

Grandpa went out, slamming the door. I followed him.

The rain had turned to snow, getting heavier and heavier. I took Giulia to the hayloft. There were only a few soldiers about the place, and those few preferred to stay in the warm, along with the mules, drinking the wine they had filched from the peasants. We climbed the ladder, and I stretched out on the hay and kissed her. I wanted to make a show of strength and determination, to take her at once, but she shoved me roughly away and looked at me as one does a stranger. 'There's someone crying… Can't you hear?'

I hadn't heard a thing.

Giulia stood up. She no longer had that ridiculous gasmask hanging on her belt.

But now I heard it too, a stifled wail. I got to my feet. I had hay all over me, even in my shirt collar, and it was itchy.

A sob. We both scrambled up the pile of hay on all fours. At the far end of the hayloft was a dark space littered with barrels and casks. The Hohenzollern thugs had stripped all the meat off the beast and left only the bones for those of the Hapsburgs. There was an acrid, sickening stench.

The cry was like that of a trapped cat. Giulia asked me for a match. I handed her the box. 'Watch it! The hay!' The match showed us the jumble of bits and pieces. A second match solved the mystery: Loretta.

She had hidden under a table, between two broken barrels.

Her face was wedged between her knees. A glimpse of her calf beneath her skirt showed a long, black graze. The frock beneath her open overcoat wasn't dirty and wasn't torn, but no doubt about it, it betrayed her roll in the hay.

'Was it the soldiers?' Giulia's face was on fire. The match went out.

'It wasn't anything,' said Loretta from the darkness.

Giulia thrust the matchbox into my hand. Her lips touched my ear. 'Hop it,' she whispered. 'There are things that can't be said in front of a man.'

I re-crossed the barrier of hay. Once down the ladder I turned up my coat collar and began to run through the thickening snow.

In the kitchen was Teresa, stirring polenta.

'Have you seen my daughter anywhere?'

I shook my head. But Teresa gave me a piercing look and wielded a dishcloth and ladle like a sword and buckler. 'It's that female...been spinning cobwebs in your brain, she has...and she's too old for you anyway.'

I stammered out an objection that Giulia was only twenty-five.

'For you she's too old, lad, that's all I can say.'

I left the room. I found it hard to stand up to censure from Teresa. With Grandma and Aunt Maria I could manage it, but there was something in Teresa which awed me. In my eyes she was the guardian of the truth, and against the truth there's not much to be done. It was lucky she hadn't pressed me about Loretta, because I wasn't a good liar.

That evening, as happened more and more, Grandma stayed in her bedroom and Grandpa, who without his wife nearby became himself four times over, set about entertaining us.

We ate in the big dining room, beneath Great-Grandma's portrait, because the Austrian officers had all gone off to Pieve di Soligo for a reception in honour of someone or other. Teresa was serving at table. Point-blank, Donna Maria asked her where her daughter was, and she said Loretta wasn't feeling well and had retired to bed. 'She has a sore backside, but tomorrow she'll be on her feet.' Adding in an undertone, 'If not I'll give her what for.' Grandpa said that there was a strange fever going around. He'd heard as much that afternoon in the *bottiglieria* where he'd been to listen into the world 'with wine before and farts behind', and that in the hospital at Conegliano there were not only wounded soldiers but also patients with 'they don't quite know what, but rumours say it's typhus.'

'You like to scare us, don't you?' said my aunt.

'A little pep in the air clears the brainpan.'

The cook, holding a dish of rissoles made of goodness knows what, failed to suppress a *diambarne de l'ostia*, and Donna Maria rebuked her with one of her looks.

Great-Grandma's portrait, hung between the two windows, was gazing down at us. She had been a most beautiful girl, with great sapphire-coloured eyes beneath a broad brow, and when Grandpa noticed me staring at the picture he commented, 'She had the bearing of a Baltic princess.'

'Why Baltic?' we all asked with one voice, but he didn't answer.

After supper we gathered round the fire. Teresa brought us a hot lemon drink. For a while Grandpa didn't even touch his cup, but then he furtively added a drop of 'something strong', because 'what you need you need'. He detested that pale yellow brew, but it would have distressed him not to sip along with the company. Aunt Maria asked him about his book. He said it was coming along, that he was trying to get the plot straight, but he had not yet managed to get his central character properly in focus.

'But in that case you haven't even started, have you?'

'I know lots about the lesser characters…But you see, Maria, it is as it is in the army. It's the sergeants and the corporals who do all the work. The privates and the officers provide numerical strength and showpieces, but the real work is put in by the ones in the middle. Give me a good sergeant and I'll set you up a good contingent.' He lit a cigar. 'Do you want to know what my story is about? It's about the world that's going all to blazes.' And for a moment he vanished in his cloud of smoke.

Teresa in the meanwhile was starting on her round of the room. There were very many candles to be snuffed out.

Twenty

THE SKY WAS MURKY, AN ENCRUSTED STEWPOT. DRAWN UP in double file in front of the church was the Hungarian contingent in full strength. It filled nearly the whole of the unpaved road down as far as the Villa gates. We were there too, all of us, not in answer to an invitation but because Grandma and Aunt Maria said we were duty bound to do so. There were no rowdy children, no barking dogs. The alleyways were hushed. Half a dozen pious old biddies, swathed in vast black shawls, were telling their beads at the foot of the church steps. Don Lorenzo had been locked up in the sacristy with half a keg of cordial, guarded by two sentries.

Von Feilitzsch was wearing, hanging from a raspberry-coloured sash, a purple cross with the monogram of the late emperor – FJ – glittering on a gold chain, supported by the beaks of the two-headed eagle. Their claws gripped a scroll bearing the words 'Viribus unitis'. They too like to call themselves heirs of Rome, I thought.

The bell weighed a hundred kilos, and it was lowered with all the necessary caution. The ropes were handled by twelve infantrymen. It hit the ground with a dull thud. A short silence ensued. The major crossed himself, and the sign of the cross swept along the line of troops like a flutter of wings. We too crossed ourselves. Aunt Maria's eyes, as she stood erect beneath the arch of the church door, flashed with anger.

The ceremony was over in a few minutes. The noise of the breaking of ranks merged with that of the approaching cart, drawn by two oxen with sawn-off horns. The bell was destined for some depot or other, thereafter to be melted down, or simply forgotten. Its voice would become a memory only.

'With the same sacred symbols, the same God,' said Grandma, walking arm-in-arm with Grandpa Gugliemo, 'we ought not to be making war on each other.'

'They lowered their eyes, did you notice? They were ashamed of what they were doing.' Aunt Maria was deeply outraged, more so even than for the sake of the raped girls. 'Field Marshal Boroevic, may you die alone with your nightmares, before the fires of hell strip the flesh from your bones!' I had never before heard her curse anyone. She usually preferred irony to invective.

Grandpa put his free hand on my shoulder and said in a low voice, 'Did you hear that? Now your aunt has started competing with Don Lorenzo.'

Grandma took her hand off his arm. 'Pipe down, you good-for-nothing.' And she took Aunt Maria's hand as she entered the gateway. The sentry – there were no longer two of them – sprang to attention, but a moment later, when Grandpa and I passed him, he pointedly relaxed into a slovenly stand-at-ease.

We all lunched together in one of the upstairs rooms. No mention was made of the bell. We ate boiled greens and hot broth that tasted of soil. Grandma didn't touch a thing. Loretta, steady on her feet but surly in the face, brought us a slice of apple tart filched by Teresa's swift hands from the gluttony of the officers eating in the big dining room on the floor below. 'All we now get is the scraps,' said my aunt, as she cut the slice into four. I glanced at Loretta. Her hands were a little unsteady, but on her lips was a smirk, and she was certainly thinking, Your leftovers is all I ever get.

While I was savouring the last precious mouthful of tart, Grandma said, 'Giulia's elder sister died last week. Don Lorenzo told me.'

Why had Giulia told me nothing about it?

'A merciful release,' said my aunt, placing her knife and fork correctly together on her plate. 'That poor girl, reduced to skin and bone. I saw her last year...yes, it was fifteen months ago, in their house at San Polo.'

'And her mother...a saint,' put in Grandma.

I looked at Grandpa. He was drumming his fingers on the handles of the cutlery and moving his lips imperceptibly as if reading. His thoughts were elsewhere. He lit a cigar and asked for an ashtray, which Loretta promptly brought him.

'It has been a terrible business,' continued my aunt. 'She was reduced to an absolute skeleton; only the face was left of the woman she was. I couldn't even look at her. Just too, too distressing.' She shook her head and turned a hard look on me. She realized that I was not in the least upset at the fate of her friend. Then she said sharply, 'You must watch your step with that Giulia.'

'You should know, Paolo, that when your Giulia attained the age of eighteen...' I knew at once from her tone of voice that my aunt was about to deliver me a lecture she'd had up her sleeve for quite a while. 'It must have been early August of...1911 because...well, it doesn't matter...That day, during the birthday party...'

But I already knew all about it. How could I not have known? In a city like Venice, the event was front page news. And for some things antennae sprout early in children. Giulia had had a lover, a friend of her father's. An old man whom everyone called 'a fine figure of a man', though what I remembered of him were his crooked teeth. That evening her lover had put his chrome-plated revolver barrel into his mouth. He'd done it in front of everyone, in front of the birthday cake a span high with all the candles lit 'while awaiting the puff of the lovely eighteen-year-old with the flame-coloured hair', as the *Gazettino* put it. A masterful coup de théâtre, with the brains spurting out and the removal of shreds of pulpy matter from the chandelier, that occupied half a paragraph in the leading article. The grown-ups – one thinks this way at the age of nine – were divided into two parties: 'She's a good lass who's had bad luck', and 'It was she who made his brains burst out of his ears'. But in such disputes, we all know, the dead have a certain advantage. 'Tombstone and Truth are total strangers,' was Grandpa's inescapable maxim. Giulia, the night of her eighteenth birthday, had earned the label of *belle dame sans merci,* not least because the suicide was a prince of the lawcourts with a wife and three children.

Until then I had always pretended to know nothing about it, but the talking-to that awaited me was just too much. 'Aunt, I know about the lawyer in Venice, a man who—'

'Was it Giulia who told you?'

'Not a word. But I have heard certain things... Do you think I don't see what happens when she walks down the village street? And then, when I was in Venice it was on everyone's lips.'

'Don't tell me that my son... that your father talked about it with your mother in front of *you!*' said Grandma, in her voice a trace of venom.

'No one has spoken to me about it. Ever.' I got up and left. I was livid.

Twenty-One

GRANDMA HAD TOLD US TO WAVE AT ALL ALLIED AIRCRAFT, meaning to give the impression that we were overcome with impulsive and consequently innocent patriotism. A subtle ploy, but wasted. The soldiers took no notice of us, and still less did the officers, who whiled away their time smoking, playing cards and drinking an insipid brandy that according to Grandpa tasted of dry dung, iron and rotting leather, 'the same taste as war'.

The captain and the lieutenant quartered in the Villa often went off in the morning and returned only at sunset, on an open lorry with two church benches screwed to the platform. They went in the direction of the Piave, where very little was happening. The baron, however, always went out mounted on his Arab, and on sunny days, in the middle of the snow-covered park, he would now and then stop and hold a conversation with it. He would put his mouth to the animal's ear and move his lips. Rumour had it that to his horse he spoke only in French, but according to Grandpa that was 'one of your aunt's vagaries'.

On one occasion von Feilitzsch told my aunt that he hated motor engines. 'They frighten horses, and for that reason our emperor – he meant Franz Joseph, not young Karl – wanted no armoured cars in his army.' And by saying so he had, if not opened, at least scratched at the tough yet fragile heart of Donna Maria.

★

It was the library of Alexandria, the story of how it was burnt down, that held the floor that evening in front of the fire. It all started with a squabble about pipes. Aunt Maria said that a gentleman can smoke a pipe within the four walls of the house, but in the street or at the inn only cigars and cigarettes were permissible. Grandpa – who loved to disagree – protested, flourishing his cigar like a dagger, until a spark flew off it onto the folded newspaper on my aunt's lap. A tiny tongue of flame set off a hubbub that ended with 'It's not as if I were Caesar! It wasn't I who burnt down the library of Alexandria,' casually thrown by Grandpa into the calm in the wake of the storm. Giulia had not spoken a word all through supper, but at this point her eyes opened wide. With fire and with flame: 'You don't know what you're talking about, Signor Gugliemo. Your Gibbon, petty bourgeois that he was, had it in for the tyrant. That night of two thousand years ago it was the warehouses on the docks that went up in flames, not the Royal Library.'

Questioning Gibbon to Grandpa was like questioning the Gospel to Donna Maria. To be gibed at by a 'flirtatious minx' was just too much. But Giulia's assertion suggested some measure of competence, and Grandpa needed a long minute to gather his resources and plan his counter-attack. He puffed at his cigar until he was stroking the moustache he thought he still had. 'Dear Signorina Candiani…Caesar was under siege, trapped in the accursed palace, with a handful of centurions, but he won! And he won because, though under siege, he fought as though he were the besieger. The torches he flung onto Ptolemy's ships set fire to everything…In short, you only have to read Lucan.'

'No!' Giulia's swarm of freckles threatened to take wing. 'Gibbon doesn't take sufficient notice of the topography of the place. It was the harbour that caught fire, and the scrolls were there ready to be shipped to Pergamum. They made a mass of money out of those scrolls, more than they did with wheat, much more…The library was a long way from the palace. That was burnt down centuries later by some caliph. For him, everything that wasn't in the Koran was the work of the devil.'

I don't know if Giulia knew what she was talking about, but the assurance with which she said it put Grandpa on the defensive. 'I'll have to re-read it,' was all he said, as he took refuge in his cigar. Luckily, a rap-rap at the door dispelled the embarrassment.

It was Renato. Grandma and Aunt Maria motioned to us to leave the room, and for once Grandpa seemed relieved. He set off for the Thinking Den with a goodbye gesture that bordered on rudeness, and I could be alone with Giulia for a while.

I gestured towards the silkworm hatchery and she followed me there. We crossed the garden almost at a run, with no over-coats. The cold air blurred the odours and the snow crunched beneath our boots. I looked up: it was a starry night. It seemed to me that the atmosphere was propitious. I kissed her, but to my surprise she turned her face away. I told her she had been magnificent with Grandpa, that she had held her end up cleverly and tactfully, and that there was something magic about her. I tried to kiss her again. This time she put her hands on my chest and pushed. I clasped her hips, but she shoved me away by force.

'What's the matter?'

'I don't want it.'

'It's so cold…'

'Stop it.'

'But what's wrong?'

A crunching of snow. We turned towards the park. 'Who's there?'

The crunching came nearer and Renato appeared from the darkness. 'Hop it, the patrol's doing its round.'

'Come with me,' I urged.

'No,' answered Giulia. 'I've got to speak to Renato.'

It was a stomach punch.

'I'm coming to see you for a moment,' said Giulia, drawing close to the major, who pulled a strange face, almost a scowl.

I stood stock still, unable to believe my ears.

'No,' said Renato firmly.

Giulia, without so much as a glance at us, ran off into the night.

I would have liked to follow her, but was rooted to the spot.

'Don't give it a second thought…better to let her go. Now, off with you.'

There was affection in his tone of voice. I felt my heart in my boots.

'Come on, get out of here! They'll be here at any moment. See you tomorrow.'

''Night.' I was weak at the knees. I opened the door to the kitchen, heard the *Aaalt!* of the patrol. But I was already indoors. I took the stairs at a run and reached the bathroom just in time to bring up my supper into the lavatory.

I took off my shoes, undressed in the dark and groped my way to bed. A glimmer of light filtered in at the windows. Grandpa was pretending to be asleep, not snoring and wearing his cap cocked at a rakish angle.

'That lass…what does she know about Lucan, or Gibbon? A petty bourgeois, she called him. Just because he detested priests. Believe me, that one's a…a pain in the neck.'

'What have priests got to do with it?'

'Buddha doesn't like Austria.'

'Grandpa…do you ever pray?' I half-closed my eyes to peer at him, but all I could make out was his rotund outline.

'I wouldn't know what to ask for. See here, laddie, if you ask for the wrong thing and you get it, where does that leave you? No, I don't pray. Right now you would like to ask God or whatever for Giulia to be yours, but no one, and especially not you, can know whether that would be a good thing. No, I don't pray. For my part I look at my Buddha. Sometimes I look at him for a whole half an hour and he says nothing. That way we understand each other.'

I said nothing.

'A word of advice, laddie: look at her less and touch her more.'

Von Feilitzsch was stroking the nose of his Arab and talking into its ear. The horse nodded its head, rattling its bridle. Walking side by side they looked like old comrades-in-arms exchanging gossip about barrack-room life or the fanfaronades at court.

Donna Maria was also leading a horse by the reins and stroking its white-streaked nose. The horse was a bay belonging to the Imperial Army and entrusted to her care through the intercession of the baron. For the past three days bad weather had confined the animals to their stables, so they were nervous, and the dazzle of the snow did nothing to calm them. The baron joined my aunt under the big lime tree at the edge of the park. After the usual greetings, they set off up the hill, leading their horses side by side.

Renato and I were following, thirty metres behind them. Our rucksacks were crammed with potatoes for the Brustolons, our share-croppers, a proud and loyal family. I liked them because of Adriano and his Pomeranian, by the name of Dog. Adriano had chest pains, a worrying symptom according to the medical officer, a moustachioed beanpole of a man, but the priest had told us, 'They're hungry! It's not pneumonia, it's hunger!' In mid-January the troops had stripped them bare down to their bootlaces. Not so much as an egg had they managed to hide. So Donna Maria, with Grandma's agreement, had decided to give them ten kilos of potatoes. The head of Queen Victoria still counted for something.

The stratagem of an outing with the baron was one of my aunt's bright ideas, because following in their wake no one would think of lightening us of our loads of potatoes. It wasn't far to the Brustolon house, just enough for the horses to stretch their legs. Major von Feilitzsch had all the signs of being mild-mannered, but early in February his provisioning problems had grown worse, so that looting was tolerated, or even encouraged, by the area commands.

'Giulia is avoiding me...I saw her for a moment yesterday and...I don't even manage to...'

'Some women are like that. What you want you have to take, not beg for.'

My ideas regarding Giulia were woolly. I didn't manage to get together a strategy, even temporary. And I was upset by the idea that I could no longer trust Renato, I was jealous, and ashamed of it.

'There are things we don't fathom...Women, they're like war...What do we know about war, and who unleashed all this on us?'

'Homer says that it's a gift from the gods, that without war there'd be very little to write about.'

'Go and tell that to the men in the trenches and see how you come out of it. You'd be lucky to have a tooth left in your head and a single unbroken bone.'

'The rape of Helen and the burning of Troy are—'

'Yes, yes…The King of Sparta betrayed, a prince shot in Sarajevo…Let's just repeat what they tell us at school! Come off it…' He gave a short laugh. 'It's a load of rubbish. No one really wanted this war, not the peoples concerned, nor the governments. It just emerged from the boiling pot of dynasties that are decrepit and worn out, but have not, alas, forgotten their old dreams of grandeur. And the spoon that stirred the pot was in the inept hands of diplomats who for generations had dealt only with ordinary matters: ships, railways, money. The enormous turmoil took everyone by surprise, Serbia, Austria, Russia, Germany, France…One mobilization followed another, and when you put millions of young men into uniform you're compelled to do something with them. Otherwise, with rifles in their hands instead of spades, they'll overturn the pot and so long to all your crowned heads.' He looked me straight in the eye. 'Women, on the other hand…they have power over us, they use their weakness to put us down and make us do what they want. It's they who corrupt us, while we, to assert ourselves, crush them. Corruption is the most subtle way of commanding, the crafty way, the woman's way.

'Horses are also feminine,' he said after a second or two. 'If you don't make them feel the grip of your knees you end up on the ground.' And with a tilt of his chin he drew my attention to my aunt and the baron, who had now mounted and were setting off at a walk.

We reached the Brustolons' in little over an hour. The baron and Aunt Maria drew rein less than ten metres ahead. They both gave us a wave.

The house was a mere hovel. The wooden shingles of the roof had in several places given way under the snow, and the wooden gutter had snapped right over the door. This was opened by a woman no taller than our king, a mere metre and a half. She looked about seventy, but was certainly fifteen or twenty years younger than that. She was bony, with little eyes close to her nose and, even if she had only three teeth, two on top and one below, she spoke distinctly.

The room was black. Black were the walls, black were the three chairs, the table, the bread store, the empty shelves around the fireplace.

'I'm Paolo Spada. I've been sent by Signora Nancy.'

'Potatoes!' announced Renato, emptying his rucksack on the table. The woman's eyes widened, became two chestnuts. I tipped my bag out too, and the chestnuts turned to plums, and when the last potato rolled down onto the blackened earth floor, for a moment they became two peaches. The woman thanked us with a volley of Hail Marys and incantations.

'Is she afraid the devil's going to eat the potatoes?' I whispered to Renato.

'The troops are worse than the devil, as she well knows.'

'How's Adriano? I'm the one who gives him history lessons. I'm helping the priest.'

The woman's eyes shrank again, small and hard: 'Schooling has never given anyone anything to eat.' With which she took a pinch of tobacco from her apron pocket and rolled a cigarette with her sparrow-like claws. Renato lit a match and held it near her face. She drew on the cigarette as if to suck in the whole Piave and, with impeccable pronunciation despite her lack of teeth, said in pure Italian: 'A curse on you and your schools and your wars…And a curse on your charity too!'

I was sorely tempted to take the potatoes back.

But the woman opened the lid of the bread bin, which was smothered in soot like everything else, fished out a rusty bayonet and banged it into the table between us and the potatoes. From the other room came a bark from Dog, startled perhaps by the bang. The house consisted of two rooms: one for sleeping, being ill and dying in, when one had to die, and the other for living, smoking sausages and eating in, when one had anything to eat. I would have liked to call out to Adriano, but we left without any goodbyes while the bayonet was still vibrating, its point buried in the wood.

On our way back we stopped and leant against a fence in front of a simple wayside shrine, from which the emaciated figure of a deposed Christ regarded us with an air of resignation. The sculptor had forgotten to give him closed eyes. I lit my pipe and handed Renato back his pouch.

'Good, this tobacco, if slightly bitter.' I was starting to give myself airs.

'Thanks be to Queen Victoria.' Renato raised his pipe heavenwards. 'Because even the enemy smokes English tobacco. When all is said and done, corruption is a universal lubricant, for good or ill.'

I too raised my pipe heavenwards. 'Thanks be to the late queen and her gold sovereigns.' I was forcing myself to be jolly. 'Who knows…Maybe Adriano has got better.'

'Those potatoes will help him for sure.'

'It hasn't been only the Germans who've reduced them to this.'

'No, toil, soot, ignorance, and now the war. The Huns are just the last straw.'

We went on our way; it was downhill all the way to the Villa.

We passed two soldiers on their way up, their uniforms patched and unlit cigarettes in their mouths. Crushed beneath the weight of their packs, they didn't even glance at us.

There was not a breath of wind. Only clouds, snow, empty houses, leafless trees.

Twenty-Two

'NOT A PENNY IN HER PURSE, NOT A TOOTH IN HER HEAD, but a whole barrel full of children instead,' sang Teresa to herself as she came and went in the steam that billowed from the cauldron. It was there, at the fire, at the heart of the kitchen, that it all began. In the cauldron two and a half litres of water were on the boil. They had to boil for twenty-five minutes 'because that way twenty per cent goes off in steam'. For Grandma the cleanliness of the bowels was more important than that of the soul.

Like all rituals, the enema demanded its liturgy, and Grandma was partial to cosmic coincidences. 'No enemas on windy days' was her dogma. With her daughter's assistance Teresa decanted the purified water into a round-bellied bottle with a narrow neck set at an angle. In the pot was one leaf of mint and one of tarragon.

Then came the solemn procession. Loretta, followed two steps behind by her mother, hands gloved in white silk as if she were a general, bore the alembic containing the precious fluid. On reaching Grandma's bedroom – which on the chosen day was always spotless from top to bottom, with clean sheets and a blazing fire – Loretta's task was to set the alembic down on the table at the foot of the bed and disappear. Once alone with 'the mistress', Teresa selected the enema. If there was snow and sunshine – the ideal day – the bag was round with a long tube, whereas if there was damp in the air the choice fell on a square bag with a short tube.

Of the most delicate phase of the ritual, the interplay of backside and nozzle, nothing is known. For the occasion Teresa would put on her lace cap – it towered white and cock-eyed over her bun – and regarding certain matters she kept mum.

If Grandma was pleased Teresa would get a reward, sometimes cash, at other times a few hours off. The cook preferred the former, because freedom is a coinage more difficult to spend.

An outstanding page in the family chronicles was the 'December Yell'. On that occasion, in the course of the ritual, Grandma gave a yell that pierced the walls, the cook rushed out of the room white in the face, and Grandma didn't speak to her for a week. At lunch Grandpa poked fun at her: 'There's nothing more tragic than a clumsily penetrated anus.'

'If you weren't the good-for-nothing that you are, a good rinsing of the bowels would do the world for you. Those cobwebs in your head all come from your infected intestines.'

Grandpa usually let it go, taking his wife's intellectual superiority in good part. But that time he came back at her tit for tat: 'Nancy, when you talk like that you sound like our P.M. Orlando when he says "I'll reduce the National Debt".'

Grandpa was on good-natured terms with the world, but he could not forgive 'that pettifogger Orlando' for having granted all combatants a life-insurance policy starting on 1 January 1918. 'In this way the youngsters who stopped von Below and Boroevic on Monte Grappa and on the Piave...they won't leave so much as a bag of beans to their families. And then they say Italians have no sense of State! But it's the State that has no feeling for the Italians.'

★

184

At nine o'clock Operation Enema could be said to have been brought to a close. Everything had gone splendidly. Teresa's pocket tinkled and her bun re-emerged from her cap. Harmony reigned at Villa Spada. But at mid-morning came news of a new decree from Boroevic. Laundry hung up outside to dry must be restricted to three items at a time. The field marshal was afraid of the imminent spring.

'And we thought we were the only ones signalling to aircraft that way,' commented Aunt Maria.

That 'three at a time' meant overhauling the code, not a very difficult matter for Grandma, who in any case was that day rejoicing in exceptional purity of the bowels, But how were we to pass on the key of the new system to Brian?

Grandma Nancy had the fire lit in the big dining room, as the Austrians didn't use it as much as before. She told Teresa to lay the table and announced that for supper we were going to have something to write home about. She kept her promise. In the evening we opened a flask of wine to go with a dish of stewed meat that was not too leathery, given the evil times.

Having interrogated our taste buds and had a brief exchange of opinions, the entire family said 'cat'.

Teresa said '*diambarne de l'ostia*'.

And all of us in chorus repeated the word 'cat', to suppress the supposition that the C might not be an R.

'I'm not saying, I'm not saying. Cook is what I am and cook's job is to cook, not talk.'

End of investigation.

The new code was as simple as it was effective, according to Grandma. We need not hurry to deliver it, as we could get by with the system of the shutters, which had escaped suspicion by the military authorities. But I was starting to feel the pinch of boredom, so I caught the ball on the bounce and volunteered for a mission. To my surprise no one raised an objection. Aunt Maria would talk about it with the steward immediately after supper.

Giulia was still avoiding me, and maybe this was my chance. Her craze for adventure would winkle her out.

Going on for midnight my aunt came to see me upstairs, where I was playing cards with Grandpa. She knocked, then came straight to the point. 'It appears that at Vidòr the Englishman shot down a captive balloon. He blew it up with machine-gun fire and then, unable to avoid the burning balloon, flew straight through the flames, risking being burnt to a cinder. The Austrian in the basket escaped by miracle. The whole valley is talking about it and Renato says we must start signalling the lorries pulling balloons, not just the troop movements.'

Next morning I went looking for the steward first thing after breakfast. He was sitting on the edge of the hayloft with legs dangling, stripping the bark off a branch with a knife. His pipe was smoking gently. I asked him if he had a plan.

'We're leaving in an hour. Your grandfather's coming too.'

'But he'll slow us up.'

'He's only coming as far as the *bottiglieria* in Solighetto, where he's at home. We'll leave him there and head up for Falzè. Your grandmother's friend is lending us his gig.'

'Go on with you...D'you mean the Third Paramour? Is he coming too?'

'No, he's not, but Signorina Giulia is. And watch it. The Third...nincompoop thinks we're all going to Solighetto just for a drink and to buy a demijohn.'

'When and where?'

'Half past nine in the piazza.'

I met Grandpa on the stairs.

'Have you heard I'm coming too?' He was as happy as a sandboy.

'As far as Solighetto.' My douche of cold water riled him a bit, but his smile got the better of it.

Giulia and the Third Paramour were seated on the box. It was a two-horse carriage, a luxury affair. But when they drew rein I noticed that the two horses were mere skin and bone. No oats for past weeks, just rubbishy fodder: hunger had struck even the livestock. Grandpa was leaning on the arm of Loretta, whose face darkened as soon as she saw Giulia.

There was hatred in the eyes of the servant, challenge in Giulia's.

The Third Paramour dismounted and helped Grandpa climb into the seat behind the box. He emitted a couple of feeble simpers and set off towards the Villa along with Loretta.

I sat beside Renato, who took the reins; Giulia sat behind with Grandpa. The inn in the piazza was empty. The innkeeper, stretched out on a bench by the door, waved to us and asked us to bring him a demijohn of red wine. 'These Krauts, they drink more than oxen in summer.'

The two nags were already breathless. Renato slowed them down to a walk.

'Lucky we're not going far,' said Grandpa.

We were stopped by a patrol right at the edge of Solighetto. The officer addressed Grandpa directly, and in French, as if Renato and I were non-existent. Grandpa opened his cloak, reached into his jacket pocket and drew out a document written in German, stamped all over and signed by Baron von Feilitzsch.

'Refrontòlo,' said the officer.

'Refròntolo,' Grandpa corrected him.

They both had a good laugh.

With a wave of his right hand the officer motioned to Renato to drive on.

Solighetto was a ghost-town, but the *bottiglieria* – where Grandpa had made friends, according to him, with the store-keepers of the army depot – was always crowded.

'This is where I leave you,' said Grandpa, giving Renato two taps on the shoulder. 'I'll wait for you till evening. If anything should happen…no, no, it can't happen. Off you go.'

On our way out of town we passed a bevy of peasant women. They were selling eggs, and one of them even trying to sell herself, but the goods were not at all appetizing. The troops were coming and going, their cloaks unfastened, their jackets all rumpled, and the eggs ended up in their bellies just as they were, cracked open and drunk raw. They paid with the money of the army of occupation, worthless paper which the women were obliged to accept, but when some tender-hearted fellow gave them a half a krone or his ration of black bread, then there was an exchange of smiles, as black as the bread or the rags of the women's clothes.

'It's a nightmare,' I said.

Renato cracked the whip. 'It's poverty,' he said. 'Poverty, like the war, seems never-ending.'

'We're in philosophical vein today,' said Giulia. She was curled up in a corner of the seat, wearing an absent air.

We aimed for Barbisano. Without Grandpa's weight the horses moved more briskly. The snow on the roadway was black and mushy, but here and there in the fields were patches of brown earth. From the leafless trees, silent black birds watched us pass by. Only occasionally did their metallic cry break the stillness.

The guns were silent, the bells were no longer, and on the hushed hills – stripped bare by winter and the ravages of armies – those raucous cries sounded to my ears like a harbinger of death.

A stone's throw from Barbisano, Renato steered the cart off the road and halted under two oaks with trunks a metre wide. 'There's a camp just round the bend, a company of Kaiserjäger. Wait for me here with the cart. No civilians allowed beyond this point.'

'Then how will you get by?'

'That's my business. Wait here for an hour and a half, not a minute more.' He waited to give me time to fish out my watch. 'If you don't see me in an hour and a half go back and pick up your grandfather. That's all you need to know. If someone spots you, you're here for a secret tryst. It shouldn't be hard to make that convincing.' With which he squeezed my knee. I smothered an 'ouch!' and smiled. I looked back at Giulia. She was frowning.

Renato made fast the reins and jumped down. He set off at a fast walk, without more ado. The horses lowered their necks to sniff at the hard ground.

'Let's get under the carriage,' said Giulia.

We lay down on the leather sheet Grandpa used to keep his legs warm when he sat on the box. I stroked her hair and she let me. She was looking at me with a kind of faked surprise that puzzled and irritated me. I kissed her on the lips, gently. She let me.

'Turn sideways… You certainly have got a nose… It's like the foresail of a yacht.'

I pulled back, but didn't manage a laugh.

'Let me smoke your pipe.'

I fished in my pocket and handed it to her, offering her the tobacco pouch: 'Shall I fill it for you?'

'I don't think that needs a diploma.'

The cold from the icy ground struck my back, even through the leather sheet and my overcoat, but there, with Giulia beside me, I had a feeling of elation that warmed me. She lit my pipe. The smoke formed wreathes against the bottom of the carriage which was our roof.

'What do you think of Renato?' I asked, trying to sound nonchalant.

She looked straight at me and blew smoke in my face with a mocking smile. 'You don't like the way I look at him, do you?'

'Why? How do you look at him?' I babbled.

Her face grew serious. Her freckles burst forth in a swarm.

'He ought to be punished,' she said. 'There's a man who ought to be punished.'

Twenty-Three

'THEIR MADONNA HAS LONG HAIR, WORN LOOSE, LIKE A cabaret chorus girl.' Grandpa was drunk and he was using all ten fingers to sketch out in the empty air what he was seeing. 'And around her yellow head...there are twelve stars, twelve of them. I counted them, and I know how to count to twelve. And all around her body, almost all the way down to her feet, are beams of light all made of gold. And the chorus girl is crushing the serpent with her feet. And on the back of the banner... because they turn it around, you know...they turn it around to show you the other side...' The cart jerked and bounced, but his voice, in spite of his state of euphoria, remained firm and confident. 'On it is a golden eagle with wings spread, and on its chest is the coat of arms of Hapsburg, Austria, and Lorraine. The right claw grips the sceptre and the sword, the left claw grips the orb with the cross of the priests...' he hacked and spat. The phlegm flew to the dirt road.

Giulia sat on the box, wedged between the steward and the demijohn of wine, the official excuse for the trip.

'What none of you know is that the coat of arms...that coat of arms contains the heraldic crests of all the empire's kingdoms and fiefdoms...Now, I say, the second escutcheon from the left...no, from the right...is the crest of Lombardy–Venetia, and we're not fooling around. The Krauts want to take back

191

their old territory, don't you doubt it for a second! And you know what this old man who's had too much to drink has to say about it? I say that they're right, by the name of San Cipresso… in that…low-life inn, with a capital I…I didn't really have that much to drink…There's an innkeeper who speaks pretty good French even if he was born in Bohemia, and the man told me that our king, who's knee high to a grasshopper, isn't worth a drop of grappa…If you try to stack him up next to their…What the devil do they call him…? Their emperor, that's what they call him.'

Renato turned and looked at him. 'I have the feeling your innkeeper must have been thinking of Franz Joseph, not Karl.'

Giulia laid her hand on Renato's arm, and he turned his eyes back to the road ahead and snapped the whip in the air. I felt a stab of jealousy, but I wouldn't have admitted it even under torture. I looked at Grandpa, who smiled and half-closed his eyes, then looked straight up at the sky, and leant closer, his mouth reeking of wine pressed close to my ear: '*C'est la vie*, laddie.'

The morning air was icy. 'That baron…There's something childish about him, and I don't trust the naïve,' my aunt spoke in an undertone. 'We need to watch out for him. The Englishman has been noticed…He always flies over twice…and always just above treetop level. And then that kingfisher of his is all anybody talks about, he's the one who has it in for the observation balloons…Major von Feilitzsch is no fool.'

'Hanging is interesting,' said Grandpa, who was walking between me and her. 'To die kicking without making any noise, a firing squad is just too…too boom! That's it. A hangman's knot is slow, a faint creak, discreet and lethal.'

'Stop trying to be a poet, Grandpa.'

'Lower your voice,' said my aunt, pointing to the soldiers who were grooming their mules.

Grandpa linked arms with us: 'Come, come,' he said, quickening his pace, 'let's go to the inn, at this time of day they serve piping hot coffee, and we'll have a chance to sense what's in the air.'

'Let's hope the coffee isn't some kind of grappa extract,' said my aunt.

'Yes, and that they're not serving goat milk,' I added.

We walked into a funk of sweat and alcohol. The innkeeper was sleepy. The non-commissioned officers were all on their feet, chattering loudly over their large steaming mugs. The innkeeper's mother was from Naples so the man knew how to make a good cup of coffee. He pointed us to a table. My aunt didn't seem displeased at being the only woman in the place and I had the impression that, as she took a seat with studied gracefulness, she might have hiked up her skirt just enough to allow a glimpse of calf, contented at the subdued stir she sent across the room.

The innkeeper ran his filthy rag over the table. 'What can I bring you?'

Grandpa, who seemed more of a sage when seated, looked the sweaty little man up and down – the man had grown a Hapsburg-style set of whiskers – with the expression of a good housewife spotting a cockroach on a clean pillowcase. My aunt came to his aid: 'Three cups of coffee with hot milk, and no grappa, if you please.'

'Madame, we're fresh out of grappa,' he said, using the dialect term *sgnappa*. The innkeeper twirled his moustache with all ten fingers: 'These Krauts drink up everything in the house and pay with tin money.'

The coffee with milk was dark, steaming, and delicious. The

cups were sparkling clean. For a moment, as I sipped it, I felt sure that this, not the taste of Giulia's lips, was the flavour of happiness. A furious whirl of canine barking rushed in: I immediately recognized Dog. The fire had just been stirred back into flame, and Grandpa stood up to hold out his hands over the heat. Adriano came in behind the dog, and slipped and fell, legs in air, to the laughter of the big mustachioed men.

'So you're all better,' I said, lifting him by one arm. He was skinny, and there was hunger in his eyes. He nodded his head up and down, and he reached around for Dog with hands that trembled slightly. I took him to our table and my aunt ordered some hot milk, a bowl of polenta, and a dish of *sopressa* salami. Adriano had set Dog on his lap. The poor animal's coat was thick with scabs of mange, and one ear had been broken by a swung stick, or some other trick of fate.

'And how is your Mamma?' asked my aunt.

The child pulled his mouth away from the polenta. 'She died two days ago.' There was no emotion in his voice. He downed the milk in a long gulp and then went on eating. Dog was eating too. Adriano stuffed nearly all the *sopressa* into his pocket: 'For tomorrow.' The fear of hunger was stronger in him than hunger itself. There was something at once candid and cruel in his tight little face, a snarl that came from deep within. As he chewed, he stared at my aunt with a look of love, and my aunt returned the glance with eyes veiled with sweetness: 'Adriano, that's your name, isn't it? Come see us at the Villa whenever you like, our Teresa...' And here she broke off, because a gigantic sergeant was glaring in our direction. He came towards us without needing to elbow his way through the crowd. His chest served as the prow of an icebreaker. He lowered his face, all whiskers and sideburns, to the child's head. He stank like a sow.

194

'I'm thinking I'm recognizing you!' he said, practically bellowing. 'You thief! You stealing my dagger!'

Adriano vanished just as fast as his dog.

The sergeant made no attempt to go after them. He shot us a grim look which he followed up by showing a rake's worth of dirt-coloured teeth. Then he went back to the bar, leaving his stench behind to keep us company.

'When this war is over, the world will belong to people like him,' said my aunt. 'Our earls, our dukes, our gentlemen, and all their *vons*…so many hulks drifting with the tide; they don't have – they won't have any strength left to throw into the battle.' She paused, looked at Grandpa, then looked at me with a hint of melancholy: 'We no longer have tears or smiles, all we want is to rest,' she sighed, and caressed my face with the back of her hand. 'It will be them, the sergeants, who will run all this misery that our fine manners only serve to offend.'

Grandpa looked down into his empty mug. 'Yes, we're sailing ships surrounded by steamers, no two ways about it.' He fell silent for a moment. 'And after the time of the sergeants, you'll see, then will come the time of the corporals of the day.'

The sound of engines emptied the inn. We went outside too, leaving a couple of old lire on the table.

Three Fokkers, flying at low altitude, were pursuing a Caproni plane with Savoy insignia. They'd gone overhead less than ten metres over the roof. On their wings were the black crosses of the Teutonic Order. The tail of our aircraft was spewing smoke. The Fokkers were machine-gunning the Caproni from all directions. The bomber headed straight for the river in desperate flight. I managed to see that the upper wing was shredded at the centre, directly above the pilot, while the machine gunner was keeled over to one side, no longer firing.

I clutched at Grandpa's arm: 'Do you think he'll make it?'

There was a burst of flame, perhaps the fighter planes had centred the fuel tank. Black smoke rose from behind a hill, to the west. The little knot of sergeants and corporals joined in a round of cheers –'Hurrah! Hurrah!' – and immediately the inn sucked them back into its fumes, amid laughter and backslapping.

We walked back to the Villa with downcast eyes.

I thought of the two men burnt alive, hoping to myself that they'd died on impact. I watched the Fokkers fly off towards Sacile, by now at high altitude, three small crosses motionless up in the sky. Not a cloud in sight. The sky was pale blue, lightly etched by the wrinkle of a flock of birds flying parallel to the horizon, the first migratory birds of the season.

An aircraft in flames, the shooting of a nightingale, the killing of a horse: we talked of nothing else all through lunch. The image of death is all the more terrible if what dies is something noble and beautiful, something that flies, that sings, that gallops. My aunt told us that she'd talked about this with the baron. She told us that the Germans see death as a blue-eyed smooth-skinned lad, smelling faintly of soap. Whereas we Italians think of it as a woman, young and nicely dressed.

'Because they think of death as "*der* Tod", while for us death is "*la* Morte",' Grandpa brusquely dismissed the topic, impatient as always when someone other than him was doing the philosophizing.

Teresa had made a roast that aroused the suspicion, something that happened with increasing frequency, that it might be cat meat; I thought it was delicious, but my aunt got up and said to the cook: 'Come with me!' I stood up and started to follow, intending to eavesdrop, but Grandma stopped me short.

'She's going to tell her that roast cat isn't fit for us to eat,' said Grandpa, 'but it won't be long before we'll be licking our fingers at the thought of a roast of that description.'

The room was filled with smoke. The chimney hadn't been scoured for months now. The rout of Caporetto had taken with it a great many professions and their absence could be noticed in many small details of life. My aunt started to cough, which was greeted with a polite smiles by the baron and General Bolzano, who was making his first entrance into the Villa.

The general was a powerful-looking man, with pale eyes and a clear voice. He was practically bald, he wore grey suede gloves. Inside him too there seemed to be something grey, something that slid out of his eyes and filled anyone who looked at him with sadness. And his eyes were everywhere. He immediately caught my interest. He reserved a long glance for my aunt and me, sensing our embarrassment, understanding the unease of being guests of the enemy in the home of one's own people, and he knew – oh yes, how he knew – that this outrage would not be lasting. When he lifted my aunt's hand to his lips, it was not merely his head that curved over it: 'Madame, I pray that you will believe that my gratitude for your patience is dictated by more than the mere obligations of courtesy.'

'Your words, General, really touch me,' said my aunt to the amazement of one and all, 'because you, like me, live in a world that no longer exists.' She pulled back her hand and flashed him a broad smile.

The general took a step back, stiffened, and clicked his heels. Looking her in the eyes, he nodded.

We were served by the attendants of the general and the major. Our palates had been seduced by Teresa's stew, which charmed even the walls and the chairs. By now, there were no longer any dogs, cats, or rabbits to be seen in the area, and even mules, horses, and rodents had become infrequent sights: no one was surprised any more.

Bolzano praised the cook's skills, saying that the dish reminded him of his childhood in Vienna at the home of his grandparents. 'We had a Friulian cook, from Talmassons, and her *spezzatino* was unrivalled.' He smiled, eyes wide open, as he stared at his empty bowl: 'Until today, of course.' There wasn't enough of the stew for second helpings, but we consoled ourselves with a second round of polenta, which was sprinkled, in the absence of butter, with Riva olive oil, compliments of the general.

The baron's attendant was a long asparagus of a man, closer in terms of the expression on his face to the vegetable than to *homo sapiens*; the general's attendant, on the other hand, was pear-shaped, and in his docile gaze it was possible to detect something of that fruit's sweetness. The pair of them worked in concert, with exquisite savoir faire: a viola and a cello in a Mozart quartet. They knew what the officers and Donna Maria wanted before they were asked, and they took care of me as well. The pear-man filled the glasses. The asparagus wobbled without ever rattling the silverware on the plates as he removed them. Their gestures, their neatly pressed uniforms, were eloquent expressions of the desire to rescue at least a memory of the courteous old way of life from the hurricane of mud and death that was sweeping away nations and families.

'If our love of good manners were ever to fade, what would separate us from the behaviour of brigands?' the baron asked point-blank. 'It's easy for the knights of the air…Pilots kill gracefully, the sky separates them.' With one hand he designed a figure of eight over his plate: 'Eagles against falcons, falcons against sparrows, but men who dig in the mud live with the stench of corpses…they see the ravaged corpses of friends and enemies mixed together in the gravel and grit and turn into dirt; how do we foot soldiers remain men?' He looked at my aunt and raised his glass; the Marzemino glittered in the candlelight: 'It's just lucky that we still have the ladies.'

I don't know why I did what I did next. But I could feel something stirring within me all the way down to the pit of my stomach and, as if the portrait of my great-grandmother as a girl, behind me, had come to life in order to speak through me, I leapt to my feet and said, in a harsh voice: 'Enemies remain enemies even at the dinner table. Even though you have fine manners, there are weapons backing you up, weapons that kill Italians, and that's something I'll never forget.'There was a rage deep inside me, and I have no idea where it came from. My aunt stared at me, uneasily, and the general seemed to have turned to stone. At that point I clicked my heels and nodded my head in the officers' direction.

'Sit down, Paolo!' said my aunt.

The skin on my face was afire. I ran out of the room and right at the door ran headlong into the pear-man who was coming back with the coffee. The tray clattered to the floor in a cacophony of hot sprays.

I breathed in the chilly air. The moon was out, a slender arc floating above the trees. I'd never noticed before that day that the moon, in our sky, is always upright, warlike. Without thinking about it, with the blood pounding in my temples, I went towards the hayloft, towards Renato's quarters. The *barchessa* was illuminated with a warm and uncertain light, and among the mules, three soldiers were throwing dice, seated on a dismantled engine. They looked up. I heard them laugh as I went by. Then

I saw Loretta emerging from the steward's quarters with her hands clapped over her face.

The following morning, at the first light of day, the biplanes of Brian's squadron flew over the roofs of the town and an avalanche of tricoloured pamphlets plugged up the downspouts and gutters of Refrontolo, obliging a company of Uhlans, expected at Moriago, to break march formation in order to act as street sweepers, thus protecting the illiterate minds of the Venetian peasants from the propaganda of the Triple Entente.

The Third Paramour had been invited to lunch and Grandpa looked like an angry owl. He wandered through the Villa declaiming, with Garibaldi's autobiography open in his left hand and his right forefinger pointed straight up at the ceiling stuccoes, where apes and tortoise, on the shores of a pale green pond, displayed their indifference to human suffering.

'You tell me about this general, a whole lifetime of adventures,' he said when he saw me, 'one of those lives tailor-made to be told as a ripping yarn…but boiled down by his own pen to a broth fit for nuns, while I' – and he looked me in the eye and lowered his voice – 'who enjoy a solid reputation as a good-for-nothing, am writing a story of money, love, and vendetta, in other words the very things…yes, the very things' – and here he lowered his voice still further, until it had shrunk to nothing more than a throttled little rivulet of sound – 'that make life worth living.'

'Then why are you reading it, if it's a broth fit for nuns?'

'You're more impudent with every day that passes! You see, laddie, unlike that fellow, that Ganymede, whatever his name is, who's never opened a book in his life…I read because I like to and…when I happen across a Garibaldi…it pains me!' I

200

wondered where he was heading with this. 'With his courage and my talent put together something could have come of it.' He was no longer talking to me, I don't think he even knew I was there. He was talking to the air, to the stuccoes, to the walls.

The beans, sautéed with onions and red chili peppers, landed on our plates with a festive sizzle that would have curled up the whiskers of even a general.

Grandma had been keeping her eye on the two rivals since the beginning of the meal, and it was clear that she'd already staved off the worst a couple of times with small sharp kicks to her spouse's ankle. A mass of insults was bubbling up inside Grandpa that threatened to sharply organize itself into a phalanx at any instant. And sure enough the phalanx poured forth the instant my aunt, who had a nose too long to mind her own business, thought of asking the Third Paramour his opinion on the financial disarray of the fatherland at war.

'When the king's coffers lie empty…'

Grandpa stole the scene from his rival by concluding the phrase in his own way: '…the subjects would be well advised to stitch their pockets shut…or fill them with crabs. And so you would appear to be a bookkeeper…the missing link between an accountant and a human being.'

The Third Paramour gulped down the mouthful of beans that for the past few seconds his tongue had been working to detach from his palate. He extracted the handkerchief from the breast pocket of his jacket and, with dishevelled grace, dabbed at his perfectly dry forehead. 'You are, you are nothing but…an Othello. That's what you are!'

'And you're a treacherous freeloader!' Grandpa, had he ever found himself in Dante's shoes, would have put tax officials, priests, and accountants into Lucifer's various mouths.

'That's still better than you, claiming to write a book that everyone knows doesn't exist.'

His voice was cracking with emotion, the poor thing wasn't used to quarrels.

'It's that cauliflower you have instead of a brain that doesn't exist, not my book. And if it wasn't for Madame Nancy…I would have strung you up from the foremast that very day,' and he waved his fists in the big-foot's face.

The Third Paramour stood up, slamming his napkin down on his plate, which was gleaming as if Teresa had just buffed it with a rag, and left, with a curt nod of his head to Grandma alone.

I felt called upon to offer my support to Grandpa: 'His cologne smells of smoked mozzarella.'

Grandpa stared at Grandma with a satisfied half-smile. He poured himself a finger of cognac from his private stock and stared into the fire, folding his napkin: 'Now I feel better.'

'My fault,' said my aunt. And she burst into laughter. To my surprise, my grandmother burst out laughing as well, until me, Grandpa, and even Loretta who was already clearing the table, were all united in a single chorus of laughter.

As Grandpa was tossing back his last gulp of cognac I said under my breath: 'After all, Grandpa, the Third Paramour… he's not all bad.'

'I believe that,' said Grandma, 'even if you turned him head over heels you couldn't hope for the clinking of a coin…He's not all bad, but he's not all good either.'

Twenty-Four

WITH APRIL THE SNOW HAD CLEARED AND BY MAY SOME of the officers began to leave. More and more lorries went through, and more and more carts, bicycles, mules and motor-cycles. They came from Udine, from Sacile, from Codroipo, from Pordenone. Skinny youngsters passed by morning and evening on their way to the Piave, their uniforms flapping on them, bent under the weight of their packs, their helmets too big for them.

The Villa had lost its importance. Lodging there with the baron were only two or three junior officers, but none of them stayed for long. Some went off west, towards the front, others eastwards, on leave. 'Like flies on a cow's rump,' commented Teresa. When he left his office, a ground-floor room on the side of the house furthest from the street, the baron spent his time with us. With Aunt Maria largely – tongues were already wagging in the village – but also with Grandpa and me. Only Grandma kept aloof, true to her principle of confronting the invader with her courteous discourtesy.

By now the baron seemed to me one of the household. I was as accustomed to him as I was to the shortage of food, the thought of Giulia or the sleepiness of the countryside. For months now there had been no sound of gunfire.

On one occasion – it was towards the end of May and the

sunshine was quite warm – von Feilitzsch saw me passing his window. He left his office and caught up with me. 'I'll come for a little walk with you, do you mind?'

We walked together for a couple of hours, during which he told me about life in Hungary, where he and his wife had been for several years, and about Vienna, where his heart lay. He told me about the pastry shops, the girls, the concerts, the Strauss family, the avenues crowded deep into the night, the cinnamon-coloured shops. He spoke to me of that world of courteous smiles, of unspoken feelings, of neat flower beds and blue drawing rooms, the leisurely world in which he had grown up. Vienna for him was a friend who had died, and he was missing her.

'You know, Signor Paolo, my father was someone who insured everything. My mother used to say he was the ideal client…the ideal gull, as it were, of every insurance agent. He would even have insured chickens if he'd been able to.'

'My grandfather says that we live in a world based on the illusion that reason is in charge, and go to one without a shadow of sense to it.'

The baron halted and closed his eyes for a moment. 'I *do* like your grandfather.'

There was the hint of a chuckle in his voice, and a slight smile on his lips. He liked to make fun of himself. When he drank tea he held the cup suspended right in front of his face for seconds at a time. 'He makes love to his cup, watch out, lad. Seems like he's soft as semolina,' the cook had said. The cook was a wise old bird, but she was wrong. The major's was not a simple character, and Grandpa had understood as much: 'The child and the soldier in him are constantly at blows, but neither manages to gain the upper hand.'

'Do you think you could kindly pass on a message to your aunt? It is something…of importance.'

I was taken aback by the baron's tone of voice. It had suddenly become harsh, even unfriendly.

'Certainly, Baron…Nothing…personal, is it?'

He halted again, and his eyes hardened disagreeably: 'What do you mean? I am a gentleman, Sir.'

I noticed that his boots were dirty.

'I didn't mean to…'

We started walking again, slowly, because it was uphill now.

'There is a squadron of British fighter planes…'

I fixed my eyes on the empty path before me, the tufts of grass motionless between the stones, the trees in the distance.

'They are British, SPADS, single-seater biplanes. It is always the same squadron that goes back and forth above the roof of the Villa, always the same. Does the kingfisher mean nothing to you?'

I quickened my pace a little. 'The king…what?'

'It's a bird. It's the symbol of that pilot, the leader of the squadron. A pilot and a half, too. He flew straight through a burning captive balloon. They'll have given him a medal.'

I struggled to show no feelings.

'Please tell Donna Maria, and also your grandfather, that to transmit to the enemy any information, of any kind and by whatever means, is a crime, and the code of warfare punishes this crime,' he said, lowering his voice slightly and stopping, so as to oblige me to look at him, 'with death. When we find spies, we hang them.'

'He got out of bed on the wrong side this morning,' said Grandpa over his cup of white coffee. He was right; Renato was not in a good mood. The major's warning had left us all stunned. Grandma thought we should stop what we were doing for a while, but how could we warn Brian to stop what *he* was doing? And at a moment like this, with the Austrian offensive due at any time…Grandma had given orders to keep all the shutters of the bay window closed, meaning 'Nothing to transmit,' and seeing all the troop movements that were going on Brian would surely get the message.

'But we can't give up now, of all times,' Grandpa had replied. 'It's now that our information is most important. That's why the baron warned us.'

Grandma had no fears for herself, but for the rest of us, for the Villa, and for me. I was not afraid; I had grown fatalistic and kept repeating one of Grandpa's little sayings, 'To do anything good in life you have to count on a bit of luck.'

'Do you think he'll hang us?' I was sitting with my legs dangling, and the hay was pricking my neck.

Renato handed me the tobacco pouch. 'He doesn't know how we send messages. And he doesn't hang anyone. And as for the information, Brian sees it for himself, flying over the plain. The roads are choked with columns of carts and there are more and more camps. Mine is a different job.'

'What is it?' I lit the pipe.

'The organization helps—'

'Prisoners to escape?' I was aiming to surprise him.

'Go on with you! Who's going to escape? Nobody wants to go back to the trenches. The deserters, they're the ones we want. It gets harder and harder to cross the river. Deserters – Czechs, Slovenians, Bosnians – they bring us up-to-date, precise information of the kind that can change the course of the fighting, not the kind we give about troop movements. One reconnaissance plane is enough for that.'

'Why are you telling me?'

'Because at this point you'd better know what we're really signalling with those shutters. They don't tell what you've been led to believe, but rather when, where, how and who will be crossing the river.'

'Why haven't you told me before?'

'Didn't need to before, but now…You might be useful to the organization…In case they kill me.'

'Tell me everything, then.' I was less frightened than excited.

He blew smoke into my eyes. 'That's enough for now, Paolo. The rest when necessary. How about stretching our legs?'

We took a turn around the village. No one was about. We paused to smoke for a while with the innkeeper, who with the return of good weather had put a bench outside the inn door. Even the inn was deserted.

'They all go to Sernaglia. All the money now goes to Sernaglia, and the girls, the ones who ply their trade, they go where the money is, in Sernaglia! Ah…times ain't what they used to be.' His pipe between his teeth, he patted the pocket of his tattered apron with his palms. 'And now this place is empty.'

This was said in our dialect, which Renato liked and understood well, though he couldn't speak it. In the village he was known as 'that bloody Tuscan', envied because he'd 'found a cushy job'. But the innkeeper had taken a liking to him, and there was always 'a drop of grappa' for us. We drank in silence for a long time, smoking away and gazing at the treetops. Then the host, showing us all the gaps he had between his teeth, took Renato aside and said something in his ear. It crossed my mind that he too was in Intelligence.

On our way back to the Villa we circled round the church, just to lengthen the walk and talk about this and that.

From far away came the boom of a cannon, then a second, then a third. The church windows rattled above our heads.

'They're adjusting their range-finders, testing their trajectories. And meanwhile putting a scare into the new arrivals down there in the trenches. Listen, now the Italians are returning fire.'

By now one roar followed hard upon another, and the rhythm increased to a continuous battering. The windowpanes were one continuous rattle. We moved away from the church.

'It's odd, this drumfire. I thought they were short of ammo.'

'A dress rehearsal?'

'Maybe. Rations have been improved these last few days. They're doing their level best to raise the morale of the troops, but I don't think they can achieve much.'

'D'you think they're in such a bad way?'

'Look at their uniforms, they're all in rags and they're hanging off them.'

He quickly led me to a spot near the chapel. With the first warm weather the stink of the latrines had intensified. I wrinkled my nostrils.

Renato took his dead pipe from his mouth. He used the stem to open a little gap between the leaves of the lime tree. 'See those lines?'

'Laundry…underpants,' said I.

'Of the emperor's officers.'

'So what?'

'Try to describe them. Take a good look.'

'Pants hung up to dry…What else? Well…rather tattered.'

'Only *rather*? Let's call them holes attached to scraps of pants.' He gave me a serious look. 'If we win it won't be because Diaz is better than Boroevic. All generals are good at coming on tough when others are doing the fighting. No, we are going to win because of those tattered underpants. You don't win if you're in rags. Do you remember that prisoner from Ancona, down at the depot a couple of weeks ago? He belonged to a captured patrol of ours. The chap who got talking to your grandfather, remember?'

I nodded.

'He had a new uniform, with all the buttons attached, and boots of real leather, not cardboard. If this is the underwear of the officers, the gods of the Danubian empire, just imagine that of the infantry who have to wade up to their chins to cross the Piave.' He replaced his pipe in his mouth. 'If you are reduced to rags then you're a down-and-out, and an army of down-and-outs never won a war. We are going to win because America has made us a vast loan. I don't think the Kingdom of Italy will ever manage to repay it, but in the meantime the war will be ours. And what goes for us goes also for the French and for the British. What's needed in combat is food, water, clothing, munitions, and all these things have to be transported and distributed when and where they are needed.' He spoke passionately, not looking at me but at the air before him. 'It's been a while now that they've been eating their mules, and now even rats are running short.' He shook his head. 'Those underpants tell their own story.'

Twenty-Five

AUSTRIANS, HUNGARIANS, BOSNIANS, CZECHS OR POLES, whatever they were they hurled themselves on the polenta. 'Take a good look at them,' said Renato. 'The four of them together don't weigh two hundred kilos.' The innkeeper stood over them, stroking his moustache and musing. Even he had got thinner. We passed them by, slowing our pace a little. It seemed to me I could hear their jaws chewing at the dry polenta.

'You see, Paolo, battles are won or lost by armies, but wars are another matter. Wars are fought by whole nations, which means banks, industries, cows, grain, petrol. Things that take time to get together, and you have to make them last for years, not weeks, do you see? These soldiers here are as brave and disciplined as ours, no more, no less, but if Austria doesn't give them enough to eat…'

'Will it be long until they make their offensive?'

Major Manca knocked out the bowl of his pipe against a tree trunk. Then, walking on with the empty pipe between his teeth, he said in a low voice, 'Yesterday I saw eleven railway wagons on a siding at the Pieve station. Flour! Tell your grandmother this. The reconnaissance planes won't see them because they are camouflaged with foliage. A massive bombing is needed, and at once! That flour is worth ten times more than an ammunition dump.'

We parted. I went to take the message to Grandma, who set to work to put it into code. She didn't take long about it. Aunt Maria said this must be the last time: 'Too risky to go on.'

Grandma objected. 'The washing line…well, we know, lots of people are doing it. But the shutters…' She had a streak of caprice in her, a consequence of that haughty character which had caused us to stay put on the east bank of the river. Moreover, the code was her brainchild.

Grandpa, on the other hand, was confident. 'I know it doesn't take much for them to hang Italians, and in war there's no sending for a lawyer. But our baron is a devotee of good manners, and good manners can be counted on. They get under the skin far more than certain frivolities such as love or faith.' With a slight smile on his lips he shot me a conspiratorial glance. 'That major isn't going to shoot anyone…The fighting doesn't depend on what happens at Villa Spada.'

'Let's hope not,' said Aunt Maria grimly.

May is also the month of the Madonna and of First Communions. I was conscripted. 'Family duty.' The glass in the church windows had been replaced by tarred cardboard – an Italian bomb had sent them into smithereens. The children all in white were chattering away in the front row while their mothers, great black praying mantises, mumbled incantatory prayers in the row behind. Don Lorenzo had banished the tribe of grandfathers, who were dozing off with their ballast of grappa, to either side of the high altar. The fathers, though, had been borne off by the war, or were toiling with the scythe. Also present were several prisoners of war in working clothes, and a few Austrian officers in battledress. My family was drawn up in the back row, so as not to attract attention. Aunt Maria sat between Grandma and the Third Paramour, and Teresa and Loretta were there as well. Grandpa's absence certainly came as no surprise to our parish priest.

The mass didn't take long. The Sernaglia sector was on the alert, and from one moment to the next the church might be requisitioned for use as an army hospital. But this early warning had been going on for days, and no one – except for Don Lorenzo – was taking it very seriously. After the reading from the Gospel, our priest launched into an invective against humanity at war. He spiced it up with a few insults directed at the occupying troops, whom he then praised for their 'devotion to the Queen of Heaven', indicating the blue and white plaster waitress endlessly smiling in the light of the flickering candles. Playing it both ways, I thought, remembering Grandpa once saying, 'They've been doing this for two thousand years. War annihilates families and nations, but God's collecting bag is always there.'

Coming to the end of his insults and eulogies, Don Lorenzo aimed a finger at the painted vault.

'Brethren,' said he, raising his voice a little, 'when a cow has a calf all Our Lord's creation rejoices. The flies have a new rump to call their home, the peasant will have milk and meat, the wolf hopes to make a meal of it, no one is sad. No lament arises from the earth. But at the birth of a man, the finest creature in all Creation, we do not know whether to be happy or sad, because God has given man the freedom to do evil. The viper that bites us, the weasel that steals chickens, the wasp that stings…these are not wicked creatures. They live according to their lights, even if they are bothersome. But Eve ate the apple because she believed in the serpent instead of in God.' His forefinger circled above his head before stiffening into a flagpole indicating the blue of the vault with its well-worn apparatus of symbols. 'I have always known that there above,' he went on, without lowering his finger or relaxing the strained rigidity of his arm, 'there is the force which moves the sun and the other stars, but the trouble is that this force also causes bad things that we do not understand, not even if we think about it for a hundred years. In fact, those who think about it too much understand it even less than those who spend all day re-soling shoes, Don Lorenzo's word upon it!' The forefinger was now lowered, and struck the lectern with a slight thump. The sermon was over and mass moved swiftly ahead until the altar boy's bell tinkled to announce the elevation. It was then that the big guns were heard. Sudden and loud. Far and near.

'They're firing from the Montello,' said Aunt Maria. The phalange of mantises broke ranks.

'If they're firing hundred-pounders they'll knock us cock-eyed,' said Teresa, and maybe her saying that aroused Madame Misfortune, for with a crash and a splatter we were all smothered in white powder and plaster.

Don Lorenzo put down the chalice. 'Dearly beloved brethren, stay calm! This is the House of God...Outside, all of us... but calmly. This way, quick, children first. *Ite, missa est.* Hurry along!' And with his hand he bestowed on the dust cloud a hasty yet expansive sign of the cross. The din the children made as they rushed out vied with the roar of the artillery. Mothers, grandfathers, prisoners and soldiers stampeded from all sides. The priest's housekeeper had thrown open the side door, and we scattered into the street, passing beneath the bell tower. The sound of gunfire slackened off, and shortly fell silent. Everyone was coughing. Me too, as I joined Aunt Maria in giving an arm to Grandma, for the Third Paramour had vanished, making good use of his big feet.

All that had fallen was a metre of the cornice, but it had whitened quite a stretch of roadway. We were white from head to foot, and in such manner we entered the Villa gates.

The salute from the sentries – the rifle butts thudding on the ground – sounded unintentionally comic: soldiers saluting ghosts.

That evening I spent with Giulia. I went over to her place just as soon as I had had a bit of a wash in the tub in the loft.

The Third Paramour's shutters were open. He had not yet washed, and was sitting there in an old armchair, white with plaster and fright. Maybe he didn't even see me, because he neither smiled nor waved. He was staring wide-eyed at the window, his long cigarette holder in his mouth. The cigarette was out. I climbed two at a time to the balcony and knocked.

Giulia opened the door, saw me and burst out laughing, 'Doesn't one wash when one calls on a lady?'

'But I *have* wash—' and didn't have time to finish. Her lips forced my mouth open and her tongue was warm and hard. Without letting go of me she steered me to the sofa and threw me down on it. We undressed quickly and then, slowly, made love.

The only woman I had come near to 'knowing' was one in the Casino di Siora la Bella, a high-class brothel in the middle of Treviso, where I had been dragged by Grandpa. I was fourteen when I lost my parents, and as soon as I turned sixteen Grandpa decided that my erotic education was up to him. It all happened unbeknownst to Grandma and Aunt Maria who, though they might have guessed something, were careful to keep it to themselves. Thus it was that on 12 August 1916, my sixteenth birthday, I found myself in a piazza in Treviso, a town which the hazards of war had not yet transformed into a fortress. We put up in a hotel which had huge windows of vaguely Gothic character giving onto an alleyway scarcely wider than a village street. We had a glass of strong liquor at the bar downstairs before going on to the brothel. Grandpa prepared me for the event with homilies slightly less sententious than usual, worked up to it gradually, said that there were certain things a man had to learn early and well, and that certain women knew how to teach, and he concluded with a piece of advice: 'Remember that even a prostitute must be treated as a lady, because this is expected of you...and in any case she deserves as much.'

So it was that my first contact with female flesh was the large pink bosom of a little dark-eyed blonde who greeted me with the words, 'Hello there, my name's Graziella, let's go and arse around, you handsome fella.' I imagine she said the same to everyone, even drooling septuagenarians, because she liked the rhyme. But what I never confessed to Grandpa was that with Graziella I had not gone through with it, out of bashfulness, I think, or maybe because that unassuming girl was shrewd enough to realize that for me that was not the moment. And when she took me back to the parlour where Grandpa Gugliemo was awaiting me, in the company of a newspaper, cigar and whisky, she told him I had behaved like a man and a gentleman; and what's more she said it in a firm voice, giving nothing away.

That evening Giulia taught me that even a woman who has you fall in love with her has something of the Graziella in her, and it is as such that you must treat her, with virility and passion, but keeping something back for yourself. I thus managed not to tell her what I felt for her. When I got dressed I felt proud of having remained myself, and for the first time since I had met her I felt sure that she too had felt something for me. Maybe she might betray me, maybe she might humiliate me, but some part of her, for an indefinable moment, had been truly mine. And that was enough.

'Where are you going? There's the curfew. Don't go out till dawn.'

I regarded her stretched on the sofa in front of the blazing wood fire. She returned my look with those strange eyes of hers. Her breasts were bare and the nipples still hard and red. 'I have to go,' I said, and out I went. My footsteps echoed on the planks of the balcony.

The Third Paramour's shutters were still wide open. He was motionless in the depths of his armchair, his spent cigarette at the tip of that ridiculously long holder. Two hours had passed and he still hadn't even rinsed himself off. He was white from head to toe and didn't even notice me passing his window.

Grandpa never spoke at random when he put on his nightcap, a rite he performed with all the grace of a fine lady. His nightshirt was rather short, not even reaching his knee, and the cap at a rakish angle gave him a touch of melancholy gaiety, like a clown putting on make-up. That night, in the dark, Grandpa and I talked for a long time. We spoke of the enemy soldiers who were more optimistic than their officers, and agreed that this was an unusual thing. 'The echoes of Caporetto are still in the air, so those bastards still think they're going to win.' Then we talked about Renato.

'I've never liked that man, he's overbearing. There's real arrogance in that man. You see? He's even pinched your woman.'

'No! That's not so!'

'Look here, laddie, there's only one thing a woman won't

forgive, and that's teetering. Get into her pants, that's the only way to keep 'em happy.'

''Night, Grandpa,' I replied. And, glad we were in the dark, smiled to myself.

Twenty-Six

THE BATTLE COMMENCED AT THREE IN THE MORNING ON 15 June, beneath a moonless, starless sky. Fog erased houses and hillsides from view. For twenty days in unbroken succession, the coming and going of soldiers had sorely tested the Villa's resources. Hot sunshine and still air only reinforced the stench wafting up out of the latrines. Unfailingly, Grandpa proffered one of his maxims: 'Soldiers may come and soldiers may go, but the shit stays here with us.'

And as the sloshing filth spilled over, the church was being transformed into a field hospital. Don Lorenzo had taken to saying mass outdoors, in the meadow between the portico of the *barchessa* and the Villa, something that turned into more and more of an irritant because his sermons were preached in an increasingly loud voice that verged on a shout, while the summer heat made us reluctant to close the windows. Still, even amidst the vast upheaval, some good had come of the situation: the Kraut field kitchen finally had something to cook, including a bit of meat now and then, and a fraction of that something would end up in Teresa's cookpot, in small part due to the baron's benevolence, and in large part because of the glittering gold in the occasional pound sovereign that Grandma, through Renato's hands, managed to drop tinkling into the pockets of the quartermaster sergeant, who had little to envy, sitting comfortably in God's lap as he was in those days.

The cannon on both banks of the river fired incessantly. Luckily the Italians, on that first day of fighting, unleashed only their small- and medium-calibre artillery, and Refrontolo remained out of range. The baron had been too busy to pay any mind to the minor matter of the escadrille that flew over-head every sixth or seventh day. My aunt said that he'd changed profession: 'Now he's a town constable, always out there in the square directing traffic.'

By late afternoon the church was already packed to the rafters with wounded men; they put the less serious cases out in the stables, with the mules. Austrians, Hungarians, Bosnians, Czechs, Poles, Montenegrins; there were even a first few Italian prisoners. Looking out the window I saw the endless line of wagons waiting to unload bloody infantrymen, who were then stretchered away in all directions. More than once, that day, I saw men without legs, without hands, their head reduced to little more than a clotted bundle of bandages. And more than once I was forced to summon all my strength to keep from throwing up. The dogfights overhead no longer made us look up. Fighter planes with Savoy insignia were constantly strafing the roads, and two of those planes were shot down. From the cockpit of one they extracted a blackened trunk that reeked of charred steak from fifteen metres away. 'Dear God, let it end,' I said over and over under my breath.

The news was bad: the enemy forces had broken through on the Montello, overrunning the front and second lines, and were about to flood the plain. But Renato was still optimistic. 'The Piave river is rising; it'll be no easy thing to fight with a river in spate at their back, and after all, the attack on the Montello can't be the principal thrust…Judging from what the wounded men have to say today, south of Nervesa it must have been hell.'

That night, even though it was summer, we lit a fire in the little drawing room near my aunt's bedroom to dry our bones: the rain was pouring down and the night was damp and chilly. No one spoke. We knew that if the Austrians pushed all the way to the banks of the Adige river, Italy would be tempted to surrender: perhaps sue for a separate peace. But we also knew that this offensive might well prove to be the Hapsburgs' swan song. Grandpa and I agreed to slip in among the prisoners and ask how the battle was faring, because the wait had become intolerable.

'Tomorrow I'll go down and introduce myself to the official in charge at the church; I want to do something to help,' my aunt announced, breaking the silence. There were no comments: for once, not even my grandpa knew what to say.

We practically hadn't eaten a thing, and Teresa angrily scolded us: 'Time to eat, masters and mistresses,' she said. 'Empty bags can't stand upright.'

You could cut the tension with a knife and my aunt, to break the evil spell, started telling us about the baron, to the astonishment of one and all. She said that his father had been a presence at court, that he was a renowned art historian, and that his mother was a saintly woman who'd lost her mind when the baron's little sister died. 'The baron was eleven years old when they committed his mother to a clinic in Zurich from which she never returned…He carries her portrait in a locket that only a mortar shell could separate from his neck.' My aunt spoke softly, looking into the fire, and there was deep feeling in her clear voice. The army, she told us, had been the refuge of a boy who yearned to do good but had little enough talent to offer. 'He's a lonely, good-natured boy, he searches for happiness but when he finds a little, he doesn't know how to live with it. He dislikes the army, even though it's given him a life and a future, and he dislikes warfare too, but he won't pull back, because... he's a child filled with uncertainty, and niggling fears...but right now the biggest fear of all, deep inside, is that he might not live up to the uniform that he wears. What Rudolf is most afraid of is dishonour.'

This was the first time we'd ever heard her call him by his given name.

My aunt wrenched her gaze away from the fire that seemed to be hypnotizing her, and looked at us one by one: 'He learnt our language so well as a way to please his father, whom he'd accompany on his trips to Italy; his father came here to study sixteenth-century painting, especially Venetian artists, and I believe he even wrote a book about Titian.' She sighed, and the flames made the green wood snap. 'He's not much of a soldier... Poor Rudolf, he's too fond of horses...and, just like me, he can't stand to see them suffer...A few days ago he admitted to me – and he blushed as he said it – that he was made aide-de-camp to General Bolzano in consideration of his illustrious birth, not his gifts as an officer.'

'These aren't the sort of things a man says lightly...I mean to say...unless he doesn't care about the woman sitting across from him.' There was a tenderness in Grandma's voice that I'd never heard before. I too was shocked, it wasn't like her to confide her inner thoughts.

'Listen, Maria...take some advice from an old man: don't let that baron slip through your fingers. One way or another, the war is going to end...'

My aunt looked at my grandfather and shook her head as if she were trying to ring a cowbell. 'The war will end and that officer has a wife back home waiting for him…Remember, challenging times bring people together as long as they last, but then they separate them.' My aunt was practically whispering now. 'The vanquished cannot forgive the victors…even if no one ever knows who really wins and who loses, because what's at stake, what's really at stake, the things that no one ever talks about, are unknown. Life goes on,' and she looked at my grandfather with her flinty green eyes, 'but you lose pieces of yourself along the way, every day.'

The windowpanes shivered. Suddenly the explosions had come closer. 'That's large-calibre artillery,' my grandfather said. 'Let's keep our fingers crossed.'

'Don't be silly, scaredy-cat,' said my grandmother, with a half-hearted laugh. 'We'll survive.'

Twenty-Seven

PAGNINI SHOWED UP IN CHURCH WITH A SLASHED WRIST. He'd tried to kill himself. Or at least pretended to. My aunt – who was wearing a white coat smeared with clotted blood – bandaged him with a grimace of disgust. 'Don't you understand what we're doing here? We're fighting to save a few... of these boys.' Pagnini left with a bandaged wrist and his face concealed under a broad-brimmed Borsalino.

The church floor was carpeted with blood-encrusted pallets, where the most seriously wounded were laid out side by side. A colonel from Cracow, fair-haired and skinny, solidly muscled, with a firm gaze, was performing surgery on the main altar. The four altars along the two aisles were occupied by one Italian doctor, a prisoner who had been captured on the Montello, and three others, all of them Croatians according to my aunt, who wasn't even certain that they were really physicians at all. The stone altars were sluiced clean with pails of water. Loretta, Teresa, the other volunteers, and I all carried empty buckets out and full buckets back in, in an endless procession.

The ditches lining the road – for kilometres, from Refrontolo to the banks of the rivers Soligo and Piave – were clogged with ravaged bodies, living and dead, locked in a mass embrace and sending up an incessant wave of moans. And 16 June had been worse than the fifteenth. The wounded were also coming in from Falzè, Susegana, Tezze, and Cimadolmo; the Conegliano hospital sent word that they'd stopped accepting patients. Wherever I turned, I saw suffering men: the garden was an endless place of torment. Around noon, a Hungarian lieutenant asked me, in dumbshow, to go with him to the inn. I followed him out. We requisitioned all the remaining grappa, with the assistance of both the innkeeper and the innkeeper's wife. 'We need it to operate, there's no more morphine.' The thing was to stun them before sinking the scalpel into their flesh, and grappa also made a serviceable disinfectant. A lorry had gone out to make the rounds of the farmhouses and confiscate all the alcohol that could be found. No one spoke, no one asked questions. My head was throbbing and I was praying, yes praying, for the day to come to an end, for the wounded to stop pouring in. In the afternoon, three lorries loaded with nuns pulled in from who knows where, and they set to work; that allowed me, Teresa, and Loretta to return to the Villa. My aunt refused to leave the church: 'I'm staying here; tonight I'm not leaving this place.' A spurt of dark red blood ran across her pinched face, as sharp and clear as if she'd been slashed by a sword: there was blood on the backs of her hands, under her fingernails, on her boots, and on the hem of the skirt that showed beneath her white coat smeared with clumps of mucus, bile, and tincture of iodine.

Even the ground floor of the Villa had become a hospital. The nuns brought everyone there who could walk, even if it was just a few steps and even if they required assistance to do so. We were without blankets, straw, or hay: the wounded were laid out on the bare flooring and they shut their eyes, all in the throes of deathly exhaustion. I looked for Renato, but he was nowhere to be found. Grandpa had shut himself up in his Thinking Den and I could hear him pounding away on Beelzebub's keys. Towards evening, while I was trying to take my mind off my thoughts with an adventure novel, he told me that he hadn't written a word all day: 'But you know, all that pounding on the keys does help to keep away the voices of the dead.'

I went to see Grandma. I found her sitting at her desk, bowed over her numbers; maybe it was her code. She looked at me as if she had seen a ghost: 'Paolo…you're a wreck…They're all so young.' Her voice was cracking and her eyes were wet. But she wasn't crying. Her swift and agile mind seemed to be hunting through the numbers for a handhold, a nugget of beauty, some accounting that made sense, anything that might tell her 'we're not all insane.'

I went back to the church, determined to give my aunt what help I could. I found her helping Don Lorenzo give extreme unction to those who were breathing their last. She held the cross while the priest blessed the young men and murmured his litanies. When my aunt saw me, she told me to leave. 'You're not needed here.' I shook my head no. 'Then lend a hand,' she said.

I knelt down and lifted an infantryman's head. There was a yellow bandage wrapped around his eyes and he was murmuring words I couldn't understand. He might have been Hungarian, but it was hard to say because he was no longer in uniform. The parish priest slipped the communion wafer into his mouth and the soldier thanked him as best he could, gripping his hand and moving one leg. The priest asked, in a soft voice: 'Who can ever forgive all this?' He glanced in my direction, dry-eyed, but what he was looking at I couldn't guess.

'I don't know,' I said.

'I don't know,' Don Lorenzo repeated. Then he stood up and went over to another boy stretched out on the floor.

'I'm Italian.' There was a grimace of pain nailed to his face.

'I can walk, take me out of here, I don't want to lie in the midst of these others…Everyone here is dying.' He was terribly pale, and his eyes were red, shot through with suffering. I understood that he was trying to shout, but all that would come out of his mouth was a tiny thread of a voice. 'I can walk,' he said again. 'Help me up.'

I looked down at the muddy sheet that covered him from the neck down: I realized that he had no legs, his body was only half there. I turned around and looked for my aunt. There was no more noise around me; the moaning and wailing was gone in my head. All that was left was what I could see, and what I could see had carried off all the sounds of the world. My aunt came over to me and grasped my hands, then she put her mouth close to my ear: 'Go to Grandpa, he needs you now.'

I left, making my way, one step at a time, over that expanse of butchered flesh, by the flickering light of a hundred candles. 'This is what cannons do,' said a voice. A voice that followed me to the exit.

It wouldn't be long now till sunset. As I was leaving, Teresa walked in. She barely glanced at me. In her hands, with a pair of oven mitts, she was carrying a basin of boiling water, with half a dozen surgical instruments in it. I went back inside, walking alongside her. She was bent over and exhausted, and I helped her carry the basin. 'Here, let me, Teresa.' She let me help without a word. She really was exhausted, and she too, just like my aunt, had black blood clotted on the collar of her blouse and on down to her shoes.

I thought about how many of those basins she must have carried. The water was heavy, and I rested it against my belly and arched my back against it.

'Come with me, son.'

A nun was waiting for us by the first altar on the right, where a young man lay stretched out, barely clinging to life. There was a pungent odour, of carbolic acid and piss, of grappa, rank sweat, and something else, something sickly sweet and revolting. I realized that it was the smell of death.

Lining the floor of the right aisle of the church were twenty straw pallets, side by side, with two soldiers on each. Loretta went over to the mother superior. The nun gave them rapid instructions, in dialect. No one paid me any mind. I was invisible. I looked around for my aunt, who was now assisting the Polish colonel operating on the main altar. Teresa and Loretta were heading over to her. I followed them. Sobs and moans, whispered words, sudden shrieks of pain, falling metal rattling onto the marble floor; oaths and prayers fused into a single murmuring stream of discordant voices. The colonel's apron was covered with blood. Don Lorenzo kept entering and leaving the sacristy with his load of communion wafers. He moved from one wounded man to the next, listening to confessions he didn't understand, scattering sketched-out crosses into the air. When he came to a prisoner, an Italian, he stopped a few seconds longer, because he understood what the man was saying. To one and all he dispensed Latin formulas.

I read the word 'water' on the lips of a *bersagliere*. In the short distance I had to cover to reach my aunt, I saw eyes sink shut and quivering bodies collapse without another moan.

The transept was for the hopeless ones. As I crossed it, I kept my eyes fixed on the floor; the last thing I wanted was to step on anyone, but my footsteps were uncertain and my mind was prey to a devastating sense of guilt, the way I felt when I walked past little children's graves at the cemetery, or the time I entered the Brustolon family's hovel, black with soot and poverty.

I stood by my aunt, tamping down my sense of nausea. With Teresa and Loretta I helped her lift a boy who had been hit by enemy fire, half his face reduced to a glistening, bloody pudding. The one eye remaining to him stared at me for an instant. I had the impression he was asking me who I was, what I was doing there. But he no longer had a mouth. From what had once been his face not even a single moan escaped. As soon as we laid him on the marble altar top, the colonel yanked open his eye, splaying forefinger and thumb. '*Raus!*' he shouted. 'You don't call me for dead men.' The doctor's face was grey with weariness.

My aunt closed the boy's eye again, then glanced over at me. 'I told you to go and tend to Grandpa,' she said, giving me a piercing look. 'Here it's forbidden, it's absolutely criminal to faint, you understand that?'

So I left the church for a second time, shuffling cautiously, dragging my feet where the recumbent bodies allowed me to. I wasn't even aware that Teresa was holding me up. But as soon as I got a mouthful of the cool evening air, I told her to turn right around and go back to my aunt.

There was no guard at the front gate. In the garden there were wounded men everywhere, men with arms strapped to their chest, men with crutches, one with a bandaged eye, another with a gauze-wrapped neck, but nearly all of them still on their feet. The field kitchen was distributing soup amidst the billowing fumes of a locomotive. I stopped before I reached the portico, I was starting to feel better. There were a few soldiers there who seemed not to be wounded at all, but they were only able to stay on their feet because they were helping each other not to topple over. They were all smoking, and they were all blank-eyed. They were staring straight head, looking at the lawn but not seeing anything.

A hand crushed my shoulder until it hurt. I turned around. 'Renato!'

'The artillery has practically knocked these men's heads off their shoulders, they're empty shells, but tomorrow's another day and maybe a few of them will recover.' He explained that some of them would remain in that state of apathy for days, others for months, and a few for good. They were empty bodies, perfectly healthy but empty, the soul, incapable of maintaining its grip, long separated from the flesh.

And so I vomited onto the steward's shoes before he had a chance to step aside. I vomited air and saliva, and weariness. I wiped my mouth. 'Sorry.'

'It's all right.'

'I'm going to see Grandpa.'

I passed through the empty kitchen. I climbed the stairs one step at a time. I heard someone behind me. It was Giulia. She'd seen me in the garden.

'You look like someone who just threw up.'

I shot her a resentful glare.

She caressed my cheek with the back of her hand while Teresa went past us on her way downstairs. She must have come home while I was staring at the demented infantrymen. '*Diambarne de l'ostia*,' she said, trailing behind her something of that warm and terrifying presence that certain elderly women possess, their hair parted sternly down the centre, indifferent to the urgency of life, firmly endowed with the strength of those who age slowly, the way domestic animals do.

I could see that Giulia was upset.

'She knows about us, but she won't tell,' I said under my breath.

'Do you think I care about that? It's just that…that woman…

she's,' and she hesitated, 'it's as if she were trying to tell me…
with every ounce of her being, every pound of her flesh: you
have to come here too, where I am, the wrinkles will take over
your face too, and the smell of your skin will change too…and
you'll wither and dry out the way that branches do, and leaves,
and plums; I'm waiting for you, here in the land where no one
desires you or loves you, and when you get here you'll stop
doing what you're doing, you'll stop being what you are.'

It was the first time that I'd seen that brazen Giulia show a
hint of fear. Fear of something as ordinary as the passage of
time. And it was then, for those few sincere, trembling words,
that I felt something strong for her.

Twenty-Eight

THE RIVER PIAVE WAS SWOLLEN, IT WAS THE COLOUR OF THE earth, the colour of the dead. That's the way that the wounded and the prisoners told it, on the morning of 18 June. The reports became increasingly confused.

'High water is to our advantage,' Renato said. 'They won't be able to supply the offensive.'

High above the Villa the squadrons wheeled in dogfights. The biplanes swooped low, like birds fleeing a darkening sky. Black crosses and tricolour cockades. We had stopped rooting for one side or the other. It was all mortar shells, mutilations, fear, and practically nothing to eat. Now when the wounded came up from the river, they stretched them out one crammed against the other, even in the Villa's big dining room; there were even a few in the kitchen, and the whole park was covered with tents.

I hadn't set foot in the church again. Only the dead ever left there: they were buried immediately, without benefit of coffin, in an improvised cemetery, tucked away out of view. The graves were dug by Italian prisoners, easy to identify by their Adrian steel helmets and their new uniforms, as often as not badly tattered, true, but still unmistakably new. Renato had talked a few of them into trading information for a bowl of Teresa's soup; she was still pulling off the occasional miracle in the kitchen. They told him that on the Montello their battalion had allowed itself to be caught off guard and that they'd surrendered without firing a shot; but they also said that further south the offensive had already ground to a halt by dawn on the 15th, and that they'd heard about it from other prisoners, captured south of Nervesa: 'They're stuck fast along the river bank, for kilometres, all the way to Zensón, and the Duke of Aosta's artillery is tearing them to shreds.' Judging from the sheer numbers of the wounded, it was hard to disagree; but others said that the Austrians were winning, and nobody really knew what to think.

My aunt, who never seemed to leave the church, had assigned me to bring canteens to the men under the portico and in the tents. All of them were thirsty, constantly. And for the past few hours it had been pouring rain like nothing I'd ever seen before. Some of them would stagger out of their tents and tip their heads back, open-mouthed, to the sky. They looked like lunatics, an army of crazed raggedy cripples. Under the portico, the young men with nothing but emptiness in their heads waggled their shoulders and stared at me sightless, gripping the canteen with trembling fingers, chilled hands, lifting the water to their lips as if those lips belonged to somebody else, as if they'd never been thirsty in the first place.

That morning, bright and early, Don Lorenzo came to the Villa. He'd lost weight, he hadn't slept in two days, his eyes were bulging out of their sockets and his face was greyer than the prisoners' uniform jackets. I asked him about my aunt, he looked at me for a second, and then turned his eyes to the wall and started scratching at the plaster with two fingers, as if trying to remove an imperfection in the mortar: 'She has four pairs of hands, God bless her.' He pulled his fingers away from the wall. 'They say that you're no layabout yourself, that you've been carrying canteens.' He gave me a look. 'Good boy,' he said, absentmindedly. So I asked him why he'd come up to the Villa.

'They're going to hang a couple of Czech boys, two prisoners; they claim that they were traitors to Austria, and one of them, whom I just heard in confession, asked me…he wants to be executed by a firing squad, he wants to die on his feet, he says. "I'm fighting for homeland, I'm not traitor," and I wanted to ask your grandma if she'd come with me to see the baron, because your aunt refuses to even discuss the idea, she won't even think of it.'

The words tumbled out of his mouth, he was talking so fast, I had a hard time following what he was saying.

'Then the baron…Has come back from the Piave.'

'He's got a bullethole in his shoulder…He's not in danger and he's resumed command. I left him in the church, he wants to be close to the dying men. But his determination is unshakable: "Hang them both, they're traitors!" That's what he said. "Look at them, all these men…They're dying for their country and for their – for our emperor." Still, I want to give it one more try, and your grandma could help me. All that boy wants is to die on his feet, like a soldier.'

'What about the other one? You said there were two of them.'

'The other one refused to talk to me…Maybe he's not Catholic, maybe he doesn't care much about dying…I asked him what I could do for him, if he wanted to confess his sins, but he just spat on the groud and said, "Place for priest in hell."' The priest made a foolish face, and looked me right in the eye: 'He must be one of those godless ones, a…Socialist.' He took off his rain-drenched hat and crammed it against his chest. 'I'm tired,' and he went back to rubbing the pads of his thumb and forefinger on a specific spot on the plaster.

'I'll take you to Grandma Nancy.'

On the stairs, I glimpsed my grandpa crossing the hallway. The second he caught sight of the black tunic he scurried into his Thinking Den, miming a military salute in Don Lorenzo's direction.

'My respects, your excellency,' said the priest in an ironic voice, without even bothering to make the expected bow.

Grandma stood up as soon as she saw us, crumpling with her left hand the sheets of paper on which she'd been writing. Her index finger was blue and the sickly sweet odour of ink wafted from the inkwell. The rain had just stopped pattering on the windowpanes, and a timid bit of blue sky was lighting up the window.

'Bad news?'

Grandma's face struck me as more surprised than concerned. Even if I'd never heard her say so, I knew that she didn't much care for the curate. Religion had never really interested her, and in any case she thought it was stupid to entrust its administration to people 'born with patches on their butts'. Unlike my aunt, Grandma Nancy believed in wealth more than rank: 'Money can be counted, and that's why it counts.'

'Yes, bad news,' said the priest, as he crumpled with all ten fingers the circular brim of his black hat, still dripping wet.

'Don't keep me on tenterhooks…Please, have a seat.' And she pointed to the little canapé that could barely accommodate Don Lorenzo's enormous posterior, emitting threatening creaks and groans beneath him.

'What can I do for you? If this is about wounded men…the Villa is already packed.'

'I'd like to ask you, Signora, to come with me and add your voice to mine when I beg this favour of the baron.'

'The baron?' Grandma went and sat down in her old

armchair. 'Are you referring to Baron von Feilitzsch? But if he's come back...the Piave isn't yielding.'

'He has one arm in a sling...and he's going to have two Czech boys, two prisoners hanged...They were fighting for the Italians.'

Grandma ran her fingertips through her hair without mussing it. 'I'm afraid he has every right to do that; the Czechs are Hapsburg subjects.'

'But Signora, perhaps...not all of them want to be...They want their independence.'

'Strange words from the mouth of a prelate...independence...'

I broke in: 'They're fighting on our side, Grandma!'

'Strength is the law. It's true in nature too...and we are animals, even if we know to add and subtract and recite a few poems by heart, don't you agree with me, Don Lorenzo?'

The priest looked at me. I had remained standing, leaning against the door jamb. I think he must have been hoping for a word of support from me.

'Yes,' said the priest, with a note of melancholy in his voice. 'But you see, Signora Spada, I don't question Austria's right to hang traitors, but one of the two young men implored me to... intercede...He wants to be shot by a firing squad, all he asks is to die with honour, and that's something you can hardly deny a Christian!' Waving his hat, he pointed at me. 'He's just a couple of years older than your grandson...'

'You could have told me right away that the boy is just asking for a few bullets. Just think, that baron is planning to hang them from a tree in my garden...but if he thinks that I'm going to let him...' Grandma was already on her feet. 'Let's go and see the baron.'

'Actually...' said Don Lorenzo, standing up and waving his

hat in front of his belly, 'actually only one of them asked for bullets, I don't think the other one cares.'

'No one is about to be hanged in my garden.'

Grandma left the room, calling for Teresa in a loud voice.

The cook came up the stairs towards us.

'Teresa, my dark blue dust coat.'

'But mistress…with all this heat?'

'My dust coat! Get moving.'

Grandma was putting on her best military posture when, directly outside the Villa's front gate, she set the baron back on his heels.

'Madame, what a pleasure to see you again,' said the officer, his left forearm pinned to his chest. His bandages forced him to make an awkward gesture as he attempted to lift Grandma's hand to his lips, and she promptly snatched it back. Don Lorenzo doffed his hat and stood at her side, boots planted firmly in a wide stance. I came to a halt a step behind them.

'I understand, Major, that you intend to hang two prisoners.'

'Two traitors, Madame.'

'The parish priest informs me that they're requesting bullets instead of a noose. I think that is a concession you can make, is is not…Baron?'

'Traitors don't deserve to die like soldiers. Many of their fellow Czechs,' and his eyes narrowed to two slits, 'are dying ten kilometres from here, in our uniform…Is that clear, Madame?'

'I disapprove.' The still air moved, a sudden gust of wind tugged at Grandma's dust coat, uncovering her thin neck. 'Where did you think you would hang them, Major? Not in my garden, certainly.'

'In…your…garden? The Villa has been requisitioned by military law, Madame. It's under my command!'

'You describe murder as duty, and armed theft as requisition.'

'Madame…it's not me…it's the war.'

'Your impertinence comes as no surprise; but to judge from what I see,' and here Grandma's nose pointed at the expanse of tents and the wounded men, 'our river hasn't brought you luck, or have you requisitioned it too, Major?'

A grimaced twisted the officer's face. Grandma knew how to twist the knife.

'Now, I'm sure you'll excuse me…The traitors will be executed at noon. Hanged with a noose, in front of the latrines. If you'd care to honour us with your attendance…' He stepped around us, because Grandma refused to retreat a single step.

'Signora, you must insist,' said Don Lorenzo, setting his wet hat firmly on his bald head, 'I beg of you, just think of that young man…'

'Go back to the church and tend to the wounded, Don Lorenzo.' Grandma's voice was calm and tough. 'Can't you see? It's over.'

The parish priest stepped aside.

Grandma Nancy gave him a smile: 'Never miss a chance to answer a challenge. At noon, in front of the latrines.'

Walking slowly and with his head bowed, the curate headed back to his church. He was a good man, and he was no coward, but he'd never be able to understand a soul as fiery as Grandma's. Grandpa said that in Nancy's heart there was ice and a parched wind, and that both forces battled it out every day, in a fight without quarter.

The sun was hot, the air was muggy, and the grass was still drenched. There was mud everywhere. The western sky was dark with smoke. Every ten or twenty minutes, the artillery batteries reawakened and began to fire, only to nod off again. The gallows poles were two larch trunks, their bark freshly peeled off, with a wooden ladder leaning against the top, which terminated in an iron hook. The smells were strong: shit, tree sap, and tar. Von Feilitzsch's uniform was spotless, but the visor of his cap was spattered with mud. Renato, off to one side, was leaning on his spade: he had just dug two graves, next to the latrines. 'We don't lay traitors to rest next to heroes,' the baron had told him.

Grandma was standing between me and Grandpa, and she was wearing a black skirt made of a coarse cotton fabric that hung down to her shoes, gleaming in defiance of the mud. Her blouse was white, ironed by Loretta's inefficient hands: the sleeves were marred by a couple of creases running down to the starched cuffs. My aunt had stayed in the church, with her dying men. There were forty or so soldiers, all with only minor injuries, some dressed in the uniform of the Honvéd, others wearing the Schützen uniform; their tattered jackets, many without buttons, were pulled back here and there to reveal their flesh, even filthier than the cloth. A spectral army: one man leaning his weight on the shoulder of the next, hands, legs, and faces wrapped in bandages; their caps and the melancholy resignation on their faces were the only things that said: 'We are soldiers.' And yet in those compressed lips, in those mute eyes, there was still something that demanded respect: the echo of an ancient renown.

Short gusts of wind kicked up revolting clouds of stench: the stink of sweat contended against the foul miasma of the latrines. Don Lorenzo hadn't been allowed to comfort the two Czechs. 'Traitors die alone, scorned by God and man alike,' the baron had said.

The first of the two – tall, broad-shouldered, his wrists tied behind his back – stepped forward in an awkward shuffle, standing straight even as he wobbled slightly. His chest was bare and he had bruises on his neck and the length of both arms, one cheekbone puffy and smashed, and a grimace spreading over his whole face. The two soldiers who were escorting him, bayonets fixed on the rifles slung over their shoulders, looked puny beside the prisoner, who still had the healthy appearance of a well-fed young man. The second boy was smaller and skinnier than the first, with his jacket neatly buttoned all the way up to the collar badges: a non-commissioned officer. His eyes were blue and he was staring straight ahead of him. 'That's him,' Grandma said under her breath, 'the one who requested...'

I felt admiration, not pity. Those two boys knew that death awaited them, only a short distance away, and they knew they were about to die before an audience of foreigners. They had made up their minds not to miss this chance to die bravely.

'Let's stand at attention,' Grandpa said.

I stiffened my back. Grandma let go of my arm and let her hands hang straight down at the sides of her skirt. Even Renato, who had certainly not heard Grandpa's words, stood at attention, his spade resting by his foot: he gripped it like a rifle.

They hanged them one at a time. First the tall one covered with bruises. No offer of a hood or a cigarette, no last words. Just the noose. It was passed over his neck by large filthy hands. The Czech climbed up onto the chair that stood next to the pole, under the hook, while a corporal scaled the wooden ladder, fastened the loop at the end of the rope to the hook, and jerked it twice to make sure it was good and taut. The first jerk of the rope prompted a moan, the second only silence. The baron turned for an instant and looked in our direction. His right hand rested on his holster. The corporal climbed back down the ladder and gave the chair a kick. I heard the simultaneous crack: of the rope, the pole, and the man's neck.

The man was kicking. He went on kicking for nearly a minute. Then he gave up, as his head bent over to one side until his ear grazed his shoulder. The troops looked on with the expression of those who had been tasting the same fetid soup for far too long. No matter how hard I tried to understand, I detected not a trace of either pity or contempt in that grim dead-eyed tribe. Perhaps as far as they were concerned nothing notable had happened. Here and there a few were even rolling themselves a cigarette. I saw a tobacco pouch being passed from hand to hand, and more than one pipe was lit. The soldiers stood silent.

The same scene followed, identical, for the second condemned man, as the first one went on swinging, though the oscillation grew slower and gentler with time. Something however disturbed the established liturgy. As the corporal was fiddling with the loop, making sure the rope was securely fastened to the hook, the young man with the noose around his neck spoke loudly and said something. What it was I couldn't tell, because he said it in the language of his people. But an infantryman, his arm bandaged to his chest, broke out of the crowd and, after hurling his cap to the ground with his one good arm, gave the chair a furious kick. The body tipped forward, face first, because the loop was not yet fixed to the hook and, given the man's weight, slipped through the hands of the corporal; he, in turn, lost his balance and came close to tumbling off the ladder. The baron, who already had his hand on his holster, instantly drew his weapon and fired as he took a step forward.

The man on the ground had a hole where his ear had once been. No blood, just a hole. From such a small hole – I thought to myself – a whole life had escaped: his parents' worries and efforts, all the fighting with his brothers and sisters, the barn-yard animals, his first night of love, the first time as a child that he had said the word 'me'. All of it gone, forever, and who knows where.

They got their hands under the body's arms and hoisted it up onto the pole and hanged it. I continued to stand at attention, but I shut my eyes. The other man was no longer swinging. Two slabs of hanging meat. Renato went back to his digging. A nod of the head and a couple of words from the baron scattered the men.

On the way back to the Villa, Grandma refused to take my arm, and refused Grandpa's proffered arm too, preferring to precede us, walking straight ahead. I turned to look back at the bodies lying there, motionless against the empty sky.

That evening I returned, alone, to the scene of the execution. I went back to the poles driven into the mud. The hanged men had been pulled down during the afternoon and Renato had buried them. The iron hooks seemed to be eagerly awaiting new prey. The birds were flying low and the song of the thrush was late in celebrating the dying of the light. The cannons were still firing in the distance, and every so often an aircraft engine made itself heard. I leant against the wooden fence and lit my pipe. I couldn't seem to tear my gaze away from those hooks. Suddenly I was caught off guard by an odd sensation, as if someone were spying on me. I turned around. Major Rudolf von Feilitzsch was standing there, motionless, not ten paces away from me, but he hadn't seen me. I thought I was seeing things, and I lowered my pipe. He too was staring fixedly at those black hooks, or at least I thought he was. His bandaged shoulder made him look ungainly, deformed. He lifted his right hand to the visor of his cap and stiffened in a military salute. He was saluting the shades floating before his eyes. When he caught sight of me, he immediately lowered his hand. He concealed his embarrassment with a smile and looked at me in that slightly childish way that I knew very well.

'So in the end that traitor got what he wanted. He wasn't destined for the noose,' he said in a firm voice. 'The truth is that all soldiers deserve a monument, a funeral song. There should be a day dedicated to the memory of every one of them, just for being soldiers, just because they were there doing what they had been asked to do. But there are too few days, too many dead men.'

Twenty-Nine

Someone was knocking at the door. I struggled to open my eyes, and I saw in the windows that colour that lies midway between night and day. Then I saw Grandpa's nightcap dangling over my nose.

'Someone's knocking.'

'I can hear,' I replied, my mouth gummy with sleep.

'Don't you think you ought to ask who it is?'

I sat up in bed: 'Don't you have a tongue of your own, Grandpa?'

'Whoever it is, it's better that they not hear an old man's voice.'

'Who is it?' I asked loudly, still sitting up on my crackling pallet.

'Renato.'

Grandpa nodded his head.

'Come in.'

The steward looked as if he hadn't slept a wink. He looked at me, then he looked at Grandpa. 'Get your britches on...Brian was shot down last night, they need us.'

I got up and grabbed my clothing from where it lay heaped on the chair. 'How did you find out?'

'That's none of your business,' he said and, staring at Grandpa, added: 'This time it could be really dangerous.'

Grandpa looked me up and down with his grey eyes, which were somehow able to express astonishment at even the tiniest things. The sky in the dormer windows was starting to turn pale. 'Do you feel like giving Renato a hand? You don't have to…'

'In two months I turn eighteen, Grandpa, and I'm Italian.'

Grandpa nodded and turned to look out the window, tugging his nightcap off his head.

As I walked down the stairs with Major Manca, I thought about him, about Grandpa. I truly did love that old lunatic.

We went out into the garden. Giulia was walking towards us. The top button of her blouse was undone and her bosom, heaving as she breathed, was threatening to rip off the second button. Her skirt let me guess at her ankles, concealed in her boots. She was about ten metres away, and already I thought I could smell her perfume. Renato too was eyeing her hungrily, but I was no longer jealous – quite the opposite, I felt as if I never had been.

'Did you think you were going to take off without me?'

'Well, to tell the truth…' Renato said.

'Everyone in Refrontolo knows that yesterday, at sunset, someone shot down the plane with the kingfisher on the fuselage.'

Renato started off. I let him go a few steps ahead so I could walk with Giulia, who was flaunting her contemptuous smile.

We crossed the park. Many of the wounded had been taken away during the night, and the road was crowded with lorries heading east, towards the old borders. In silence, we passed small groups of soldiers stretched out, or sitting on the grass, next to their sopping wet tents. Between the latrines and the hooked poles two stretcher-bearers wearing lab coats and fezes were burning bloody bandages. There was the smell of carbolic acid in the air, and the wind reeked of burnt flesh.

No one paid us any mind. There was no sign of armed guards around the camp. The only sentinel post that we saw, on the top of the hill, consisted of four soldiers who looked for all the world as if they were sleeping, with their backs resting against the columns of the little temple.

The clouds had cleared. 'If Brian survived, he's certainly waiting for us at his house,' said Giulia.

'He went down three kilometres north of here,' Renato's voice was tense, 'and I doubt he survived, but the only way to know is to go and see.'

Once we were within sight of the Englishman's hovel, the major ordered us to crouch down. We stayed there for a few minutes, silent and vigilant.

Renato was very still, and I could read in his face how hard he was trying to conceal his fear.

'I'll go,' said Giulia. 'If it's a trap...they won't shoot at a woman.' She started off before we could raise any objections.

I was about to stand up but Renato's hand stopped me. 'She's right, we can see the door clearly from here, we can get moving if we need to.'

'Are you armed?'

'Of course,' he said, with his chin in the grass, pulling a semi-automatic pistol out of his pocket. 'You see? It's just like the one our baron carries. Steyr makes pistols for officers who stay behind the lines, or for the top brass who only read about the trenches in the newspapers...Still, they never jam.'

Just then I realized that I was no longer afraid. 'Giulia is useful to us, isn't she? With someone like her around, there's lots of things they might not notice.' A recklessness verging on euphoria was beginning to sweep over me. If there was one thing I ought rightly to have been afraid of, it was that giddy feeling, but I lacked the necessary mental clarity and, for that matter, the wisdom. There was no one around, and the few groups of

men we saw, the lorries and carts were all heading for Conegliano, Sacile, or Vittorio; it was the 22nd of June, so we couldn't
have known that Boroevic's army corps had already begun to
fall back.

I looked at my watch and slipped it back in my pocket. I saw
Giulia swallowed up and then, a few seconds later, spat back out
by the door. She waved for us to come ahead. We stood up, our
britches and shirts dripping wet.

The smell of mould and damp wood washed over me. From
a shutter pushed ajar, a strip of light entered the room and cut
the floor in half. On a bench shoved against the wall, I could just
make out the silhouette of a man. I walked over while Renato
shut the door and shot the bolt with a screeching of rust. Giulia
had one hand pressed against the forehead of the man stretched
out on the bench. 'It's him. He tried to get up as soon as he saw
me, but he fell back down like a tree.'

Renato leant over his friend, pushing Giulia aside. Brian was
motionless, his eyes shut. Renato slipped his right hand under
the back of his neck and gently lifted his head. The Englishman
let a moan of pain escape his lips and his eyes flickered open:
'Oh, nice to see you...You wouldn't have a tumbler of whisky,
would you?' He flashed a row of white teeth.

Renato pulled open his jacket. He turned to look at Giulia,
who had wrapped her arms around me. 'We need some air here.'

Giulia went over to the window and pushed one of the shutters open, then immediately pulled it shut again, taking care not
to make a noise.

'What is it?' I asked in a low voice.

'Soldiers.'

'How many?' asked Renato.

Giulia held up three fingers.

Renato bent over Brian again.

'I've hit my head, right here, behind my ear, I can't stand on my legs; *gira*, everything's spinning.'

German voices, loud and raucous. Just a few paces away from the door. Renato gently laid Brian's head down on the bench, then stood up and went over to stand by the door jamb, pulling out his Steyr as he did so. With his eyes he signalled to the two of us to hide, waving the barrel of his gun towards a large black armoire on the far side of the room. I crept over to it on tiptoe and pushed Giulia into it ahead of me; she flattened back to make room for me. The door refused to close all the way, leaving a gap of two centimetres. I hugged Giulia to me and held my breath. The men outside were talking loudly and laughing. Perhaps they're just hooligans, renegades out looking for a place to hide from the fighting, I thought, maybe they're not looking for Brian at all.

I could feel Giulia's breasts warm against my chest. In the silence, I thought I could also hear Renato breathing and Brian gasping and wheezing.

Then the German voices fell silent. Giulia pressed her nose against my neck. I breathed in the scent of her hair. There was banging on the door, first once, then twice. Again, those voices, but now they were shouting. More banging, louder now. The door squealed – the hinges, then the bolt. A shout and the thud of a kick: the door collapsed with a crash. Two shots, then a third. I hurled myself out of the armoire. Renato was standing there pointing his gun, and he fired again, straight into the backs of the two men stretched out on the floor in front of him, face down atop the door wrenched off its hinges. The third man was a short distance further back, just outside the doorway, dragging himself on one elbow and spitting blood and saliva.

Renato stepped through the door and nailed him to the floor with a shot to the head. He reloaded as I hurried over to him. His movements were quick and sure. He looked around, like a hunted animal.

I turned to look at Giulia who had emerged from the armoire and covered her face with her hands.

'Give me a hand, we have to get out of here.'

'What about Brian?'

Renato grabbed the foot of the soldier with the hole in his head and told me to grab the other. We dragged him inside. 'Now they're going to be looking for whoever murdered their men,' I said, and I realized that Renato was no longer swaggering boldly: that frightened me more than anything else.

'You, Signorina, stand guard, over there.'

Renato went over to the Englishman who seemed to be sleeping, as if nothing at all had happened.

The light that came in through the door landed right on the murdered bodies.

'Hurry,' said Giulia, 'we need to hurry.'

Renato was sitting at the foot of the bench upon which the English pilot lay outstretched and unconscious. He held his head in his hands and was staring at the corpses. He stood up: 'These days a plate of beans is bigger news than a couple of gunshots, but for Brian…we need to take him up to the Villa, we have no choice.'

'To the Villa? But if they find him we're all—'

He cut me off mid-sentence with a glance. 'I can't abandon him.' For the first time since I'd met him, I saw dismay in his eyes. 'He'll get better, taking him up there is my concern… tonight. You two head back and tell no one about this.'

'Not even my aunt? She might be able to help us.'

'No one! Whatever happens, you were never here. Brian and I can take care of ourselves.' He gave Giulia a fleeting glance and Giulia threw her arms around his neck. Renato grabbed her by the wrists and pushed her away from him: 'Get the boy out of here,' he said. 'Now!'

Giulia stepped through the door without turning around: 'Get going, Paolo, are you deaf?'

I was certain – I was suddenly certain at that moment – that the two of them were lovers, or at the very least had been. I said nothing, I didn't even bid farewell, I just left with my eyes lowered. My head said: it isn't true, you're seeing more than you ought to here, you're making a mistake; but my heart knew.

I crossed the open ground between the house and the woods at a run, dragging Giulia by the hand. The air had again begun pulsing with artillery fire.

Part Three

Part Three

Thirty

THERE WAS SOMETHING VULNERABLE AND FUNNY ABOUT
Brian's face. I watched him as he slept, clutching his pillow.
Grandpa, next to me, shook his head as he stared at him: 'To
hide him here, of all places…Wouldn't the barn have been
better?'

Brian had been taken to the Villa, by night, by the steward
and an Italian prisoner who'd been helping him to dig graves
for the past few days. He'd had ten or so almost unbroken hours
of sleep, and that morning, the twenty-third, when the heavy
artillery finally fell silent, he woke up.

Soldiers went by along the municipal road that skirted the
garden, marching towards Conegliano, Godega, Sacile, and
Pordenone, where a rest awaited them. My aunt, who had come
back to the Villa, told us that the Hapsburg soldiers blamed
the defeat on their officers, not the unit-level officers but their
elderly generals with their trembling fingers, their hearts muffled
by compromise. 'They don't think much of the Italian infantry,'
she told us, reporting something she'd heard from the baron, I
imagine, 'though they have great respect for the officers in our
trenches; in any case, they fear our artillerymen, who tore them
to shreds.'

'The river fought its battle too; the high water destroyed
more bridges and footbridges than our planes could,' Grandpa

had said at dinner, 'and now the real trouble starts, for us, and especially for the peasants: an army with the breath of defeat on the back of its neck…We can kiss goodbye to the peace and quiet of the past few months.'

Brian opened his eyes wide. He looked bewildered. 'How do you feel?' asked Grandpa, leaning over him slightly.

The pilot didn't reply and looked at me: 'Thirsty,' he said. The water pitcher was half full and I poured him a glass. Brian took a long drink, which ended with a grimace. '*Pecàto*…too bad it's not whisky.' Then he burped softly and smiled, sitting up with some effort on the pallet. 'Feel better, too much better,' he said in broken Italian. 'Am we winning or' – and here he reverted to English – 'are we beaten?'

'The cannons can no longer be heard; Austria has gone home…on a stretcher,' Grandpa had regained his laughing face, 'and this time we gave *them* a licking!'

'*Sic transit gloria mundi*,' said the Englishman, biting down on the ample Latin vowels.

Two sharp raps at the door. Grandpa slipped off his jacket and threw it over the pilot's face, where he lay flat on the pallet. I sat down in front of him. The knocking came again, sharp and angry.

'Who is it?' asked Grandpa, with a fake sound of surprise.

The door opened slowly. Loretta came in, white as a sheet. 'They've arrested Renato,' she said in a faint voice.

'Renato?' Grandpa's face darkened.

Footsteps on the stairs. Heavy footsteps. Loretta stood aside. A sergeant entered the room, revolver levelled, and behind him came a private with a rifle slung over his shoulder and a bayonet in hand. The sergeant, a man with a small cascading moustache whom I'd never seen before, passed us in review, lowering his gaze to look at me where I sat, shielding the Englishman; then he holstered his gun and reached me in three paces. He looked me straight in the eye with his yellowish eyes. He grunted something I didn't understand. I didn't move but just kept looking steadily back at him. Then he grabbed me by the armpits and lifted me to my feet. His hands were hard, a pair of vice grips. He delivered a sharp kick to the jacket that lay in a heap on the straw pallet, and the jacket emitted a groan. The revolver whipped out of the holster. It had a long black barrel. I stood aside as Grandpa pulled me close to him. My legs were shaking. Then Brian hoisted himself to a sitting position and pulled the jacket off his face. The sergeant had kicked him right in the cheekbone. The Englishman got to his feet, his face disfigured by a grimace of pain. 'Coming,' he said, staring at the sergeant's revolver, while the private slipped the bayonet into a loop in his belt and grabbed him by the arm.

The non-commissioned officer barked something in Grandpa's direction; he remained silent but did not drop his eyes. Loretta burst into tears, covered her face with her hands, and ran down the stairs as the soldiers left, slamming the door behind them.

I threw my arms around Grandpa.

'We've been sleeping side by side for months...and this is the first time that you've hugged me, laddie.'

'What now?'

'We can only put our hopes in Donna Maria,' he said in a soft voice, walking over to the dormer window, which was open. Brian, staggering, was walking flanked by the sergeant and the private. We watched as they crossed the garden; they were going to the baron's office.

Thirty-One

IT HAD BEEN RAINING FOR HOURS. THE TABLE IN THE BIG
dining room had been set at the baron's orders; he had sent to
Pieve di Soligo for lamp oil. That afternoon, Teresa had ironed
the one lace tablecloth that cunning and a bit of luck had allowed
her to save from the looting. The invitation had been conveyed
to my aunt by a sergeant who, according to Grandpa, had the
charming manners of a guard dog on a chain. Von Feilitzsch
wanted the whole family to be present; and he even had the
impertinence to arrive a little late.

When he came in, I stood up, as did Grandpa, but the baron
gestured for us to remain seated. He flashed a quick smile at
the ladies and told the cook's daughter to go ahead and serve.
He knew that he would offend both Grandma and my aunt by
addressing one of our servants directly, and they both feigned
indifference.

From the roasted flesh the cartilage of three thighs protruded.
The two chickens were a gift from the baron and he, with a hint
of coquettishness, told how he had won the fowls with a single
roll of the dice from Major General Serda Teodorski, the commander of the garrison of Sernaglia. Loretta wore white gloves
as she served. The baron and my aunt, seated face to face, were
scrutinizing each other without a smile. My grandparents were
sitting at the two ends of the table, while I sat next to my aunt

259

and looked at the portrait of my great-grandma on the wall behind the major, set between windows illuminated by the last light of day.

Grandma always said that a gentleman reveals himself at table: whether that's a dining room table, a card table, or a conference table. We all sensed that, on account of the two chickens and their thighs, our reputation as respectable people would somehow be put to the test that night.

Loretta's hands shook slightly as she stood by Grandma's shoulder; the old woman took an angular wing and a small piece of breast meat. Then it was my aunt's turn, who opted for the risk of taking the thigh, leaving at least one of the three gentlemen present – I enlisted myself, duty-bound, in that category – with the burden of drawing on his native reserve of good manners. The baron hesitated for a scant second before plopping the thigh onto his plate, surrounded by a plentiful helping of boiled potatoes. Grandpa looked over at me, but I don't think he felt much pain as he renounced the opportunity to make the handsome gesture, and his plate too welcomed a juicy thigh, accompanied by its drumstick and a fitting portion of potatoes. Still, I was happy to console myself with breast and drumstick.

The clacking of forks filled the dining room. The weight of the humid air bore down on everything. Grandpa and my aunt never lifted their eyes from their plates, while Grandma ate as if it wasn't her mouth that was chewing her food, staring all the while straight at the baron who looked up every so often, pleased to see us all nicely subjugated, humiliated by our gluttony.

'We are indebted to you for the kind of dinner you'd expect in peacetime, Major,' Grandma Nancy said abruptly, as Loretta was making the rounds, serving second helpings.

'I was hoping to earn your forgiveness for the departure of

Donna Maria's horse,' the baron replied, with his customary courtesy, but I thought I detected a hint of resentment in his tone.

Taking a thigh and setting it on her plate, my aunt looked up: 'With everything that's happened in the past few days...Those two young men hanged from iron hooks, all those dead men, down in the church...Do you really think I have had time to think about my horse?'

'I thought...forgive me, Madame...but I thought that you liked horses more than human beings.'

'That's what I thought myself,' said my aunt, looking down at her food.

The reserve supply of good wine was down to the last drops and Grandpa had been reduced to diluting what wine he could get with water: 'It's going to be weak in any case, we might as well have plenty of it.'

'But here we're missing a thigh...and a drumstick,' the baron pointed out. 'There were two chickens.'

Loretta took a step backwards, straightening her back, and the serving plate in her hands trembled.

'It was my fault, Major,' said my aunt. 'The cook and her daughter shared them, at my invitation, of course.'

Loretta blushed. Then mouths and forks resumed the fervent ballet in which they were engaged, giving way to a silence that was barely broken by the clatter of metal, until an abundant salad of lettuce, arugula, and cress cleansed our palates.

Gradually, as the time approached for coffee to be served, small and increasingly anxious cracks begin to run through the silence. We weren't at all comforted by the thought that the chickens were a gift. 'Nothing comes free of charge, and a gift costs more than anything else': this was one of Grandpa's axioms, and for years Grandma had insisted that there was a mathematical basis to that truth. I knew that if Grandpa and Grandma agreed on an axiom – something that happened only rarely – it became a law of the universe, neither more nor less certain than the law of gravity.

'Ladies and gentlemen,' said the baron, patting his lips with his napkin and setting down his demitasse, 'I've invited you together to inform you that you're all under arrest.' The baron felt the need to pause at this point, and he filled the interval with a faint cough. 'Until matters have been thoroughly cleared up, your comings and goings will be kept under surveillance. You'll be able to go to chapel and to stroll freely in your garden and the immediate surroundings, you can even attend mass, but any other excursions you may make will have to be under guard, and I'm referring especially to you, Signor Guglielmo, and to you, Signor Paolo.'

'You have no authority, Baron, only power,' said Grandma as she got to her feet and looked the officer in the eye. 'Your only law lies in your weapons.'

'Madame, mind your tone! We've found three soldiers buried in the woods…and that pilot…we're familiar with his insignia.' The major was speaking in a low monotone; his voice sounded like someone else's, and he was enunciating his sylla-bles distinctly.

'Are you telling us,' my aunt broke in, 'that from now on this house has become a prison?'

'For a few days, Madame, but only for a few days, I hope. Tomorrow the Englishman and your…steward…will be inter-rogated by two officers from our office of counter-espionage.' The officer pretended to cough and then, after a pause that he used to raise his empty glass to his lips, he added: 'Apparently Signor Manca knows quite a bit about it.'

Grandma sat down again.

'Your severity, Baron von Feilitzsch,' said my aunt, 'is prompted by your anger at your defeat, and…it does you no honour.'

'Severity, in wartime, is a duty to which there is no alternative, Madame.'

My aunt stiffened. The portrait of Great-Grandma Caterina was suffused with the glow of the fading light of day. And while Loretta made the rounds of the room to trim the lamp wicks and light the candles, the major muttered something that no one understood. Then he looked me straight in the eye and added, in a clear voice: 'To conceal an enemy is a crime: neither your youthfulness nor your grandfather's advanced age constitute an excuse, nor will they serve to shield you. I had warned you, Signor Paolo!'

Grandpa cleared his throat, but said nothing.

'Then this is a very serious matter,' said Grandma, standing up again. Her pale face, looking as if it had been carved with a hatchet, riveted our attention. 'Indeed! My husband and my grandson hid an enemy of yours, but he was their – our – friend. You are an officer, you understand the meaning of honour, wouldn't you have done the same thing in their place?'

'Madame,' and the major got to his feet in turn, 'what I might or might not have done is of no importance. The soldiers who were killed were under my orders, and now it is up to me to do justice.' There was sadness, but also satisfaction in the officer's eyes, and he turned his back on us and left without clicking his heels.

Thirty-Two

THE SENTINEL STOPPED GIULIA AT THE FRONT GATE. IT was the first time such a thing had happened. One of the soldiers unslung his rifle and, holding the muzzle low, sketched out an indolent figure eight with the tip of his bayonet on the parched dirt. Giulia took a step back. The other soldier went to the *barchessa* at a run and re-emerged immediately with a young lieutenant, polished and buffed to a high glow.

The officer offered Giulia his arm, he stroked her hand, and together they walked into the garden. I realized that duty and love of country count for very little in the presence of a shapely bosom and the inviting smile of a woman willing to lead you on.

Grandpa, who had been shut up in his Thinking Den for the past several hours, joined me at the window. He leant out, at my side: 'Ah, Signorina Candiani...come, we need to talk.'

I followed him to the desk which – one of Teresa's miracles – was bare and uncluttered, with not even a speck of dust. Now Beelzebub reigned uncontested, a black and silent queen, while the little Buddha had been exiled to a place among the books and stacks of paper on a shelf.

'Look how neat it is, have you given up writing?'

'Writing...doesn't suit me. It's such an unnatural thing to do...my pages wander here and there, just like Pagnini's feet... Go ahead and light your pipe, I want the smell of your tobacco.'

I sat down and pulled out the leather pouch.

Grandpa's eyes were slow and dull. 'You know that they'll kill us, don't you?'

'The baron said that we are forbidden to leave the Villa, but… Aunt Maria has a certain amount of influence over that man.'

'Last night, that friend…of Maria's tried to warn us, don't you see? It's time to cut and run.'

I struck a match and lingered for a moment, with the flame just a finger away from my pipe.

'Those three soldiers…if Renato buried them in the woods… then we've been betrayed! And then the Englishman…We were reckless and foolish, and now Austria wants its pound of flesh.'

I raised a hedge of pipe smoke between us.

'Grandma has asked your aunt to begin negotiations with the baron. There is nothing that can be done for Renato, but perhaps for you…' The smoke thinned. Grandpa's eyes were glistening. 'You have to run away, go hide at Giulia's, you could make your way to Venice, perhaps even with her.'

'What about you? Grandpa, are you going to stay here and let them hang you? And anyway, how would I get to Venice?'

Knuckles rapped at the door. Grandma entered without waiting for a reply. 'Guglielmo…did you tell him?'

'We're talking about it now.'

Grandma looked me in the eye.

'Grandma…I don't want to escape. I don't even believe that the baron wants to kill us. He stormed and shouted yesterday, but I don't believe…'

'This is wartime. And in wartime, certain things…sentiments…everything loses importance, and everything becomes dreadfully clear. Renato and the pilot are going to be interrogated…harshly. It's not about the code or the information that we transmitted…Now the baron has three corpses to avenge.'

'But, when it happened…I was there! You weren't, Grandpa.'

Grandpa slapped his hand down on the desk. 'Paolo, listen carefully to what I have to say. There are three corpses with the two-headed eagle on the collar badges, and three Italians is what Austria is going to want to see dangling at the end of ropes. Renato is the first…but we are the ones who concealed the pilot, you understand? Von Feilitzsch has no choice…now…I've seen plenty of the world, but you…you need to take it on the run!'

Grandma nodded her head yes: 'I'll let you talk, you men understand each other,' she said, and left the room.

Everything had happened far too fast. I couldn't seem to make sense of things. And I wanted to see Giulia again. My pipe went out.

Grandpa stood up and opened the window behind him. 'Come, laddie, let's go for a walk in the garden, fresh air will help clear our heads.'

Giulia was deeply upset. She had used all her charms and wiles to learn what was going on, but she had been unable even to gain an audience with the baron. All we knew was that two officers were on their way to interrogate Brian and Major Manca. 'I know that one of them is tall and skinny with dark eyes, a medical officer,' she said, caressing my cheek and speeding up her stride a little. Taking advantage of the benevolent distraction of the soldier with a rifle slung over his shoulder, who was following us twenty paces back, we took refuge in the silkworm hatchery. There was still a hint of the disgusting smell of sulphur in the air, and there were streaks of soot on the dry walls. A breeze pushed in through the little window, and outside the soldier was strolling back and forth, whistling. '*Non più andrai, farfallone amoroso.*' I shot the bolt. 'It's the baron who set that guard on our heels,' and, as I was getting out the last words, Giulia was already kissing me. She kissed greedily, and I was even more voracious than she was. She slipped her warm hands under my shirt as I unbuttoned her blouse and lowered my lips to her hardening nipples. We tumbled on the cold damp dirt. Then she sat atop me and rode me until I couldn't see straight. I felt the churning blood inside me take control. That's when I turned over and got on top of her while she was still moaning. I thought I could hear the soldier singing his mocking little ditty still louder: '*Non più andrai…*' The blood was exploding in my groin, in my chest, in my temples. Until, stifling my shout of pleasure, I collapsed on top of her, with all my weight. That's when I heard two sharp blows at the door.

The guard was kicking the door and the bolt made the sound of a hammer. We jumped up and quickly got dressed, smoothed our hair with our hands, and looked at each other as if we were saying goodbye. We walked out and the soldier assaulted us with a phrase in German. Then he added, in a courteous tone and in fractured Italian: 'Now you will stay where I can zee you, official orders.' He'd done us a favour by letting us be alone, out of some sense of rascally camaraderie, perhaps, seeing that he next slapped me on the back while staring sly-eyed at Giulia.

We headed off towards the chapel. The Austrian let us get a dozen steps ahead of him before starting after us. Giulia, wordless, eyed me with a gaze that was really a question mark.

My legs felt rubbery and loose; I was happy. And happiness doesn't know or say, happiness just is.

Thirty-Three

'WHAT EVER HAPPENED TO KNOCKING?'

'The door was open.'

'Sit down.'

'Do you mind if I light up?'

The priest smiled. 'Afraid of a whiff of my bad breath?' He looked me right in the eye, as his fingers groped for his breviary.

I stuck my pipe back in my pocket. 'Now don't tell me that you're going to urge me to flee too.' The damp patches on the plaster sketched out an unknowable archipelago.

Don Lorenzo kept running his fingers back and forth over his filthy, tattered breviary. He looked into my eyes: 'There's no reason to get yourself killed.' He lifted the breviary high over his head and slammed it down onto the table; the violent noise made me jump in my chair. 'You're still just a boy, and you think that death has nothing to do with you, you think it's something for others to worry about. You're a fool, this is war, and they're out for blood, Italian blood to avenge German blood. It's a pretty simple matter, it's not hard to figure out. You're not immortal, my boy!'

I found the priest's sudden presumption offensive. But I also realized immediately that he was right. I wasn't afraid of death because I couldn't sense it coming, I had a whole life ahead of me, I had no time to die, I had too many other things to do.

That's why I'd been indifferent to the words of my grandparents.
I believed that death wasn't meant for me. I'd seen it, I'd caught
a whiff of its scent in that cursed church, I'd seen how it drops
down unexpectedly onto men shattered into bits by cannons,
I still had the death rattles of the wounded in my ears, I'd seen
those empty men, the ones whose souls had fled far away, who
stood there mindlessly staring at the canteen. I knew what war
was, and I knew fear from having experienced it myself, with
Renato and with Giulia, and I'd seen those boys, who weren't
much older than me, hanged by the neck until they were dead.
Still, I didn't believe in death. I looked at the breviary that the
priest's fingers were gripping and twisting. His lips were pressed
tight, his face was hard under his bald head shining with sweat.

'How am I supposed to escape? The river is swollen and
then…there's a man with a bayonet out there who follows me
everywhere I go.'

The sacristy door creaked behind me.

'Signorina Candiani!' The priest was surprised. Giulia sat
down beside me.

'Now I understand…Paolo, you don't want to disappear…
you want to be with her. So it's the devil who has made you
blind and deaf!'

Giulia brushed my cheek with the back of her hand.

Don Lorenzo got to his feet and levelled his forefinger at my
face: 'You foolish refugee from a penitentiary, you need to stop
thinking with your groin, your brain is up…' – and here he leant
forward to touch my forehead with his sweaty finger – 'here.
Not down there.' His finger, propelled by the length of his arm,
pointed at the place he meant.

I stood up, but Giulia placed both hands on the table, her
fingers spread like duck feet, and looked me up and down:

'The priest is right, you need to run away, and fast, the clock is ticking!'

Don Lorenzo turned to look at the blank wall. 'God Almighty be praised,' he said. He touched the little crucifix hanging there. He ran his fingers through his hair and then started pacing from one end of the sacristy to the other, eyes fixed on the floor. This was his sacristy. An inland sea, whose shores, inlets, and grottoes he knew intimately. He skirted sharp corners and objects without looking. 'Yes, the clock is ticking...' and he went on walking, brushing past the armoire, the credenza, the tripod that held the holy water, his head bowed, his hands gripping his breviary. 'Perhaps the baron...is only waiting for Major Manca to give in and talk.' His voice betrayed his anguish. He stopped, stuffed the breviary into a pocket of his tunic and placed his fists akimbo on his hips, as his gaze grew flinty: 'Paolo...if they question you, remember to say nothing. They'll think you're doing it out of pride, out of patriotic loyalty, but if you try to lie they'll trip you up, make you contradict yourself.'

He pulled open the drawer under the table and extracted an envelope that he tossed in front of me, grim-faced. 'This is for you, a letter. It's sealed. Carry it with you in your jacket wherever you go, from now on. This was an idea of your aunt's: it says that you are serving your novitiate in this parish...Even if there's a war going on, we're still the Holy, Catholic, Apostolic Church...and Austria respects us! If they catch you while you're trying to escape and find it on you, it could save your life, they won't shoot a novice, or at least, they'll take him to his parish priest...first.' He suddenly swung around towards the door, as if he'd sensed a threat. He pulled a foot-long knife out of the drawer. The blade glittered in his hand, then next to his face, over his shoulder. He let it fly.

271

A thump. There was a rat, twisting and writhing, pinned to the foot of the door. Giulia and I exchanged a glance, speechless, horrified.

'I got you, you bastard!' The priest cackled and, under his breath, added: 'Not all bastards come from Vienna.'

That corpulent priest was as quick and agile as a street thug. A smile stretched from ear to ear and his enemy, whether that be Satan or the Austrians, was gone: in that rat, run through and through, its paws stretched wide in the sign of the cross, the priest saw not a creature from the sewers, but a delicacy to be savoured at his blessed leisure.

I slipped the letter into my inside jacket pocket. We said farewell and left by the church door, avoiding the door where that foul creature had been crucified.

Thirty-Four

'NO ONE WANTS TO TALK STRAIGHT ANY MORE, NO ONE WANTS to look me in the eye.' Teresa punctuated her lament by spitting into the piece of canvas she was using to shine the copper pot. 'Donna Maria wants you, laddie, out in the garden.'

My aunt linked arms with me. I was becoming her shadow, she asked me to accompany her everywhere. She was afraid of losing me, and she was afraid of losing Grandpa. We walked in silence. The afternoon air was sticky, filled with cicadas and small birds. Nearly all of the soldiers had left; many of them, at the field marshal's orders, were helping the peasants with the harvest, which luckily promised to be more abundant than expected. We skirted the latrines and then the family cemetery. There lay the Valt, Rainer, Bozzi, and Spada families. They lay beneath Istria stone, an ironed sheet barely greyed by the rains, here and there marked by saxifrage and winter ice. The graves of the recently buried soldiers, in contrast, with the turned soil already green with weeds, made me think of the unmade beds in a barracks abandoned in haste at dawn. My gait sped up a little, and my aunt kept pace.

'May the Good Lord console their mothers.'

'Grandpa thinks that you care more about the horses, and he's not the only one who thinks so.'

'With the horses, I can let myself go.' She looked at me and

smiled, squeezing my arm. 'You men weren't made to understand things; you're summoned to action by a primordial
instinct; all you care about is doing things and taking care of
things; you're afraid to stay in one place.'

Then, I'm not even sure how, we started talking about books,
and the topic turned to my mother, who used to read to me until
I fell asleep. I already knew how to read perfectly well at age
five, but I liked to have books read to me. I don't think it was
sheer laziness; it was because I liked the sound of my mother's
voice, and the way she could make me feel the presence of the
characters, their fear, their strength. I even asked her to read to
me when I was nine and ten years old. She enjoyed herself, and
often she'd dream up her own stories, while pretending to adhere
to the book, down to the smallest details. I let her do what she
wanted, I'd never object, except when she tried to soften certain
instances of cruelty that I actually savoured with great relish.

According to my aunt all books worthy of the name tell the
story of a continuous flow that resembles the glittering of river
water. 'It's not the destination of the journey that matters...I
don't read books to find out how they end...The glittering that
dazzles me along the way, that's what I like. Look at our Villa, our
roads filled with invaders, nothing will ever be the way it was,
not even after we've kicked them out of our country, these foreigners. Everything passes and everything leaves its mark...and
yet everything remains, we slowly fill up with wrinkles and...'

I was about to start crying, and I covered my face with my
hands. My shoes lay still in the grass.

My aunt embraced me. 'You won't die,' and she took my
hands away from my face, gripping my wrists so hard that it
hurt. 'You aren't going to die because I won't let you, and that's
a promise. If it's the last thing I do, I won't let the baron kill you.'

I dried my face with my fingers. We looked at each other. Those eyes, green and still, knew my terror.

'What about you, Aunt Maria, do you want me to run away too?'

'Yes.'

'Get across the Piave…but how?'

'Tomorrow or the day after, at night, alone. Grandpa agrees. He'd only slow you down and after all…after all they're determined to hang a Spada, but you're just a boy.'

Aunt Maria pointed me to the chapel. 'Let's go in for a minute.'

The door squealed; it had been some time since the hinges had been given their regular dose of oil. The dankness swept over us with its pungent coolness. Far from the altar, the baron was on his knees in a corner. His eyes were half-closed and his head was bowed slightly forward, both hands together. My aunt told me to wait where I was. She crossed herself and, lifting the hem of her skirt just slightly, knelt down next to the baron.

They began talking intently in a low buzz, even though there was no one to overhear. Her lips were close to his. They ignored me. They stood up, I pretended to be praying raptly, tipping my head slightly forward, and to make it more convincing, I muttered under my breath, 'Angel of God, my guardian dear…' As a child, I was somewhat concerned at the thought that God didn't have time for me, that He had too much to do taking care of the other matters of the world, so I had become fond of that other, little, private god all my own, my guardian angel. 'Be at my side, to rule and to guide,' I said, in a slightly louder voice.

'Amen,' said my aunt. At her side, grim-faced, stood the baron.

'Signor Paolo…No one must know of this meeting. Three men have been killed and now three men must die. You are just a boy…but so was one of those killed, only two years older than you. I don't like ordering executions, but this is the law of war… and then there's that pilot, the Englishman.'

'He was wounded and we…we are Christians.'

'Colonel Herrick is an English pilot, and anyone who conceals an enemy…is an enemy of ours, and we kill our enemies, because that is what armies do, they kill…now…as the commander of the garrison, I have a certain degree of freedom… some leeway, not much, but let's just say that I could manoeuvre sufficiently to save someone's neck…'

'Someone's…neck, Major?'

My aunt gripped my arm and forced me to look at her: 'If you know who killed them, you have to tell the baron! You have to tell him, you and Grandpa had nothing to do with it!'

Could it be that my aunt was asking me to betray Renato?

'That little serving girl came to talk to me.'

'Serving girl?'

'That's right, the young one, not the cook but her daughter, she came to see me and she told me things that I can't pretend I never heard.'

Loretta must have followed us that day.

'That servant,' the major went on, 'told me…'

'Loretta is an idiot and the things she says count for nothing.'

The officer stared at me through slitted eyes: 'That idiot, as you call her, led us to—'

A soldier threw open the door. It was the attendent. There was a brief exchange of phrases. The major crossed himself hurriedly and left without a word of farewell. My aunt took my right hand and squeezed it hard: 'The officers from the secret service have arrived…' We too left the room, and we saw them immediately.

They looked pretty beat up. They were white with dust to the tips of their caps. The first one, a barrel of a man – he was sweating like a pig – was walking up the lane through the park leading a lame mule by the bridle, while the second, tall and skinny, had dismounted from a bay horse that, even without the weight of its rider, seemed overburdened by its Pantagruelian pack. I offered my arm to my aunt and we joined them outside the stables, where they were handing over their mounts. As we approached them, my aunt slowed down and contemptuously offered her right hand to the fat man, who displayed the full amphitheatre of his teeth with a gap in the middle. His eyes were tired, hard and sky blue, and when he grasped my aunt's hand it was only her prompt withdrawal of it that kept him from smearing it with a streak of slobber. The other man, in contrast, chose to snap to attention and click his heels, so that a cloud of dust billowed over us, snapped into the air by his patched trousers.

'Not even during wartime…do you go around looking like that,' said my aunt, lengthening her stride. When we got to the gate, we tried to leave but the two sentinels standing guard lowered their rifles to bar our way. We heard one bayonet scrape against the other.

Thirty-Five

GRANDMA WAS SO INTELLIGENT THAT SHE SOMETIMES FORGOT to understand her cook. Teresa, for her part, was sufficiently intelligent to overlook '*li strambéssi de la paróna*' – the eccentricities of her mistress. But when Grandma's silence lasted a whole day, even Teresa felt called upon to comment. '*Paróna, el diambarne ve ciàma?*' Mistress, is the devil calling you?

Grandma stopped drinking her hot lemon concoction and replied with a bitter smile. She found it hard to put up with the idea of sharing confidences with the woman who administered her enemas. But the tragic present had swept away all boundaries. 'That major,' said Grandma with reddened eyes, 'wants to hang us from hooks.'

There was a crash. Fragments of enamel covered my shoes, along with a splat of hot water, while the pitcher rolled until it hit the moulding. Standing motionless only a few steps away from the table she'd just cleared, Teresa was swept by a shiver, her face bright red, while silent tears rolled down her cheeks. Grandma stood up and did something I'd never have believed if I hadn't seen it with my own eyes: she threw open her arms and gathered the cook in an embrace. And the two women hugged, their breasts crushed together, melting together their tears and their rage in the muggy heat of that July evening.

I entered the church, hoping to leave the grey chill behind

me. Once I got over the sudden impression of darkness and absorbed the pleasant, damp coolness of the place, I glimpsed Grandpa sitting in one of the last pews. With the evacuation of the wounded, the church had turned back into a church again, with a few candles flickering under the statues of this saint and that. It had taken elbow grease and the muttered imprecations of a platoon of church ladies to restore it to a decent condition.

To see Grandpa sitting there was like finding a hair in one of Teresa's cakes. I went over and sat down next to him. He looked at me without smiling.

'Your reputation as a priest-hater is starting to wobble, Grandpa.'

'To everything there is a season, and today doesn't go hand-in-hand with sarcasm…I'm thinking, *thinking*, and I prefer to do it out here, in the fresh air,' he glanced at me again, 'where that cop of a grandmother of yours isn't going to come bothering, plus today she's doing her enema and she woke up with her heels on backwards.'

In his voice, which he was doing his best to keep on the usual ironic note, I heard anguish and bewilderment. I decided to leave him to his thoughts. I hadn't had time to walk down the last step of the church courtyard before I heard the priest's heavy footsteps behind me. 'Signor Paolo, wait.'

I turned around. A whiff of his breath curdled my nose and my guts. When he caught a glimpse of the look on my face, the priest stepped back. 'Yesterday, the non-commissioned officers invited me to eat with them at the inn, and the soup had…more grappa than soup. And they sang songs with lyrics like Krieg-Sieg, Not-Tod, and then they said things, things that bode ill for us…for you.'

He turned to look at the soldier with his rifle slung over his shoulder; the man had just hoisted his butt up off the bollard on which he'd been sitting, he never lost sight of me for a second. 'Let's take a little walk together, Paolo...just out to the gate... This morning, at dawn, your servant, Loretta, came to say confession.' He linked arms with me and we headed off towards the Villa, while the soldier followed us, moving at a slow, short gait. 'Those damned people know everything, you understand, everything. I can't tell you anything more...sacrament of the confessional...but they know everything!' We were walking with our heads bowed, and we shortened our gait to make the walk last longer. 'Austria wants to exact a tribute of Italian blood... Last night they loaded the Englishman onto a lorry heading for Udine. And they're not giving Renato anything to drink...in this heat...he's toughing it out...but...after all, they already know everything. And Donna Maria has less power than she thinks, certainly much less than she hopes. After losing the battle, they certainly can't afford to let their immediate backlines deteriorate into a threat.' The words were galloping over each other in their haste to get out of his mouth, as if he were afraid of losing some: 'The idea of executing the Spadas...a family of nobles! Dogs don't eat dogs, the peasants say.'

'But maybe...'

He stopped and jerked me around so that I was forced to look at him. 'What I know is that they won't be satisfied with hanging the steward.' He started walking again, slowly, slower and slower, head bowed: 'They won't touch a hair on the ladies' heads...but you...you need to run for it, tonight, tomorrow could already be too late.'

There was something in the priest's voice that was at once desperate and imperious.

'They're spying on everything, even my mail, and I can't send you to a monastery…you have no choice but to get to the other side of the river.'

At the gate there was a single soldier standing sentinel. He looked weary, a boy no older then eighteen or nineteen, skinny as a stick, with a heavy helmet riding low over his ears.

'Tonight, come to church to hear vespers, at the end of prayers I'll hear your confession in the sacristy, and you can escape from there. After that…well, after that, good luck, and may the Good Lord protect you.'

Thirty-Six

I SPENT THE AFTERNOON TALKING OVER THE DETAILS OF MY escape with my grandparents and aunt. The priest's plan was discarded immediately because the baron had also put a guard at the sacristy door. I shoved a blanket, a knife, a burlap sack with some dried polenta and a tin full of red marmalade into my rucksack.

Grandpa and my aunt and I studied a military map that was two years old, but it was all we had. I told them that Renato had taught me how to move through the woods, an exaggeration they pretended to believe. Grandma told me to leave town immediately, and warned me not to try to get in touch with Giulia: the baron had just had her arrested and shipped off to Conegliano with a Red Cross convoy.

When we made our farewells, late that night, the moon was out, huge, round, and riding high in the sky. 'You won't get lost.' Grandma hugged me with all her strength, but she held back her tears, as did my aunt. Grandpa concealed how moved he was by talking about his Gibbon and his Beelzebub: 'I'll leave them to you, you'll certainly be able to make good use of them. Join up with the deserters at Falzè, that's where they cross the river. But if everything goes wrong, just head north, towards Follina, and from there towards the mountains, and you'll see, you'll find someone willing to help you...' There was a strange confidence in Grandpa's voice; when I wrapped my arms around him and hugged him with crushing strength, I felt him choke back a sob. We were just a footstep away from the door that gave onto the courtyard; the women of the house had left us alone. Grandpa twisted the knob that extinguished the flame in the lamp. I pulled open the door and slipped out. I didn't hear the door shut behind me, and I didn't turn to look, knowing full well that Grandpa was standing there, behind me in the dark, watching the first things I would do.

I ran all the way to the wooden fence, crouched down, and stayed there, listening. The first patrol went by only a couple of minutes later. I had to figure out how much time I'd have to reach the woods. There was a stretch of open ground I'd have to cover and it was such a bright night. I pulled out my watch. I saw two soldiers making their rounds outside the wooden fencing, circling the enclosure in an anticlockwise direction. The first patrol I'd seen was making its rounds inside the fence, and walking along a clockwise circuit. They went by me at a distance of less than three metres. Two minutes and forty seconds had passed between the first patrol and the second one. I took off after waiting for fifty seconds. To make sure that they didn't spot me, I'd have to reach the dense vegetation in no more than a minute and a half. I ran. I didn't bother to keep my back bent to stay low. Once I reached the treeline I stretched out on the ground, face down. I lay there motionless, scanning the bare terrain behind me. I struggled to catch my breath. I watched as the patrols went by. Hapsburg punctuality had worked in my favour. Once my heart stopped racing, I got up and started walking. I hiked for two, perhaps three hours. Every so often I would stop and stand listening to the woods, but each time I did that a wave of anguish swept over me. I saw two owls and

I frequently heard animals moving in the leaves, but I know that those weren't the dangers I needed to worry about. I was hunting for certain paths I'd travelled with Renato. I stopped by a large rock. I spread out my blanket and wrapped myself up in it. I pulled out my knife. I waited for a shaft of moonlight to catch the blade, and I sank it into the soil, not more than a foot away, well within reach. I gnawed on a bit of dried polenta and I gulped down a bit of marmalade. Then I swallowed a mouthful of water and wine – my canteen was still full. I didn't want to get sleepy, but I needed to rest my legs. The wind shaking the highest branches and the rustling of the underbush kept me alert. From there, I could see several stars, three, perhaps four, that the moonlight was unable to dim. I tugged the blanket around me. The air was warm, but a chill rose from the damp soil, and I could feel it in my spine. I heard an owl hoot. Then an odd thought caught me off guard: my father. I saw him smoking his pipe in an armchair in the drawing room, serious, focusing as he read a book that smelt of mould. I never thought about him. I'd thought of my mother, yes, more than once, I'd even thought I'd heard her voice in the long hours of partial sleep, but since the time of the Great Disaster the image of my father had vanished from my mind. Grandpa had done his best to take his place, and he'd succeeded, even if Grandpa was an old friend to me, while my father had always been, and continued to be in my memories, a stranger: merely a collection of details that my memory had set aside. In this corner I could hear his voice; in that other corner I caught a whiff of the scent of his cologne, or glimpsed his serious face, lost in a secret elsewhere that, with a rough and off-putting manner, he even protected from my Mamma's gazes. 'Now I'm alone, hunted, and afraid,' I whispered in the darkness. I took a deep breath, filling my lungs.

The smell of damp earth, moss, and wet bark pervaded me. The stench of the war was gone. And I dropped off to sleep.

There was light all around me when I came to. I'd fallen asleep with my hand wrapped around the hilt of the knife. It was Grandpa's knife, and the hilt was made of a warthog tusk filled with twenty centimetres of steel, the edge of which showed on both sides. It sliced like a razor. I wondered, as I got to my feet, whether I'd ever be capable of using it to kill someone. I shook off the cold by banging one shoe against the other. I drank a little water and wine and ate a healthy helping of dried polenta after spreading marmalade on it with the blade of the knife. I felt strong. I'd survived the dangers of the night. I stuffed everything back into the rucksack, except my knife, which I slid at an angle into my belt. By day it was best to avoid the trail. I studied the map, but it wasn't going to be much good to me unless I left the woods. I was suddenly afraid that I was lost. I tried to get a look at the sun, which had just risen, and used it to orient the map: the proper direction was south by southwest. I started hiking again.

Every half an hour I halted, to check my direction and make sure, by remaining perfectly still as I listened, that no one was following me. Around noon, with the sun straight overhead, I caught the smell of the river. The forest was dense at that point, and I could see neither fires nor houses. I heard the sound of planes overhead and hunkered down. I wasn't capable of distinguishing the insignia. These weren't scout planes, but a dozen fighters. The noise made me think of SPADs. I got back to my feet and followed my nose towards the river's smell. After a few minutes the woods thinned and opened out into a clearing. There was a house.

I crouched down and remained in hiding. I'd learnt a lot of things from Major Manca. To calm my nerves I took a swallow of water and wine. And I kept listening, my eyes peeled for anything. The shutters on the house were open. I was too far away to see inside, but someone was there. It wasn't just the smoke that told me so: all around the place, the grass had been mown for a distance of thirty paces and, on one side of the house, under the overhang of the roof, there was a stack of firewood. Leaning against the firewood were a spade and a rake, their handles crossed together like newlyweds in a church. The door swung open and a woman emerged with a wicker basket; she went over to the stack of firewood and filled the basket. Just as she was about to go back inside, she stopped on the threshold and turned around. She couldn't see me, but out of caution I retreated a little further into the shadows of the thicket. She looked in my direction, like a doe scenting danger before seeing it or hearing it. She set down the basket and loudly called a name. Another, much older woman came out, her back curved, dressed all in black. The old woman went back in and emerged with a rifle. She started walking towards me. I didn't move. The old woman was coming closer. By now she was just ten paces away.

'Come out into the open! Who are you?'

She had a courteous voice.

I slowly rose to my feet.

'I'm alone, I'm unarmed.'

'Come out of there! Hands up high.'

I put my rucksack on my back, raised my hands, and came out into the open. The rifle barrel was aimed straight at my chest.

'What are you doing here? Why are spying on us?'

'My name is Paolo Spada, I come from Refrontolo, and I must have got lost.'

'Give me that!' She jerked the rifle barrel at the knife that I had stuck into my belt.

'I'm looking for help, I don't want to do you any harm.'

'The knife!'

She came closer and aimed the rifle right in my face: 'Take it out with your left hand and keep your right hand up in the air.'

I did as I was told. When I handed it to her, she took it without removing her right hand from the trigger, but the weight of the weapon forced her to lower the muzzle. For a second I felt certain that, if I moved quickly, I could have ripped the rifle out of her hands.

'You're just a boy…' she noted, though there was no surprise in her voice. 'Come in and walk behind me, I don't want any sudden moves.'

I walked in under the curious gaze of the younger woman, who was Giulia's age, with raven-black hair and large light eyes, the colour of tea. She smiled at me and I smiled back.

Inside the house, the odour of poverty was notable for its absence. And that was an odour that I knew all too well. In Venice, I'd smelt it in homes I'd entered, on occasion, with a servant visiting her family. It had something to do with the odour of ashes, chickpea soup, and inadequately dried clothing.

What struck me immediately was how neat the room was. Four chairs stood around the table, set for a meal. There was water in a glass pitcher on the table. A carafe of wine. Silverware flanking two white dishes. Set over the fire was a steaming pot; under the table, a hemp mat.

'Put down your rucksack,' said the young woman, as the old woman lowered her rifle. 'You're probably hungry, I imagine.'

I nodded my head.

'Luisa, take our guest to wash his hands.'

It suddenly dawned on me that I must have looked like a wild man. Luisa waved for me to follow her. I walked through a bedroom that was bare but clean. Then Luisa showed me to a vat full of water, over which dripped the spout of a pump. On a counter stood a bar of soap.

'I'll leave you alone here…The latrine is back there, you have to go out that door.'

'*Grazie.*'

I felt an almost childish sense of relief: I was eager to entrust myself to those two women, and to let them trust me. I washed my face, hands, and neck, and I went out the back door to use the latrine.

We ate in silence. A soup whose contents remained a mystery to me but was delicious. They'd even baked some bread made of white flour. Until I ate I hadn't realized just how hungry I was. Luisa had a warm, round face, a faint blush to her cheeks, while her mother had chilly features, carved into hardwood.

'Who are you?' Luisa's voice was just as warm as her face.

'I'm running away…from Villa Spada, maybe you've heard of the place.'

'A hospital, during the battle,' said the mother.

'Ah…yes…I know who lives there…'

The mother gave her daughter a glare that shut her up: 'Luisa listens to all the gossips, when she goes into town, and there's a lot of nonsense in circulation.'

'What town is this, where are we?'

'Just a kilometre from the Soligo river, the waters have subsided, you could get across easily…I could accompany you… You're heading for the Piave, aren't you?'

'No,' said her mother, 'it's out of the question…If your father were here…'

I turned to look at the rifle that stood leaning against the door jamb.

'The fighting took my husband. The highland of the seven villages, in 1916...and that's not his rifle, a deserter sold it to me...in the days after Caporetto.'

'Let me go, Mother, I'll take him as far as San Michele al Ponte and come back; it's not a long trip, I know the way.'

'We've suffered enough...We've been left alone here.' The woman stood up, brushed back her white hair, and started clearing the table, wordlessly.

'I'll do fine on my own. All I need are some directions, I have a map.'

The girl had got up to help her mother. I joined her at the sink to pitch in.

'Your eyes look tired, lie down on the pallet over there, we'll wake you up as soon as it's dark.'

At sunset, the woman gave me a bag of dried figs and a slice of hard cheese wrapped in a length of sky-blue canvas. She returned my knife with a slap that was meant to resemble a caress.

'I can't give you the rifle...My daughter will see you to the levee along the Soligo, but I want your solemn promise that you'll send her back to me as soon as you get there.'

'Rest assured, Signora...and *grazie.*'

'Good luck to you then.'

Luisa led the way, and she kept a fast pace. We slipped into the depths of the woods almost immediately and for ten minutes we walked north, then we turned left, skirting a clearing. It was quickly getting dark. Suddenly, the vegetation forced us to slow our pace; I pulled out the knife and cut a few thorny branches. We made our halting way forward for another fifty paces or so, then we heard the river and stopped for a moment, relieved to listen. Luisa turned around and lifted her finger to her lips.

I didn't hear anything. Only the water flowing past. 'What is it?' I asked in a low voice.

'Germans, straight ahead…twenty paces.'

We hunkered down close together, behind an especially big tree.

'Odd, there's usually never anyone here, they fill their canteens upstream from here.'

'Let's wait…maybe they'll leave.'

She put her mouth to my ear: 'Yes, the water is shallow here, and the current isn't strong, the river widens out.'

After a couple of minutes the soldiers started talking. They were Hungarian, their voices reached us loud and clear. They were fiddling around with a camp stove – one of those little metal devices that run on oil – and we could smell coffee and the odour of their sweaty jackets because we were downwind.

'Go back to your mother, I'll get across as soon as they leave.'

'I'm not going to leave you alone now of all times. Maybe they sent them down especially to guard the ford.'

To my surprise, Luisa pulled a knife out from under her skirts, with a long slender worn-out blade.

'What are you doing?'

'Best to be ready,' she whispered, and stroked my cheek with her left hand.

She didn't even give me the time to be surprised. She waved for me to follow her. We moved slowly, on all fours, getting steadily further and further from the river. Once we felt safe enough, we walked upright, keeping the river bank on our right. By now, we had the darkness to protect us, but it made it almost impossible to travel, as the moon hadn't yet risen.

Luisa turned around and waved for me to get down.

'Let's wait here,' she said.

The air was chillier than the night before. It had rained in the mountains. Luisa wrapped her arms around me: 'This'll warm us up.'

'What are you doing?'

'It's cold...what, are you afraid of going to hell?'

'No, not of going to hell, but...'

She moved away from me. 'Maybe you're right, it's time for me to get back to my mother...good luck.'

I must have nodded off. I got to my feet. I no longer had the knife. I looked for it in the grass, then I peered inside the ruck-sack. With a sigh of relief, I found it and slid it into my belt, then I headed for the water. The moon was low, riding just over the hilltops that rose on the far side of the Soligo. The river bank was deserted. I sat down and waited until I could clearly see the far bank. I didn't know how deep the water was at that point, but the current was slow and I noticed a log lying crosswise in the middle of the river.

It wasn't hard to get across, except for the last few metres, where the icy water unexpectedly rose almost to the middle of my chest. Once I was on dry land I realized how cold I was. I was shaking, but I couldn't run the risk of lighting a fire. I stripped off my clothes, wringing out each article one by one, dressed again in haste, and set off: I needed to get warm.

The moon had lit up the face of the river, and I followed the stream until I saw the black shape of the bell tower of the church of San Michele al Ponte. I slowed down and my right hand found the hilt of my knife. From there on I could run into enemy patrols. I skirted the town, staying close to the forest. The windows were dark and no smoke rose from the chimney pots, as if the houses had all been abandoned. I hastened my steps, because the silence of that place was scarier than the noises of the woods.

Thirty-Seven

EVERY SO OFTEN I STOPPED TO CHECK THE MAP. I WAS TRY-
ing to economize on my use of matches, which I only lit very
carefully, after lying bellydown on the earth, behind a rock or
else using my rucksack as a shelter: a tiny flame can be seen for
a long way. I was no longer walking in the woods, now I was
on the cart road, and I only abandoned it when I glimpsed the
campfire of a bivouac.

I was pretty sure that I was midway between Materazzo
and Donegatti, but I couldn't seem to make out the rooftops
of Trame, which ought to be straight ahead of me, according
to the map. I walked on for another half an hour, returning to
the road to make better time. My feet were shattered, my legs
were rubbery, but I was determined not to stop. I came to a
ruined town, a tumbled heap of rocks, fallen walls, and blocked
lanes. That's why I'd been unable to see those houses: Trame
was nothing but a pile of rubble.

'Italian cannons.'

I swung around, grabbing the knife from my belt. I barely
had time to focus on a tall, massive silhouette before I felt my
wrist seized in a vice grip. I choked back a shout.

'Hurry, get off the road, there's a patrol not three minutes
from here.'

In spite of the pain in my wrist, I hadn't dropped the knife, and I proudly slipped it back into its sheath.

We hurried away from the rubble of Trame and in less than a minute we were in the woods. Immediately afterwards we saw the patrol go by, four soldiers sloshing with alcohol, barely able to stay on their feet. They were walking slowly, making no noise. It took a good five minutes before they were out of sight; they were zigzagging as they went, in grim silence.

'They're not on a happy drunk,' said the man.

'Who are you?'

'We've met. Lieutenant Muller.'

'I remember, you took me to Renato…Major Manca.'

'How is he, have you heard anything?'

'Under arrest.'

'I know that, he's not the only…friend we have in Refrontolo.'

'The reason I ran away is—'

'Save your breath, I can fill in the rest.'

He stood up. I did the same.

'We can't go though Falzè or Mirra. We'd do better to cross the Soligo and head for Mercatelli, we can find a boat there.'

He started off without another word. He walked quickly, so fast that I had a hard time keeping pace with him, and he never turned to see if I was following him. Suddenly, he stopped and looked me in the eye: 'Do you know how to shoot?'

'I can identify a weapon at first sight, calibre and make…'

'Answer me!'

'No. I've never fired a gun at anyone. I've only shot a few bullets into trees…one time I killed a roe deer with my grandpa's hunting rifle.'

The lieutenant pulled a revolver out of his pocket and put it in my hand.

It was heavy.

'It will never jam on you, just cock the hammer and aim at the chest, the centre of the chest.'

He set off again. I walked after him, hefting the revolver as I went. I went over it, trying to find out everything I could with my fingers and, where possible, with my eyes. 'It's a Tettoni, an import, am I right?'

The lieutenant said nothing but just started walking a little faster.

When we re-crossed the river, day was already dawning. We stripped bare and wrung out our clothing. The lieutenant handed me a hunk of cheese and I held out the tin of marmalade. Then we ate some dried figs. We set off again with our wet clothing sticking to our skin. We needed to move quickly and find a hiding place before the bivouacs stirred to life: we were too close to the Piave to be able to walk around in broad daylight.

I kept the revolver in my left jacket pocket so I could grab it faster with my right hand. I'd managed to keep it from getting wet. Even if I was afraid of it, something drove me to want to use it, to be forced to kill in self-defence. I could feel a dark, molten mass building up inside me. I was strangely aroused.

We stopped around nine. We gulped down the last few pieces of polenta and shared out the cheese that Luisa's mother had given me. For a few minutes, as I sat eating, I thought back to her, and Giulia. Their faces appeared before me, and I was astonished that I couldn't clearly remember the moments of pleasure, only certain scattered details that poured into my head, only to slip quickly away.

'Get down!'

I flattened myself to the ground behind a log. I saw that the lieutenant had his revolver in his hand. I pulled out mine. The voices were coming from the trail. Two, three. One voice was a woman's. Then a shout: 'No!'

I looked at the lieutenant; he was tense, motionless, listening.

The German voices exchanged short phrases, imprecations. The woman had started screaming, and her screams grew louder and louder. From his position the lieutenant could see, but I couldn't. I craned my neck: a soldier had grabbed a girl and was dragging her into the ditch. The other soldier was laughing and tagging along; he laughed and laughed.

'They're raping her,' I said.

'Don't move.'

The screams died out, resumed, then fell silent.

'Aren't we going to do anything?' I didn't realize I had raised my voice.

'Shut up!' said the lieutenant, but it was too late. A soldier was coming towards us, his rifle levelled, bare-chested with his belt undone.

The lieutenant emerged from his hiding place and fired. The soldier fell forward, face first. I was frozen in place. A second shot made me jump. The lieutenant dropped right in front of me. I looked up. Not five metres away, the other soldier was taking aim. He was practically naked, that's the only thing I noticed – that and the rifle barrel pointing straight at me. I lifted my left hand to the gun that I was already aiming and I pulled the trigger, once, twice. The soldier fell to his knees, his rifle splayed in the middle of the path. Without thinking twice, I walked towards him. He had one hand pressed against his chest and the other held high, in a gesture of surrender. His eyes were large and dark. And he was looking at me. I stopped two metres away from him. He was looking at me, shaking his head *no* as blood oozed down onto his belly, his exposed genitals.

My right hand was shaking. Once again, I raised my left hand to the grip of the revolver, but the barrel of the gun refused to stay still. He was looking me straight in the eye, with one hand held high: '*Nein*,' he said, '*nein!*' and he shook his head *nein* too, over and over again. He wouldn't stop. I don't remember pulling the trigger, but the bullet blew his face wide open and blood splattered everywhere.

I took a step back. My mouth was dry. I looked around. There was no one on the trail. I leant over the lieutenant. The rifle shot had splayed his throat open right up to the chin. His eyes were staring at the sky, opaque. I closed them. My hand was no longer shaking.

The girl's jacket was torn. She was barefoot. Her hair and her face were smeared with mud, and her features were pinched in an expression of extreme alarm. Her eyes were fastened on my revolver. I realized I still had it clutched in my hand; I pocketed it and took the hand the young woman was holding out to me. We started running, running through a field of corn and there, in the middle of the field, we stopped to catch our breath. I dropped to the ground and, from a sitting position, took off my rucksack. She squatted down, pressing her hands between her legs with a grimace of pain. The shocks of corn rustled overhead.

When her grimace faded, I saw that she was pretty. She had a high forehead, unlined, and pronounced eyebrows, blue eyes that looked straight ahead of her. Her fine nose was well shaped. Her fleshy lips were pressed together in anger and disgust. Only then did I realize that she couldn't have been older than sixteen or seventeen, at the most.

'What's your name?'

'*Ti…te parli da sior…e ti gà le man de quei che no gà mai lavorà.*' She said in dialect that I spoke like a gentleman, and that I had the hands of someone who'd never done a day's work.

'My name's Paolo, what's yours?'

'You don't need to know my name.'

Without the lieutenant there was no point trying to reach Mercatelli.

'I have to get to the river,' I said.

'I'll take you.'

She was on her feet and walking before I could get the ruck-sack back on my shoulders. It wasn't easy to keep up with her. She moved through the corn, and then through the woods, like a wild animal whose den was there.

The darkness and the pouring rain forced us to take shelter in an abandoned sheepfold, about thirty metres above the cart road that ran parallel to the rampart of the levee: the Austrians had fortified the levee and equipped it with machine-gun nests, plazas for light artillery, and munition dumps. From there I could see the oxbow curve of the river Piave. Not even the furious rain was loud enough to drown out the sound of the river flowing past.

'If it keeps up, it'll be hard to get across the river. The water is quick to rise.'

She told me not to try to cross here, where soldiers might see, but to go further on.

I objected that I needed to rest for a little bit, that I didn't have it in me to take another step. The girl nodded and slipped all five fingers of her right hand into her mouth to let me know she was hungry. I shared with her the cheese and the marmalade, greedily gobbling down my portion. Then I stuck my cupped hands out so that they'd fill with rain. I'd lost my canteen. The girl asked me to give her my knife. My objections met with complete indifference: without that knife she wasn't willing to stay near me. When I gave it to her, she waved it in my face, then she demanded that I put the revolver under the rucksack, and then she pretended to go to sleep. I tossed and turned on the straw. I was drenched, exhausted, and – enveloped in the stench of manure – I did my best to get my thoughts straight.

Thirty-Eight

WHEN I OPENED MY EYES I TURNED TOWARDS THE GIRL: SHE was watching the raindrops bounce off the stone enclosure of our shelter, while the tip of the knife blade struck the upright supporting the lean-to roof overhead, rising and falling in time with some inner cadence. She didn't look at me, and if she had, she wouldn't have seen me. Before me I saw the blank eyes of Lieutenant Muller, then the soldier I'd killed, even though he was trying to surrender, even though his eyes, his face, and his voice kept telling me not to. I imagined a noose tightening around my neck. The girl kept driving the tip of the knife into the wood.

I picked up the rucksack to get my revolver.

'Where did you put the revolver? My revolver!'

The girl kept chopping the tip of the blade against the wood, faster and faster. She was far away, she couldn't hear and she couldn't see. I tried to speak to her in a gentle voice. I spoke in dialect. But she went on driving the knife into the upright supporting the rafter. I looked outside: the rain was falling harder and harder, and the river was roaring.

I felt a spurt of something hot on my face, I clapped my hand to my cheek and I turned to look at her: she'd sliced her throat open and the blood was still spurting out. Suddenly, I couldn't breathe, and I shouted: 'No-o-o!' I yanked the knife out of the girl's rigid hand. I don't know if she was already dead, she was no longer convulsing, and that cut throat gaping open was something horrifying to behold. I ran outside. I wanted the falling rain to wash me clean; my face and hair must have been covered with blood. I cleaned the blade by rubbing it on the grass. Luckily, there wasn't a soul in sight. I was shaking, I was sobbing. Finally I fell to my knees. And I stopped crying. I wanted to stay alive. I couldn't seem to think. It was raining so hard that I couldn't even see the cart road, and I practically couldn't hear the river any more. I started walking, after sliding the knife under my belt. The rain was blinding me. I walked for ten or twenty minutes; I wanted to put some distance between me and all that blood. Without meaning to, I found myself standing in the middle of the cart road. I crossed the road and headed for the river. The barbed wire fences were in the midst of the stream, and at this point, the levee had collapsed. I realized that I had wound up amidst the enemy's defensive structures. They seemed to have been abandoned, the bunkers were empty. The Austrians must have taken shelter in some nearby house to stay dry. I knew that all the civilians within a distance of two or three kilometres had been evacuated. I ran my tongue over my lips. I still had the taste of blood stuck to my skin. I rubbed my face with my hands and I drank water by tipping my mouth up towards the sky. It was out of the question to try to ford the river. I was a good swimmer, but I knew that stronger swimmers than me had drowned in that river. I ventured down the levee that had been washed away by the current. There was barbed wire sticking out of the water here and there, and I imagined the spine of a sea monster lying on the riverbed. I went into the water, putting just my shod feet in first. I wanted to test the strength of the current. I had no alternative, I decided to run the risk.

'I have to get past that stretch of wire fence and stay on my

feet while I'm doing it,' I said to myself, 'otherwise I'm finished.'
The water was up to my knees, I'd got within a metre of the iron
barbs. 'I can do it, I have to!' I said.

A shot.

'Halt!'

I turned around. There were two rifles aimed at me. I looked
at the river, I saw an islet.

'Halt!'

I felt someone grab me by the shoulders. There was an arm
around my neck. I twisted free. There was a sudden pain, dull
and powerful, in the middle of my chest.

The pain climbed up from the back of my neck to my forehead and my temples. I was lying flat on my back. I moved my
hands. Straw. I half-opened my eyes. There were men standing
and sitting just a few paces away from me. I couldn't hear any
sounds. I'd gone deaf, completely deaf. I laboriously lifted one
hand to the nape of my neck. It hurt. I was wet. I could feel
water in my shoes. I was cold, I was trembling. I could feel the
tremor in my chest, on my lips, in my elbows, in my knees. And
I slipped into a state of lassitude that shut my eyes.

A sharp jerk brought me awake, and I realized that there was
a very heavy blanket on me. To the right and left I saw two rows
of seated soldiers, four on one side, five on the other. Someone
spoke to me, but it was in German and I didn't understand. A
second thump confirmed that I was riding in a lorry. The sun
was shining. I saw it because the grey canvas was raised on both
sides. I was breathing fresh air. I hurt all over.

The soldiers stood, silent. Every so often one of them would
look at me. I lifted my left hand to my belt: the knife was no
longer there, and deep inside I blessed the girl who had hidden
my revolver from me.

The lorry was moving slowly, but it kept bouncing and jerking and every jerk was a stab of pain to my chest and back. I shut my eyes. They'd certainly searched me, someone must have read and deciphered Don Lorenzo's letter, that is unless the water…I hadn't even read it, because I wanted to make sure the seal remained intact, but the curate's words surfaced in my mind: 'If they catch you, this could save your life.' Perhaps they were taking me back to Refrontolo. That's good, at least I wouldn't die among strangers.

Thirty-Nine

BY THE TIME I WALKED INTO THE BARON'S OFFICE, I HAD regained my strength. My head, chest, and back no longer hurt. They'd locked me up in a little room over the inn for a couple of hours, across from the Villa, and no one had come to visit me. I had eaten two mess tins full of boiled potatoes and a round-eyed corporal with reddish whiskers who reminded me of an owl had offered me 'a drop of dark-red wine'. During the months of occupation, he'd learnt the language of the peasants, and he spoke it fluently, practically without accent; he was in the same line of work, and he told me about his home near Salzburg; he also said that the peasant girls along the Soligo were more beautiful than so many Madonnas, and a little less holy, luckily for him.

The corporal led the way into that office wallpapered with maps of the Veneto region, of Trentino and Friuli, where the old boundaries were outlined in pink and the rivers were a bright blue; on the desk, which looked as if it had just been neatened up and had a vague scent of wax, a portrait of the emperor with his young son sitting in his lap enjoyed pride of place. The non-commissioned officer had me sit down in front of the baron's desk, then he stepped back a pace and stood at ease. And so we found ourselves contemplating together, in the room's dusty half-light, the sepia-tinted photograph of Karl I, over which the evening light, filtering through the dirty glass, extended a grey film.

The baron entered the room like a mountain stream in spate. He sat down without glancing at me. The collar of his jacket was unbuttoned. He dipped his pen in the inkwell and signed a sheet of laid paper densely covered with an angular handwriting. Only then did he raise his head and look at me. He pushed his shoulders against the backrest and caressed the armrests. He dismissed the corporal with a wave of the hand.

'So we're supposed to believe you're a novice? Whose idea was that letter? Your grandmother's or Madame Maria's? That doesn't matter...I'll lock you up with your grandfather and Major Manca, I have no choice in the matter.' He swivelled the chair so that his back was turned to me for a few seconds as he looked at his emperor, and he added: 'The corpse of a young peasant woman was found...in a sheepfold by the river Piave, not far from where you were arrested...Would you happen to know anything about it? She had a revolver hidden between her legs...two of the bullets in the cylinder had been fired, one of which, in all likelihood, had killed a private...You see, Signor Paolo...there aren't many revolvers of that kind, it's Spanish, and I know that the Italian army imported quite a few...but I'd imagine you know nothing about it...' There was a half-smile playing about the baron's lips. 'Ever since you became a novice, weapons are no longer of any interest to you, I believe...That peasant girl was lying dead less than three hundred metres from the point where you climbed down into the river...Her throat was cut with a knife blade, and you had a knife on your person when they caught you...An unusual hilt.'

I said nothing.

'You can smoke...I have some tobacco...'

'I'm afraid I lost my pipe in the river.'

The major opened the desk drawer and pulled out a small burlap bag tied up with a hemp cord. He loosened the knot with studied slowness. He thrust in his hand and pulled out a balled-up handkerchief, then a leather pouch and my Peterson pipe. He leant against the backrest and looked up at the ceiling. 'This is what they found in your pockets, Signor Spada.'

My fingers were trembling, I felt my face turn red, and my head was spinning a little. I cleared my throat and doing my best to speak in a normal voice, I said: 'Yes…I'd be glad to have a smoke…but the tobacco…must be drenched.'

'Try some of mine…I almost never smoke…Only when I feel too much alone.' And the baron pulled a tin box with a yellow label out of the drawer: 'It's Dutch tobacco, blond and dry.'

'Thanks,' I said. 'I hope the water didn't ruin the pipe.'

'It's a handsome pipe, I'd admired it already…before… your escape…Is it a gift from a woman? Perhaps the Candiani woman, your friend?'

'No. I got it from…Grandpa.'

'Ah, your grandfather…a singular man.'

I filled the Peterson with the baron's tobacco, and my hands were no longer shaking, but it was as if my head were stuffed with cotton balls. I lit it, hoping that it would help calm my nerves, but my hands started shaking all on their own. I blew out the smoke in a puff meant to draw a curtain between me and the officer.

'Well, what do you say, did the Piave ruin it?'

'No, it draws wonderfully well.'

Von Feilitzsch looked at me with a mocking smile: 'Wonderfully well? Yes, I believe you…'

Suddenly it dawned on me: I hadn't had the pipe in my

pocket, I'd left it in the rucksack, and I'd left the rucksack in the sheepfold, near the woman with the slit throat.

'I have nothing to say to you, Major,' and I stuck the lit pipe into my pocket, snapping the lid shut with the heel of my hand.

Two sharp raps at the door. The corporal stuck his head in: 'Fräulein Spada.'

'Paolo! God be praised!'

The baron stood up.

'It's all right, I'm fine,' I said, walking towards my aunt. As she embraced me, I felt myself being swept away by a sense of euphoria, as if a weight had just lifted.

'Have a seat, please, Madame.'

The corporal closed the door behind him on his way out.

My aunt pushed her chair against mine and gave me a long, searching look. She'd overdone it a bit with her eau de Cologne. Anguish and tenderness were battling in her gaze. On the San-gallo lace that lined the collar of her white blouse was the enamel pin with the soaring swallow and the blue sky: she was con-vinced that the motto in the oval – *Je reviendrai* – brought her good luck.

'Even far from here, your boy got himself noticed.'

'He ran away…who wouldn't have done the same thing, Baron? And you won't even let me see Uncle Guglielmo…how is he? Donna Nancy is worried to death.'

'He's all right, I gave orders to allow your cook to make food for the prisoners…including Signor Paolo…now.'

Aunt Maria caressed her temple, and her fingers lingered over a hint of a wrinkle that marked her forehead.

'Madame, I know why you've come here…uninvited.'

'I have to talk to you.'

'After the time we spent together…Our walks, the horses…' The baron held out his right hand until it almost brushed her left hand, lying white upon the black desktop. 'Yes…our horses…but here we all have to make a special effort,' and he withdrew his hand while hers slipped down onto her knees. 'I…I, Madame…' the baron's face twisted slightly, and suddenly he seemed to have aged ten years, 'I saw my men come up in that river, bob to the surface out of that water, like your potato gnocchi in the pot, do you understand me, Madame? Gnocchi in boiling water. By the dozens, by the hundreds, the men I commanded came up, bobbing to the surface like gnocchi, my soldiers…and General Bolzano, my general, lost his mind. I watched him lose his mind, he wound up among the Italians, killed with his own dagger, and so I led the soldiers back myself. The retreat over the river…the pontoons torn to piece by the mortar fire, and the planes with their machine guns strafing us over and over.' With his right hand he covered his mouth. Then his whole face. 'I saw my boys die, platoon by platoon, as they were boarding their boats, as they ran over the footbridges from one islet to another, and the screams…the cannons were tearing everything to pieces, everything, bridges, pontoons, soldiers… and the heavy machine guns…those bodies in the stream…' – he looked at me for an instant, lifting his face from his hands – 'young men like you…all that blood…bobbing to the surface like gnocchi.'

Then her eyes sought his. And his eyes saw hers, those dark green eyes, underscored by black crescents.

'Madame, listen…Soldiers were murdered in occupied territory. The law of war demands that I have Major Manca executed by firing squad, along with his accomplices, your uncle and your nephew. That's without adding that, during his escape, the young man…further aggravated his…' Our gazes met for a moment. 'I am responsible for the lives of the soldiers I command. There's the laws of war…and that serving girl, whatever her name is' – and he waved his right hand as if shooing away a fly – 'told us the whole story, in front of my officers. That girl hates you, she wants to see you suffer, all of you. Major Manca claims that he did it but…I found the Englishman in your attic, with Signor Guglielmo and Signor Paolo.'

'Baron, listen…Rudolf…listen to me, I beg you.' Leaning slightly forward, my aunt placed her fingertips on the edge of the desk. 'Renato's life for the lives of your soldiers…why can't that be enough? It was him' – and she swallowed a gob of spit – 'not Uncle Guglielmo who killed those men, and Paolo here… he wouldn't even know a revolver if he saw one…'

The officer cocked an eyebrow.

My aunt stiffened her back and placed both hands on her knees. She was trembling.

The baron stood up and put both hands behind his back. Then, with three taut paces he rounded the desk and came even with my chair. Leaning forward stiffly, he placed both fists on the black desktop and lifted his eyes to the portrait of his emperor. The sepia was faded, Karl had both arms around his little archduke who was staring out wide-eyed at the world and holding his right hand pressed against his father's knee while his left hand vanished into the large hand that, on the ring finger, bore the dynastic seal. The young emperor wore the uniform of a Hungarian general and at the centre of his chest, bedecked with medals, was the Prussian Iron Cross. His gaze wasn't especially imperial, it was just the gaze of a concerned father looking at his little boy. There was no joy in the monarch's features: the rotund face, the jug ears, the fleshy, unsmiling lips. The baron lifted his fists from the desk and opened both hands, palms upward, pointing to the photograph. 'Madame,' he said, 'do you think that this man looks like a sadist, or particularly bloodthirsty?'

'No, he has the face of a good man.' Donna Maria stood up and looked her adversary up and down. 'A sad man...and gentle.'

'I think he's a good man, but the soldiers still love Franz Joseph, even if he uncorked this bloodbath' – and he bowed his head for a moment – 'they don't feel protected under Karl. You see, Madame,' and the baron resumed his seat behind the desk, while my aunt remained standing, 'I believe that subjects are like children, and soldiers more so than anyone else. They want a firm hand on the reins, a hand that never falters, they can never forgive that...and they're right, because dithering and indecision, in wartime, cost lives, and pity can seem...and believe me, often is...like the doctor's pity...what is it you say in Italian... the doctor's pity lets the wound become infected...right? If the prince gives the impression that he doesn't know what's best for his soldiers, for his realm, then the magic of the royal throne flickers out and everything collapses. Do you understand what I'm trying to say, Madame Maria?'

His eyes sought hers. And her eyes responded, green, absolute.

'Rudolf, I beg you' – her voice was breaking with emotion, as I did my best not to breathe – 'at least spare this boy...If your emperor were here, he wouldn't deny this pardon.'

The baron coughed into his hand. He stood up, but immediately let himself fall back onto his chair. With nervous fingers, he pushed aside the sheet of paper that I'd seen him sign and, after clearing his throat, he said in a firm voice but without looking up: 'I can't.'

'Baron' – my aunt's voice had darkened and roughened – 'I'm not indifferent to you, there is a' – she looked down and shot me a glance out of the corner of her eye – 'a certain feeling…that has grown between us, in these terrible, endless months. But now I'm imploring you for a favour, imploring you! You can't deny me this. You mustn't, there must still be some way to…'

The major looked her in the eyes: 'There isn't.'

I was tempted to say something.

'He could escape,' said my aunt, 'and they could start looking for him the morning after he runs away…That would give him a few hours' head start. Austria would still have her revenge, Renato is a soldier; my…uncle is a Spada, you'd have their lives to set an example!'

'There's already been an escape, and it cost more blood. Innocent blood.'

'Rudolf, I beg you, I'm on my' – my aunt looked at me, and put her hand on mine, without sitting down, and then looked the baron straight in the eye – 'I'm down on my knees.'

'I have murdered soldiers to avenge, and an enemy pilot who was given safe harbour, and—'

'Major, war is murder, always and invariably…all you want is to set an example: killing gentlemen isn't the same thing as killing peasants! After the battle, the troops' morale has hit bottom; your high commands fear the uprising of the populace, once the final clash has begun, isn't that right? Moreover, you'll have an easier time confiscating the crops if the peasants see their masters dangling from hooks high atop poles. That's what you think, and that's what the field marshal thinks, that's what General Teodorski thinks. But by refusing to show mercy, you contribute…I'm talking to you, Baron von Feilitzsch, because you're here…You contribute to the destruction of the civilization to which you and I…and this boy…belong, and that civilization is more important than the fate of the Hapsburgs themselves, or the House of Savoy. You won't like the world that is coming into existence any more than I will: there will be no room for pity, nor for that gentility of manner that we care…so much about. With your severity you think you're doing justice, but it's the other way around, Baron, you're just blazing a path to a time when a corporal will claim the title of general, and the people will make fun of us, of you…because we're children of the horse, not of the plane…' My aunt was a dynamo, and I sat glued to my seat, listening in astonishment. 'But when our courteous manners are long forgotten, when the superfluous is viewed with contempt and haste rules the world, foolish brutal men will wield the sceptre and therefore, when the universal deluge washes over us, there will be no ark in readiness.'

'Madame…Madame…'

Donna Maria went to the door and pulled it open. But before she left she turned around with stormy eyes: 'God damn you to hell, Rudolf von Feilitzsch!'

Forty

THEY LOCKED ME UP IN THE SILKWORM HATCHERY, ALL alone. No delicacies from Teresa: they gave me black bread, dried polenta, and very weak coffee. The smell of sulphur that still impregnated the plaster mixed with the odour of the tobacco that the red-whiskered corporal had given me. It smelt slightly of the stables, but I didn't really mind. That man had taken a liking to me. 'You're a good kid, you know…even if your nose looks a Genoa jib.' One time he stopped to talk, and he told me that one of his sisters had died, that he hadn't been able to attend her funeral, that in Vienna these days they'd been eating dogs and smoking straw for months, and that it was just stupid to carry on the war.

The window was tiny, the glass was filthy, and the light that chased away the darkness in the morning was just a strip of dust containing all the colours of the rainbow. Everything had happened as if in a movie, where you can see the images but the reason for what happens remains, at least to a certain extent, unknown. I felt responsible for Lieutenant Muller and for the peasant girl who had slit her throat with my knife. I thought about Giulia, Grandpa, and Renato. I thought about death, and the noose that awaited me. Sometimes I'd stand up, put my face just a few centimetres away from the wall, and breathe slowly. Then the picture of the Austrian I'd killed would surface in my mind. He'd tried to surrender, he'd tried to say no, with his face, with his eyes, with that raised hand, with the other hand pressed against his wounded belly, but I'd fired anyway, and I'd enjoyed doing it. I told myself that it wasn't true. But what I remembered was a sense of euphoria, not pity: I'd acted confidently, obeying a will that I had a hard time believing was mine, and the sensation of triumph was there, horrifying. Then I'd throw up, spitting saliva and remnants of undigested food into the bucket we used for our excrement.

I remained there three days until, on the morning of the fourth day, the corporal with a red moustache came to get me, accompanied by a soldier with a rifle slung over his shoulder. We crossed the courtyard: it was drizzling and there was a good scent of wet grass. I thought about Grandpa, and I decided that certain people are like hundred-year-old oaks. When they're felled, they leave a hole in the earth, a hole that the seasons struggle to erase. The corporal opened the storeroom door with a key that was a hand's width long. The soldier shoved me inside and shut the door.

'I can't say I'm happy to see you again.'

It was Renato's voice, followed by Grandpa's embrace.

In that big room, the harrow and the plough sat rusting. The floor was rammed earth and there was a small high window from which you could see the treetops and a small patch of sky. There was also a pallet made of dry straw, which we managed to make serve as a bed for three, as well as a table, four stools, a pump that spat water only when it felt like it, and a tin pail that served as a chamberpot. There, for years, the demijohns of olive oil and small barrels of vinegar had been stored, and the whitewashed walls gave off a rancid stench that turned the stomach, though I quickly became accustomed to it. The meals, thanks to our cook and Grandma's silver coins, were reasonably plentiful and tasty, and Renato was starting to recover. The baron had learnt very little from him, but what little he'd learnt was enough for him to make a good show with his superiors.

Teresa was the angel of victuals, our tie to the outside world. Grandma and my aunt had been permitted only one visit, and they had devoted their time with us to Grandpa's ankle, which was swollen: when they arrested him, he had resisted, and he had a swollen cheekbone too. The medical officer had stopped by for a minute and a half, and he'd said that what was needed was ice, ice and time, but the icebox was out of order and the time remaining to us little and shrinking.

'There's that serpent of a daughter of mine, who's no longer my daughter,' Teresa would say each time she set the mess tins down on the table. Until finally one day Renato, tired of hearing her grumble, whispered something in her ear. Teresa glared at him with black thunder in her eyes, then lowered her head and for the first time left the room without a *diambarne de l'ostia* and without asking if there was anything she should report back to the mistresses.

When I told the story of my escape, I said nothing about the death of Lieutenant Muller, I just said that he had managed to get away. Renato understood that I was keeping something from him, but he pretended he hadn't. He told me that Giulia was a spy too, that she'd been working with him in the I. S., and that my suspicions were foolish. I, in turn, pretended to believe him. Grandpa always looked at me with large, sad eyes. And I never knew what to say to him.

We did what children, ostriches, and savages do: we said nothing about our impending executions, we talked only of the errors made by General Cadorna, the Church, and the Widow's

Sons; and about the Socialists and the downfall of the Romanovs.

Time passed slowly in prison.

At night, I heard Renato talking to himself, and Grandpa snoring as he'd never snored before. In my dreams – and I dreamt with my eyes wide open as well as when I slept – I saw Giulia, and those few, intense, precise moments of passion came back to me, as I watched and listened to them again. The thought that she wasn't the woman for me, that I'd never wanted to grow old with her, did nothing to console me, I still loved her, I loved her even though she'd betrayed me.

Certain memories crushed me with their weight: I'd seen the Czech kicking as he dangled from the hook, and the other one shot, and all those men who'd died in the church, all those broken men begging for water, and who knew what they were seeing. And I'd killed, too.

The things I'd miss would be the electric smell in the air after a summer thunderstorm, I thought to myself, the smell of new mown grass, the smell of Teresa's *spezzatino*, and the smell of Giulia's hair. From time to time I'd think of how upset Grandma would get because I was a donkey when it came to arithmetic, and how my aunt would take the slightest phrase as a pretext to slip into one of her brown studies.

We took turns sweeping the cell with a sorghum broom, while the major and I shared the duty – from which Grandpa was exempted – of cleaning the tin pail at the pump, a pump that heehawed vigorously but produced very little water.

At first light, the guard brought us a mirror and a razor. Grandpa let Renato shave him, but Renato preferred to do his own shaving. I also managed to take care of my own shaving, even if the mirror was a fragment no bigger than my hand. And when the guard, who watched over the ritual with his rifle at his foot, confiscated the mirror and the razor, he pretended – he did it every time – to listen to our complaints about the broken pump.

It wasn't long before I started keeping my ration of grappa for myself instead of giving it to Grandpa. I started to develop a taste for alcohol. I liked that sense of giddy sleepiness, the pleasant illusion of freedom you get from slightly disjointed sentences. Finally, one morning, around seven – we'd just had our coffee – we were driven out of the cell by three bayonets: one poking at each back. I assumed the time had come.

The cool of the night had vanished. And the white sky was turning light blue. We understood that our turn hadn't yet come when they marched us up to three caskets: the baron wanted to make us witness the funeral of the murdered soldiers. They lined us up, between the latrines and our little cemetery which had only seven headstones of ours, surrounded by thirty or so untidy mounds of dirt.

'They're empty,' said Renato, in an undertone.

'What?' I murmured.

'Those coffins.'

They were made of roughly nailed deal planks, and the infantrymen who carried them weighed less than the boards themselves. They lowered the coffins into the grave one atop the other. The baron put together a brief speech and the platoon snapped to attention. All told, the ceremony couldn't have lasted more than ten minutes. They took us back to our cell.

'How did you know they were empty?'

'With this heat and without ice, how could you keep three corpses? Freshly unearthed some time ago, to boot.'

'Have you seen the road?' asked Grandpa. 'White, empty, without so much as a barking dog, without a single cat on the

walls. And outside the stables there were three men with car-
bines at their feet and bayonets.'

'The soldiers must be starving,' said Renato.

Grandpa and Renato talked about politics a lot. They did it to
stave off the fear of death. At first I found it offensive, because
they tended to exclude me from their discussions, but in the end
it wound me up and every so often I'd weigh in myself, on one
side or the other.

As far as Grandpa was concerned, the king had staged a coup,
sidestepping parliament, and had driven us into that bloodbath
even though he was well aware that Italy lacked both the military and financial resources to sustain a long war – and even
the deaf and the blind knew, back in April and May of 1915,
that this was not going to be a lightning war. Renato retorted
that the king had had no choice, that Italy relied on France and
England for its supplies of raw materials, from wheat to coal, to
say nothing of the debt of honour that the country had towards
Queen Victoria's empire.

'France and Prussia helped us out, but only at two points…
there was a common advantage…but you can't forget that that
follower of Mazzini, without the English, would never even have
been able to land at Marsala.'

I jumped in: 'Look out, if you touch Garibaldi, Grandpa's
liable to…'

But that time Grandpa's counter-attack failed to drive deep,
after a moment of hesitation that robbed his offensive of all its
impetus, he almost seemed to go over to the enemy's side: 'Maybe
Italy is a failed ambition…nothing more than a geographical
expression…Metternich was right…and the plebiscite that legit-
imized the annexation of Venice to the newborn Kingdom of
Italy was a fraud: who really believes that so few voted against it?'

'What!' Grandpa's outburst had lit up Major Manca's eyes and unshaven cheeks. 'A geographical expression...yes, absorbed into the soft belly of the Kingdom of Sardinia, though. Don't forget that Victor Emmanuel II' – and here Renato's pipe went out – 'never changed his name when he became the King of Italy. He was the Second when he was King of Sardinia and he's still the Second as King of Italy. Ah, yes' – and he lifted the lit match to the pipe – 'we hardly created ourselves with our hands, we were not our own makers, we Italians...well, the Piedmontese...maybe...'

'A little royal house from the mountains with a big appetite for revenge...but, Major, you say that the English wanted a monarchy that could settle matters with the Roman Catholic Church, and the Masonic Grand Orient supposedly lent a hand...I could admit you're right, in fact, I do, but you see... history doesn't work that way, with such well-oiled mechanisms, neat situations...it would be too convenient.'

Renato wasn't caught off guard in the middle of that no-man's-land by that offer of a truce: 'If you want to argue... you need to simplify matters...and a mortal vice-grip clamped down onto the pope at Teano. The pope's worst nightmare had come true: there was a single king ruling the entire peninsula, and so things turned ugly...from Teano to Porta Pia took just ten years.' He emitted a nice big puff of smoke into the air between Grandpa's face and his. 'If our Teresa were here, she'd say: *Diambarne de l'ostia!*'

The idea of bringing the cook into the discussion, and calling her 'ours' had been a masterful move: and so, with a more convincing smile than was customary with him, Grandpa acknowledged that the major certainly knew how to talk. At that point, I caught the ball on the first bounce and sealed the armistice: 'The unification of Italy was a whiplash from the war between Protestants and Catholics.' It wasn't original with me, but Renato pretended not to know that.

'Compliments on the concise summary, laddie,' said Grandpa, and he raised his mess tin to drink a toast. I imitated him while Renato rummaged under his pallet. Concealed in the straw he had half a bottle of cognac, stolen from who knows where by Teresa. We raised our dented goblets towards the stone roof. 'It's been centuries,' I said with a knowing air, 'since those bastard priests started scheming to keep the north and the south of the boot from joining together.'

Renato gulped his down all at once and slammed his mess tin down on the table: 'The power of the British empire's foreign policy.' He walked over to the window, scratched a match head across the sill, and relit his pipe. 'But even England is powerless now...This war is sweeping away all dreams of greatness.'

'What are you saying? Renato, you've always said that the Triple Entente...the English...will win the war.'

Renato didn't bother to turn around, he just went on smoking quietly and looking at the clouds. It smelt like rain. 'Once you take the negroes with you into the trenches you're done for. In India, in Africa, everywhere...The English have always presented themselves as gods, gods that build bridges and trains, gods that drive automobiles, an empire is an empire only as long as it's able to rule dreams and pretend that it's part of a divine cosmos: let them once see that the blond Saxons are sinking up to their knees in the shit-filled trenches, with slaves from overseas falling at their sides, white and black, row after row, like picket fences, mowed down by machine-gun fire...if the negroes see this, and now they've seen it, then it's over. Nothing can make men equal more than sharing a fate of mud and shit;

322

down in the filth gods become men. So the bloodbath is going to sweep away race and rank, and the great nations are bound to become smaller, and it's not necessarily the case that this will make the world a better place.'

'You're even more cynical than Grandpa.'

Grandpa squeezed my shoulder with strong fingers and looked me in the eye: 'The major isn't wrong and I'm no cynic! The problem…the real problem is that cretinous generals might well be replaced by cretinous sergeants.'

'Quite likely,' said Renato, turning around and letting his pipe go out, 'since Europe, in the past forty months, has discarded a couple of generations of officers, the ones who knew languages, the ones who might have read a book or two in their lives.' The first fat drops of rain splashed off the stone window sill. 'Let's stop talking about it! And let's have another…'

'*Goto de forte*,' said Grandpa, holding his mess tin out towards the bottle. 'A drop of the strong.'

Forty-One

THE THIRD PARAMOUR THANKED THE GUARD WHO OPENED the door to him. The butt that was still emitting a plume of smoke from the tip of his cigarette holder entered the room just a hair ahead of the tip of his shoe. A few short steps took him to the table where he placed his panama hat. He raised his eyebrows to focus on us. First he sought to lock eyes with me, then with Grandpa, and finally deigned to exchange a glance even with Renato, who was looking back at him, up from under, from where he lay stretched out on his pallet, his thumb pushing tobacco into his pipe.

For a while he talked about this and that, my grandma and my aunt, the damp weather, the dog days just around the corner, until our silence forced him to come to the point: 'There was talk of helping you to escape, but that no longer appears possible.' He dropped his gaze and picked up his panama hat, and from the grimace on his face you'd think the thing weighed twenty pounds: 'It's scheduled for tomorrow.'

Grandpa slammed both fists down onto the table: 'And you're the one they send?'

'The baron wanted to spare the ladies…and he wanted it to be a friendly voice, a voice speaking Italian…Donna Nancy and Donna Maria were able to arrange…for you to be spared the noose…it will be a firing squad.' He was speaking in a low voice, both eyes fixed on the floor, his fingertips nervously glued to the brim of his hat.

Renato went over to the window; there was a patch of vivid blue amidst the treetops. Not even a trailing shred of cloud in the sky. 'Nothing remains to be done but one simple thing... Tell the ladies that they will not be disappointed.' Renato was looking at that small patch of sky: 'We'll show these animals who the Italians are.'

Grandpa adjusted the rickety stool under his butt: 'Yes,' he said, with a glance at me. 'I'll be standing firm on both legs when they shoot me.'

Pagnini's eyes remained glued to the floor: 'Well...I've said what I came to say. I can only add that I'm truly sorry...That's it.'

Grandpa stood up and went over to him, they looked each other in the eye.

'Your wife is a courageous woman...She's not afraid of anything.'

'I know,' said Grandpa.

The Third Paramour's hands threatened to crumple the panama hat: 'A miracle...can always happen.'

'Dear Sir,' said Grandpa, staring at him, 'I've been here on this planet a few years longer than you, these two eyes of mine have seen plenty of things, good things and bad, so many things, but no miracles, I've never seen miracles, and I've never given any credence to the jabberings of priests.'

I thrust my hands into my pockets, and without a word I joined Renato at the window. My head was empty, and there was a brick where my stomach ought to have been.

The bolt squealed open. Don Lorenzo's silhouette filled the door. Thunderbolts surrounded his bald head.

'It's time for me to go, let me leave you to the parish priest,' said the Third Paramour, scuttling off with his panama hat jammed down over his forehead, practically crushed to a pulp. His feet really were too big, it was hard to think of him as smart.

Don Lorenzo grabbed a stool and sat down with his back to the wall. Then I noticed that he had a wine bottle in one hand. He pulled four small wine glasses out of his tunic pocket. 'I have this fine bottle, all that's left to me.'

We all sat down. It was a dark red wine and in the dusty light filtering in through the window it turned ruby. As he poured, the parish priest glanced sidelong at our faces. 'Terrible things all happen together,' he said in a grave voice, pushing one glass after another to the centre of the table.

'What else has happened?' asked Grandpa, and this time his voice quavered slightly.

'That girl, that foolish girl, God forgive her…has gone and hanged herself. And her mother, Teresa, the poor woman, hasn't stopped screaming since this morning. Like a wounded wolf. In the stables…with a soldier's belt…she hanged herself from a rafter.' He looked up and stared us in the eye, one by one. 'I don't know what's happened,' and he ran both hands over his cranium. 'She'd been with him, he confessed that, but he said that he had nothing to do with her death…The belt was his, that's true, it was the young soldier's belt, but he had nothing to do with it…She didn't kill herself over the young soldier, and I believe him, as does the baron…Loretta had come to see me, she'd said confession, and that's why I believe her…I wouldn't tell you if you didn't know it already…but she was the one, it was Loretta who told the Austrians to come…'

'Poor Teresa, poor thing,' said Grandpa, downing his wine in a single gulp. He slammed the empty glass down on the table. 'Poor…poor Teresa.'

The priest's glass, and mine, and Renato's all slammed down on the table, too.

'Perhaps someone wants to confess their sins.' Don Lorenzo looked at the major, who said nothing, just stared at a spot in the middle of the wall and said nothing. 'There's always time for… God's eyes are large and He can forgive anything.' He fell silent for a moment, ran two fingers inside his sweat-yellowed collar. 'Now I have to leave you, I'll come back this evening, for the sacraments.' He stood up and went to the door, rapping sharply on the wood – the sound reverberated. I heard the bolt squeal.

'Poor Teresa, poor thing,' said Grandpa, bowing his head and shaking it from side to side. He refilled his glass and drank, this time sipping, his eyes lowered, staring at the tabletop, the fingers of his left hand lingering around a knot in the wood. 'She deserved a better daughter.'

Renato, who was again standing at the window and had resumed staring at the little patch of blue high above the tree-tops, murmured: 'You're right…she really did deserve a better daughter.'

Grandpa's fingers spread open like a duck's foot on the table. He cleared his throat and, raising his voice slightly, spat out one of his maxims: 'Stupidity and bad luck play snap even in the homes of the wealthy.'

Forty-Two

DEAR NANCY, I'M AFRAID THAT THESE WORDS WILL BE ALL *that is left of me, and the thought saddens me. It especially saddens me to know that you will grieve, but I know how strong you are, and I know that the subtle strength of your intelligence will keep you company. Our boy has become quite clever; when Renato and I quarrel about the fate of Italy, he snickers to himself, and he considers us – he of all people! – a pair of urchins, as foolish as we are astute.*

I stopped. 'Grandpa, this is embarrassing, I don't want to read your letter.'

'Read it and stop talking!'

The baron brought us dinner and told us that even if the two-headed eagle is caught among the crags, its talons shattered, in the name of past glory it's determined not to give up. He was filled with anger. He talked to us a little about his family, apparently they're starving worse in Vienna than here, he said that he feels sure that it won't be long until he catches up with us 'where you're heading': he waved his hand in a gesture you should have seen. I asked him if he'd let me embrace you one last time. He said no. The law of war. But he conceded us the favour of allowing us to be shot, so I asked him for one more: being tied to the pole. You understand, I don't want my legs to give out at the end, I want to die on my feet, consarn it, we need to show these bastards how you die, we can't let ourselves be outdone by those Czech youngsters. The baron couldn't refuse, and it made me happy, because I'm not that confident of my own courage, to you I can admit it.

I'd also like to ask you for something, and it's important. Burn all my papers. You were right, I never was able to write the book and if Beelzebub managed to produce a few handsome pages, a few good phrases, well...I'm pretty sure that was chance. Burn it all, better for it to vanish, better nothing that something paltry. You know me, I lacked the strength, perhaps I had the talent to achieve something, but not the courage, that's something I always lacked.

But you, Nancy, you always had plenty of courage. Stay close to Maria: she's a proud woman, just like you are, but she holds in too many tears. I hope that, once this bloodbath is just a distant memory, our lovely Villa can once again hear the sound of laughter as it once did. Places have a bad habit of outliving us. So take care of it, then, and when you happen to remember me I hope you'll forget the tantrums and the sarcasm. In turn, I promise that when I look down from up there I won't be unkind about your enemas, and if I run into some stuck-up almighty mathematician I'll tell him not to put on airs, because I married a woman who was the best mathematician of them all. One last thing: you were right about Renato, he's quite a guy, the devil take me, he's got the gift of the gab, just think he had the impertinence on more than one occasion to argue me to a standstill with the things he says about our country's history. He must be one of the Widow's Sons, I even asked him but he just didn't answer, which looks to me like a confirmation, best I can tell.

Of course, as a major of the Intelligence Service he leaves something to be desired: with that bitch Loretta, unless I miss my guess, he must have dallied more than once.

And one more thing, don't forget to wrap your arms around Teresa for me.

330

I loved you the way I knew how, Nancy, and now I'm going to have to let you miss me. Stay strong and impose your will, the way you've always done. Don't change. Ever. Yours, Guglielmo.

I handed the letter back to Grandpa and turned my face to the wall, choking back my tears.

Forty-Three

GRANDPA HAD NODDED OFF. THE CRICKETS WERE ALREADY making their noise. And the lamp wick was short, the oil was about to run out. The flickering flame made me think of my pipe. I stuck my hand in my pocket. I walked over to Renato who hadn't moved from the window all afternoon. He handed me the matches. I stood next to him, smoking and looking out the window.

'Lieutenant Muller bought the farm in that firefight...didn't he? You're not that good a fibber after all...'

'I thought I'd learnt...'

'Soldiers die, it's not your fault. And the one you killed...You did the right thing...you could hardly take him prisoner!'

Then I asked him about Giulia and told him about my moments of jealousy, but he pretended surprise.

'I enlisted her in the I. S. That's why certain meetings took place.'

'Even if I've never really learnt to tell a lie properly, Renato, I can spot one when I hear it.'

'We're short on oil, this damned lamp.'

The smoke from our pipes crossed. His eyes locked with mine.

'You've carried yourself well in this battle, you should be proud of it.'

'Are you afraid, Renato?'

'I'd like to live.'

'So would I.'

'Is it the thought of what we won't experience or the past not lived…that sticks in your throat?'

We heard the guard's heavy footsteps. The door flew open. Don Lorenzo had a little box with him.

Grandpa sat down on the pallet, rubbing his eyes.

'If you're looking for suffering souls, here you see three, Don, but I don't think there are any confessions in the offing.' Grandpa's voice was gummy.

'What's that?' asked Renato, pointing at the box.

'It's a field altar, Major, I use it to hold the consecrated wafers.'

'I'm afraid that these three little lambs will remain lost.'

'Signor Guglielmo…Signor Spada…you shouldn't talk that way, your grandson is little more than a child, he should…'

'I won't say confession, Don Lorenzo, and it's time to quit calling me a child. Tomorrow morning, at dawn, they're going to kill me. My life is over, I've loved and I've killed, and my life is over. Yes, I'm eighteen years old, but I'm about to die, and I have a full lifetime behind me!'

Don Lorenzo was caught off guard by the anger in my voice; I hadn't realized I was practically shouting. He wiped his brow with his filthy handkerchief, and turned to look at Renato.

'What about you, Major? The time has come to look inside yourself and ask forgiveness. God loves us even when we don't deserve it…He loves us because His image is inside each of us… We were born human beings and that's enough for Him. Pride gives bad advice, Major Manca, and now your time has run out.'

'I'm happy you're not asking me.' Grandpa laughed one of his laughs and pulled me close to him.

'I really don't know what to do with your God,' said Renato 'but I still have something to say to you…Let's go over in that corner.'

Don Lorenzo pulled his stole out of the box and the major followed him into the dark corner, carrying two stools.

Grandpa and I turned to look out at the dark sky. Every so often he'd take a drag on my pipe, which I was passing to him. The voices of the priest and the major came to us, muffled. There was a star atop the dark trees.

'Is there any wine left?'

I turned towards the table; the bottle was there. I picked it up and shook it. 'Not even half a drop, Grandpa.'

'Cognac?'

I pointed at the bottle lying on its side on the table: it had lost its cork.

'Leaving condemned men without a drop of alcohol and in the company of a priest is a genuine cruelty.'

'Sober as you are, Grandpa, you might even be tempted to confess your sins.'

'What sins? I still haven't murdered anyone.'

My face darkened.

'Forgive me, laddie…you know, I wish I had…Look, you have nothing to blame yourself for, it was him or you, or are you feeling guilty about that peasant girl?'

'Guilty? No. That's not it. I'm afraid, Grandpa. Afraid of all that darkness out there, of the nothing that's waiting for us.'

'I know. So am I.'

The priest and Renato emerged from the dark corner. The parish priest had removed his hat. He'd marked his forehead with a red circle that seemed to flame in the dim half-light, for a moment.

'Will you do what I've asked you, Don Lorenzo?'

The priest nodded gravely. 'Yes...I'll do what I can,' he said, staring at the major.

Then the priest took the letter from Grandpa.

'Signor Paolo, are you sure you don't want to say confession? You'll feel better afterwards.'

'I don't doubt it, but you see...I'm not sure I want to feel better. I'm just sorry to do you the discourtesy...'

'You've become a cynic, just like your grandpa.'

He didn't know he was paying me a compliment, or perhaps he knew it all too well.

Forty-Four

I'D EVEN GOT A LITTLE SLEEP.

Day hadn't yet dawned when I opened my eyes, the flame of the lamp was rising and falling and Grandpa was hard at work on the table with a package. The twine refused to yield to his haste.

'Donna Maria sent us these,' said Renato, who was very pleased to see his major's uniform again. 'I haven't worn it in more than a year…It was the innkeeper who kept it for me, for two gold sterlings…but I ought to leave it to our priest…Yesterday I asked him to replace me in certain of my duties…He even seemed to be moved.'

We stripped off our filthy clothing and took turns washing up at the pump which gave us water in drips and splatters. I had a white shirt and summer wool trousers, ironed with a crease; Grandpa was wearing his light-coloured frock coat. We had no mirror so we combed our hair, each asking the others for advice.

'What remains to be done is fairly simple.' Grandpa was making an effort to seem calm; he was doing it for me.

The sun hadn't yet peeked over the hilltops when the door swung open.

Don Lorenzo was the first one through the door. He wore a round, broad-brimmed hat and had his breviary in his hands. Then came the corporal with his little red moustache. It seemed that his eyes were less round this time, less owlish.

It all happened in a hurry.

We walked out in a line, Grandpa first, me in the middle, Major Manca last. We were escorted by four men. Rifles slung over their shoulders, bayonets fixed, tattered caps.

The light that swept over me made me half-close my eyes. I took a deep breath and filled my lungs with the scent of wet grass. The whole village was lined up along the iron bars where they used to tie up the mules. There were even children with mud-daubed faces. When the men saw us go by, they doffed their caps; the woman had snarls on faces wrapped tight in dark scarves. The children were excited.

It didn't take us long to reach the poles with the iron hooks. They'd added a third. I understood that after the bullets, a noose awaited us. I didn't much care, in fact, it seemed like an honour to me, to swing, in plain sight, like the heroes in my books.

The air was clear, and it smelt of damp earth and rain-drenched grass.

A company of Honvéds, lined up in double file, waited with rifles resting at their feet close to the wooden fence, where the field hands were clustered for the show and were doing their best to quiet the children who were pointing, consumed by eager curiosity.

The firing squad consisted of twelve men, but they weren't in Hungarian uniform. They were all veterans, and the baron had hand-picked them. For certain jobs, he didn't trust youngsters.

I saw Grandma standing next to my aunt. Grandma was wearing her black veil, which dangled over her face from the brim of a grey hat, and Aunt Maria had her enamel seal clipped to the strip of lace at her neck.

A gust of cool air ruffled the skirts.

I saw the dawning sun gleaming on the iron hooks high atop

the poles. Then the four men escorting us brought each of us to stand next to a pole and ran a rope under our arms. The baron had been true to his word. As they were tying us up, Grandpa, who was on my right, looked at me with resignation in his eyes: 'You know, after all these years I've even grown to love the vertical position.'

I turned to look at Renato, but he was ignoring me. His eyes stared straight ahead, and he refused the black blindfold, spitting on the ground as he did so.

I shook my head when the red-moustached corporal offered me one. 'I'm sorry, son,' he whispered.

Grandpa too refused the offer, shaking his head.

I looked up at the Villa. And on the second floor, at the corner window, behind the panes I glimpsed Teresa's rocky silhouette.

The stench of the latrines began to make itself known as the day grew progressively warmer. Don Lorenzo went on muttering prayers with his breviary shut in his hand. When he came to my pole, he made the sign of the cross with his thumb on my forehead, but I jerked my head away in annoyance. In front of Grandpa he sketched a cross in the air, and salted it with a bit of Latin: '*Proficiscere, anima christiana, de hoc mundo.*' Then he stood aside.

I looked at my aunt's face, as she stood there holding Grandma by the arm. Her face was pale. A sparrow landed by my foot. I moved my foot so I could see it fly, but it just hopped a short distance away. Then I noticed the birds of the morning, a sound that had always been there, but which I'd never listened to.

The baron stood next to the soldiers with their rifles at rest position. He unsheathed his sabre. He issued an order. The first row of soldiers knelt. I looked towards the Villa and saw that Teresa had opened the window; a shaft of sunlight was glinting off the glass pane. I turned towards the tenant farmers and field hands who were standing erect along the whole length of the wooden fence. Now even the children stood silent. And the women were lined up just as orderly as infantrymen. No one had summoned them, they weren't there merely out of curiosity, or to show their respect for us, or because they hated us; they had all come to let the enemy know that nothing is forgotten, that everything is known, and that everything comes with a price. The baron spoke my language and those peasants didn't, he gripped his fork and lifted his glass the way I did, and those peasants didn't, he'd read many of the same books I'd read, and those peasants didn't even know how to read, but at that moment I felt that that war, that damned filthy war, had put me and those peasants on one side, and the baron and his men on the other. And just then, if those miserable poverty-stricken men could have laid their hands on their pitchforks, they'd have cut the baron's throat, not ours, even if the resentment they nurtured for us was far more justified, and dated back over the generations.

The rifles were pointed. I saw that the rifle barrels were swinging slightly. I didn't think we could be such a hard target to aim at. I tried to look the soldiers in the eye. For a moment I lifted my head and I saw the sun gleaming off the hook awaiting me. Then the spark of light on the baron's sabre moved. I saw it fall; I heard it swish, I believe.

Forty-Five

A RING OF LIGHT, A BALL OF FIRE. SWINGING. A PENDULUM that made me feel as if I was falling off a cliff every time it went past, as if there was air beneath me, an abyss of air and hot wind. The ball of fire went on swinging.

There was a voice, a woman's voice.

The sky was white, the purest white.

The ball wouldn't stop swinging.

'Stop that ball, stop it!'

'God be praised…He's awake.'

I recognized my aunt's voice. I opened my eyes. My eyelids were heavy, and I felt pain, a sharp stab of pain in my leg. There was a man with large black sideburns, and a smell that gave me a sense of nausea. Everything looked blurry, as if I was immersed in steam. The man was wearing a white coat, and it looked to me as if he had tubes running into his ears and he was using an icy tentacle to sting me in the chest.

'It's all okay…Paolo.'

'That light…Why is it moving?'

The man with the white coat reached up his hand and stopped the light bulb that was dangling over my face. With his thumb, he lowered first one of my eyelids, then the other. 'You have a couple of bulletholes in your right lung, one on the left thigh, and a flesh wound on the temple…I'd say you had the devil on your side, I've never seen such luck.'

'What are you talking about…? Where am I?'

'Mezzavilla. The hospital. My name is Bresci, Aldo Bresci, from Ferrara. Lieutenant physician, taken prisoner on the Kolovrat, nearly a year ago, now…' He was smiling, he had a mouthful of teeth – so many teeth, and all gleaming white. 'I've been helping out here since the battle in June. I was almost done with my shift when they brought in an Italian boy on a stretcher. He'd been shot by a firing squad but apparently they'd spared his life: no bullet to the head, as regulations would normally demand.'

The doctor's voice was deep and gentle. I felt a burning sensation in my thigh, but nothing in my chest, even though I could barely move because I was bandaged all the way down to my crotch. My aunt looked at me with glowing, incredulous eyes. There were two other iron hospital beds next to mine, both empty. It took me a full half an hour to come to, to understand what had actually happened.

The doctor had started speaking German to a woman who had the insignia of the Red Cross on her blouse, while my aunt went on telling her story. Her excitement and joy at the sight of me, alive, had pushed Grandpa's death out of her mind.

She told me everything, down to the last detail. And I had to make her repeat it to be sure that it was really true.

When the baron had walked over to me to deliver the coup de grâce, he'd noticed that I was moving my head. At that point, my aunt had run headlong across the few metres that separated her from the baron, and thrown herself between me and that levelled pistol. The baron ordered a corporal to shove the intrusive woman aside, but he simply uttered the words 'Xé un segno del Signor' – 'It's a sign from God' – and planted his feet by Donna Maria's side, as Grandma hurried to support them.

'You should have seen the faces of the baron, the two ladies, and his corporal...'

She told me that after that they'd hoisted Grandpa and Renato up onto the hooks. She said nothing about Grandpa. 'The major...you know' – her green eyes filmed over – 'the major had his left foot closer to the ground, as if death had decided to make up for the wrong that life had done him, by lengthening his shorter leg.'

Forty-Six

THE WAKE WAS HELD IN THE SACRISTY. GRANDMA NANCY, Teresa, and my aunt stayed up all night, and early the next morning the whole town filed through, one by one, like the beads of a rosary, passing before Grandma, who held her head high, without her veil, dry-eyed, and said to each one: 'They're more afraid than we are.'

In the afternoon, Renato's coffin was placed on a lorry headed for the river and Grandpa's was taken to the church for mass. A short mass; everyone was there, the innkeeper and the innkeeper's wife, Attilio and Adriano. With a masterful touch, Don Lorenzo reduced the sermon to a few measured sentences, concluding with 'public evils always come to everyone's front door...but so does the mercy of Our Lord.'

The parish priest accompanied the corpse to our little cemetery, next to the camp latrines. Four peasants lowered the casket into the grave. Then they crossed themselves and struck a sorrowful pose, while Don Lorenzo sprinkled a little holy water and a handful of Latin onto the deal planks sunk deep into the earth.

The event was less widely discussed than the baron had expected, and when Italy's armed resurgence finally came, groups of armed men aided the advance of the sharpshooters who were pushing the imperial army back towards Vittorio, where it would soon be annihilated.

The Villa was reached by the troops led by General Clerici on 30 October, after a brief but intense barrage of artillery fire on Refrontolo. That same day, Teresa captured a large rat. Her culinary skills transformed it into a hare: a roast that delighted both my palate and her mistresses' palates. It earned her great praise and even a small, but still entirely welcome, tip.

The Hapsburg eagle, a shadow and relic of the eagle of the legions, had lost itself in the sky blue of the House of Savoy. I didn't take part in the celebrations of liberation that for nearly a year crisscrossed the country, on one Sunday after another: 'Victories have little to say, it's defeat that teaches a lesson,' said Grandpa. And what could all those big-bellied gentlemen with their black top hats and tricolour cockards know about it, as they clambered onto the stage making promises of pie in the sky in the sweet bye and bye to one and all?

'The syntax of things could kill us,' Grandpa had written in one of his rough drafts, which Grandma hadn't had the heart to burn, 'but it won't; we'll take care of it ourselves, crickets venturing out into the snow.'

Coda

September 1929

GRANDMA DIED OF SPANISH FLU A FEW MONTHS AFTER THE war ended, a war that left traces – fading over the years – of half a dozen mortar shells in the park. When I have time, in the summer, I make it a point to call on Aunt Maria. She's a woman who lives alone, intense, still beautiful. I try to stay for a couple of weeks when I go. We talk about the latest books we've read, and now and then about 'that character', our Duce who just won't stop rinsing the laundry of his Socialism in the holy water font. There's a tacit understanding between us: we never talk about the war, about what happened at the Villa, about the gallows poles with their hooks. But a few days ago I asked her if she ever has occasion to think about that major from Vienna, Baron von Feilitzsch. Without glancing at me, she ran her forefinger over the rim of her cup, making it sing, as Teresa's grunt moved off into the distance. Then, her eyes focused on her coffee, in a faint voice, she said: 'No.' At that point I turned to look at Teresa. She looked grim, carved out of the evening light, just a few steps away from her kitchen, with her thinning hair pulled back into a bun. She was looking at the hills. I sense that she'll never leave here, that she's like the grass, born to stay in one place, at the centre of the miserable splendour of everything that goes past.

'*Diambarne de l'ostia.*'

347

Note

This story is based around certain events that actually happened, described in Maria Spada's book, *Diario dell'invasione* (privately printed, Vittorio Veneto, 1999), but it is still fiction, and any resemblance to real persons, living or dead, is purely coincidental. The places where the events occurred, however, are real and historical.

A. M.